Dead of Night

Ghosts & Magic #1

By M.R. Forbes

CHAPTER ONE

About that job...

I APPROACHED THE DOOR ON my elbows, dragging myself like some kind of mutant lizard along the stained brown carpet that lined the eighth floor hallway of the Hotel Paramour. It had taken me almost ten minutes of left arm, right arm, rinse, and repeat to get from the first door, now thirty feet or so behind me, to this one, and at that point I was just about ready to stand up and walk the final few steps, if only to give my lungs a chance to expand again.

It only took a few repetitions of my favorite mantra, 'I don't want to die', to convince myself to stay prone and keep snaking.

Left arm, right arm, left arm, right arm.

I finally got my eyeball to the bottom of the door, fortunate that it had been hung with as little care as anything else in this dump.

"Now that we have the details out of the way… Did you bring it?"

Peeking in under the frame, I couldn't see who was speaking, or even tell where the voice was coming from. What I could see were three pairs of feet, two on one side of a desk, and one on the other. They were all angled somewhat cockeyed, which told me that the targets inside were sitting. The closer feet, they were packaged up in standard-issue brown boots. The other guy was wearing some nice shiny loafers, probably a Gucci or a Prada.

"Yeah, we've got it."

There was a rustle. Someone pulling something from a plastic bag. The thunk when it landed on the desk said it was heavy. At least I was in the right place.

"Mr. Black will be pleased with your success," Gucci said. "We've been having a lot of trouble getting the drops picked up lately."

"We heard. If you had put the money up sooner, you wouldn't have had to lose so many packages."

I slid forward a few more inches, lifting my eyes to the rusted doorknob above my head. I really wanted to open the door, and I didn't want to be seen or heard doing it. What would be the odds of that?

"Since we're on the topic, Mr. Black has another job if you're interested."

Laughter. "If the money's right, we're interested."

A soft chuckle. "Of course. The money, my friends, is sure to be to your liking."

I reached up, my hand moving ever so slowly towards the knob, boney fingers finally falling onto it with the softness of a feather. Even so, just touching the surface caused the door to emit a slight snap.

"You hear that?" one of the booted men asked.

"It's an old building, Rodge. Shit probably creaks and groans all night."

"Like your mother?"

"Shut up."

I started to turn the knob, a fraction of a millimeter at a time. It was a movement so precise I doubted many people could have repeated it. It was that control, that attention to the art that had made me everything I was today. It didn't seem like much, crawling around on the floor of a shitty hotel like a worm, but from time to time it paid at least one or two of my bills.

"So what's the job?" Rodge asked.

I ran my mind through the profile I'd been given of the targets. Roger Excelon, and his brother Tim. They were a pair of accomplished ghosts, experienced heavies who were making their move up into the big-time. Their normal work orders consisted more of guard duty than active carrying, but defense never made the same kind of coin as offense, and to be honest, their backgrounds did make them more suitable for pickup and retrieval.

The third guy was a fixer, an associate of Mr. Black's whose role was to arrange the resources for the given job. There had been no way to know who he would be, which made him a wild card that I was only slightly nervous about. I had planned this thing right, and allowed for the unknown variable.

"Another pickup. A little more sophisticated this time. Mr. Black has a rival, and that rival has something that Mr. Black wants. Need I go on?"

"Nah, I get it."

Rodge's laughter was the perfect cover as I finished twisting the knob and carefully eased the door open about six inches. It wasn't enough for me to get into the room, but I didn't want to get into the room. Yet.

"It sounds like there might be some violence involved," Tim said. "Violence costs extra."

"Yes, of course it does. I imagine there may be some violence. Dragons very rarely wish to part with even the smallest trinket from their hoards, if you know what I mean."

"I'm not much for metaphors, but yeah, I think I know what you mean. How much?"

I heard the sound of wood scraping wood; a drawer being slid open. Then I heard the sound of something plastic bouncing on the desk.

"Two million," Gucci said. "Payable in advance. The only way you lose it is if you die."

3

"Up front? You trust us to do the job when we've already been paid?"

It was Gucci's turn to laugh. "I trust you not to be stupid enough to double-cross Mr. Black. Besides, you two came highly recommended. You don't build a reputation on lies, and guards don't build a reputation on theft."

Right arm, left arm. I pushed myself back from the crack in the door so I could think. Two million was a good haul, a lot more than any of the other jobs I had ever been offered. I could cover meds for a year with that kind of take. Of course, Mrs. Grey wouldn't be very happy. The question was, how not very happy? I'd been ghosting both for and against her for the last three years, and she seemed like a reasonable sort. Then again, I'd never actually crossed her.

I felt an itch in my throat and a constriction in my stomach. It was a reminder of the decision I was trying to make. The bottom line was that I was only getting a hundred thousand for this little dance, and for the price it didn't seem that important if one of Mr. Black's fixers got through it alive. I'd still take out the Wonder Twins, which had been Grey's goal from the start. How mad could she be for that?

Decision made, I squirmed back into position.

A beep told me they had run the card and confirmed the funding. Two million in bitcoin, digital currency, available to whoever brought the card in for transfer, minus a fee, of course. It crossed my mind to just finish the job and steal it, but I knew Black would send a goon squad over to sweep the scene once I was gone, and if the card was missing and the job ignored, they'd be all the more focused on finding out who had pulled the hit. There was no part of me that wanted to cross any of the Houses' kill teams.

I felt another urge to cough, and I tightened my throat and fought against it, my eyes drawing tears for the effort. Not yet. It was too soon. I glanced down at my watch. One more minute.

"Looks like the money's good," Rodge said. "We have a deal."

"Excellent."

I heard Gucci's chair squeak, and the sound of another drawer being pulled open. His voice was deeper and more firm when he spoke. "Take this. It has the address, an image of the target, and a shitload of reconnaissance data. Call the number when the job is done, and then wait for confirmation. You have forty-eight hours to check-in before we send a team looking for you. Understand?"

"Not a problem. This isn't our first tango."

"That's why Mr. Black wanted you."

I checked my watch again. Twenty seconds. I reached down to the inside pocket of the black nylon trench I was wearing and brought out a pair of small cubes made of carved human bone. I held them tight in my fist, whispered softly, and prepared to toss them into the room.

"That's all I've got for you two right now," Gucci said. I heard the chair move again, and the sound of springs. Whoever Gucci was, he was a fat-ass.

The other two chairs shifted. Rodge and his brother also stood.

That was when the window shattered.

Ten seconds early.

"Shit."

I forgot about my sneak attack, gathering my feet under me and standing up. I could hear the commotion in the room, shouting and gunfire, and the unmistakable thump of bullets finding flesh.

I threw the dice in at the same time I slammed the door open, grabbing the sawed-off shotgun from the makeshift holster under my coat and leveling it at the dynamic duo. It was the first time I had seen this pair, a couple of ogres with massive builds, coated in tattoos and looking plenty mean. Heavies for sure. They had been pumping bullets into my companion in the window with custom made firearms, but now they turned to watch the dramatic entrance, their eyes following the bone dice.

My first round sent heavy buckshot scattering everywhere, digging into their skin and ripping through, sending blood splattering against the paisley wallpaper behind them. I tracked my eyes to Gucci, finding him standing in the corner, looking exceptionally calm.

"You're early, dammit," I shouted at Caroline. She had never been pretty, but the gunshots had ripped off half her jaw and an ear, and torn a nice chunk out of her thigh.

The dice rolled to a stop.

My eyes returned to the ogres, who were bouncing back from the first hit. They were bloody, but it looked like all it had done was piss them off.

"That fucking hurt," Rodge said. I could see his muscles clenching and rippling, tensing to pounce on me. His partner was swinging his huge semi-automatic my way. One shot from that thing, and my head would be painting the hallway.

I looked down at my dice. Lightning. Doubles.

"This is going to hurt more."

A wail sounded from all around us, a high pitched shriek followed by a hint of *something* from the dice. I felt the beating of my heart hang and stop. I felt the pain of a dying man. In front of me, the leathers dropped their weapons, screaming and spasming. Right now, they would be feeling like their entire bodies were burning in intense flashes of pain, nerves overwhelmed and minds unable to process the explosion of sensation. Their size wasn't a benefit against Lightning.

"Caroline!"

She had finally gotten into the window and raised the gun I had given her. Fingers broken, her aim sucked, but she managed to get two of the sixteen armor-piercing rounds into each of the ogres' foreheads. They weren't able to do much to stop it, and they both toppled over, dead. I watched the black shadow of their souls being pulled into the dice laying on the floor, and then turned my attention to Gucci.

He was still standing in the corner, unfazed by the death of his hired help. His eyes travelled from me to Caroline and back. "A necro?"

I re-holstered the shotgun.

"I didn't think there were any more necros."

"We're a dying breed." The dry humor made him laugh.

It made me cough.

"Did you come to off me, or just those two?"

The instructions had said no survivors. I hadn't made up my mind about that. "I heard you talking to them about a job. Two million."

He smiled. "Who are you working for? If I had known there was a necromancer floating around, I might have given you a call first."

Except I didn't advertise my specialty. Even Mrs. Grey didn't know what I was about. She had hired an assassin and a thief, not a necro. That was why I wasn't sure about leaving him alive. It might be better for business in the short-term to let the secret out, but it wasn't a good long-term plan.

"Don't let the stories fool you. I'm not half as cool as they would make it seem."

In the stories, necromancers could control legions of the dead, kill with a touch, that sort of thing. I had no such luck. My animation efforts were limited to one corpse at a time, and my control of them was a little bit shaky. I couldn't kill with a touch either, and the death magic... it was all wrapped up in the pair of dice, a game of chance, and it always required a payment in souls after use, one way or another. I was still around because I made the most out of what I had, not because I could work some hocus-pocus.

"Tell that to those two brutes," Gucci said. He held out his hand. "My name is Wilson."

I didn't take his hand, or offer my own. He pulled it back.

"Fine. You want the job? It's yours. Take the card and the specs, they're both buried somewhere under those empty mounds of muscle. Give a call when it's done." He stepped forward, to go between Caroline and me and out the door. Caroline grabbed his arm.

"Hold on." In my mind, I was running the probabilities, considering the odds. He knew what I was, and I was supposed to have killed him in the first place. I could finish this job, and take on the new one. Mrs. Grey would be happy and Mr. Black likely wouldn't give a crap about some random underling.

His eyes flashed a bright blue. "I know what you're thinking, necro. I urge you to reconsider."

Real power, or a scare tactic? Looking at him, he seemed like the type who would blab, and I wasn't ready for my predicament to become known to the Houses.

I let Caroline hold him for a few more beats. In the end, it was the shoes that made up my mind. Shiny black shoes belonged to dealers and salesmen. In a past life I'd preferred sneakers; simple and functional. Now I wore matte black boots, because anything else stood out too much in the shadows. Shiny was ostentatious. Shiny drew attention. Shiny made you look like you were bragging. I resented people like that, because they thought they had something I didn't.

A future.

"I'll take the job," I said, holding out my hand.

"Forty-eight hours. Call the number. If you don't, a kill team will be on you, and they won't give a shit that you can raise the dead."

I glanced over at Caroline, who let go of Gucci's arm. He brushed his sleeve and reached out, wrapping his meaty fingers around my flesh coated bone.

"When you call, give them your number and your handle. Mr. Black can use-"

His eyes widened, and he looked down at his hand, still in my wasted grip. He could feel it now. The death of my flesh, the poison that I carried. I had been sentenced a long time ago, and it had made me what I was today. I had learned to fight, and to cheat, and to survive.

I couldn't kill with a touch.

I needed to keep contact.

He tried to pull his hand away, but my grip was a vice. I'd always had strong, nimble hands. Doctor's hands. He tried to call on his own power, if he really had any, and was silenced when Caroline shoved her fist into his mouth and held fast. He could gnaw her fingers off, she wouldn't notice, and the voice was how the energy was released. He tried to kick and flail, so she used her other arm to brace him, her deadness not understanding the limits of living muscle.

"I prefer to keep my anonymity," I said, trying to explain to him why he needed to die. "Those shoes tell me you talk too much."

He couldn't do anything else, so he began to scream, the sound dampened by the hand in his mouth. We watched the necrosis travel up his arm, turning it a sick shade of green. Blood started to run from his nose, and he began to convulse and gasp.

It wasn't a pretty thing, death. It didn't spare your dignity, or your feelings. It just took you; sometimes by surprise, and sometimes with plenty of warning. If you were lucky, you had time to prepare yourself, to prepare your family and your loved ones, or in my case to spare them from the ugliness. If you were unlucky, like Gucci, you just dropped. Then again, maybe it was the other way around. Maybe he was the lucky one.

Either way, maybe the world would hear about your passing, and maybe someone would care.

Or… maybe not.

CHAPTER TWO

Sweet Caroline.

I DROPPED THE BODY TO the floor and then turned to Caroline, pointing at the watch hanging from her pale wrist. "Ten seconds. You almost got me killed."

Double lightning was a stroke of luck. Not all of the rolls were as effective or immediate.

"Mmmfffrrpfff." Without her jaw, she wasn't going to be saying anything intelligible.

"It's just so typical, Caroline. I should have expected you'd come in too soon. You always want to be the center of attention."

"Mmmmrrrrpppffff."

"Just stop trying." I walked over to the two brutes, bent down and picked up the dice. They were still warm. I blew on them once and put them back in my pocket. "Help me roll them over."

She shambled up to Rodge and bent over, grabbing his arm and lifting. As he rose from the floor, I could see the plastic card laying in a pool of his filth.

"Put him over there." I waved towards the window, and she complied, but not without a grunt of opinion. "Just put him over there."

I tried to take a deep breath and wound up coughing. I could feel the disease churning in my stomach, the malady that was going to take my life one of these days. That was the ultimate downside to being a necromancer, and the reason there were so few of us.

To wield the power of death, you had to be dying yourself.

Rodge's body thumped back to the floor.

"Get the card, and wipe it off."

"Mmmrrrrffff."

"Just get the card."

She came back over and picked it up, holding it gingerly between her thumb and index finger, like any of the bodily fluid clinging to it could hurt her. She brought it over to the other brute, wiped it clean on the back of his jeans, and then handed it to me.

"Thank you." I shook my head and rolled my eyes. She smacked me on the shoulder and grumbled her complaint. "Noted, and ignored." I put the card in my pocket with the dice.

It was a bit of good fortune that the glasses hadn't gotten crushed in the fight. I found them laying a few feet to Tim's right, waiting patiently on the carpet.

I held them out in front of me, remembering the first time I had owned a similar pair. They had been pretty new at the time, a marvel of technology that nobody really saw much of a need for, and only the truly bold had the guts to wear in public. Mine had been foisted on me by the medical director, who thought it would be a great idea for all of the surgeons to wear them in the operating room. Not only could we record the surgery, both for posterity and in the event of litigation, but we would have instant access to our charts, notes, and surgical plans. Never mind that you had to talk to it like it was a precocious two year old to get it to do what you wanted.

Seven years had passed, and the things had evolved the way all technology did, even though the market for them was still shaky. There wasn't as much interest in recording your life as the makers had assumed, probably because most people weren't billionaires who could do exciting things whenever they wanted to. For some of us, our lives were living hells that we'd never want anyone to have to suffer through.

Even so, the glasses were common enough for the Houses to parse their jobs on. They could preload any info the ghost might need and give them quick and easy access to schematics, dossiers, schedules, and whatever other intel they had gathered on the target. Even better, there was no more speaking involved. They could essentially read your mind.

"MMmmmrrrfffrrrmmm."

I looked at my watch. It was a classic Rolex, a heavy lump of metal with a mechanical movement and softly ticking hands. My mentor had given it to me the day I'd finished my residency. "You're right. Let me just take care of the body and we'll go."

It wouldn't do to leave Gucci laying there, his flesh rotting and covered in gangrene. It would be too obvious how he had died, and the last thing I wanted was obvious. It was a good thing I kept the right kind of equipment for this situation.

I reached into a pocket and pulled out a stainless steel flask. I uncapped it and took a whiff of the kerosene, and then spread it across Gucci's body. Once it was good and wet, and the flask was empty, I took out a match. It wouldn't do much more than burn off the clothes and toast the flesh, but it didn't need to. The odds were good that they'd believe a pyro had done the dirty work. Like the man had said, necros were rare.

"Mmmmmrrrfffmmm."

"I'm coming."

I lit the match and tossed it onto the corpse, waiting a few seconds to make sure it caught. Satisfied, I followed her to the window. Gucci would have had a monitor implanted near his heart that would tell someone in Mr. Black's chain the moment he ceased to be alive. While I wasn't too concerned that they would know I was the one who ended him, I was concerned about that information being discovered so soon. It was better to do the job and call it in, and let them learn about me that way. If the job was important enough, and for two million up front it sure seemed like it was, this particular sin would be forgiven.

We descended the fire escape that Caroline had been waiting on for the last sixteen hours, out of view of the window. The dead were perfect for stakeouts, or for anything that required waiting extreme amounts of time without a twitch. That's why it twisted me that she couldn't wait an extra ten seconds. That's why I knew it had to be intentional. Even so, it was going to be a shame to have to retire her before I went home. She had been a good night's digging, a fortunate gem in a pile of trash. Too many people didn't die pretty, and were too damaged to work with, their bodies desecrated in any number of ways. I'd needed someone who could walk out into a crowd, and in the end I had come to enjoy her company.

That was the thing about animating the dead. They weren't like zombies in the movies, or the people who got cursed with the Rot. They weren't mindless bodies following some programmed command to eat brains. When you brought a corpse back to life, you were pulling their soul from wherever it was souls went and forcing it to re-inhabit the flesh, no matter what condition that flesh was in. You were putting the person back in there, albeit with a reduced ability to express their own free will. Reduced, not gone, and it was the strength of the summoner's will, and the will of the soul, that determined how much control you actually had. Caroline was a stubborn one, and while my will was strong enough to get her to do what I wanted, it wasn't strong enough to keep her from bitching about it.

Anyway, she looked like any other corpse now. Bodies like that were a dime a dozen, and despite my attachment she was too unreliable to be worth keeping around. She'd need to be replaced at some point.

Not tonight. I was too tired tonight.

We reached the alley, and I told her to wait while I walked across the street to the public lot where I had left my van. It was a large, white delivery van, an old thing with rust eaten corners and 'Flowers by Jack' in large, faded blue script along the sides. It got me where I needed to be and had plenty of room in the back for a couple of big coolers.

That was the other thing about the dead. Bringing them back didn't change the chemistry of a rotting corpse. If the day had been warm and sunny, Gucci would have smelled Caroline long before she had gone through the window.

I hopped in the van and closed the door, pausing once to cough my lungs up before I started it up and drove over to the alley. I checked the mirrors a few times for onlookers before backing it in, climbing to the rear, and opening the receiving end.

"Come on." I extended my hand, and Caroline took it, her flesh cold in my grip. I pulled her up, and then leaned out to swing the doors closed behind her.

"MMmmmffffff."

She had lifted the lid of one of the coolers, and was standing at the edge.

"Not tonight, Caroline," I said. "If you had come in on time, maybe you wouldn't have gotten your jaw blown off."

Or maybe that was the point. I didn't know if the souls I called back *liked* being back. They didn't seem to be capable of answering that question. Sometimes I wondered if it just depended on where their soul was otherwise. Other times, I just wondered where otherwise was. The only thing I knew for sure about the beyond is that when whatever lived in the dice claimed its prize, there was nothing I could do to get a refund.

That was one of the things that drove me to stay alive. Fear, the great motivator. I knew some of the secrets of death. It didn't make it easier to accept. It made it harder. I didn't want to be ping-ponged back and forth between otherwise and my wretched corpse, or eaten by whatever evil thing had been spelled into the bone dice. I didn't want to think that there was no final resting place, no comfortable end to existence. Yes, I was aware of my hypocrisy, but knowledge and fear had moved me from Jeckyll to Hyde.

Caroline tried to sit shotgun, and I had to urge her out of sight. I could only imagine how the police would react to seeing a woman with half a face. I was playing with corpses. I had no desire to show off that skill set. She settled for the floor right behind my seat, her stream of satisfied mumbles doing their best to reach through my deadened heart and make me feel guilty for both keeping her around, and for planning to bury her again.

I coughed long and hard enough to leave myself gasping. Touching Gucci had been a risky proposition all the way around, and now I would need another hit of meds much sooner than I had noted in my calendar. It was going to cost me half the haul from Grey's payment.

I rolled the van out of the alley at the same time I leaned over and opened the glove box, pulling out a thin sliver of clear substrate with a small bit of aluminum at the bottom. I slid my finger up along the surface, and it turned into an opaque screen.

"Call Danelle."

The phone began to ring, and I placed it on the dash and hit the speaker button. A moment later, she answered.

"How'd it go?"

"No pleasantries? No, 'how are you feeling', or 'hey, it's good to hear from you'?"

"Cut the shit. Did you finish the job?"

Danelle was my agent, my business partner. She handled the negotiations. She was also my alter ego, the person who the Houses thought they were hiring when they called in about getting an assassin or a thief.

She had been one, once upon a time. She had taught me everything I knew about this life, introducing me to this career back when I was nothing but a lost soul trying to escape the pain of what I had been forced to do, and making every effort to forget that I was dying.

Then a pyro had toasted her legs and left her in a wheelchair.

"Call it in," I said. "Two dead ogres, one dead fixer."

"The dice?"

I sighed. She had a strange fascination with the dice that she refused to let go of. "Happy. I can't say the same for myself. I had to touch the fixer."

A pause at the other end. "You need more meds?"

"Yes."

"Christ! By the time I cover everything else we'll be lucky to eat this week."

I let out a weak, fake laugh. "If it's any consolation, I don't eat that much. Especially after the meds."

She didn't laugh with me. "Give me an hour, and then go meet Dalton at the shop."

An hour was good. I had another stop I needed to make in the meantime. "I do have a bit of good news for you. I'll give it to you when I get home."

"Can I eat it?"

I hung up.

It took me about ten minutes to make the drive over to Graceland, and another five to get back to the plot where I had dug Caroline up. I'd been real careful with how I'd moved the earth, in preparation for this very event. This time I had a helper with a second shovel, and we reached the coffin within a quarter of an hour.

"Thanks for everything."

She was in the pit, standing in the base of the open casket.

"Mmmmmffffff."

It sounded like a goodbye.

"Just close the lid behind you, and I'll let you go. I won't be calling on you again."

She paused a moment, and her hand lifted up in a curt wave.

I returned the gesture. "I hope wherever you're going, it's a good place for you to be."

Caroline laid down in the box, and then reached up and pulled the lid down. As soon as it was closed I let go of the tie that was controlling her, feeling the specter of her soul float free of my grip. Internally, it was like I had been holding air in my esophagus for too long and had just belched it out.

I succumbed to a bit of coughing then, putting the back of my hand to my mouth and taking a moment to stare at the blood when I moved it away. I needed to cover her up and get my ass over to Dalton. The touch had left me in worse shape than I thought. Maybe he'd been a user after all.

Magic. It had been mother nature's best kept secret, hidden in the form of not-exactly-magnetic fields that wrapped around and through the earth. According to people who knew better than me, it had always been there. It was just that us humans couldn't feel it, or see it.

Then the Earth's polarity had shifted.

It was called geomagnetic reversal, and it hadn't happened in about forty-one thousand years. For whatever reason, this shift did something to the not-exactly-magnetic fields, powering them up to the point that they began to have strange effects on us surface dwellers.

Some of us became what we called sensitives. We could feel these fields emanating around us, and in some cases we could even hear them as a constant thrumming and pulsing in the ears that we just couldn't shake.

That was me, five years ago. That was me, before I got sick and started the quick downward spiral towards death. I had always been able to hear the buzzing and thrumming. I had always known I was sensitive. In this world being sensitive meant learning to live with the noise, and knowing there was a power out there that others had access to but you didn't. It was like being first in line at the most exclusive nightclub on the planet and having the bouncer tell you to fuck off.

It was the medicine that had brought me across the line, from sensitive to user. It was black market, experimental, and illegal. I didn't know who made it, what it was made of, or where it came from. I hadn't even known there was a whole underground of remedies to all sorts of nasty things out there until I had gotten one of those nasty things, and been lucky enough to hook up with Danelle.

At first, I didn't understand that I'd finally gotten into the club. I began to feel the fields. I was able to bring the energy into me. I was also getting sicker and sicker. My hair fell out, my skin turned a gnarly grey, and no amount of sexual attention of any kind could get me aroused. I was sure I was close to death.

Only, I didn't die.

The things I touched did.

I'd been rightfully terrified, but Danelle had kept a level head about it, and once again become my guide. She was maybe a little too excited to find herself with a necro sleeping on her couch, but she saw the potential, and began to teach me everything she knew. She had more experience with magic than any sensitive had a right to, because she was supposed to be a user. She'd been bred for it, and when it didn't happen her father had disowned her for her 'failure'.

I set about the task of closing the grave, down one partner to help me shovel. It was tough going, as weak as I was, and I had to stop more than once for a fit of heavy coughing. By the time I finished leveling the dirt I was dead tired. Too tired to even make my way back to the van.

I sat down against Caroline's headstone, a plain slate of beveled marble with her name, dates, and a simple epitaph:

'Beloved daughter. God is blessed to have you in His Kingdom.'
I felt the familiar twang of guilt, and I wiped a wayward tear from my eye. I'd never asked for power over death and the dead, but when you were in my situation you needed every advantage you could get.

I didn't want to wind up like Caroline, with a small bit of stone and a sentimental phrase to send me off into the great beyond.

I wasn't ready to die.

CHAPTER THREE

Is this medically necessary?

"YOU LOOK LIKE SHIT, PARDNER," Dalton said when I stumbled through the door to his pawn shop.

It was eleven at night, a little early for peak in the dusty old storefront, where a mint guitar hung in the bullet-proof glass window, claiming to have been owned by Elvis Presley. Nobody but Dalton actually believed that it had.

I winced in pain, holding back another cough. "When have I ever come to you and not looked like shit?"

His sharp smile was annoying. So was the life in his dark, almond shaped eyes. "Gina!"

A few beats later she joined us in the center of the shop. The King's greatest hits were radiating through the hidden speakers above me, and to either side rested shelves covered in mounds of crap I couldn't believe he had given money for, or that anyone would ever buy. They probably wouldn't, but what did it matter? Was there any pawn shop around that wasn't a front for something?

She was a total counter to her cowboy-obsessed husband. Where he wore flannel and high leather boots with faux spurs, she wore tight black leather and fishnets. His head was covered by a fedora, her hair was dyed green and pink. Either way, both styles looked warped on the pair of Chinatown refugees.

"Hey, Conor. You look like shit, man."

I gave her the same unpleasant look I had given her husband.

Dalton smiled at her, leaned in, and kissed her cheek. "He's in a bad mood today."

"When is he not in a bad mood?"

"Did Danelle send the payment over?" I could feel my stomach knotting up, and my lungs complaining as their seizing accelerated. There was this notion among the ignorant that magic meant crazy power with no consequences. It would have been great if I could wield it like Gandalf and smoke a pipe after, but it just didn't work like that; at least not for me. Touching someone meant accelerating my own illness. I'd almost killed myself in my decision to keep the secret.

"Of course. She sounded pissed about it though, bro."

I expected as much. It wasn't the cost of the medication that made her angry - the meds were keeping me alive way past my use-by date. It was the other expenditure she hated, that we had fought about tooth and nail for weeks, and would still be fighting about if she hadn't lost her legs and become dependent on me to keep a roof over her head.

"She'll get over it. She always does. You have everything set up?"

"Yeah, come on down. You're the next contestant."

It was Karen, and Molly, that gave her fits. My ex, and our daughter, who was two years, one week when I was diagnosed, and two years, one week when I had abandoned them in a fit of self-loathing and with the bright idea that they'd be better off without the burden of my slow burnout. Once that stupid decision had been made, I'd been too much of a coward to go back, and so I sent them money instead. Maybe they knew it was me, but probably not. I'd paid to have myself declared dead three years ago so they could collect the life insurance.

I looked around. "I'm the only contestant. How many people take these meds, anyway?"

"Come on, pardner. You know I can't tell you. HIPAA and all that."

That statement got me to laugh, despite the pain.

We made our way behind the counter, into a back storeroom that was even more cluttered with worthless garbage. Trays filled with wedding bands, tree-like wooden dowels buried in necklaces, and a whole wine barrel filled to the top with firearms.

"It amazes me every time I come back here," I said.

"You know what I like about this front? It's the stories, Conor. Every pathetic dude who comes in here has some kind of pathetic story, and if you can sort through the alcohol induced shit, you can be entertained for a while. Then, when I'm hanging with my buds, or maybe going down to Chinatown to see my mom, I've got plenty of stuff to talk about to make them feel better about their own situation."

There was an old rug laying across the floor, and he knelt down and folded it back, revealing a trap door. He dug his fingers in the corner and lifted it out of the way.

"Do you have a story to make me feel better?"

He looked at me, his left lip curled in an Elvis smile. "You? Fuck, no."

We climbed a simple wooden ladder ten feet down into a small hallway that adjoined the operating room. You'd never know from all the mess and crap up top that anyone would be able to maintain a perfectly sterile environment below it, never mind one that was used for all kinds of sewing, sticking, and cutting of live people.

"You know the drill." Dalton rolled up his sleeves and went over to the sink, starting his scrubbing.

I took off my trench coat, then the black hoodie beneath it, and then the white tee beneath that. A few minutes later I had removed my black pants, swat boots, and boxer briefs, and had washed away the bacteria in a hot spray of water from a nozzle next to the operating room door. I grabbed a freshly laundered towel and wiped myself dry, trying to ignore the mirror.

I wasn't a pretty man. I looked as sick as I felt. My body was rail thin, with grey skin clinging so tightly to muscle and bone that it looked like it had just been laid on top of my skeleton. My head was way too big for my body, my face was small and sharp, and my eyes were sunken and sullen, with no sign of brightness inside the almost wholly black orbs. I had no hair to speak of, and every breath I took carried a hint of pain and decay. I could still remember when I had been healthy, and almost handsome. At least, Karen had always told me I was the most beautiful man she had ever met. It had been enough for me.

The sink turned off, and I heard the snap of latex gloves. I turned the knob to unlock the operating room door and walked in, my body shaking from the clean cold. I grabbed a fresh sheet and laid it over the table, and then sat down.

"Just make sure you don't touch me." Dalton entered the room and went over to a safe, bolted into the floor. He put in the combination and heaved it open.

"It doesn't work like that, and you know it."

I watched him pull out a sterile bag which contained the medicine. It was nothing but a small, round capsule that contained who-knows-what. By itself, it was nothing too bad. The problem was that it couldn't be taken orally. It had to be injected.

"It had just stopped hurting, too." I leaned back and twisted a little, exposing a nasty pucker of scarred flesh that served as a twisted target for the treatment apparatus.

"Sorry, Conor." Dalton picked up the injector from the table next to the bed. It bore a vague resemblance to a gun, except the nozzle ended in a needle that was thick enough for the capsule to blast out of. He popped the side of it open and dropped the capsule in. A small bottle of compressed air went into the back, and would fire the little pill through my innards.

He flipped it on, and brought it to my stomach. I closed my eyes while he lined up the needle and jabbed it through the scar tissue. It gave pretty easily, having been penetrated so many times before. Even so, his precision was almost embarrassing. Dalton was a black market merchant who had learned medicine on the internet, and he was almost as good of a surgeon as I had been.

I grimaced through the pain. In the beginning I had taken his offer of anesthesia, but over time I'd realized the stuff he was giving me made me feel worse than the pain did, and cost a lot more to boot. Now I just grinned and bore it, and even watched the procedure with a calm expectancy. Every time I saw the blood start running down my abs I waited for it to be a thick black pus.

He put his finger on the trigger. "The hard part."

I nodded and took a few deep breaths. He'd have to get the capsule in pretty deep. Whatever was in it would spread throughout my system and attack the ugly cells that the base was producing, keeping the factory in check for up to a month at a time, unless I touched someone and caused it to go into overdrive. Why it couldn't actually destroy the mass that was causing the trouble I didn't know, and neither did Dalton. When I asked, he would only say, 'they're working on it'. Whoever 'they' were.

"On three," Dalton said, shifting the device in his hand, changing his aim.

He'd have to get the positioning just right, or it wouldn't travel to the right spot, and would open too soon and be relatively ineffective. It had happened once before, and I'd only gotten a week out of the treatment. Even worse, the whole thing was buyer's risk. Too bad it didn't take, I had to pay full price all the same.

"One…"

I closed my eyes, mentally preparing myself for the pain that would follow.

"Two..."

I sucked in one more deep breath, and held it tight.

"Three..."

There was a puff of air, and then I could feel the capsule moving down deep towards the base of my gut. I felt the burn of it, the hot agony of it pushing through my innards. It was a thousand stabs at once, dense and tight and unbelievable. In an instant, the needle retreated, and I felt the coldness of the air against my flesh again.

I opened my eyes, reaching up to wipe the tears away from them. Dalton put the injector down and grabbed some thread, stitching me up in less than a minute. Then he took a damp towel and wiped away the excess blood.

"Not so bad, was it?"

"Go to hell."

He laughed. "Would you let me stay there?"

"Would you want to?"

"Go put your clothes back on."

I hopped off the bed and left the operating room, grabbing my stuff and getting myself back into it. Every movement hurt again, the stitches in my side bringing back the old, familiar pain. The payment card fell out of a pocket as I swung the trench back on.

"What's this?" Dalton asked. It had landed at his feet. He picked it up and twirled it in his fingers. "Haven't see one of these beauties in a while."

"Payment for my next job." I held out my hand to take it back.

He looked up at me, his brows arching in concern. "You know this is Black's, right?"

"Yeah."

"Does Dannie know about this?"

"Not yet. I'm going to tell her as soon as I get home."

"She's not going to be happy."

"I know, but I think I can ease her mind. There's two million on that card."

25

M.R. Forbes

Well, I hoped I could. There was no love lost between Danelle and her father, and that normally meant an embargo on jobs sourced through House Black. Then again, our jobs didn't normally pay two million.

He whistled and handed it over. "I don't think any purse is high enough for Dannie when it comes to Black."

I shrugged. "I guess I'll find out."

Now that I was dressed, Dalton wasn't afraid to reach out and grab my arm. It didn't matter how many times I told him it didn't work that way, he still treated me like a leper.

"I would think long and hard about taking this job, pardner. There's a reason the value is so high, and no offense, but you're small shit compared to the types that usually take this kind of work."

I reached for his hand, and he whipped it away before I could make contact.

"Tell that to the corpses Mr. Black was going to hire."

I left the pawn shop without another word.

CHAPTER FOUR

Never had a friend like me.

DANELLE AND I LIVED IN a tiny two bedroom house on the outskirts
of the city, close enough to make getting in for jobs easy, far
enough to make being under scrutiny hard. The house itself was
nothing special - beige paint badly in need of a touch-up, a patched
grey roof, and boards over half the windows. It was the kind of
house you'd think somebody had killed someone in, and if you
ventured into the basement you would have realized that wasn't
too far from the truth.

Maybe I'd never killed anyone in the house, but I had a few
murdered corpses stashed beneath the stairs.

Dalton's words were still resonating with me as I pulled the van
between the posts of a rusted fence and up a driveway that in a past
life had been a solid block of concrete. He had stolen most of the
wind from my sails about the job, and the throbbing in my side was
mangling the rest. I wasn't excited about stepping over the
threshold and having Danelle confront me about botching the work
for Mrs. Grey and needing to touch someone. I was even less
excited about telling her I was going to be working for her father.

Dalton was right. I should have reconsidered. Danelle was the
only reason I had survived so far outside the two months the
doctors had given me. She had been the one who had found me, a

depressed mess wandering through a dangerous part of town at the wrong time of night, almost begging someone or something to come and kill me. She had been a little late - I had already been mugged and beaten up a bit - though in retrospect it had been for the best. She claimed she'd smelled the aptitude in me even before the treatment had introduced me to the actual power I could wield. She'd also admitted that when she saw me laying in the street, she thought I was gorgeous, despite the swelling in my eye and jaw.

She'd fixed me up, nursed me back to health, and got me talking about everything. I'd spilled my life out to her, and found myself crying in her arms as she rocked me to sleep. That was the first week. We'd kissed once, but I'd just left Karen and Molly behind and she was nice enough not to take advantage. For reasons that were still unclear to me, we hit it off. She claimed it had to do with the zodiac. I thought it was because she was an idiot.

Still, the romantic part of the relationship had gone nowhere. The night of our first job together, we had gotten a little too excited, had a little too much to drink, and woke up the next morning in one another's arms. By the end of that day I'd come to the conclusion that our night of sweaty, messy sex had been way too awkward, in a brother-sister incest kind of way. She had concurred. It never happened again.

I shut down the van and shoved open the door, wincing as it squealed. I had been hoping to make a more subtle entry, but had been betrayed again. The kitchen light went on.

A deep breath. A review of excuses. I hopped out of the van, slammed the door closed, and made my way around to the back, to go in through the kitchen door. She was waiting there when I opened it.

"Hey, Dan."

She was sitting in her wheelchair, a red blanket folded tight over the remaining stumps of her legs. Her thin, muscled arms snaked down to where her hands rested on the wheels, ready to roll forward over my feet at her first spark of discontent. The long, dark hair of her Native American ancestry flowed out around her angled face, and her dark eyes were on fire. There was nothing even hinting at contentment in her voice.

"Do you know what we have left, Conor?" She pointed to the laptop on the kitchen table. "Four thousand."

"That's more than enough for rent."

"What about next month? You just finished the fucking job, and we're broke."

I hadn't expected to reach the moment of truth so quickly. My heart pounded while I reached into my pocket and found the card. I dropped it into her lap.

"I have another job."

She looked down at it, and then back up at me. The fire in her eyes had blossomed into a nuclear blast. Her anger had gone from a controlled yell, to a seething whisper. "That's Black's card."

"Put it in."

"Conor-"

"Put it in."

She growled and rolled herself into position in front of the computer. She took the card and waved it in front of the screen.

"What the hell?" She looked at me. "Where did you get this?"

"From the job for Mrs. Grey. The two ogres I fed to the dice were supposed to ghost it."

I could tell she was conflicted. As much as she hated her father, she liked having a home, and food in her stomach. It was enough to cool some of her temper.

I waited patiently while she cooled down a little.

"I don't know, Conor. No job that pays this well is going to be no-frills."

"You don't think I can handle it?"

"I'm not oozing confidence. Especially since you didn't exactly get through this last one without a hitch."

Ouch. She knew how to hit me where it hurt. "That was Caroline's fault. She came in too early."

"I told you not to bring her. She always has to be a drama queen. Where is she anyway?"

"She got hit in the jaw. I put her back to bed. Anyway, you know I didn't have anyone else who can be seen in public."

Her face softened. "I'm sorry, Conor. You could have used Mr. Timms if all you wanted was a distraction."

I shrugged. "Cats are harder to keep in line than people. Talk about a disaster." Not that the slightly decomposed feline couldn't be useful at times. That just wasn't one of them.

She sat and stared at the computer screen for a few minutes, not saying anything. When the tension had gotten thick enough, I broke it with capitulation.

"I don't have to do it."

She turned the chair and motioned for me to kneel down at eye level. "You had to do it the minute you took the card. Welcome to the big time, Conor. They've been tracking its movement since it left the hotel."

Damn me for thinking I was smart again. "Oh. Shit."

"Yeah. If that isn't bad enough, they'll probably think I'm the one who took the job. Mr. Black's failure of a daughter trying to get in his good graces."

"I'm sorry, Dannie. I didn't know."

She laughed. "How could you? You're a small-time thief and a so-so hitman. You should just be glad none of the Houses know you're a necro." She licked her lips and held the card up again. "I was pissed at you before you came home. I'm even more ticked now." She let loose a huge, heaving sigh. "What's done is done. I'll get my due once you finish the job, if you survive. Did you get any kind of data dump?"

I nodded, pulling the glasses from another pocket. She took them and put them down next to the laptop. "I'll transfer the data so we can both review it. You need to go clear out as much as you can keep in the van from the basement. We'll have to burn this place down."

"Burn it down?"

"I swear, Conor. How the hell did you graduate medical school?"

"Come on, Dannie. You know the treatment takes it out of me."

She rolled over to the counter and opened one of the drawers, pulling a small, thin cable from it. "How long do you have to finish it?"

"Forty-eight hours."

She looked even more unhappy. "Right. So, what do you think they're going to do in forty-eight, if the job isn't complete? They're going to come looking for you, tracing your steps backwards. One of those steps leads to this house, and an invalid in a wheelchair who can't defend herself. The kill team won't care whose daughter I am while they're putting a bullet in my brain."

She plugged one end of the cable into the laptop, the other into the specs.

"First, you're hardly unable to defend yourself. Second, you're assuming I'm going to fail?" I hadn't failed to finish a job yet, even if one did wind up a little sloppy from time to time. She had no reason to think I couldn't do it, and it was starting to make me equally angry that she didn't believe in me.

"I'm not assuming anything. I hope you're flawless. That doesn't mean I'm putting my life on it, not when I don't have to. We can torch this place and set up shop somewhere else, after the job is done. Next time, you'll be smarter."

"Now you're making a huge assumption." I smiled, my anger rescinded.

"There's a jug of kerosene in the basement. Get your toys out of here and then dump it over anything that'll burn."

I felt like garbage for forcing her out of the house, but what I could I do? She was right, what was done was done. I was grateful she was handling it with the same grace and efficiency that had made her such a good ghost. I reached out and took her hand on my way by, giving it a quick squeeze before leaving the kitchen. She returned the affection and added a small smile.

Pissed, but always dependable.

There was a plain white door tucked under the stairs to the second floor, which led down into the basement. I pushed it open, and then reached up and pulled the string on the fixture that illuminated the steps. They were simple wood planks, old and cranky, and they complained with every step I took to the bottom.

Once there, I hit the other light and glanced around. The basement stayed cool most of the year on its own, and a huge humidifier kept the air dry, which meant I didn't need to stick all of the bodies in freezers. Instead, I had them lined up along the walls, in seated positions like the world's most fucked-up collection of dolls. I knew how sick it was, but I'd been ghosting for three years. I also knew how useful they could be.

Bringing the dead back to life was easy enough, once you knew what you were doing. In its simplest form it was a test of will - mind over matter. I could hear the thrumming of the magic around me, a decent pocket of energy that had been the reason we'd chosen this house. That, and the cheap rent paid in cash. I could feel it too, a charge in the air that tickled my skin when I stood still enough.

There was a brick wall between being a sensitive and being a user, but once you made it over that didn't mean you were on the same level as every other user out there. Wizards varied with regard to both power and ability. Most of us had an affinity towards a specific frequency or range of frequencies within the magical fields, and that was what made someone an illusionist, or an aquamancer, or a necro. Those that could work with the whole range were the rarest of the rare, and those that could do it well were even rarer. The only ones like that I knew about were the heads of each of the Houses.

When the reversal had taken place and the fields became active, it was the Houses that had helped bring some kind of order to the chaos of a world where not only had magic suddenly become very real, but so had a number of other things that had once been thought to only exist inside of fairy tales, movies, fantasy novels, and nightmares. The new humans weren't limited to alternate homo sapiens. The fields affected everything, and not all of it was friendly.

It was the masters of the Houses that had also figured out that this whole thing had happened before, all those years ago, during the fairly early days of man when the last reversal had occurred. Scientists had called it the Laschamp event, after the lava flows that proved its occurrence. Considering the shift before Laschamp had happened almost a million years ago, the one after should have continued for hundreds of thousands of years, meaning we would have had magic and everything that went with it from our humble beginnings as neanderthals.

Instead, it lasted somewhere between two hundred and five hundred years.

So what had happened? The working hypothesis was that a single wizard had found a way to force the polarities to shift back, and in doing so had not only destroyed our access to magic, but had also killed anything that had ever absorbed the power, including himself. It always seemed too convenient to be true, but the Houses pointed to the sudden and tremendous population growth of what would evolve into homo sapiens, the only human types that weren't killed in the blast. Knowing what I knew now, and putting myself in that position... I couldn't say I wouldn't have done the same thing.

In any case, the Houses had been a single House once. A conclave of the most powerful wizards to evolve from the shift, who joined together during the original crisis to help keep the world running smoothly. Of course, given time they began to argue about what they should be doing with their power, and so the conclave went rock band and split up. A pretty even balance of power emerged among the many now fragmented Houses, and with none of them wanting to challenge one another openly, they looked to anonymous agents, ghosts, in their constant see-saw battle for control.

Sometimes it was about money, other times it was power, and most times it was to stop one House or another from getting too much of a foothold. Whatever their individual reasons, in the end it wound up being the best thing for the world at large, because it prevented any massive, open wars from developing. When you considered that conventional warfare was bad enough on its own, the idea of adding magic to the mix only made it all the more terrifying.

The other benefit was that it helped keep a good portion of users under control. As long as they had strong enough mojo, any that didn't already belong to the Houses were recruited into the fold whenever possible.

Except for necros. They didn't recruit necros. They had no use for the dying, or the dead, and there was a standing agreement between them not to promote death magic, because they feared it as much as I did. That was why it was better to keep it a secret. Better to stay anonymous, to let Danelle be the contact, and just do the jobs.

Which is why I was standing in a cold, musty basement, surrounded by corpses.

CHAPTER FIVE

Looks easy enough.

TAKING IN MAGICAL ENERGY WAS two parts genetics, one part skill. The genetics part had to do with being able to absorb the energy and store it, like metaphysical fat cells. If you couldn't store the energy, you couldn't use it, because you had to build up enough to make it *do* something. That was sensitives in a nutshell. Once you stored the energy, you needed to know how to release it. That was the skill part. I didn't know what controlled the frequencies different wizards were able to access. I only knew it was related to DNA, and that it theoretically could be bred into or out of people. That was Danelle's story at its root.

She was a failed experiment.

I was a pharmaceutical anomaly.

Life was spectacularly unfair that way.

I pulled the energy in and held it, like taking a deep breath and never letting go. Then I walked over to one of the corpses leaning against the wall. His name was Rayon, and he was a hulk of a man that put Rodge and his bro to shame. During his life, he'd been a body builder, with a strong addiction to both human growth hormone and cocaine. It had been the cocaine that killed him. Not from an overdose, but from an angry dealer who wanted to get paid. He had a bullet hole in his forehead, and a deep cut along his neck. He also walked with a horrible limp, since they'd played with him a bit first and cut his achilles. He was too big to be stealthy, so I used him more for mundane lifting than anything else.

I put my hand to the dead forehead, releasing the held breath of energy with my voice. "Come on, Rayon. Time to wake up." Except for the name, I didn't think the words were that important. The vocalization was.

My hand warmed from the energy flowing through it. A few seconds later, Rayon blinked.

"Awww, why me?"

The animation left a connection, a gossamer thread of energy that reached from his soul to me. It was the tether I used to control them, to make them do what I wanted, and to hold them in this world. The further they got from me, the more free will they had, their nascent personality taking over and sending them wherever. Until they got too far. Then the connection was lost altogether, they got dropped from their bodies, and any passer-by could just come across a wayward corpse. It had almost happened once in the beginning, before I had known better. I was more careful now.

"I need you to help me get some of the others out of here. We're ditching this place."

He stretched out his limbs and groaned. The dead didn't need to stretch, but their souls still thought they did. "You look like shit, man. How long's it been?"

"Since I woke you last? I don't know, a month?"

"Feels like forever." He stood up, towering over me. His decaying flesh probably stunk, but I had developed an ambivalence to it. "How many are you taking?"

I hadn't thought about that. I turned in a circle, looking around the room. I had about a dozen bodies out of the freezers, and three more in them. I also had a small collection of cats, dogs, birds, and mice. You'd be surprised how useful birds and mice could be.

The idea of leaving any of them bothered me. As sad as it was, they were like family. Still, I only had so much room in the van.

"Take Evan and Kerry from the freezer and put them in the coolers. I have to think about the rest."

"Okay." He lumbered off to one of the Frigidaires, his awkward steps shaking the floor.

Evan was a former member of the Chicago S.W.A.T, which made him indispensable as firepower, despite the fact that his body was a mess. Kerry had been a ghost, before she'd first lost her left hand, and then lost her life. They were my two go-to zombies, when I didn't need to worry about them being seen. True, the wounds could be disguised, but the rotting flesh and visible muscle and bone couldn't, at least not without it being beyond suspicious.

I looked over the others. Mr. Timms would come for Danelle's sentimentality, but otherwise the animals were easy enough to replace. The rest of the people? I wanted to bring them, but I couldn't. Not without a place to bring them to.

That included Rayon.

He was more gentle than his mass would indicate as he lifted Kerry's stiff form into his arms and headed for the stairs. I stopped him before he reached them.

"What's up, boss?" he asked.

"Rayon, I... uh... You need to stay here, when we're done packing."

I never knew what to expect from them. I never knew if they would be happy, like Caroline had seemed to be, or if I was punching their ticket for a permanent ride back to Hell. Rayon just stared at me as though I'd lost the tether, and then he nodded.

"I'm too big. I get it."

"I'm leaving all of you here."

"Not Evan and Kerry. I bet you're bringing Mr. Timms, too."

"Danelle would kill me if I didn't." There was a long, silent, uncomfortable pause. "What's it like, when you aren't here?"

"I don't know."

I had asked the question more times than I could count. That was the only answer I'd ever gotten. I hadn't expected anything else, but I kept trying anyway.

"Do you want to go back?"

"I'd like to be alive, but I can't have that. This is closer, so I like it well enough. Otherwise, I don't care."

I stepped out of his way, having resolved none of the guilt I was feeling. He went up the stairs and into the kitchen. I heard him greet Danelle on his way out to the van.

She was still at the kitchen table. The glasses were resting on top of her head. "I don't know, Conor."

I pulled one of the chairs over and sat next to her. "You don't know what?"

She leaned forward and turned the laptop so I could see the screen. "The job is to get into Mrs. Red's house. Her house, Conor!"

"I can get into a house. We've both done it before."

"This isn't just a house. This is a House house. No, not just a House house. This is fucking Red's house. My father is a cheap-ass, only paying two million for this job. It's suicide."

Each of the Houses went by a color, and usually the color fit their personality. It was easy enough to guess from that why Danelle was concerned.

"He thought the two ogres could do it."

She tapped a few buttons on the laptop. A 3D image of the home popped up. It was your typical east coast mansion, with a huge lawn, big driveway, lots of fountains, columns, and rooms. I'd stolen a flash drive from a place like it once. For a thief, the size was an advantage. It made it that much easier to hide.

"I'm not so sure he did." She tapped a few more buttons, and the view panned in. A bunch of red dots appeared. "Each of those dots is a guard."

38

"Users?"

She shrugged. "No way to know. Probably not. Take a close look though, Conor. Every line of sight from every room is covered." She zoomed through the walls, turning the point of view so I could see what she was talking about. "Mrs. Grey wanted those two dead. How do we know Black didn't too?"

"He was going to pay two million for it? When Grey was only offering a hundred thousand?"

"Now you're pretending that the Houses are logical."

"Now you're deluding yourself that they aren't." I leaned forward and pushed her hand aside so I could take control. I moved the camera up and out so I could get a bird's eye view of the property. "Did they include kinetics?"

"Shift plus K."

I hit the keys and watched the red dots move back and forth in a loop. Just getting this kind of data would have cost Black a million or more.

"There are two possibilities. One, this job is legit, and the pay is high because the risk is high. Ogres may not be subtle, but they can take a beating. Two, Black wanted those two dead, and he wanted Red to kill them. He's already gotten number two for free, and you said I'm stuck, so I might as well bank on number one and claim the prize."

"I have a third possibility. He wanted those two dead in that house for a reason, and since you fucked it up you're going to take their place."

I bit my tongue, and watched the loop a few more times.

"Right there." I pointed at the screen. "I can make a break in the whole thing. Twelve seconds."

Danelle laughed. "You can't get from the wall to the house in twelve seconds."

I looked up as Rayon came back in and shuffled past, his heavy feet ratcheting up the volume on the basement steps.

"I'm iffy, but Kerry definitely can."

"Conor, no." She sounded angry again. "You can't trust her on a job like this."

"Why not? She's fast, she's quiet."

"How is she going to vault the wall without a hand?"

"Good point." I went back to examining the kinetics, ignored Rayon when he passed by with Evan over his shoulder. "I only need to take out one of them." I pointed to the red dot near the back door. "Clean break to the target. What is it, anyway?"

Dannie took command of the keyboard again. "There's a picture." She pulled it up on the screen.

It was mottled grey, vaguely oval, and about eight by six inches in size.

"A rock?" I asked.

"I don't know. It looks like it. Maybe it's enchanted, like your dice?"

It seemed like the best explanation. The Houses spent a lot of time and money vying for artifacts from the Laschamp. If they'd known about the dice they would have gone crazy trying to get a hold of them, despite the fact that they could only be used by a necromancer.

"Forty-eight hours. Well, forty-six now. We need to high tail it out of here, and then I need to get to…"

"Connecticut."

I should have guessed from the render. I shifted so I could look her in the eye. "I know you aren't thrilled with this, Dannie, but we've been scraping by for how long? I finish this one job, and we're set for a year at least. A whole year where we don't have to worry about how we're going to eat, or if we're going to get taken by something on the street, or if I'll even be able to afford the meds and stay alive another month. I know you don't want to do anything for your dad, but you know we need this."

She pursed her lips. "You shouldn't have taken the card. I've got enough of a reputation to keep getting easy jobs for a long time. Easy, safe jobs."

"Like the hit on Carlos Jimenez?"

She couldn't help but flinch at the name of the pyromancer who had taken her legs. They hadn't clued us in to the fact that he was a user, and so we'd been reckless in confronting him. He'd lit the match and tossed it at her, and all it had taken from there was a release of energy, and the small flame had spread into a fireball. She'd crumpled to the ground, screaming out in the kind of agony I could never have imagined, while I had to figure out a new approach to killing him. Shooting pyros was a tricky proposition, because they could take the muzzle flash and throw it back in your face, even as the bullet killed them.

In the end, I'd rushed him. He had tried to lay his hands on me, to burn me with his touch. We'd grappled for a minute, and he put a hole right through my hoodie before I got in a lucky punch, causing him to fall and hit his head on a coffee table. It broke his fall, but not before it broke his neck.

There were no hospitals for ghosts, and so the first night was agony. The next three weeks weren't much better. Dalton had come by to do what he could at a nice profit, which included amputating her legs to just above the knee, and I only slept about sixteen hours over the whole span of time.

"Fuck you for mentioning it. You know what I mean."

"I'm sorry, Dannie. It's just... I'm tired of living this way, and I'm even more tired of dying this way. I'm doing this job with or without you."

She reached out and put her hand on my face. "With me, Conor. I'm not about to abandon my best friend, even if you are being a jackass."

"You say that like it's something new."

CHAPTER SIX

It's not easy being green.

WE LEFT THE HOUSE TWO hours later, after clearing out our meager possessions and pouring kerosene on anything that would burn. The back of the van was surprisingly empty: two corpses in the coolers, an old steamer trunk filled with tools of the trade, and a couple of dumpy old fabric suitcases containing ninety percent clothes, and ten percent memories.

Outside of what I carried, my most prized possession was a picture of Karen, Molly, and myself that I'd found on Facebook, printed from an inkjet on thin copy paper and framed in clear plastic. It was my reminder of better days, and the perfect life that had gone sour because of a breakdown in my molecular construction. I don't know why, but when I looked at it I almost felt normal again. I almost believed I was still a human being. I'd laid it on top of my pile of dark hoodies, black tees, jeans, pants, underwear, and socks, so meager that I couldn't even fill my suitcase completely.

Danelle's stuff wasn't much more impressive. She had a greater range of blouses, camis, sweaters, tights, and jeans, but her own memories were limited to a photo of her with her brother before she'd been disavowed, and another of her with her ex-husband, before he'd been caught on a job and killed.

It was a sad life, but it was a life.

"Thanks, Rayon," Danelle said, after the big zombie lowered her gently into the passenger seat. "I'm going to miss you."

"Really?" He seemed surprised.

"Really."

He gave her a half-smile, turned, and shambled back towards the house. I was standing at the front door, holding a lighter.

"It's okay, boss." He could tell I was feeling guilty. I don't know how, but he could. "I don't know what I'm going back to, but something tells me its better than what you've got." He looked back towards the van. "With one exception, maybe."

I couldn't believe he was trying to cheer me up, when I was about to turn him to ash. Then I remembered what I had packed into the van.

"Maybe you're right, with one exception." Danelle and I made lousy bedmates, but we'd clicked everywhere else. I patted the zombie on the shoulder, and handed him the lighter. "You know what to do. Maybe I'll see you on the other side someday. Just not too soon."

His answer was unexpected. His face turned eerily dark, his eyes narrowing and his lip curling in an almost-snarl. "Stay away as long as you can. If you think it isn't safe for you here, you have no idea what's waiting."

A lump rose into my throat. "What the hell are you talking about?"

Rayon's face regained its peaceful neutrality. "What?"

"What...the...hell?" My heart was pounding, and I could feel my muscles tensing up. I'd always been afraid of death. Having it threaten me was new.

"I don't know."

"You don't know?"

"Sorry, boss."

I stared into his blank brown eyes, searching for some shred of whatever had caused the outburst, and finding nothing. "Whatever, Rayon. Go do what you need to do."

I headed back towards the van, trying to calm the pounding in my heart. The door to the house creaked open and smacked closed behind me. By the time I slid into the driver's seat and turned to look, the flames were licking at the windows. I could see Rayon through them, his hand raised in a wave, smoke swirling around him.

I found the thread connecting us and cut it. A second later, his body fell from view.

"It never gets easier, does it?" Danelle asked.

I turned the key and brought the van to life. My hands were quaking against the wheel. "That depends on the corpse. Evan's useful, but he's an asshole. Ray was a good one, though."

I put the car in reverse and backed it out of the driveway. The smoke from the house was getting more noticeable, and I wanted to be gone before the neighbors called the fire department. I could only imagine what they'd think when they went into the basement. There was a reason we'd paid our rent in cash.

"Where to?"

I sucked in my breath and held it, hoping it would calm the tremors Rayon's words had caused.

Danelle dug the card out of a small backpack at her feet. "We need to cash this in so we can lose the trail."

"Why didn't you just do it at the house?"

"Too direct. We need to route it through a few other holdings first, so it will be harder to trace back to me."

She was still worried I was going to blow it, and her father would find out she was involved in his business. Even if he thought she was working for him. It was nuts, but that was the depth of his disappointment.

"They're going to take twenty percent."

"Money well spent. Even if you finish the job they're going to try to trace the funds, just so they know who they're dealing with. Black doesn't like anonymity."

"I thought that was the whole point of being a ghost? I take it you have a contact in mind?"

She smiled. "Of course. Head down to the Loop."

"It's two o'clock in the morning. The banks aren't open."

"Don't be stupid. This one is."

We crossed over the LaSalle Street bridge, into the canyon between the high skyscrapers that made up the bulk of the financial district. The buildings rose up around us, giant skeletons of steel with concrete and glass skin. Lit interiors brought faint, speckled glows to the exteriors, as overnight janitors prepped the offices for the next day's transactions and underground financiers worked the mundane magic that kept the world moving with as little disruption as possible. Most people didn't know how much the Houses actually controlled. Then again, most people probably didn't care to know.

"You're sure this guy is freelance?"

The streets were almost empty this time of morning, barren but for the occasional vagrant with nowhere else to go, or a patrolling squad car. Most people went inside and locked the doors once it got late enough, including pieces of the criminal element. Even if you were a ghost, it wasn't always a safe place to be.

Not since the reversal.

Not since the monsters.

"I'm sure. There's a lot of coin to be made catering to unaffiliated clientele. Turn right up there, go two blocks and pull over."

"As long as you have enough balls to openly defy the Houses." I made the turn and counted the two blocks, and then stopped the van at the side of the road. The street was deserted.

"You see that alley?" Danelle pointed to an especially dark spot between two buildings. "Go in there, all the way to the back.

There's going to be an emergency exit. Go inside, and climb up to the sixth floor. If anyone tries to stop you, tell them you're there to see Mr. Clean. If they still won't let you by, do what you have to."

"His name isn't really Mr. Clean, is it?"

"Close. What does it matter? Oh, and just so you know what to expect, he's a goblin."

"You're kidding?"

She gave me the evil eye. "Do I look like I'm kidding?"

It wasn't that I was racist against leathers. I had worked a shift in a clinic that treated them almost exclusively. Their mistrust had been palpable, but when you set a broken bone, or treated a case of ambrosia, they were as grateful as anybody else. My surprise was more because this Mr. Clean had somehow beat the odds and made something of himself. The fact that he was doing it in the same thread of reality as the Houses only made it more impressive.

I got up and moved to the back of the van, unlatching the steamer and lifting the lid. There was no order to the way we'd packed the guns, we'd just piled them in as we found them, and so I grabbed the first pistol I saw. It was a standard issue piece, matte black and plain in appearance. I shoved it into the back of my pants, under the trench coat. I dug around a bit to find a second handgun, and gave it to Danelle.

"I'm not leaving you here alone, either."

The place where we had stopped was pretty light on energy, but it was enough to get Evan up and moving. I lifted the lid to the cooler and reached in, pulling on the fields and sending the magic through me and into the corpse. I was still a little freaked out by what Rayon had said, and my voice trembled when I called him back.

"Captain Evan Williams. Time to deploy."

The cold, glassy eyes became a little less cold and glassy. A skeletal arm reached up and grabbed the edge of the cooler, and his half-face created an angry sneer.

"You know I hate when you call me like that, asshole. You were never on the force, so don't act like you're my C.O."

"Just get up," I said. I didn't like Evan. I never had. I respected him for the badass he had been when he was alive… excluding the fact that he'd gotten blasted in the chest by his own wife after he'd almost beat her to death.

He lifted himself from the cooler and stepped out, his bone foot making a hollow sound when it landed on the floor of the van. "Well? What do you want?"

"I want you to defend the van. If anything tries to give Danelle trouble, take care of it."

He glanced over at her and sighed. "Invalid duty again?"

"Fuck you, Evan," Danelle said.

"Back at you. It's not like I have a choice." He looked over the collection of weaponry. "Still no M-16?"

"Do you know how much those things cost?"

He picked up the Bushmaster. "This is close enough, I guess. You want me inside or outside?"

"Stay inside unless there's trouble."

"Fine. Now get lost."

I went back to the front of the van. "Any last words?"

"Try not to touch anyone. We can't afford to boost you a second time in the same week." She handed me the card.

I nodded and went out through the drivers side, circling around the back of the van towards the alley. The street was still deserted, and the quietness left me feeling edgy. Even so, I made it to the rear of the building without incident.

The door was there, just as Danelle had said. I tried to push it open. Locked. I looked around while I dug my hand into another pocket, locating my set of picks and bringing them into the open. I moved myself so my body hugged the door while my hands worked the picks, and the picks worked the tumblers. The door was open inside of five seconds.

I slipped in, using as little space as possible. I was in the inner emergency stairwell, a narrow, dimly lit vertical expanse of metal grated stairs. Looking up, I could see a pair of size twenty feet three floors above me. They weren't moving, so I could only assume the wearer hadn't heard me come in.

Which left me with an interesting choice. Sneak up on him and take him out, or let him know I was here right now. I tucked myself into the shadows and watched him for a minute while I tried to decide. Danelle had known there would be guards in the stairwell, which meant they could probably be reasoned with.

"Hello," I said, raising my voice and stepping out of the shadows. The pair of feet shifted, and then a large head leaned over the railing, looking down at me.

"How'd you get in here? I didn't hear nuthin'." His voice was deep, and it echoed through the stairwell.

I ignored his question. "I'm here to see Mr. Clean."

"What for?"

I held up the card, making sure it caught enough of what little light there was that he would understand.

"Who's the ghost?"

"Daaé." Every ghost had a handle. That one was Dannie's.

He stopped looking down at me. There was some rustling. His voice carried in the narrow enclosure. "Got a ghost here... Daaé... Mr. Clean... yeah, okay." His head re-appeared. "Come on up, slow like. Keep your hands where I can see 'em."

His small, dark eyes followed me a I wound my way up the steps, walking as lightly as I could so that the soles of my boots barely made a sound on the steel. I wanted him to know I could have snuck up on him, if I'd wanted to.

Even when I reached the third floor landing, I still had to look up. The leather was nearly seven feet tall, and my head only hit his thick chest. He glared down at me past his wide, flat nose and smiled, holding out a meaty hand. "Gimme your piece."

I returned his smile and slowly reached under the trench to remove the gun from my pants. I dropped it into his waiting palm.

"You'll get this back when your business is done. Head up to the sixth."

I didn't say anything else to him. I stepped past his hulking form and climbed the next three flights of stairs. I coughed once when I got to the top. The downward spiral was beginning again already.

There was another orc behind the stairwell door, and he opened it for me when I arrived. He looked a lot like the first, but with straighter black hair and a fancy silver earring. His ordinance was heavier too, a fully-automatic assault rifle with an extended clip.

"You Daaé?"

"I'm the only one on the stairs."

He grunted a laugh. "Smart ass. Third door on your left. Don't touch anything."

I nodded and walked by. I was in a long hallway with a pink marble floor and a scattering of doors on either side, each leading to a different financial office. All of them were likely owned by one House or another, through all sorts of shell corporations and entities that made them difficult to trace all the way back. The third door on the left belonged to 'Simon & Williams Accounting'. It was the only one whose lights were on. Looking through the small glass window, I could see a receptionist desk with a pretty young woman sitting behind it. I turned the handle and walked in.

"I'm-"

"Daaé," the woman said. She was a petite thing, with shoulder length blonde hair and delicate features. I could see the tips of her ears poking out through strands of gold.

"Does Mr. Clean have a thing against homo sapiens?"

The elf smiled. "My mother is a traditional human, so I would say probably not. You can have a seat over there." She directed me towards a row of chairs.

"I have to wait?"

"You don't like to wait?"

I approached the desk. I was six floors up and a hundred feet in from the street, and I could feel my line to Evan wasn't as strong as I'd like. "I left my friend outside in the van. I'd prefer her to still be there when I get back."

She looked like she actually cared. "Just a minute."

She stepped out from behind the desk and walked past me to a door on the left, giving me a whiff of fruit and spices. It wasn't perfume, elves just smelled that way, even halves. I took a deep breath to gather it in. For the dying, it was like taking a hit of life.

Of all the new humans, elves were the most integrated into the society of the now 'traditional' humans, to the point that half-elves were becoming somewhat common. Others, like the orcs, goblins, ogres, and other so-called leathers were still fighting for equal rights, fair job opportunities, and all of the socioeconomic bullshit that had plagued the prior minorities for so long. It was amazing how quickly that racism had been forgotten once a few new races had started manifesting.

In the beginning it had been much worse, with a whole lot of 'cides. Suicide, fratricide, infanticide, genocide. Until the Houses had put an end to it, even going so far as to force the major governments to parcel out land where the leathers that didn't want to deal with all the crap could do their own thing. That move had ended the threat of open warfare, and limited the problems to simple hate and segregation.

We never learned.

She came back in. "He'll see you now."

"Thank you, Miss…"

"Salazar."

"Miss Salazar. I don't deserve your kindness."

Her eyes were soft and sincere. "You look like you could use all the kindness you can get." She flashed me another smile, gave me another fruit and spice walk-by, and motioned towards the door.

I pushed through a frosted glass door into an open space filled with low-walled cubicles and computers. A light from a flat monitor provided the path to Mr. Clean. I could see him already, a small-statured man with a bald head and a subtle green pigmentation to his thick skin.

"Daaé," he said when I reached him. He turned his head from the monitor, the screen filled with numbers. He stood and stuck out his hand. "My name is Sal, it's a pleasure."

It might have been a test, but unlike some, I didn't hesitate to shake. "Thanks for seeing me."

"No need to thank me, no need at all. I don't mean to be rude, but I'd like to get this business concluded so I can get back to more important matters. I would have made you wait, but my assistant Gloria took pity on you. Do you have the card?"

Pity? I held myself in check and found the card in my pocket. He pulled it from my grip.

"I'm sending it through about two dozen accounts, so it will take a couple of days for the funds to show up."

Great. I might be dead before I saw the statement. "How do you know where to deliver it?"

"Don't worry about that, pal." His fingers flew along the keys, and screens flashed one after another. Then he put the card in front of it and scanned it. "Done."

Two million sitting in our account in two days. All I had to do now was finish the job, and time wasn't on my side. "The kill team can track the card's path back to you. How do I know you won't snitch if they come for me?"

He turned his chair back to me. "Who said I wouldn't snitch? This protection is only good as long as you finish the job. I've got a business to run, and I run it by misdirecting the Houses, not misleading them. Now, if you don't mind." He waved his hand, shooing me away.

I stood there for a few more seconds, but Sal didn't notice. He'd already put his attention back on the monitor, and was flitting through screens faster than my eyes could follow.

"You still here?" he asked, without turning his head.

I thought I should say something, but what would be the point? I turned and left.

When I reached Miss Salazar, she looked at me with a sad expression. "It's just the way he is."

I nodded, but didn't say anything.

Pity?

CHAPTER SEVEN

No rest for the wicked.

"Boring night," Evan said, the minute I opened the door to the van and slid back in behind the wheel. I pulled the door shut and looked over at Danelle.

"That was pleasant."

She laughed. "Clean? It's just his personality, but can you blame him? Goblins don't have it easy, even among the other leathers."

"Next time you can watch Wendy Wheelchair, and I'll go take care of business." Evan opened the steamer trunk and tossed the Bushmaster back inside. "I'm going to get rusty, as little action as I've been seeing lately. Either use me or let me sleep, but this guard duty bullshit is getting old."

I wasn't in the mood for Evan's mouth. "Stand down, captain."

He groaned through his teeth while he climbed back into the cooler. It didn't matter how much he hated me, he wasn't in charge. "I hope you die before you need me again." He pulled the lid closed, and I cut the cord.

"The money's being transferred as we speak, minus four hundred thousand, but it won't show up for a couple of days." I started the van and pulled away from the curb, out onto the empty streets. Unlike Evan, I was grateful for the quiet.

"One less thing to worry about," Danelle said. "Now we just

need to find a new place to live."

"You aren't making the trip to the coast with me?"

She gave me the 'stop being a dumb ass' look. "What use would I be to you? I can roll this thing pretty quick, but all it takes is a flight of stairs and I'm out of the action. Let's just find somewhere for me to hole up, and I'll see if I can dig up anything about what it is you're going to try to steal."

"Fair enough. There's plenty of lousy hotels outside of O'Hare. Just pick one that doesn't have valet. I don't think they'd like the surprises in the back."

She found my cell in the glove compartment and hit the internet. I navigated us out of the Loop and made my way to I-90 while she searched for a good rate.

"How about the Best Western?"

"Free continental breakfast?"

"And free wi-fi."

"Jackpot."

By the time we pulled into the parking lot a little bit later, Dannie had already managed to score me an executive coach seat on a four o'clock flight to Connecticut. She'd also arranged for me to pick up a car there.

"I don't know what I'd do without you," I said, as I opened the passenger side and helped her with her chair. In truth, I did know, but it was a ritual we'd started whenever she would help me arrange a job.

She smiled and put her hand on my cheek. "You'd be dead. In a ditch. Or maybe an alley." She released my face and vaulted from the van to the chair with practiced ease.

Her answer wasn't too far from the truth. After all, she'd found me half-dead in a gutter.

"Can I help you?" Our rep's name was Jonathan. He was a heavyset man with a goatee and a light wisp of brown hair. When he looked at me, it was with an odd mix of fascination and disgust.

I thought it was ironic, considering that he was killing himself on purpose.

"I made a reservation online," Danelle said, getting his attention. "Daaé."

He ran his fingers along the touchscreen, doing some turns and taps. "Credit card?"

She reached into the lip of her bra and grabbed her plastic, resting it on her index finger and thumb. She flicked it up, flipping it so that it twirled end over end and landed cleanly on the desk.

"Wow, nice." Jonathan picked up the card.

"You've been practicing," I said.

"A little."

Jonathan swiped it, did some more random tapping, and then prepped a couple of room keys for us. "Room 207. The elevator is right around the corner. Go up, follow the signs." He handed me the card-keys and the credit card, and looked over at Danelle. "Are you sure you don't-"

"She's sure," I said, cutting him off. It was obvious to anyone that Dannie had no legs, but that didn't mean she liked being treated that way. A handicap room would have been easier to manage, but she wasn't interested in easy. She wanted to live her life the way she had before, in every way she could.

I could understand that, even if I couldn't do the same.

"Okay. Enjoy your stay."

I nodded my thanks, collected our luggage, and followed Dannie to the elevators.

"You've only got three hours before your flight," she said while she rolled on board for the short ride up.

"I thought I'd go over the kinetics a few more times. I need to synchronize."

"That's a good idea."

We found our room and made our way inside. It was a standard three-star hotel room, with a queen bed, a writing desk, an armoire with a flat-screen, coffeemaker - the usual. It hadn't been renovated in a while.

"Home sweet home. You better make it back. I don't think I can stand being stuck in this place for more than a few days. The colors are awful."

"Do you say that about me?" I wore black ninety percent of the time. I wore gray the other ten. Colorful threads didn't look good on me. They tended to accentuate the pallor. "You know, if I die, you still get to keep the money."

"Only if I can convince the kill team that I had nothing to do with it. What do you think the odds are that they'll even give me the chance?"

"I already feel guilty."

She rolled over to her luggage, lifting and heaving it onto the end of the bed. "I'm not trying to make you feel guilty. This is death or death for you, I get that, and I hitched my wagon to yours a long time ago. We're in the shit together."

She unzipped her bag and pushed past the clothes to where the laptop was resting. She pulled it out and wheeled it over to the desk. I didn't try to move the chair out of the way for her. I knew she'd take care of it. It wasn't that she'd never accept help, but only if she knew you would have done it even if she were still fully operational.

Her upper body was strong, and she lifted the desk chair in one arm and spun about in a tight three-sixty, dropping it next to the table. She replaced it at the desk, opening the cover of the laptop and navigating back into the kinetics. We watched the dots a couple more times, and then started going over my route.

I found my other watch in another pocket. It wasn't the same one I had used to time my assault on the hulk twins; this one was more modern, with a curved, full-color screen and a buffet of apps installed on it. I opened up the timer app and reset it. I preferred the old-fashioned kind of watch because I didn't need to worry about the lithium running out of ions in the middle of a run. In this case, I needed the extra features.

It took another hour and a half and dozens of repetitions to get a clean plot of the inception, from the moment I snuck over the ten foot stone wall at exactly 10:31pm, to the second I put my hand on the prize at 10:39:08.

Eight minutes going in. It was a long time. I wasn't going to tell Dannie, but it made me nervous. So much could happen in eight minutes. So much could go wrong, and I had bet both our lives on it. Of course, she wasn't the one being threatened from the great beyond. Remembering what Rayon said gave me a new chill.

"That's it," I said, hitting the screen and setting the last timer. Once I started the countdown, it would vibrate on my wrist as each checkpoint was reached. If I hadn't made it... I didn't want to think about not making it.

"You still have a little time." She closed the lid of the laptop and rolled over to the window. I had parked in a good spot, leaving the van visible from our room. She wasn't looking for that though. She was looking to see if we were already being tailed.

"Anything?"

She reached up and lowered the blinds, closing them tight. "Not so far. Hey, did you see the news this morning? There's some Senator in Iowa pushing a meta registration bill."

"This again?"

In the sixty years since the reversal, and the forty since the Houses had smoothed the brave new world over, there had been what seemed like a bi-annual effort to force 'metas' to declare themselves. That was the fancy term the politicians used for wizards. The line of thinking was that we were inherently dangerous, because we could create destruction seemingly out of thin air. First, for most of us it didn't work like that. Second, guns were still a whole lot more dangerous than users were the vast majority of the time, and not everyone who owned a gun was subject to the scrutiny that we tended to fall under.

Dannie rolled her eyes. "The Houses will get it lobbied out again. Personally, I think she's just looking to line her pockets a bit more."

"She should introduce a subhuman equal rights bill if she just wants to get someone to pay for her next trip to Bora Bora."

There was no end of the groups that wanted to keep the leathers down and out, to go with the few that wanted to welcome them in. On one hand, I could understand the discomfort with having your CEO be a ten foot tall, muscular, greenish brute with long teeth jutting out from the corner of their mouth. It was a little intimidating. On the other, they were people. They looked different, and they had varying intelligence levels depending on their types, but we had the same origins. Some, like the ogres, even had their own specific usefulness. Fukishima would still be melting down if it hadn't been for them and their immunity to radiation.

We fell into a somewhat uncomfortable silence. We were trying to fill the gap while we waited for my flight. The fact was we were both nervous as hell about it. I'd done sneak and grabs before. So had she. We were good at them. This... This was the major leagues. This was serious business. If it wasn't for the fact that it was too late to go back, way too late, I would have been really tempted to call it off.

Dannie turned on the television. "I hate waiting on a job."

I flopped down on the bed with my jacket still on, while she flipped channels until she found some late-night news. We got past the commercials for the latest invention in slow cooking, what to do if you have diabetes, and class action lawsuit notices. It faded to a pretty young thing in a short, tight business suit.

"This is the scene from Nevada's Death Valley Yard only a short time ago," she said. The video skipped off her to some amateur footage of a line of armed men in uniform, standing atop a high wall and firing down. "According to sources, a riot broke out in the yard at around eleven o'clock, when one of the inhabitants allegedly assaulted and killed a guard."

More gunfire. Growling could be heard from off-camera, along with shouting and screaming.

"The ferals imprisoned inside overwhelmed security before breaking out into the yard itself. Reports have come in that the containment team was successful in regaining control of the situation, but not before a half dozen of the inhabitants managed to escape through a rear exit that had been abandoned during the riot."

The camera was shifting all over the place, from the men firing down into the yard, and then to the yard itself. Spotlights had been aimed at the chaos, and in it I could see the ferals; the third kind of new human. These were the creatures that were supposed to go bump in the night. The weres, the wendigo, the vampires and the like. People who were people, but who had changed in ways that made them violent, unpredictable, and an overall danger to the rest of our dysfunctional society.

The camera scanned across them. The different blocks of the yard would hold the different kinds of ferals, grouped so that they wouldn't kill one another. This one was for weres. Dozens of dead lay motionless in the bright light of the yard, their tough bones and thick, furry hides ravaged in bullet holes, blood pooled around them.

A lot of people, including leathers, hated the ferals, and would find the scene exciting. I killed people who were in the business, who knew what they were getting themselves into and the risk they were taking. My prior life had been dedicated to saving people. I saw only sadness and futility in it.

In the beginning, when the ferals had first appeared, there had been rightful terror. They needed to eat fresh meat to survive, and their new mental state didn't give them much room to discern between wild game like boar and deer, and human beings like their neighbor or their little sister Susie. Of course this led to them being hunted down without regulation or control, in many cases by their own families. Like all things fighting to survive, they had found one another and joined together, creating growing packs of violent, cannibalistic wanderers.

There was a lot of death then. A lot of destruction. Time passed. Science. We learned that one, it wasn't their fault, and two, it could happen to anyone. The mutation wasn't straight genetics. It was like a virus, able to be carried without showing symptoms, and passed along like HIV. The really shitty part? The number of people carrying it was growing, as if feral human is what we were meant to be.

"Its so sad," Dannie said.

The gunfire stopped. The camera zoomed out to take in the whole yard. There was no motion.

"According to Peter Mays, the Director of the Death Valley Yard, eight guards were killed in the riots, along with forty-six of the two hundred seventy-eight ferals in Block 'C', making it the third deadliest feral riot in history." The young reporter shifted her eyes to a new camera angle. "Residents of the area around the yard have been advised to be on the lookout for the escaped ferals, and Homeland Security has mobilized search units to locate the escapees. The National Feral Control Board has scheduled a news conference for ten o'clock tomorrow morning in response to calls for action on increasing feral violence."

"They put people in cages, and expect them to be happy?" Danelle said.

"What do you want them to do?" I didn't like the situation, but the alternative was worse. It wasn't even that the yards were like true incarceration. Their goal was only to contain, to keep the ferals out of society at large and to avoid the mass killings on both sides. That had been the 'compromise' that had calmed the whole episode.

Of course, ferals were still out there, and new ones were 'born' every day. While most were captured and contained as soon as they started the change, there were always some that got away. The smart ones kept themselves hidden in places like Yellowstone, but the smart ones weren't that common. Most tried to go back to the places they knew, and found themselves out on the streets at night with their fellow monsters.

"I don't know. Put them on a reservation?"

I knew her well enough to know she was only half-joking.

CHAPTER EIGHT

Thanks, Grandma!

FIVE YEARS EARLIER...

"COME ON, kiddo, we're going to be late for day care." I leaned over and scooped Molly into my arms, ignoring her complaints. It was tough for a dad to compete with the colorful monsters that laughed their way across the television.

"No," she said. She was two, of course it was her favorite word. I kissed her cheek and found the remote, shutting off the television and heading for the kitchen.

Karen was waiting there. She was ready to go, looking fantastic in a red blouse and dark slacks. Her short hair turned forward behind her ears, and her eyes sparkled when she saw our daughter.

"Cutting it close again, Conor." She reached out and took Molly from me.

My cell was on the counter. It was already eight-thirty. I had twenty minutes to get to the hospital to prep.

"I should be getting the results of the biopsy back today." I tried to say it casually, matter-of-factly, like it was no big deal. It came across flat and nervous.

"I'll come by, if you need me. I know you like to play the tough guy, but you aren't going through this alone." She put her hand on my face. I gave her my best forced smile and tried not to start crying again. They had said there was a good chance the tumor was benign. They were my friends, my peers. They wouldn't lie just to make me feel better.

"No," Molly said again. She wasn't talking about anything. She just liked the sound of it.

"I'll be fine."

I had told myself that a thousand times every day, in hopes that repeating the mantra would make it so. They had found the growth almost by accident, after a skiing incident had broken one of my ribs. The rib had healed okay.

The jury was still out on the tumor.

I put my arms around her, and she swung Molly aside so I could give her a kiss.

"Good luck," she said.

She was worried. She wanted to be there. Part of me wanted her to be there, too. I couldn't bear the thought of hearing bad news in front of her. If it was malignant... I needed my own time to deal, without worrying about her. In any case, there was no guarantee they'd have the results today, and I had a surgery scheduled this morning. The logistics weren't in favor.

"I love you," I said, kissing her again. We'd been married eight years, after being matched by one of her best friends. We'd hit it off right away, a so-called fairytale romance. A year to the wedding, and then five years of trying, some IVF, and a lot of prayer to get Molly into our family. We were close before she joined us. We were closer since.

"I love you, too." She put her head on my chest and kept it there for a minute. She was being strong for Molly. I was being strong for both of them.

"I love you, kiddo." I kissed her pudgy face again, her head turning to avoid the moisture. Then I let go of them both, grabbed my cell, and picked my blazer from a hook next to the door. "I'll call you if I hear anything."

I moved out the door into the garage, and dug out the keys to the Tesla from my blazer pocket. It was one of the originals, and I kept it in great shape. I circled around to unplug it, and then got behind the wheel. I backed out into the street.

Our house wasn't anything special. Fifty years old, four bedrooms and a small yard. It was modest for a surgeon, but it was the kind of place Karen had always dreamed of living in, and she loved it. That meant I loved it, too, and I really did, if only because it was in a low magic zone, and kept the sensitivity from becoming too overpowering.

I'd splurged a bit on the car, but I did have to keep up some kind of appearance in the hospital parking lot.

As I drove, I could hear the pulses of the fields shifting and moving through the earth around me. It had been with me as long as I could remember, but for some reason I was more in tune with it today. It wasn't just the magical energy that was clearer. The sky looked more blue, the air felt more clean. Even the morning traffic barely registered. I was in a weird state of happiness and lust for life that I hadn't felt since Molly was born. I turned on the radio, and started singing along.

My voice trailed off in the middle of the first tune.

That was the moment I knew I had cancer.

###

"It's malignant, isn't it?"

I was sitting in the office of Dr. Robert Anders. His assistant had been waiting for me when I'd come out of surgery, and after a quick shower I'd put my slacks, shirt, and blazer back on and headed up to see him. I knew I should have been more scared, more nervous, more something.

I was resigned.

When the realization had hit, it had done so with such force that nothing short of God's own voice in my head could have convinced me otherwise. I had done my best to stay in denial, and to be positive for Karen. All alone, left to my thoughts, there was nothing to deny.

I was going to die.

I'd remembered my grandmother Sophie then. She lived to a hundred and four. She made it through the reversal, survived the riots and the feral virus, and managed to avoid the Rot. I'd asked her once how she'd been able to survive so long.

"Nothing in life can scare me as much as death," she had said.

She'd borne that out when she had gone screaming from this world, her eyes wide in terror and her voice hoarse. I had made the mistake of being there when it had happened. I had made the mistake of knowing her at all. She'd passed her fear down to me.

He was sitting behind his desk. Seventy years old, an expert in his field. Like Sophie, he'd also been born before the change, and that meant he had seen a lot of bad shit in his time on Earth. He had also given this talk, and worse ones, too many times to think about. Even so, it hadn't become rote. He hadn't become hard. His eyes were soft with compassion, and his lip quivered when he answered me.

"Yes."

I nodded and pursed my mouth. Rob had been the first person I'd met at the hospital. He was the smartest guy I'd ever known. He had more experience in his pinkie than I had in my whole body.

"How long?"

He opened his mouth, and I knew he was going to give me all of the disclaimer bullshit that he had to throw in there, so that the hospital was safe from legal trouble.

I put my hand up to cut him off. "How long?"

"Six months at best. I'm sorry, Conor. In my professional opinion... less than three."

Three months? Ninety-days? I had been expecting the worst. I had underestimated. I clenched my stomach to keep myself together. I thought about calling Karen. To tell her what? 'Hi honey, I'm going to be dead by Christmas. Now that I've dropped that bomb on you, can you please drive over here without getting into an accident?'

"Conor?" Rob stood. "Look, I know this is hard…"

"I know you do," I interrupted. He had told me stories, and it wasn't like I was a novice. I'd made the 'I'm sorry' speech before. I'd lost people in the operating room.

"You don't deserve this. You're a good man."

I sat in silence. Deserve had nothing to do with it. It was just bad luck. He was twice my age, and in three months he would open his eyes, kiss his wife, get out of bed, and come to work. I'd be sucking dirt.

"If you need anything…"

There was so much a doctor could say to a typical patient. So much they could try to explain, and help them prepare for. So many words they could use to fight through the shit situation both parties found themselves in. Doctor to doctor? There was nothing to say. There was nothing to do. I knew what I was in for. I knew how people fell apart from diagnosis to death.

Three months.

I got to my feet and walked out without another word. My face felt like it was on fire, but it was cold to the touch. My heart was racing, and all the clarity that had brought me to the truth of my situation had fled the moment it had been confirmed. People passed me in the halls. They said hello. Maybe I was cordial and polite, maybe I brushed them off. I don't remember.

Somehow, I made my way to my own office. I closed the door behind me and slumped in my high leather chair, the chair I had dreamed of sitting in from the day I had first played with a stethoscope. I took my phone out of my pocket and held it up. I found Karen in the contact list a dozen times, but I never made the call. I was too afraid my hurt would get her hurt.

I did the only thing there was left for me to do.

I cried. Silently. In agony.

Some people think doctors are superheroes, immune to all of the garbage in life that downs lesser mortals. I was the furthest thing from a superhero. I was anything but strong. I wanted to be. I wished that I could be. I had everything I could ever want, and in three months it would all be gone.

I didn't want to die.

CHAPTER NINE

A legend in the making.

I CALLED DANNIE THE MOMENT I woke up, which was the same time the plane hit the tarmac at Bradley International in Hartford.

"I'm here. Which rental place did you book again?"

"Thrifty." She sounded tired. "How was the flight?"

"I got some sleep. Did I wake you?"

"No. I've been working since you left. I can't find anything even remotely related to the rock you're tracking."

"You didn't think you would." Neither did I. The Houses didn't tend to be interested in things that anyone else knew anything about, although there had been occasional exceptions. I reached into my pocket and found the dice, wrapping them in my hand. You couldn't Google them either.

"Not in public circles, no. I went a little further than that. I called Arlen."

"Are you sure that was a good idea? I don't really need to know what it is in order to carry it."

Arlen Brown was a Professor Emeritus of archaeology at Washington State University. One of the foremost experts in most things pre-Leschamp. Nice guy, a little weird. I liked him overall. The problem was that his specialty was valuable enough to earn him work from a number of the Houses, if not all of them.

Considering the job was a direct hit as opposed to the usual strafe, I didn't like the idea of giving him any information he could pass on, intentionally or not.

"I know, but I'm still not happy about this." She paused, waiting for me to argue with her. When I didn't say anything, she kept going. "Two million to two ogres for a grab? Ogres aren't exactly known for their light feet and quiet gait."

"I thought we had this discussion already." It was all I could think of to say. I might have been walking to my death, just like I was every other day of my life. It was fifty-fifty, and fear of what came after notwithstanding, we needed the money. People had done more for less.

"We did, and I know you think it's a risk worth taking. I wanted to see if I could at least get the odds in your favor, so I asked Arlen about the stone. I sent him a picture."

"How much did that cost?"

"A hundred thousand."

I was tempted to be upset. We'd already lost a quarter of the take, and I hadn't even attempted the job yet. "I'm worth that much to you?" I asked.

"Someone has to bring back Mr. Timms for me."

"What did he say?"

"He'd never seen anything like it."

"That's it?"

"Yeah."

"A hundred thousand, and he gave you a phone shrug?"

"And an apology, and credit for a future inquiry."

"But no money back?"

"No. He did confirm that I'm right to be concerned."

I looked out the window of the plane. We were approaching the gate. It was raining. "Stuck between a rock and a Black House." I was screwed the minute I touched that card. "I don't do this, we spend the rest of our lives trying to evade a kill team. Clean already said he would turn us in without batting an eye."

"I know. I'm not trying to throw your game. I just want you to be extra careful. If they're meaning to hit you, hit them first, and then take whatever the hell that thing is and get out. Hell, if you make it through a trap alive, you might become the next Quidsy."

I laughed at that. Quidsy was a ghost legend. A legend that retired young with all the cash he had earned, only to wind up feral. The rumor had it that his lover had put him down and then gone to collect the thousand dollar 'containment' reward. "I don't think I want to be the next Quidsy."

"You know what I mean."

The airplane doors opened, and everyone stood up around me, rushing to get their carry-on and get off. I sat patiently in my aisle seat, putting my hand to my mouth to stifle a cough. "We're at the terminal. I'll call you when I get to Fairfield."

"Okay. Let me know if you need anything."

"Thanks for worrying about me."

"Everybody deserves to have someone to worry about them."

"Even assholes like me?"

"Especially assholes like you."

CHAPTER TEN

Pit stop.

THE RAIN WAS COMING DOWN hard when I pulled over at a gas station in Fairfield. It was still early in the morning, which gave me lots of time to get myself together before the run. I navigated the Ford Focus I'd been assigned to a spot in front of a convenience store and pulled out my phone.

I stared at it for a minute. I told Dannie I'd call her, but I had nothing to say, and after her earlier pep talk I wasn't feeling like anything we chatted about would be helpful. I also knew she would worry more this way, and maybe a part of me preferred that. I pocketed the phone and got out of the car, lifting the hood of my sweatshirt up over my head to keep from getting too wet.

The look I got from the clerk told me I wasn't their typical clientele. His eyes followed me while I cruised the aisles, grabbing a Coke and a package of Twinkies. It was pure sugar, but I'd found that sugar helped after a treatment. It might have been a placebo thing, but I took what I could get.

I was headed for the counter when a redhead in a sharp suit yanked the front door open and ducked inside, dragging her umbrella behind her. She gave me a cursory glance and made her way through the store, quick and easy, sure of where she was headed. The clerk and I watched her go, and gave each other a knowing eye. She had that look to her, the one that made men dream. The one that could take that dream and run it right into the ground, or ram it back into your throat.

"Three-sixty," he said after he scanned my junk food. We had bonded over the woman, but he still seemed a little uncomfortable with me. I was willing to bet he didn't get too many half-dead guys in long trench coats and hoodies in these parts. This was a rich neighborhood, where thousand dollar suits and Mercedes held court. I was moving on up.

I found a five in my pocket and dropped it on the counter. I smelled the woman before I felt the heat of her behind me. She was wearing some fancy perfume or other.

"Some weather," she said behind me.

I turned around.

"I think I passed an ark a few miles back," I said. I gave her a closer look. Narrow face, huge brown eyes, plenty of makeup. Her red hair was the real deal, and flowed smoothly across her shoulders.

Her laugh was a little bit raspy, more scratchy than sultry. "I like that. I'm going to use that one, if you don't mind?"

The clerk held out my change. I took it and jammed it into my coat, and then picked up my stuff from the counter. "You could, but I have it trademarked. I'll have to put you in touch with my attorney." I forced a smile. My flirting skills were rustier than the Titanic.

She put her haul on the counter: a loaf of bread, and a package of Twinkies.

"Nice choice in processed snack foods," I said, shaking my own golden bars.

"I guess great minds think alike." She pointed behind the counter. "Can I get a pack of Camels, too?"

That explained the laugh. I slipped away without another word. Smokers pissed me off on a personal level. I had gotten cancer, and

I'd never smoked a day in my life.

I was sitting behind the wheel, tearing open the Twinkie when she came out. She'd parked her Lexus next to my econobox, and she glanced over at me as she got behind the wheel, and then one more time when she backed out and sped away.

It took me two minutes to eat the snack, after which I pulled the car out and around to the side of the building. It had a service station attached to it, with the bay doors facing the rear. I looked around before I shut the engine and got out, circling to the office door. The TSA probably wouldn't have liked most of my standard equipment, and so I had left my picks back with Danelle. That didn't mean I was defenseless. A Glock had travelled with my suitcase in cargo, along with a WWII era combat knife I had picked up at Dalton's shop.

I turned the knob on the door. I expected it to be locked, and they didn't let me down. Picks were one thing, hairpins were another; they didn't even set off the metal detectors. I bent down and pulled it from my sock, shoved it in the lock, and had it open in about thirty-seven seconds. It was a poor performance, but this was just the warmup.

I moved past the air fresheners and other random car-related impulse buys, pushing open the door to the shop itself and moving inside. There were no cars in the bays, and the only light came from fluorescents bleeding in through the small windows. I walked the space, keeping my attention to the corners. I was in the back when I found what I had been hoping for.

A rat trap, with a victim still attached.

I knelt down and picked up the trap. The kill was still pretty fresh, the corpse in decent enough shape. I let it loose of the spring and put my hand to it. "Come on, little buddy."

It didn't take much energy to bring back a rat. It twitched under my fingers, and then skittered forward with a slight limp in its gait. Perfect. I dropped the connection, sending it back to its eternal sleep, and scooped it up in my hand. "You'll make a good accomplice."

I carried the rat out to the car, put it in the glove compartment, and checked my watch. Ten in the morning. I had a little over twelve hours before my planned heist.

I was going to need them.

CHAPTER ELEVEN

Slipping a Mickey.

RED'S MANSION WAS NEAR THE shore. It would have been on the shore, except she had about six acres of lawn in front of her house that abutted another couple of miles of beachfront. The rear was just as large, and it was the reason I needed so much time.

Rats didn't exactly move very fast. Especially dead ones with limps.

I parked the Ford well away from the mansion. The car would be too out of place in an affluent neighborhood, and I didn't question that it would draw the wrong kind of attention. I would have gone for something a little sportier, classier, and expensive, but the short notice had left our options slim. The end result was that I was going to have to sneak my way to the wall that surrounded the house, and then sneak myself away *after* I had lifted the stone. As far as I was concerned, that second part was the most dangerous of all. My plan left me seventy-one seconds to get out of the house and over the wall. That was a full sprint on my best day, and my best days were behind me.

I hadn't survived this long without being resourceful, and I made it to the outer edge of the property unseen and thankful that the rain had faded to to a steady drizzle. I crouched behind some thick shrubs and peered over at the brick wall, to where cameras rested near the top and swung back and forth, covering the entire perimeter. I would need to take them out of action later, but for now, I focused on listening for the pulse of the magical field. It was stronger on the other side of the wall, closer to the mansion, but a sliver of the energy was still leaking out to where I was sitting.

It was more than enough to breathe life into the rat again.

"Come on, Mickey. Time to go to work."

I held him in my palm while he shuddered. His nose started moving, sniffing its way along my flesh. That was the instinct that always remained; the hunger, and the desire to satiate it.

I placed him on the ground and moved behind the trunk of a wide tree, positioning myself with the bottom of my waterproof trench beneath my ass, so it wouldn't end up soaked on the damp grass. I was in the middle of a copse of foliage between Red's property and whatever wealth lived next door. It was meant to be a barrier, and it was perfect for keeping my body hidden.

I say body, because I had one more necromancer trick up my sleeve. I closed my eyes, and eased myself along the thread of magic connecting me to the rat. Not my physical self, but my consciousness, my senses. A moment later, I was looking through Mickey's eyes at the massive world around me.

Discovering the trick had been an accident. There was no necromancer handbook to reference, and Dannie hadn't been able to locate a living peer to pick their brain. One night before Mr. Timms had passed on, the cat had grabbed a mouse in our kitchen. It was a good soldier, and it brought Dannie the prize, but he had been a little too rough with it. Curious, I had brought it back from the dead, and watched it sniff and scuffle. I had this thought that it would be neat if I could make it run around, to give Timmsie something to play with. It started running then, and the rest was trial and error.

Most importantly, and most obviously, it didn't work on people.

We were too evolved, our souls too developed and independent. I had managed to stick on Mr. Timms for about thirty seconds once, but cats were hard to control. Birds and mice worked best.

Of course, I hadn't actually transferred my existence to the rat. It was more like a remote control, where I was getting the feed of what Mickey experienced from the safety of my own brain. Not that my brain was totally safe. If I saw what the rat saw, I didn't see what my eyes could have seen. I was an easy target if anyone happened across me.

I guided him through the grass, skirting to the base of the wall. There was no doubt the cameras had seen Mickey go by, but it was unlikely they would find him suspicious. I ran him along the wall, all the way around to the iron bars of the front gate. It was easy to slip under them unseen, and make our way along the lawn.

The house wasn't close for a person. It was a marathon for a rat. I moved Mickey forward in stages, letting go of the sight and returning to check on my own surroundings during intermissions, while I allowed him to sniff the ground and pick up some choice morsels. He was dead, and he didn't need to rest, but I did.

Eventually, he reached the house. I could see the feet of guards walking back and forth in their patrol, unassuming men in black suits, but they were looking forward, not expecting to get infiltrated from down low. I skirted Mickey over one of their shoes, to the foundation of the mansion. I just needed to find a way inside.

I kept near the house, tracing its edges and searching for even the tiniest opening. It was a huge place, and just clearing the front side took almost half an hour. It was also well-maintained, with no obvious paths to get in.

I left Mickey to his own devices, pulling back my sight and opening my eyes. I took a deep breath and muffled a cough, and checked my watch. Six o'clock. No wonder I had to pee. I figured Mickey was in as safe a spot as any, so I moved off behind a further tree and relieved myself, and then returned to my position.

Mickey was still where I had left him. I only had a few hours left, and I really wanted to get into the house. My aim was to make sure the stone was where Black's ops had said it was, and that it was a real thing, whether Arlen knew anything about it or not. It wouldn't mean it wasn't a trap, but I'd already seen through my rodent accomplice's eyes that the guards were following the path in the kinetics.

Mickey ran along the far wall, near the limits of my reach. I was ready to give up when I spotted a small vent just above the base of the grass. I moved him inside and skittered down a dryer line, hopeful that there was some way out of it, and that nobody picked that moment to wash some clothes. A tiny crack in the hose was all I needed, and I pulled my little buddy out and down the rest of the tube, and then on to the floor.

I was in the basement. The room was large and clean, with a couple of industrial washers, a huge laundry bin, and a servant who was humming while she put some cleaning agents back on a shelf. She didn't see Mickey, and I got him under the bottom of the bin before she turned around and headed away. I raced along behind her, following her feet as she climbed the staircase back to the main floor. I slipped through just ahead of the slamming door, ducking under a decorative table before I could be spotted.

I saw the guards walking the halls. They were all human, wearing sharp dark suits and carrying light assault rifles. They could have been users, but it was impossible to know without intel or witness. I was going to assume they were, because it would be better for my health.

In my mind, I matched them to the kinetics. It was a tricky proposition since I had to adjust for the time differentials, but despite the poor judgement I had shown in taking the job, I was good at doing the math. If the pattern was off, it wasn't off by much.

Since I knew how they were going to move, it was easy to avoid them. I darted from one piece of furniture to another, and then shoved myself under the corner of a runner that ran the length of the hallway. A young girl dashed by; eight or nine, in jeans and a sweater, headphones on her ears.

I didn't know Red had a kid. It was an unexpected wrinkle. How could I be sure she'd be out of harm's way? She was young enough she should be in bed by then, and if all went according to plan, nobody would know I had been there until I was gone. I brought Mickey out from under the rug and kept going, through the hallway until I got to the library.

The door was closed, but there was just enough space underneath for me to squeeze my rat through. Even from there I could see the stone, resting on a pedestal in the center of the room, with a large track light shining down on it, displaying it with pride. It was real, and it was there. In fact, other than the little girl, everything was just as it should have been.

Mission accomplished.

I kept Mickey moving into the room, in search of a place to leave his corpse where he wouldn't be noticed for a few hours. The whole room was lined with bookshelves, but they were floor to ceiling, with no space under or between. I would need to leave him in with the books.

It wasn't a problem. Mickey climbed up over the top of one, and then I forced him down into the rear, squished behind a brick sized novel with a leather binding. I brought myself back from the sortie, opened my eyes, and checked my watch. I had two hours left to wait.

This was going to be a piece of cake.

CHAPTER TWELVE

Like taking candy.

I HAD THIS RITUAL BEFORE I started a run. I'd been doing it since my first time leading a team in the operating room, and had continued it into my new profession, back when Danelle was still dragging me along and showing me the ropes. Those first few had been true cake work - a couple of burglaries, a couple of package drops. In and out, no questions asked. Dannie had handled all the details. All I had to do was show up and not get us caught.

I bent from the waist, stretching out my limbs. I did a few jumping jacks. I did some neck stretches. I cracked every knuckle on my fingers. I yodeled the whole time, though it probably couldn't be called yodeling. Caterwauling, maybe? I knew it looked ridiculous from the outside, because Dannie had said as much during the fit of laughter that usually traced my progress, and I had gotten the same reaction from the O.R. nurses. She said I could be a Youtube star if I were to upload a video of the calisthenics. I could imagine Molly seeing her dead father making a jackass out of himself on the internet. Talk about awkward.

Anyway, I kept the yodeling as little more than a whisper, and tried to minimize the movements as much as I could, but I had to go through the process. It was to loosen up my body, and my mind. It was to calm my nerves and get 'in the zone' as best I could. My first move was to hop a ten foot stone wall, without being caught by the security cameras. If that had been the only move, it would have been nerve-wracking enough.

I still needed to get into the house and past the guards.

The armed guards.

I had my gun in a shoulder holster, hidden by the trench. I took it out and hit a small switch on the bottom of the grip, and then held it up to my ear. A soft hum came from the barrel. I checked my watch. Ten thirty and thirty six seconds. I opened my timer app and watched the time vanish in front of me. At exactly ten thirty-one, I hit the 'start' button, turned off the backlight, and eased my way to the corner of the tree.

I watched the cameras swivel. At the moment of intersection, I aimed the gun and pulled the trigger.

There were no bullets. There was no sound. The gun wasn't a gun at all. It fired a micro sized electromagnetic pulse. The two cameras had just been burnt out and gone offline. I expected the disruption would be noticed right away, it was part of my plan, and I would be over and gone by then.

I sprinted from the tree to the wall, gaining speed until I planted my foot and pushed up, reaching forward with one hand for balance, and up with the other for height. I gained a few feet, planted my other foot, and gained a couple more. It was enough to get my hand on the lip of the wall, and I pulled myself up without difficulty. Even then, I didn't slow. I took two steps and jumped forward off the wall, dropping down in a break-fall roll and getting back on my feet, coming up running.

10:31:26. A quick glance in both directions showed me I had made it past step one. I came to a stop against the side of the house. Twelve seconds to get across the yard. I had made it in ten.

Two guards turned the corner at either end of the house, making their way across the grass. I dropped to my stomach behind the bushes and pulled myself along the ground towards the rear. I had two and a half minutes to get to the back of the house. It wasn't a long time, but it felt like forever.

One guard helped another onto the top of the wall. I risked a look back to see him bent over, checking the cameras. My heart was racing, my breath coming heavy. I clenched my teeth to keep from coughing, and kept putting hand over hand. I spent way too much time slithering like a snake.

10:34:58. I reached the rear of the house. The back opened up to a stone patio abutting an olympic-sized pool. Outdoor furniture lined the patio in front of a massive barbecue grill. The guard was standing right in front of the sliding glass doors, his hand to his ear, listening to the report from the others on the wall.

Getting over that wall had been the hardest part. This was the second hardest. There was no cover here. Once I turned the corner, I was going to be an easy target.

I reached into my pocket and took hold of the dice. I rolled them between my fingers. Every job had a bit of chance with it. Every job required some bit of luck. I pulled the dice up to my mouth and breathed onto them. "Guard at the door," I whispered, exhaling some of my power, and some of my decay.

They grew warm in my grip, a dark energy leaking out of my fist. I ducked down, and tossed them at the patio.

The echoes of the dice rolling across the stone caught the guard's attention. He didn't know what they were. Almost nobody knew what they were. He watched them skip and turn, in a strange rotation that didn't follow any known laws of physics. He impressed me then, taking his eyes off them and looking for the person who had sent them on their journey. He saw me a second later, and his rifle went to his hip.

The dice had already stopped moving. The magic hit him, and the rifle dropped from his hand. Blood began to pour from his eyes, his nose, his ears, his mouth... anywhere there was an exit point. I didn't need to see the symbols, I knew what they were by the reaction. Blood and Snake. My luck was still good. He toppled over without a sound.

10:35:47. They would find him when they came back around. I needed to get into the library and grab the stone, and make my way out the front before that happened. I ran over, picked up my dice, and checked the slider. It was unlocked, and I slipped inside.

I was in a quaint living area that was too modern for the more classic style of the mansion itself. There was a hallway at the rear, that was split by a second. I ducked behind the couch as a guard walked across my view, glancing over to the back. My dead guard should have been walked left to right, while one of the pair at the cameras crossed around the rear. I had broken that pattern, but the rest of it had continued, or so the guy in the hallway thought.

10:36:14. I got up off the floor and walked down the corridor as silently as I could. I ducked into a bathroom when the guard passed by again, and then turned right behind his back. A quick dash forward brought me to another door. I pushed it open and ducked into a bedroom that had been converted to a studio. An easel sat in the center, holding a half-painted portrait of a nude male model. A draped table was in front of the easel, waiting for its muscular and apparently well-endowed partner to return.

10:37.04. I heard the footsteps of the guard move past once, and then back again. Just as he crossed my hiding spot, I twisted the door open and put my arm around his neck, cutting off his air and pulling him backwards into the studio. He struggled against the grip, but I had done this often enough to resist despite his greater physical strength. I kept tugging him backwards, getting his whole body in. By the time I laid him on the floor, he was out cold.

10:37:49. I sprinted down the hallway and turned right, going down another short hall and coming up against the door to the library. I turned the handle. Locked. Damn.

I hadn't expected that. I pulled out my hairpin and stuck it in the lock, counting off the seconds in my head. My performance at the gas station had been shit. I needed to do a lot better. I closed my eyes and manipulated the pin. Five... four... I got it unlocked. Three... two... I pushed it open just enough. One... I gently eased it closed. I didn't make it all the way, but it wouldn't be obvious from a distance.

"Impressive."

I took a deep breath and closed my eyes.

CHAPTER THIRTEEN

Lady in red.

"TURN AROUND, LET ME SEE your face."

I couldn't see who was talking. She was female, that much was obvious. Older, and used to giving commands. I lifted myself to a stand and slowly rotated. The pedestal sat in the center of the room. The woman was standing next to it.

"I was wondering where this had come from." She was holding Mickey, dangling him by the tail. "It was my understanding that the Houses had an agreement regarding necromancers."

I had been right about older. Mid-fifties, maybe. Asian. She was slender, with shoulder length black hair lined with silver. She was wearing a shiny red suit with a white blouse underneath. A huge ruby hung from a gold chain around her neck.

I ran a pale gray hand along my hairless scalp. "What gave it away?"

"You came to take this?" She ran her hand along the top of the stone.

"Guilty. You aren't supposed to be in here."

She tossed my rat to me. I caught it instinctively. "Neither are you, but you're correct. I'm supposed to be in China right now."

She wasn't afraid of me, that much was obvious. Her clothes, her age, the massive ruby... They all gave me a solid idea of who I was dealing with.

Mrs. Red.

I had been scared the second she asked me to turn around. I was beyond terrified now. I was caught, like Mickey had been. She didn't need to call the guards to dispose of me, unless she didn't want to dirty her own hands. Either way, I was going to die.

I fought against my nerves, working hard to find my breath. I wasn't sure what else to do, so I tried to stall. "So why are you here?"

She rubbed the stone absently. I had heard Mrs. Red was a spitfire, but the woman in front of me looked more like a mourning grandmother, a victim. A tear ran from her eye.

"They told me Katherine was sick. They said she had the Rot. When I landed, they said they couldn't wait, that the Rot had taken over."

For years we'd been fascinated with the concept of zombies. Then the reversal happened, and with it came the Rot. It was the disease that started the whole walking dead mythos, and it was just like the movies. A fever, chills, death. Then your body started moving again, in time to a new drummer, motivated only by a desire to eat living tissue.

Unlike the movies, it wasn't that easy to get. Saliva to an open wound from someone or something with the virus would do it, but it was easy to avoid getting bit by a zombie. They didn't move very fast. There had been no hordes of walking dead, or world-breaking apocalypses; just a random stray victim from time to time, who could maybe take one or two others with them before they found themselves with a bullet, arrow, knife, or other blunt instrument lodged in their brains.

Whoever Katherine was, I couldn't imagine how she had gotten it here. I knew some animals could carry it like rabies, even if they never got symptoms. Maybe she had been bitten by an infected squirrel?

I felt the cold deadness of Mickey's fur in my hand. Or maybe she'd been bitten by a rat? Was that why she was telling me? Did she think I was responsible, and she wanted me to know about it before I got the toast treatment?

"It wasn't me." I held Mickey out towards her. "I only came for that, and I don't kill children." Did I really think I had a chance of getting out of here alive?

The tears hit her cheek and ran off her chin, leaving wet splatters on her suit jacket. "It wasn't a rat bite."

"Who was she?"

"My responsibility. The daughter of a deceased friend. She was only nine."

The ringing of alarm bells in my mind was sudden, and loud.

"What is it?" She must have seen my expression.

"Little girl, about this high?" My heart had already been pounding, my adrenaline already pumping. An overwhelming feeling of dread joined the mix. I thought getting caught was bad.

"Yes. How did you-"

I dove away from the door just in time, as the loud popping of gunfire echoed through the hallway, and bullets ripped through the wood. The lady in red wasn't so lucky. The shots slammed her hard, knocking her backwards into a bookshelf. Whoever they were, they were crack shots, or they could see through the door or something, because they managed to leave the stone and the pedestal totally unharmed.

I crouched in the corner, finding the knife and holding it at my side. The gunfire stopped. I could hear two pairs of feet coming down the hall.

"Come on, Mickey. Back at it," I said, reaching out for the rat. It came alive as it had before, sniffing and turning. When the gunman kicked the door open and saw the motion, he turned his rifle on it and let loose. I used the distraction to get the knife to his neck and cut his throat, fighting against the nausea that rose up as a result.

This way of killing was too personal for my taste.

If he had been alone, I would have been fine. The guy behind him opened up, and it was all I could do to get out of the line of fire and keep the other guard in front of me, catching some of the rounds and deflecting others. A bullet whizzed past my ear, the hot slug scorching it on the way by. I shoved my victim, trying to push him into the other guard, but he backed up and then jumped over.

I recognized both of them. They were supposed to be defending the place, and instead they were making their own move on the stone. What the fuck was this thing that they were staging a bloody coup to get it?

He smiled when he saw me, the muzzle of the gun swinging my direction. I was in the open, and all I had was a knife.

A sudden flash of energy bolted across the room, catching the guard full-on. He shook and rattled as the power coursed through him, and then fell to the floor. I whipped my head around, to where Red was laying propped against the bookshelf, bleeding out but still alive.

I stared at her for what felt like forever, but it was only a couple of seconds.

"They're going to blame you for this." Her voice was faint. A soft chuckle followed. "I should have known. I should have seen this coming."

I stood up and looked towards the door. I needed to get the hell out of here. "I was just supposed to steal the stone."

Her laughter was louder, mixed with a choking gurgle. "Then steal it, necromancer. It's the only way you might live long enough to continue dying."

I walked over to her and crouched down. Her eyes were turning glassy, but she didn't look afraid. "Dannie was right. I was supposed to die here, wasn't I?"

"Live, die, it doesn't matter. You aren't important . You're just the ghost. *I* was supposed to die here. It was supposed to be taken, but not by you." She looked over at the smoldering guard. "Eight years, and they got to him. *You* need to take the stone. Don't let them get it. Bring it to Jin." She reached up and took hold of the ruby. "Take this with you. She will know I sent you. If she survives, you survive. There is no other way."

I stared down at her. I never should have picked up that goddamned card in the first place. I needed to get away from there. I needed to get back to Danelle and get her out of Chicago before Black's kill team...

"I was paid by Black. The card came from Black."

She coughed up some blood. "It wasn't Black."

"How do you know?"

"It wasn't Black," she repeated.

There was no motion down the hallway... yet. "Why should I help you?"

"Help yourself. You'll die if you don't do as I say."

I crouched in front of her, trying to decide what to do. If I left without the stone, I could get away for now, but someone would be coming after Danelle and me. Whether it was Black or not, any House could fund a kill team. They would figure out who had done the job, and they would find us, and we would be dead.

I could take the stone, and call it in like I was supposed to. If I had been set up, I would just be painting a big fat target on my ass. The fact that they had convinced Red to be here when I walked in... Danelle had been right. Those two ogres were supposed to be dead right now.

Red was right, too. Her rope was the only one not already tied into a noose.

I had been stupid for taking the job, and for dragging Dannie into this. I had been stubborn and greedy, with a side of desperate.

Why couldn't things be simple?

"Where can I find Jin?" I leaned over her and reached for the necklace.

"New... New York." She was struggling to speak. All the color had gone out of her. She reached up and put her hand on my wrist. "The House... you don't know... secrets... protect the treasure."

"Treasure?"

Her eyes shifted past me, towards the pedestal. She took one more deep, gasping breath, and abandoned this world for whatever came after.

My head was spinning while I took the ruby necklace from her corpse. I would have loved more answers, but my magic didn't work on users. Instead, I got up and walked over to the guy that Red had toasted.

"Wake up, asshole."

Without his name, it took a lot more effort to bring him back. Without his name, it would make him harder to control. Under any other circumstances, I wouldn't have even tried it. Thankfully, the fields were strong here, and it helped spare me from some of the burden.

The corpse moaned, and sat straight up. His clothes were whole, but his body had been scorched beneath them, leaving the flesh burned and blistered.

"What the hell?" His eyes zipped around the room, frantic.

"Not yet." I didn't like to bring fresh kills back. They tended to spend too much time being shocked and confused that they weren't in Kansas anymore. Death was a bit of an adjustment. "Get up,"

His eyes found me as he rose to his feet. He looked down at his barbecued complexion.

"You fucking killed me?"

"You would have killed me first, but no. Red took care of you." I turned back and put my hand to the stone, shocked by the warmth of the light shining down onto it. It was soft and smooth, and didn't weigh anything close to what I had been expecting. I held it in the crook of my arm like a football. "Who paid you to turn on Mrs. Red?"

"Turn on?" He shook his head. His expression was still one of shock. In this case, it was at least making it harder for him to resist my control. "No, we wiped the original set last night. Stuffed 'em all in a big laundry bin downstairs, and then this woman did us up in makeup so we'd look just like them. Paid? I don't know. I just do the dirty work."

"Who organized the team?"

"Some fixer or other. He wore these fancy italian shoes."

Shit.

"How many of you are in the house?"

He looked down at the other guy's body. "Six, and Carla."

"User?"

He nodded.

"What kind?"

"Water."

She must have been the maid downstairs. "Close?"

He shrugged. "They should have been blasting your sorry ass by now. I thought necros were against the rules?"

What? I bent down and grabbed the other assault rifle from its former owner, and then I moved past him to the hallway. I didn't hear anything. At all. "Lead the way, smokey."

He didn't have a choice. He raised the assault rifle and walked up the hall ahead of me.

"It's clear," he said when he reached the crosswalk.

I joined him there, looking out from behind. The gunfire was still ringing in my ears. There was no way every living thing on the property hadn't heard it.

"Do you know what this thing is?" I asked him, shifting the stone in my arm.

"No. Don't care either."

"Even though you died trying to get your hands on it?"

"Especially because of that."

We walked down the hallway. There was nobody there. We

turned right and headed past bedrooms and bathrooms, a game room with a pool table and a large formal dining room. We spilled out into the foyer through a pair of mahogany doors.

Carla and the rest of the goons were waiting for us.

In a pile on the floor.

Their throats ripped out.

Bloodstains ran along the marble. They had been killed elsewhere, and dragged here. I checked my watch. 10:43:54. There were only two ways someone could have done this. One, they had started the killing before I had even gone in. Two, there was more than one assailant involved.

Either way, this whole thing was getting exponentially more fucked up by the heartbeat. A third team had been sent to take out the second, after the second had taken out the first and... well... me?

"Go on out and make some noise."

He looked back at me, his dead eyes still able to show some fear.

"They can't hurt you, you're already dead. Go." I pushed a little harder on him through the tether. He walked ahead, into the midst of the gore. I turned around and headed back the way I had come. I should have gone back out the rear in the first place.

No. That was stupid. There was no chance I was going to be able to get away on foot. I needed to get to the garage, and hope that they kept the keys with the cars.

I tried to remember the blueprint as I ran, my mind flowing over the red dots and the outlines of the walls. The garage was off the west wing, the other direction from the way I had come. I traced my steps back to the library, forgetting about caution in my mad dash to get away. I skidded around corners and sprinted along the hallways, my finger on the trigger of the assault rifle, ready to blast anything that appeared in front of me.

I shoved open the door into the garage at the same time I heard the gunfire. It only lasted for a second or two. I don't know what happened to my new partner, but the speed at which he'd been silenced caused me to spin around and take aim.

There was nothing there.

I backed into the garage, looking over my shoulder. There were four cars, lined up in a row. The closest was an Escalade. I wasn't about to be picky. I tried the door. Unlocked.

A dark shape hurtled through the doorway, cornering with impossible dexterity and rocketing towards me.

It was over before I could think.

I pulled open the car door, using it as a shield, and was thrown backwards to slam into the side of the SUV from the force of my attacker smashing against it. My shoulder lit up in throbbing pain, taking the brunt of the force so I wouldn't drop the stone. I clenched my teeth, pulled off the car and ducked down, looking below the battered door.

Six feet of muscle and fur, a large semi-canine head with sharp, nasty yellow teeth. A fucking werewolf? It was laying on the floor, blood running from a gash in its head. It seemed dazed as it tried to pick itself up.

Today was full of surprises. The Houses weren't supposed to use necromancers. They were even more not supposed to use ferals. Ferals were efficient killers, vicious and violent, but they were also beyond difficult to keep in line. That a House had chosen them on purpose to head-up this orgy of chaos and death was chilling.

There was no way to know if this one was alone, so I assumed it wasn't. I ran around the Escalade to the next car in the line, a Lexus sedan. I made it into this one without a catastrophic event, found the keys above the visor, hit the button to open the garage door, and started the engine.

I looked over to find the big bad wolf, but it must have still been on the ground. I put the car in drive and hit the gas, blasting out of the garage. I saw another dark form coming from my left as I accelerated - a second werewolf. He pounced forward towards the car, and nearly caught me, his shoulder smashing into the rear quarter panel. It rocked from the force, the wheels skidding and spinning, and then righted itself. I watched the feral fade in the rear-view, a hulk of a thing with mottled black and white fur. He stood and watched me for a second, and then retreated back to the front of the house where a brown version waited.

I kept going, gaining speed as I reached the front gate. I expected it to be closed. I was wrong. It was sitting open, undamaged and unguarded. I knew there had to be a reason for it, but in the moment I didn't care.

Someone had done some serious work, and spent some serious cash in order to take out Mrs.Red and get their hands on whatever the rock resting on the passenger's seat was. My survival had just thrown a big wrench in their scheme, and I had a feeling they had the will and the means to throw something even bigger and badder than a few werewolves back at me.

The one thing I knew for sure: I would never, ever take a job without consulting Dannie first, ever, ever again.

CHAPTER FOURTEEN

A case of the munchies.

I WASN'T STUPID ENOUGH TO keep the Lexus for long, especially with the dent in it. The only way I could have made myself easier to find would have been to turn around.

Instead, I drove the car back to the Ford, and then drove the rental car back to the gas station. I thought about calling Dannie a couple of times while I was driving, and dismissed it. Now that the adrenaline was wearing off, it was leaving me shaken and more than a little punch-drunk. I shouldn't have been driving, but I didn't want to stay too close to Red's mansion.

The parking lot was empty when I got there, save for a beat-up old Honda that had to belong to the clerk. He'd parked it around the corner from the main lot, which was pretty stupid of him. Then again, this wasn't the kind of area where you'd need to feel too protective over a hunk of rusty Japanese metal.

I didn't steal it right away. I parked in the lot and just sat for a few minutes, my heart racing, my cough kicking up and leaving my throat dry. I glanced over at the stone in the passenger seat, and shook my head. I couldn't believe I had just fucked up my whole miserable life for a rock. My life, and Danelle's.

It was more than a rock though, wasn't it? It had to be. It was worth killing Mrs. Red over. It was worth hiring feral thugs to ensure there wouldn't be anyone to blab about what they had been involved with; a risk that was already minimal among ghosts. It was well-organized, and well-orchestrated, with multiple levels of deception and double-cross.

And I had screwed up the whole plan.

I was the wrench in the gears. The gremlin. All of that planning, and my unique combination of magic and undeserved dumb luck had gotten me out of there alive. It was great in the short-term, but long-term?

Maybe there wasn't a long-term. There was going to be at least one kill team moving after us, maybe in addition to the feral hit crew. If this thing was valuable enough to kill the head of a House over, I couldn't be sure there wouldn't be more than one player racing to get to me first. Red had told me to go to Jin, whoever that was. I didn't see any other choice.

It took me less than sixty seconds to gather the rock, pick the lock of the Honda, hot-wire it, and drive away. I watched the mirror as I did, but the clerk didn't seem to notice that his car was being stolen.

Actually, I hadn't seem him at all.

I hit the brakes, threw the car in reverse, and backed up to the door. Turning my head and looking in the windows, I could see the register, but I didn't see the employee. I got out of the car and went in. I wasn't concerned about the guy, I was afraid of the implications. When I found him laying in one of the aisles with puncture wounds in his neck and his body cold and shriveled, my fear was confirmed.

I was half-expecting damage from a werewolf attack, so it was a surprise that a vampire had done him instead. It had left him in a cleaner state, but I felt bad for the guy. There was nothing pleasant about being bit. From everything I had heard, getting drained was one of the worst tortures imaginable, and since the venom left your muscles paralyzed, you couldn't even scream.

The bloodsucker virus, as it was so colloquially named. It was a food borne disease that came from tainted meat, the shitty kind that got sold in shady deals to shady people, who passed it off as good and sold it forward, mainly to the lower class. People ate the meat, and those with the right genetic susceptibility got infected, starting a chain reaction that turned them into creatures that were worse than any myths or legends could have imagined.

They weren't people anymore. They were barely even ferals, and more than one politician had run their platform on getting them classified with the Rot zombies so they could be exterminated instead of controlled. The problem was that they were still alive, that they had never actually died. That made them people to a lot of people, but the hunger for blood was constant, the ability to think outside of that eradicated. They became nothing more than a human shell for a single drive, albeit a human shell with enhanced strength and agility, and a tolerance to take a shitload of damage before they even realized they were injured.

That there were werewolves and vampires here together couldn't be a coincidence. That someone had managed to get a vamp to follow a command? The concept scared the shit out of me.

"Why did they kill you?" It wasn't worth the energy to bring him back to answer. "To keep the vampire satisfied, so it wouldn't turn on its handlers? To make it look like the carnage at Red's house was the work of some random band of rabid ferals? Does it even matter?"

In the end, it didn't. I was wasting my time, and staying too close to the scene. Whatever the reason was that the clerk had to die, it wasn't my problem.

I grabbed a box of Twinkies and a six-pack of Coke on my way out.

CHAPTER FIFTEEN

I love New York.

"WHERE THE FUCK HAVE YOU been, Conor?"

That was how Dannie answered the phone. Not that I could blame her.

"I've been better."

"Seriously? That's how you're going to answer me?"

"I'm too tired to be more expressive."

"The job?"

"You were right."

She gave an exasperated sigh. My terse answers weren't doing anything to help the nerves I'd frayed. "About which part?"

I returned her sigh with one of my own. "The worst part. I almost died tonight, Dannie, and not in a pleasant way."

All of the anger fell away. I'd kind of expected it to go down like that, once she'd switched from pissed to worried. "What happened?"

"Not enough time to tell you everything. The bottom line is that you need to get the hell out of Chicago, before something bad happens to you."

There was silence on the other end, and then a solid exhale. "How am I going to do that, Conor? You know I can't drive the van. I can barely even wipe my ass on my own."

"You're being overly dramatic."

"I'm being realistic. How am I going to get out of here?"

I looked up and watched a road sign for I-95 go overhead. "What about Dalton?"

Her cold laughter was enough of an answer.

"Come on. You've got connections everywhere. You're telling me there isn't one person you can call? We've got money to pay them, or at least we will."

More silence while she thought about it. "Okay, yeah. I think I know somebody. You're going to owe me your life for this."

"I already owe you my life. I'm going to owe you more. I need you to bring the van."

"What?"

"The van. I need the van. More to the point, I need Evan and the guns. Somebody is going to try to kill us. You can be afraid about that later. Right now, you need to get us organized while I try to hunt down someone named Jin. Mrs. Red told me they could help out."

"Conor, you're my best friend, but I fucking hate you right now. Mrs. Red? What the hell is going on?"

"There's no time. You need to get moving. All I can say is that the whole thing was a setup, a massive setup, and Mrs. Red and the stone were the prize. Now it's just the stone."

"Red is dead?" It came out in a whisper of disbelief. "They killed the head of a House?"

"I said I've been better. Dannie, go do what you need to do, and call me when you get to New York. That's where I'll be."

"Shit. Okay. I'm moving on it."

"Oh, and if you see any ferals... Drop them on sight." I paused, and then remembered the most important part. "And be careful. I'm sorry I fucked everything up."

"You be careful, too. You can't help fucking things up, it's part of who you are."

At least I got to hang up laughing.

It was only an hour drive from Fairfield to the New York skyline. I was halfway through it, traveling south on I-95, when three massive armored trucks rolled by, headed in the opposite direction. The letters "USFC" were stenciled on the sides, white text on dark blue plating. Feral control. I couldn't see them through the tiny slits and mirrored glass that served as windows, but I knew what was inside. All of the cities had routine USFC patrols moving through them at night, keeping an eye out for the wrong kind of human.

I knew where they were going, and why they were going there. I could only hope they didn't try to trace me back to the scene. I hadn't noticed any cameras on the inside of the mansion, and the one at the convenience store was a fake, but that didn't mean my face hadn't been caught somewhere.

There was nothing I could do about it now. I watched the mirrors until the trucks faded from sight. A minute later, a news van came trailing behind them. My foot eased down on the accelerator, getting me up to a healthy seventy-five. A couple of extra minutes couldn't hurt.

Jin. It was nothing more than a name to me, some silhouette of a... I don't know what, that had some connection to Mrs. Red. Male, female, human, user... I had no idea. I couldn't even be sure they would be friendly if I ever did meet them. It could be they'd see I had the stone, and kill me on sight. Wouldn't that be ironic?

I had a destination, but no destination. New York was a huge city. It was an easy place to get lost, which was good, but a hard place to find someone, which was bad. A three letter name wasn't going to get me much further than the two hundred dollars I had in my pocket, and I wasn't hot on using plastic until I had a better feel for the depth of the shit I was in. Mr. Clean may have laundered our deposit nicely, but he couldn't do anything for our withdrawals. Regardless of how the link in between was made, I would be screwed, and Clean had already admitted he would squeal like a baby if a kill team came knocking.

It was better to wait until Dannie got here, if I could manage that long. She would be able to help me get a better line on Jin, and Evan was the best kind of backup I could get. It did leave me wondering who she was going to reach out to for the ride. Ghosts knew other ghosts by reputation, and by handle. We didn't keep contact lists of one another, and we didn't socialize outside of the Machine. We were anonymous to each other most of all. Hell, the POTUS could be a ghost, and none of us would know.

I scanned my brain forward and backwards, trying to come up with a name. I was sure Danelle knew people I didn't know. While Black had cast her out for not being even a small portion of the user he was, she had made some inroads with people inside the family's circle who weren't as unemotional as her dear old dad was. They would help her out just because, as long as they wouldn't get caught.

Those thoughts, and a million more encircled my brain like angry wasps while I finished the drive into Manhattan and ditched the car in mid-town. I pulled it up along the sidewalk, tucked a package of Twinkies and a Coke in my pocket, wiped my prints off anything I had touched, got out, and walked away. I kept the stone tucked under my shoulder, out of sight beneath my trench, and wandered off into a dark alley a few blocks down. It wasn't an ideal situation, but it was the middle of the night, and even most places in the city that never sleeps took a breather this time of morning, keeping the path clear for the new kind of night jobs.

That wasn't to say the city was deserted, because there were random folks out doing whatever people did at three in the morning. There was a tension to it, a caution. You never knew what kind of person was out here, when the new world became the most dangerous. They knew they were taking a risk, and they were willing to take it. That made them inherently unsafe.

I found a spot to sit behind a dumpster, leaning back against the graffiti-covered steel and taking a deep breath, and then stifling the cough that wanted to follow. I had tried to conserve myself, and I had done well all things considered, but raising the grunt at Red's mansion was going to speed up my decline. The realization that I was likely cut off from Dalton and my treatments brought a level of anxiety and fear into my breathing. If this thing went on too long the kill team wouldn't be able to get me, because my sickness would kill me instead.

Was that irony, too?

CHAPTER SIXTEEN

Famous.

I DIDN'T DARE GO TO sleep. Even the homeless knew well enough to stay alert at night, and rest during the day. The police and feral control tried to keep everything as safe as possible, but nobody wanted to be the statistic. Nobody wanted to be 'that guy'. There was bad shit out there, it was guaranteed, and that was good enough.

The alley was deserted when I entered it, and it stayed that way for the five hours I spent tucked behind the dumpster, cradling the stone in my lap and listening for the sound of anything coming down the pipe. Every once in a while I would glance up at the walls on either side of me for good measure, but the coast stayed clear.

Dawn broke, daylight began to filter through skyscrapers, and normal life pushed itself back into gear. The sun even made random appearances through patchy clouds, and in the brightness of the light I almost forgot for a moment that I was up the creek and I hadn't just lost the paddle, I'd lost the boat with it.

I left the alley with a high degree of caution, scouting the passerby in search of anyone who looked like they were looking for something, or someone. This crowd was ninety percent sapiens, with the occasional dwarf or elf mixing in, and a couple of twelve foot ogres cleaving a path through them on their way to wherever.

It was a picture of modern civility and society, a lustrous surface to a universe with a tarnished underbelly. It had been thirty years since the Houses had helped settle the fighting, but I'd seen some really twisted shit move through hospital doors that only proved we were still animals at heart, even if we were coming with more varied packaging. I understood the rules, I understood the reasons, but some things... some things just left you with that huge pit in your stomach, and did damage that could never be undone.

Her name was Kayla. She was eight years old, and an orc. I could remember her like it was yesterday, laying on the operating room table, her body and soul tortured beyond measure. It had been seven years since I had helped her to a quiet end.

It was a memory that would never leave me.

I'd gone six or seven blocks before I decided to slip into a diner and grab something to eat. The waitress tried not to be too obvious about her fascination with my condition as she brought me to a table. I ignored her forced smile while I ordered a cup of coffee and some scrambled eggs, and then pulled out my phone.

"Where are you?" I asked.

"Cleveland," Danelle said. "We had to stop at a gas station. The radiator hose sprung a leak or something."

Shit. "You have a mechanic working on it?"

"Amos is handling it."

"Amos?" I wasn't familiar with the name.

"My chauffeur. You don't know him."

"Are you being intentionally cryptic?"

"He's an old acquaintance, and he owed me a favor. He's pissed that I called him on it, and he's even more pissed that I'm making him drive me to New York, but at least he's doing it. We should be there tonight."

"Has he seen-"

She cut me off. "No. I padlocked the coolers and told him to mind his fucking business. He saw the armory though. He called it a 'nice little collection of pea shooters'."

The waitress brought my eggs, the plate clattering in front of me.

"Where are you?" Dannie asked.

"Diner in Manhattan. I'm trying to lay low until you get here, unless you can gift me with some wisdom on how to find a random person I know next to nothing about in a city of thirty million people."

"You know I can, or you wouldn't have mentioned it." I heard rustling through the phone, and then the tapping of a keyboard. "I cross-referenced recent flight manifests into New York with the state tax database, and then spent some time trying to connect Mrs. Red to the 161 Jin's that could potentially be in the area. I narrowed it down to three."

"Holy shit. You did all of that in the last five hours?" She had impressed me before. She had outdone herself this time. "How did you even know where to start?"

"You haven't seen the news?"

"I spent the night behind a dumpster."

She laughed at that. "Serves you right. It's plastered everywhere this morning. Apparently, a gang of ferals tore the shit out of Fairfield late last night. They killed forty-three people and torched six mansions before control caught up to them."

Six mansions? Torched? It made sense. "They wanted to make it look random."

"They did make it look random. Or at least, they moved in a straight line from the highway down towards the coast, hitting everything and everyone that crossed their path like a pack of wild animals. Now you've got control and the Army involved, trying to calm all of the well-to-dos whose idyllic little community just got ripped apart."

"Which means the investigation is going to be open and shut, and nobody will ever catch on to why there were really there." I couldn't help but smile. "Clever."

"It works out well for you, because they won't be looking too hard for anyone to refute their claims that it was just bad luck for the community."

"It only works out because I got away. I wasn't supposed to."

She was silent for a few seconds. "I know." Another pause. "Anyway, nobody knows who the leaders of the Houses actually are, right? I mean, we assume they're wealthy because of how much power they have, but its not like you could have walked up to Mrs. Red on the street and asked for her autograph. At least, you couldn't know that you were talking to Red when you did."

"Somebody knew who she was."

"Of course the other Houses know each other. I've never heard of them being so direct before."

If there was a war brewing between the Houses, it was the rest of us who were going to suffer. Not just the ghosts, but everyone on Earth. I shook from a sudden chill. "So who was she?"

"I don't know how the media got it and I didn't, but according to them the house you were in last night belonged to Kai Sakura."

"It isn't ringing any bells."

"I'm surprised at you. Kai Sakura owns Parity Limited. They're huge into med tech. Not only do they make all of the fancy gadgets and gizmos you used to use in the hospital, but they have an R&D division that tests over three hundred new drugs every year. It's one of the biggest in the world."

I still didn't know the name, but I could picture the Parity logo in my mind. It was nothing fancy, a butterfly bursting out of a strand of DNA, in front of the company name in a basic font. "You're going to have to do a little better than that. How does this relate to Red?"

"I think Red was his wife, Mei Sakura. I've got a pic I'm going to send over. You tell me."

It only took a second for the message to come in. I flipped the cell over to the image. It was a blurry shot of a woman getting into a car, a black Escalade that looked too familiar.

"Yeah, that's her."

"That's what I thought. Like I said, I narrowed it down to three."

"Okay, so who are they?"

"I'll text you the addresses. I haven't had time to do a full profile, and probably won't before I get there. You can either wait around and stuff your face, or you can go visit them."

I heard the squeak of the van door opening up, and the creaking of the seat as someone of apparent bulk got in on the driver's side.

"I think I fixed the damn crap radiator. Let's see what we've got." The jangle of keys was followed by the turning of the engine. It rumbled to life. "No smoke. Good sign."

"Amos, I take it?" I asked. His voice was a scratchy bass, and he sounded way too heavy to be a decent bodyguard.

"Yeah. He's got the van going again. We'll see you tonight."

"That your friend?" I heard Amos ask. "Tell him his van is a piece of shit."

"Conor, be careful."

Then she was gone.

I picked up the fork and ate a few bites of the eggs. The text came in with the addresses not long after. Two were uptown, one was downtown. It would be more efficient to start with the cluster, but I decided I would head downtown instead.

Mei Sakura was Mrs. Red. She had been killed in an ambush, but it seemed that her husband was still alive. Had he known about the attack? Did he even know who she really was? It was strange to think that two people could be together and have a secret like that, but maybe it was just safer for everybody that way.

What about the ferals? Dannie said control caught up to them and killed them. Had they known they were running to their deaths? The organization of it, and the presence of a vampire made me question if they were even in control of themselves. If they were… what was so important about Red and the stone that had brought them to that kind of self-sacrifice? If they weren't… what kind of magic could master them like that?

I could feel the stone resting on my lap, hidden by the top of my trench. Forty-three innocent people had already died over this thing. I wasn't innocent, but I had no desire to join them. I took three more forkfuls away from the plate of eggs, gulped down some of the coffee, and left a twenty on the table.

I had been to New York before in a past life, to attend a surgical conference on intestinal failure and transplant. At the time my interests were targeted more at high-end restaurants, a suite at the Waldorf=Astoria, and buying nice things for Karen. When I stepped out onto the street and checked the address on my phone again, I knew enough to know I had no idea where I was going.

I stood at the corner and waved down a cab, careful to keep a good grip on my package without letting it slip from under the trench. It was a burden to have to carry the thing around, and at the same time I was grateful to hang onto it. The oblong rock was the bargaining chip for both my and Dannie's life.

A yellow cab braked hard and cut over, coming to a quick stop alongside me. I grabbed the door and swung it open, jumping inside and quickly moving the stone back out of view.

"Address?" the driver asked. I glanced up at him. Human. Maybe Mexican? He had short black hair and a couple of days of stubble on his neck.

"You know where Gold Street is?"

"Near the bridge?" He turned his head to look back at me. His eyes darted from my face down to my coat. "You gonna rob me?"

I looked down. The bulge of the rock could have passed as a piece, the way it was draped by the trench. "This? No. Just a souvenir from the Museum of Natural History." I lifted the coat so he could see the corner. His eyes didn't show any recognition. "Its a reproduction. I'm trying to get it to my niece without scuffing it."

He smiled and nodded. "Gold Street?"

"Yeah."

He turned around and got moving, while I wondered if I was making the right decision. Whoever killed Red knew who she was. What were the odds they knew about Jin as well? I could be riding a cab right to a corpse, another ambush, or worse.

"Hey," I said to the driver. "You know what? I changed my mind. Do you know any cheap hotels near there?"

He didn't answer right away. "Mmmmm... yeah, I think so. You want to go there instead?"

I didn't want to, but it had to be a bad idea to keep carrying something Red had called the 'treasure' around with me. "Yeah."

"Okay, man."

He dropped me off half an hour later. I laughed when I saw the rusted, slightly crooked sign of the hotel he'd picked for me - the Bright Sun. There was nothing bright or sunny about it, but if it was cheap, I was game. It wouldn't do to have Danelle's friend pull the van into the Ritz.

The attendant at the front desk was a heavyset woman with curly white hair and a smile that showed she was trying, despite it all. Unlike the waitress, she didn't have to force it. "Good morning, sir."

"Good morning. I'd like to rent a room, but I was wondering if you have parking on-site?"

She laughed. "Welcome to New York. We do, but it's fifty a night."

"How much is a room?"

"Forty-five."

Living was cheaper than parking. I smirked at that. "You take cash?"

Her smile turned a little crooked. "I can give you a deal for cash. Ninety for yourself and your car."

"Done. I'll pay one night at a time. I'm not sure how long I'll be here."

"Not too long by the looks of you." She said it with the same sweetness she'd been wearing since I walked in. "Let me get your key." She typed into an ancient computer, its beige shell splattered with grease, or blood, or something. A minute later she went to a rack behind her and lifted a key for me. "Room 601. Enjoy your stay."

I wondered what the likelihood of that was while I walked over to the elevator. It was already waiting for me when I hit the button, and I stepped inside and directed it to the sixth floor. As soon as the doors had swung closed I put the stone on the floor, and then reached up and found the emergency access door. I flipped it open and pulled myself up, just enough to survey the top of the elevator. If the mechanism broke while I was gone I would be in trouble, but I didn't trust that the stone would be safe in my actual room. I dropped down and retrieved it, and then reached up and positioned it out of sight against the mechanism. I closed the door and straightened my coat before hitting the button to go back to the lobby. I didn't need to see my room right now.

"Is everything okay?" the attendant asked as I walked back past the desk.

"It's perfect. Just going to get a bite to eat."

Her eyes followed me from the hotel, leaving me with the feeling that I had done the right thing.

CHAPTER SEVENTEEN

The necro and the Jin.

IT WASN'T HARD TO FIND the address Danelle had sent me, now that I was close. I traced my way down a few blocks and over a couple more, until I was standing in front of a tall, somewhat run-down high-rise apartment building. I looked over the address again, just to be sure this was the right place. It was.

I was pretty certain that the Jin I was looking for didn't live here. If she was close to Mrs. Red, she was probably loaded, or at least comfortable. This place looked anything but. Since I had made the trip, I figured I might as well go in and check it out, though I was glad I hadn't brought the stone with me.

There was no security in the lobby. There was a desk for a guard, a suggestion that they had made the effort once, but it had probably gotten too expensive to maintain and had been abandoned. Beer bottles and food wrappers were scattered along the dingy floor, and the elevator doors had graffiti all over them. I paused to reconsider my reconsideration, and forced myself to forge ahead. I couldn't risk missing Jin because I'd been too quick to judge.

Of course the elevator didn't work. I hit the button multiple times, stood in front of it and waited. When nothing happened, I leaned my ear in and listened for the hum of the motor, or the creaking of the winches. Nothing. I found the stairs and started climbing.

The steps were as filthy as the lobby, and also deserted, leaving me to wonder if there was anybody living here at all. A stone plaque on the outer wall had confirmed I was in the right place, but the right place for what? The possibility began to creep into my mind that the data was bad, the address a front to keep people like me, or whoever had screwed me away from Jin. If the address was the penthouse, I might have stopped and waited for Danelle to arrive with Evan. It was on the tenth floor, and I had already climbed six.

My hand drifted to my pocket as I pushed open the stairwell door, finding the dice and wrapping around them. The feel of their curved sides brought me comfort, and I needed it.

The hallway was the scene of a massacre.

Two dozen bodies were scattered across the floor on either side of the elevator, used and thrown aside like the food wrappers down below. There were all kinds of puncture wounds and jagged tears through flesh and bone, leaving severed appendages and entrails mixed in with the corpses, and sending out a smell that would have made me gag if I weren't already used to death and decay. Even so, the sight of it made my stomach turn, and I clenched my teeth and gritted myself against the resulting nausea.

I should have gotten out of there. I should have turned and ran down the stairs. Every instinct told me to, and I would have if I hadn't heard the whimper.

It was small, and frightened. It was coming from down the hallway. Shit. I listened for the fields, getting just the barest whisper of a ping back. It was only just strong enough to be accessed from this height. I wasn't about to risk pulling the energy in before I knew I needed it, but it was good to know it was there. I steeled myself and stepped forward, closing the door softly behind me. My boots squished against the carpeting, wet from all the blood.

I don't want to die. That was the thought that always ran through my head at times like this. It was a thought that had served me pretty well so far. I gripped the dice more tightly and removed them from my pocket. I wouldn't have much time to use them if I needed to. If I tossed them without naming a target they would choose at random, and I wasn't excluded from the pool.

Not that I heard anyone else. Maybe whoever was in there was alone. Maybe they had somehow survived their injuries and were a few breaths away from death. There was little I could do for them in that case. This place was a nightmare. What the hell was I still doing here?

Tiptoeing through a mess of dead bodies, my boots getting bathed in their blood, that's what. It was a new experience for me, and I fucking hated it.

I examined the bodies as I crept past them. All traditional human, all men, all between twenty and forty years old. The majority were asian, Japanese I think, with a couple of mean-looking caucasians thrown in. They wore suits, blazers, jeans, t-shirts. Random clothing, but their presence here was anything but random.

The doors to the apartments I passed were hanging open. Televisions were still casting flickering light in a few of them. I could picture the scene in my mind. The ferals coming into the hallway, maybe busting into Jin's apartment. The other people on the floor hearing the ruckus and moving out to intercept. Moving out... not hiding.

Protecting them, or at least trying to.

My initial reaction to this place had been that I was way off-base. That whoever Red had asked me to find would never be living the slum life. The carnage here was suggesting otherwise. Unfortunately, it was also suggesting I had gotten here second, and I was going to be shit out of luck.

Another whimper brought me out of my head. It was stronger

this time, and it sounded strained. A third, louder cry made me stop moving. I waited while my heart pounded through my chest, and then inched forward towards 1024 - the apartment that was supposed to belong to Jin Mori.

I didn't trust that whoever had killed these people had left. It would have been stupid to drop my guard. I kept myself near the wall opposite Jin's door, crouching low. As I did, I saw that one of the bodies nearby was armed, a gun in a hand that was positioned unnaturally behind his back.

I rolled the dice in my fingers. They were what they looked like: an element of randomness, of chance. My luck was running pretty lousy right now, and that made me hesitant to trust them.

I put them back in my pocket and glanced from the gun to the doorway, figuring my route, running through it a few times in my mind. If I fucked it up, it could mean my life.

Screw that. I took three long, quick steps towards the corpse with the firepower, swung low to scoop it up, ripped it from the dead hand, dropped to a crouch, and turned to fire into the room in one quick motion.

I didn't pull the trigger.

A girl was hanging from a motionless ceiling fan, her face and clothes bloody, her lifeless hands gripping the bottom of the belt that had been wrapped around her neck. She was young, too young, and pretty. Japanese, with short, bobbed hair and delicate features.

She was dead.

I kept the gun out and aimed into the room, walking forward. I swung the weapon back and forth as I entered, making sure I was alone. There was a door on either side of the living room, whose furniture had been thrown into the back corner to make space for the hanging. Those doors were open, too.

The whimpering had been coming from somewhere in here. I reached up and put my hand to the girl's face. It was still warm.

She had been dying when I had come in, which meant she hadn't been hung too long ago.

The floor creaked. The door on the right pushed open a little more, and a pale figure with dark hair burst through it. I turned and fired, but my attacker was too fast. The bullets chipped the wood around the doorframe, and a hand slashed across my wrist, opening the skin and trying to make me drop the weapon. I brought my other arm up and around, catching the vampire in the jaw. It was enough to get it off-balance, and I slipped back and away, gaining a couple of feet of space and setting myself for round two.

It turned and glowered at me with bloodshot brown eyes and a twisted scowl. Its fangs dripped the poison secretions that would paralyze me if they managed to break the skin, and its lithe muscles flexed with anticipation.

It had been sitting in the room, waiting. For me? For something else? Vampires didn't wait. They were either hunting, or sleeping. That was it. Like the creature that had done in the clerk, this one wasn't acting quite right.

That didn't make it less dangerous.

My left hand held the gun, but it could take a dozen rounds and still kill me before it would even register the damage. My right hand dove into my pocket to find the dice again. They were warm in my grip, which was good. The vamp wasn't going to wait for me to use them, which was bad.

It leaped towards me, a hissing screech preceding clawed fingers. I put three rounds into its chest as I backpedaled into the wall, and then rolled to the side while it scraped the plaster and turned to track me. I put my left side towards it and brought the dice to my mouth, whispering into them at the same time the claws raked my forearm, tearing through my coat and hoodie, but not quite getting the skin. I leaned in and shoved it back, and then dropped the dice at its feet.

Fire, and fire. The dark magic flowed out of them towards the vampire, and it screamed as its skin exploded in burns and blisters. I kicked it away from me and brought the gun up to shoot it a few more times.

I didn't need to. Six more pops sounded behind me, and six bullets made a nice cluster in the feral's skull. It tumbled backwards and didn't move.

I turned around and aimed at the interloper, only to find a similar weapon trained on me. Another young woman, her features close enough to those of the hanging corpse that I knew they were related. She was a little older, a little prettier, her thick black hair in chunks instead of a bob and elongated ears pushing out between dyed purple locks. She was wearing a flower-printed camisole and cotton sweatpants, her feet bare.

Her eyes were red from crying. They were narrowed with anger. She said something to me in Japanese, and then glanced at the girl.

"I'm not with them," I said. I lowered the gun.

She walked over to me in four quick steps, shouting something at me in Japanese and putting the barrel of the gun against my forehead. I didn't move to stop her. I didn't move at all.

"I'm not going to hurt you. I was trying to kill the vamp."

Her eyes shifted, looking at the mess of a feral behind me, showing me she understood English.

"I'm looking for Jin Mori."

She pushed the gun harder against my forehead.

"Whoa. Wait a second. I came to help. Mrs. Red sent me."

Her eyebrows creased and her head tilted slightly.

"Prove it," she said, with only the slight hint of an accent.

"I need to reach into my pocket."

"Slowly."

I did as she asked, dropping the gun to the floor and digging into my pocket. I found the necklace there, and lifted it out into the open. "She said to bring it with-"

There was a crash as the stairwell door slammed open. Her eyes widened, and she reached out with her free hand and grabbed my bleeding wrist. "This way."

I tugged against her, the blood making her grip weak. I broke free and swooped down to grab my dice. "Where?"

She ran ahead of me, across the living room to the room on the other side. I wasn't sure why she was going that way. We weren't going to be any safer staying boxed in, but I followed. She had come from somewhere.

We were in a bedroom. She went past the bed and vanished into the closet, reaching out and tugging me in, and then closing the door, even as I heard the growls and claws moving through the hallway.

"We're hiding in a closet?" I asked, keeping my voice low. "How is this going to help?"

She put her finger to her lips and knelt down, moving her hand to the wall below a row of blouses and dresses. A small, hidden door slid silently away.

"In here," she said.

I got down on my hands and knees and crawled through the opening, into a tiny room that was obviously only intended to hold one person. It had a couple of pillows, some bottles of water and a few cans of food stacked in a corner. I shoved my back against the wall.

The woman followed after me, climbing up into my lap, and then putting her hand to another part of the drywall. The secret door slid closed, leaving us in claustrophobic darkness.

CHAPTER EIGHTEEN

Too close for comfort.

I COULD FEEL HER BREATH on my neck. I could smell the sickly sweetness of her sweat mixed with the scent of fruit and spice that was so common with elves. The warmth of her body pressed down on mine, settling onto my lap as best she could. I couldn't see anything. In another place, another time, the whole thing might have been exciting.

We didn't speak. I could hear the ferals in the hallway, the creaking of the floor as they entered the apartment. They must have found the vampire, because they yapped at one another excitedly and the feet shifted around again. By the sounds, I was guessing there were three of them.

Two left the apartment.

The other moved into the bedroom.

Pounding heartbeats passed in silence.

The feet moved closer.

The door to the closet creaked open.

I could feel her muscles tensing on my lap, and I was sure my own were tensing as well. We waited for whatever was on the other side of the wall to react, to figure out we were right there, and start scraping away in an effort to reach us. Instead, the feet turned and moved away. The bed creaked as something heavy bounded onto it, and an impact sounded when it landed on the other side. Only then did I take a breath.

We stayed silent for another minute. I could feel her hair tickling my cheek, her breast pressed against my shoulder. I could feel the throbbing of my wounded wrist.

"We're lucky it didn't smell your blood," she said, breaking the silence. "We need to put pressure on it." Her hands gripped at the sleeve of my hoodie in the pitch, exploring until they found a tear. "This may hurt." She grabbed the ends and pulled, ripping it apart into a single strip of cloth. She wrapped it tight around my wrist and tied it off.

It hurt, but nowhere near enough to affect me. I was used to pain.

"Who are you?" she asked.

"I'm nobody."

"You came looking for Jin. Mrs. Red sent you. How did you know her?"

I could feel the heat rising to my face. There was no point being dodgy. "I was hired by a fixer who claimed he was working for Mr. Black. The job was to break into Red's house and steal something."

"The treasure? You were set up."

"To put it mildly. I feel like I'm the only one who didn't know what was going to happen."

Her breath waved against my neck, making the hairs stand on up end. It had a warm cinnamon smell to it, and we were so close I couldn't help but take it in with my own.

"We expected someone would make a move on the treasure. The house was guarded..."

"They took out the guards and replaced them with ringers. They killed Mrs. Red. I was there. She told me if I wanted to survive this, I needed to bring the necklace to Jin. The girl-"

"She was my sister, Natsumi. She was sleeping in the other

bedroom. She didn't make it in time." Her voice trembled.

"You're Jin?" I hated myself for feeling relieved that she was still alive, when her sister was dangling from the ceiling fan in the living room.

"Yes."

"What happened?"

"They got here before you did. I never saw them, but I heard the fighting. Did they kill everyone?"

"Yes. They were trying to protect you."

"Only a few of them were users, and only a couple were armed. No one was supposed to know I was here. No one was even supposed to know I'm related to Mrs. Red."

I felt the weight of her head against my chest. She rested it there and sobbed, as though I had known her for more than five minutes. I was stiff, unsure how to react to her.

"They were my family, my friends. They didn't deserve this. Natsumi... we heard them coming. She tried to get to safety in time. They caught her. I could hear her screaming and crying. Someone asked her where I was. A woman's voice. They hung her there for me to find. They wanted me to see."

"They left the vampire for you, too."

"I didn't know it was out there. I could hear Natsumi crying... choking... dying. I was afraid to come out. It is my duty and place to survive, even though it meant letting her die. When I heard the gunshots, I thought my aunt had sent a team to save me. Now I know the truth."

She had been waiting for a whole team. All she had gotten was me.

"I'm sorry." The words were like trying to salve a wound with salt.

A few minutes passed while she cried into my chest. I was tentative as I moved my hand to her back and lightly held her. I couldn't have a woman crying in my lap and not try to at least be a little comforting.

Then, she just stopped. She lifted her head and I felt her arms moving while she wiped at her eyes.

"Do you have a name?"

Her face was right in front of mine, her breath washing against it. Her voice had changed. The sorrow was gone, replaced with cold anger.

When I didn't answer right away, she laughed. "The ghost who saved my life. You don't call yourself anything?"

"Daaé."

Her hair brushed my face when she shook her head.

"I don't like it. It's too feminine for you. You should have been the Phantom."

I should have been dead. Any name was better than that.

"I have a job for you, Phantom, if you're willing to consider it."

If I could have seen her face in the blackness, I'm sure her eyes would have been burning through me.

"The last job I took didn't go so well."

"Perhaps together we can change that. To murder my aunt in cold blood... The Houses don't move against one another like that, not without reason or purpose. Their power, their rule, is a delicate thread that holds civilization together. The treasure is valuable enough to steal, not to risk an all-out war over."

"What are you saying?"

"It was only a matter of time before a new major power was born outside of the Houses. We are still evolving, still changing. You're a ghost. You know what the Houses are, where they came from, what they do."

"Yes."

"It has been sixty years. Three generations since the reversal. Did you think those who first rose up would be the only ones to master the magic so fully? Did you believe that no others would rise?"

121

The idea of it made me shiver. The Houses were always working with and against one another, but they had rules, and they knew the consequences. "No, but the Houses control-"

"The Houses control the controllable." Her body shifted, and her forehead pressed against mine. It was warm and sweaty, full of life. The last time I had been this close to anyone had been that one night with Danelle, and it had been less than memorable. "Just as I could control you, right now."

Her voice softened, becoming sultry and charged. Her lips met my own for just a moment. In the absolute darkness, I was tempted, more by memories than reality. It had been so long since I had felt this kind of touch. I closed my eyes, remembering.

Then I put my hand to her face and gently turned it away. "You can't. Not like that."

"Then you know what I'm saying. Most have a price, but there are some that do not. The Houses don't dare risk a confrontation with an equal power without discussion. The consequences of initiating an open battle between such wizards would be disastrous."

"What if that other power confronted you first?"

"Then the others would say that we should be even more cautious. An aggressive enemy is the worst kind. I agree with them to a point. That is why I need your help."

"Me? You don't need me. You need a whole team. Or at least someone anonymous. They know who I am. They've seen me. Hell, the only reason I had the job is because I stole it. I thought it would be my big payday, my ticket to living to see next year." I banged the back of my head softly against the wall, feeling stupid again.

"My sister is hanging from the ceiling in my living room, Phantom. This enemy... They are using ferals to do their dirty work. No one was supposed to know I exist at all, and yet I was attacked. I can't sit here and wait for them to kill me, and I can't afford to be cautious while they dismantle my House. I need to find out who is behind this and put a stop to it, and I can't do it alone. You're the only person I can trust."

She surprised me. From her crying, I had mistaken her for a weak, scared victim. I didn't feel any of that now. What I sensed was what I had expected Mrs. Red to be.

"You don't know you can trust me."

"I have to take my chances. There is no one else."

"I don't even know if I can get you out of this closet alive."

"But you'll try, for a price."

"I'll try because I can't shake a kill team on my own. Your House has resources, contacts…"

"What is your price, Phantom?

"I want to survive. I want to take care of my ex-wife and our daughter. That's all."

"A necromancer who's afraid of death?"

I considered making a comment on what I'd learned about the other side, but the image of her sister stopped me. "I have other responsibilities. I have a friend to take care of, too. She's on her way to New York to help with this mess. I owe her my life."

I felt her lips again, this time on my cheek. "I will do what I can. I know we just met, but I sense you are an honorable man. Whether we live or die, remember that."

Honorable? There was nothing honorable about abandoning my family. It was an old wound, and I felt it spread open.

"You're sure this is the work of a new House?" I asked, shifting the subject.

"I'm not sure of anything. What I can tell you is that I was raised to inherit House Red at the time of my aunt's passing. Since I turned eighteen, I have been apprised of every action we have taken with and against the other Houses. They may discourage hiring necromancers. They would never use ferals."

"The payment I received was from Black."

"It was counterfeit."

Neither Dannie or Mr. Clean had noticed anything strange about the payment, and Gucci had been authentic enough. "I don't think so."

Silence.

"It wasn't Black," she said at last.

"The payment card was real."

"It wasn't Black." Her steel tone told me she was sure of it. Mrs. Red had made the same claim, so I didn't keep arguing. "Either the card was a very, very good fake, it was stolen, or it was exchanged."

"Exchanged?"

"A ghost took a payment from Black for a job. He then traded that payment card for another of higher value from a different House. It isn't unheard of."

"The ghost would have to be in on it."

"Yes, which means there's a trail that leads back to the source, however faint it may be. If the card was fake, we need to know who made it. If it was stolen, who took it. If it was exchanged, who traded it."

"First we need to get out of this closet."

We fell into an alert silence, listening for the werewolves. Jin had said there was a human with them, a woman, most likely a user. With them, or controlling them?

The building was silent around us, and in the claustrophobic darkness it felt like a tomb. We were safe for now, but we'd need to leave the panic room at some point. What would happen then? Was I only delaying the inevitable? If we were lucky, they believed Jin wasn't home, and had left the apartment to keep watch near the entrance. If we were lucky, we would be able to sneak past them.

Considering my recent misfortune, I wasn't holding my breath.

I closed my eyes and listened for any hint of the ferals. At first I didn't hear anything. Then the silence was filled with a soft snore, a light whistle that would have been adorable anywhere else.

With nothing else to do but wait, I relaxed as much as I could and let my own fatigue take me.

CHAPTER NINETEEN

The girl with the dragon tattoo.

I OPENED MY EYES, BUT I still couldn't see anything. My feet were tingling, the circulation cut off by the weight of Jin on my lap. It was an odd first waking thought, but I wondered what the word for elf was in Japanese?

"Jin?" I put my hand on her shoulder and gave her a light shake.

She moved against me with a soft moan. I felt the weight of her head leave my chest, and she sucked in some drool that must have spilled over onto my hoodie.

"I'm sorry."

"A little spit never killed anyone." I shifted around until I could reach my watch. The light from the face bathed us in a blueish tinge. We'd been asleep for two hours. "There you are."

Her eyes were swollen from crying. "Do you think it's safe now?"

I let the light fade away. There was no point wasting the battery just to look at one another. "It better be. My feet are asleep."

She shifted again. "Listen."

We sat in silence. A few minutes passed. There was nothing. It was time.

"We have to take our chances."

"Your dice-" she started to say. I hadn't realized she'd even noticed them.

"Magic, yeah."

"They're old."

"Very."

"They don't use the fields."

I didn't like to talk about them. It made me feel... I don't know... dirty. "No. There's something... in them. A soul, a dark soul. It's trapped, I think."

"I saw you use them on the vampire. I don't think it's trapped."

That's why I didn't like to talk about them. The idea that something wanted to be in there, wanted to take the souls, gave me a chill.

"They aren't unlimited use." My control over them was an illusion. They only worked when *they* wanted to. Sometimes, they weren't hungry. Some souls, they didn't want. "How many rounds do you have?"

I heard the sound of the gun sliding against the floor. I hit the light on my watch again so she could check her clip.

"Six. Not enough to stop a werewolf before it gets its claws into one of us."

"We could piss it off, though. The fields are tickling this floor... You should be able to draw enough energy in to do some damage. I can cover you."

She didn't say anything. She slid the clip back into the gun and handed it to me. "Maybe they think I escaped. Or that I was never here. Maybe they left?"

I didn't feel that confident about leaving the panic room, but we couldn't stay trapped forever. One of us would need to pee sooner or later. "There's only one way to find out. Open it up."

Her weight shifted again, and she put her palm against the wall. The panel slid aside, allowing the dim light of the closet to filter in. She crawled out on her hands and knees. I followed behind.

Once we were both in the closet, I went over to the door and eased it open, just enough that I could peek out through the crack. I could see her bedroom was empty. I could also see through the doorway, to where her sister was hanging.

"Are you ready?" I asked.

She set her jaw and nodded. I opened the closet the rest of the way and stepped out into the room. I held out my hand to keep her back while I tiptoed to the bedroom door and snuck a look to the entry. The vampire had been hiding in the other bedroom. Had they left another guard there?

I raised the gun and circled around the back of the room, so I would have time to react if anything jumped out at me. I made it to the other side, ducking and twisting as I cleared Natsumi's door. Her room was empty. The whole apartment was clear.

Jin was standing in front of her dresser when I returned to the bedroom, her flower-printed cami on the floor, her bare upper-half in an artful profile. Her skin was porcelain and smooth, and she had a red dragon tattoo that wound from her side over the top of her right breast. It was bright and intricate, the work of a serious artist. It disappeared a moment later under a plain black bra, followed by a tight, long-sleeve shirt with a high neck.

"I can't go outside in my pajamas." She looked straight ahead, her face a mask.

"You're so sure we're going to make it outside?" I watched her sweats come off.

"I don't want to die in my pajamas either."

A pair of slim black pants covered her up again. I hadn't realized I was distracted until I wasn't distracted anymore.

"The apartment is clear. I think the floor is, too. If they're still here, they'll be watching the exits."

She was moving as I spoke, going back into the closet and pulling out a pair of black sneakers and putting them on. "What do you suggest?"

I had been pondering that for too long, and I still had no

confident reply. I wasn't wholly convinced we would get out of this. I found my phone in my pocket. I could call Dannie, see how close she was. Maybe we could hide for a few more hours until the cavalry arrived?

I let it go. I'd just be getting her killed, too.

"Is the elevator really broken?"

"Yes. It's stuck on the roof."

"It could be that they won't be watching it, then. We could climb down to the ground floor."

"What if they're waiting in the lobby?" Her head turned towards me, and her eyes sparkled. "I have another idea." She went over to her night stand and opened the top drawer, pulling out a set of keys. "The elevator goes down into a parking garage. I have a bike stashed down there. They may have positioned someone to wait for us, but if we can get to the bike we might be able to outrun them."

"Outrun werewolves? That must be some bike."

She smiled. "Oh, it is. It was a gift from my aunt."

We hadn't left the bedroom yet. I walked over to her and put my hand on her shoulder. "You don't have to look. I can lead you out."

She put her hand on mine. "As I said, Phantom, you are an honorable man, but I must say goodbye."

"They might hear us."

The look she gave me shut me up. I nodded and walked out ahead of her, going out and checking the hallway. It was clear.

"Help me take her down."

I went back to where she was standing, her face still set in stone as she looked at her sister. I held Natsumi's legs and lifted while she unbuckled the belt. Once she was free, I lowered her to the floor as quietly as I could.

"You can bring her back?"

"I can't animate users."

"She wasn't a user."

I looked at her sister, her face purple, her eyes bulging. Not a user? "Sensitive?"

Her head whipped around, and her angry eyes regarded me. "Does it matter?"

Not for bringing her back. It mattered because Jin was the heir to House Red, and if she was a full-frequency wizard, her sister should have at least been sensitive. Which meant...

"You aren't a wizard, are you?"

I wanted her to yell at me. I wanted her to tell me to go fuck myself, and how dare I insult her like that. I wanted her to prove me wrong.

Her face changed. First it turned back to stone, and then it flushed. She bit down on her lip.

"I was chosen because I was the best option out of a pool of poor options. We never expected I would need to take on the role. As you may be aware, powerful wizards like my aunt often live much longer than the average person. She was barren, and someone had to be selected and prepared." She brushed her hair away from her ears. "When I was born with the elf mutation, she decided to raise me as her replacement. She believed the empathic ability that comes with the mutation would allow me to... fake it... better."

I didn't say anything. Fake it? The only thing that kept a House alive was the potential of its head to rain fire and brimstone down on anyone who fucked with it. A House without a wizard at its front was broken. Irreparably broken. Even if I got Jin out of here, it was only a matter of time before her ruse was uncovered. It was only a question of when she would die, and House Red would be no more.

"Do the other Houses know?"

Somebody did. I was sure that was one of the reasons all of this had happened to begin with.

"They aren't even supposed to know I exist. I always assumed I would never need to take control, that my aunt would outlive me. Do you want to cancel our agreement?"

She kept her eyes on mine, waiting for me to react.

I took a deep breath, licked my lips, and shook my head. "No. I took the job, and like it or not your enemy is my enemy. They want me dead as much as you." I put my right hand on her sister's wrist. "This might be a little weird for you. I don't like to animate people I know."

"Please. She can help us."

I knew she could. That was why I was willing to do it. The fields weren't very strong up here, but I wouldn't need to exert much will on her to get her to do what we needed. She would follow her sister, or so I assumed.

I took a deep breath, sucking in the magical energy. It was a longer reach, and it felt more like trying to drink a thick milkshake. "Natsumi. Wake up, Natsumi. Jin needs you."

The bulged eyes focused, her lips moved, and a soft groan escaped.

"Natsumi?" Jin put her hand to her sister's face.

"Jin?" Her larynx had been crushed by the belt, leaving her voice barely audible.

"I'm sorry. I'm sorry I didn't save you."

Natsumi lifted her arm and put it to Jin's face. "No." She tried to say something else, but the damage didn't let her.

"We need to move," I said. "Natsumi, the ferals that killed you are probably still here. You need to help Jin get out of the building alive."

She got up without effort. Her body was still in good shape. She wasn't showing signs of the confusion, which impressed me. She wanted to come back. She wanted to help. That part of her personality was overriding everything else.

"Take the lead," I said. "I'll cover the rear. We're going down the elevator shaft to the garage."

She walked out into the hallway without hesitation, practically daring any of our enemies to be waiting for us. Jin stayed close, and I followed with my head turned so I could see behind us. I was amazed by how light the thread between Natsumi and me felt.

We made it to the elevator doors. Natsumi dug her fingers between them and pulled, her magic-powered muscles stronger in death than they had been in life. The doors succumbed, moving aside and allowing us access to the shaft. Jin and I leaned in, following the empty space all the way to the bottom. I looked up, just in case.

The path was clear.

CHAPTER TWENTY

Here boy!

THE CLIMB DOWN THE ELEVATOR shaft was tense, but it was also fast. Natsumi and Jin were both plenty agile enough to go hand-over-hand along the guide wall, and I was more experienced with this sort of thing than I had ever planned to be. We reached the third sub-level of the garage within ten minutes, standing together in front of the sealed elevator doors, trying not to make a sound while we listened for any indication of someone, or something guarding the exit.

In the end, I knelt between Natsumi's legs with the gun aimed upwards to where I imagined a werewolf's head would be. Jin crouched behind us, trying to stay out of view and ready to dash past towards her ride as soon as we got the door open far enough. We hadn't heard anything on the other side, and I was optimistic that we had evaded our enemies.

It had been way too easy.

Natsumi dug her fingers between the doors and pulled. A crack appeared, allowing some of the dim ambient lighting of the garage to trickle in, and introducing us to the smell of garbage and damp cement. My finger rested on the trigger of the gun, and my eyes strained to stay focused.

She moved them further aside. There was no sign of life down here. All I could see were a couple of rows of old beaters, and a great deal of empty spots. That, and a motorcycle. A gorgeous, tricked out, futuristic blend of carbon fiber and chrome with thick, smooth rubber and a tiny but powerful electric motor resting mid-chassis.

Natsumi moved out into the garage, her head turning to scan the area.

She only made it two steps.

A dark brown blur snatched her up like a linebacker, slamming into her and throwing her across the garage. Jin started forward out of pure protective instinct until I caught her wrist and redirected her. "Get the bike. She can't feel it."

The motorcycle was only twenty feet away, but it might as well have been a mile. The werewolf only needed one bite to realize his prey was already expired, and he was turning around even as I moved from the safety of the shaft. I trained the gun on him, holding my fire, waiting to see if he would charge me or Jin. I needed him to charge me.

My other hand was in my pocket, reaching for the dice. They were cold to the touch. Disinterested. The werewolf broke for Jin.

Fuck.

She was halfway to the bike, and she must have seen it coming, because she turned as it approached, seven feet and six hundred pounds to her five and a half and one hundred. She braced herself as it charged, crouching low and skipping aside, maneuvering around its grasp with acrobatic efficiency. It skidded to a stop and spun again, snarling in frustration. She dashed towards the motorcycle.

I blasted the wolf in the head.

A perfect shot right between the eyes. If only the bullets had been armor piercing. If only weres didn't have ridiculously solid skulls. It yelped in pain as its head snapped back, but it recovered within seconds, dropping to all fours and rushing at the new threat.

Bang! Bang! Bang! Bang! I snapped off four more rounds, catching it in the shoulder, the thigh, and the chest. I succeeded in pissing it off, but not in slowing it, and I scrambled backwards, slipping on some old oil or shit or something and falling onto my ass. My hand hit the cement and sent the gun sliding away, leaving me unarmed and helpless with a monster bearing down.

Somehow I managed to get my knife into my hand, even as the werewolf was landing on top of me. Huge jaws approached my face, and I brought my forearm up and pushed against it, holding it back for as long as my strength could manage, which wouldn't be very long.

I heard only a soft whine when the motorcycle came to life. At least Jin would make it out of here. The were's teeth were getting closer to my face. My injured arm was breaking down, and a claw dug hard into my shoulder. I cried out and stabbed wildly with the knife, burying it in the feral's side and earning myself a deeper wound. Its jaws were only inches away from my face now, the last thing I would see before I left this world and traveled to one that was even more frightening.

I heard the screech of tires, and I felt the displacement of air. All I saw was a red blur out of the corner of my eye, and then the wolf was gone, slammed and knocked aside by the bike. More screeching tires and it was coming back towards me. Jin skidded it like a pro and put herself between the werewolf and me.

"Come on."

I was hurting, but I forced myself to get up as fast as I could. Once I was on my feet I could see past Jin to where the wolf was getting back up, recovering from the blow. It stumbled towards us on its hinds, gaining speed.

"You are so fucking slow!" She grabbed my trench and pulled me towards the bike. I got my leg over as the werewolf neared, claws reaching for her.

Natsumi stepped in front of it. Her throat was shredded, her face torn. She raised the gun up, sticking it in the werewolf's open mouth. The teeth chomped down, but too late. She fired, and a line of gore exploded from the back of its head.

"Go, go, go," I said, wrapping my arms tight around Jin. She glanced back at her sister one last time and peeled away, angling towards the ramp. I looked back at Natsumi too, waving goodbye as I let go of the thread. She collapsed in a heap.

The bike rocketed forward, only the slightest whine coming from the electric motor, the lightest touch from the smooth wheels. Jin hit the ramp without slowing, jostling me and making my shoulder feel like it was about to fall off. The bike swayed but didn't topple, and she ripped into the turn, gaining even more speed.

We hit the next platform, and she pegged the throttle, sending the bike launching forward even faster towards the ramp at the other side. Two werewolves were racing down it. One of them was huge and black, with a patch of white fur.

"There's no other way out," Jin shouted back at me, alerting me to the fact that were about to play chicken with a pair of ferals. Ferals that Danelle had told me were dead. Whatever control had killed, they had the wrong fur balls.

We raced towards them. They ran towards us. The distance felt like it took forever to close, but it was more like three seconds.

"Don't let go." The wolves leaped towards us, high enough to get over the bike, low enough to rake us with their claws.

If I hadn't been on the motorcycle, I wouldn't have believed it. Somehow, she turned us sideways, leaving us in a serious skid that brought my head only inches from the ground. The wolves flew over, too high to hit us, and the friction of the wheels caught up to the maneuver, physics and Jin's balance pulling the bike upright. She twisted it again, bringing it straight with only a few small wobbles, and continued towards the ramp, leaving the weres behind.

"Holy shit!" I yelled, my adrenaline pumping so hard I didn't even feel my shoulder any more.

We hit the first level and sped towards the ramp, reaching it safely and bursting out of the garage. It was evening, and it was dark, a heavy rain soaking us in seconds. Jin slid the bike out into the street and aimed us north past the building. I turned my head to look towards it, just in time to see someone coming out of the lobby.

The redhead from Connecticut. I should have known.

I gave her the finger while she watched us ride away.

CHAPTER TWENTY-ONE

She slimed me.

WE KEPT RIDING, WEAVING THROUGH the evening rush, using the sidewalk when we needed to and trying to put some distance between us and them. If the ferals decided to take to the streets, they would be able to pace a bike in traffic.

"Where are we going?" I asked, shouting above the sounds of honking horns and wind. How she kept the bike from wiping out on the slick pavement was a mystery.

"As far away from here as I can get."

"The stone is back that way."

"Do they know where you hid it?"

"No."

"Then you can get it later."

Me. Not we. We had gotten out of there alive, and she was falling into her role. In that moment, a thought made my heart nearly stop. I was a ghost. I wasn't supposed to know who the heads of the Houses were, and here I was holding tight to one. When this was over, she'd have every reason to have me killed. Every reason to send her own team after me and erase my sorry ass.

We threw a nice puddle onto a pair of old ladies in fancy raincoats and cut around a parked car, riding between the lanes on our way to... where? I wasn't going to worry about it. Jin seemed like she knew where she was headed, and she wasn't going to kill me just yet. We had a deal, and I knew she would honor it, just the same as I would. I would need to make sure Danelle didn't know who she was, or why she was important. Let someone else be in charge of House Red. She could be a favorite niece. It wasn't even a lie, just an omission.

We maneuvered through mid-town, heading uptown and into Harlem. I found a little bit of humor when we wound up riding right past the cross streets that housed the addresses of the other two Jins on Dannie's list. She brought us down a couple of side streets, and then angled the bike into an alley between a pair of average looking apartment buildings.

She slid off the bike and ran her hands through her short hair, squeegeeing some of the water out of it. She was soaked to the bone, her clothes clinging to her body. I had fared a little better, my waterproof trench protecting part of me. Even so, my hoodie felt heavy and tight against my torso.

"My friend Reva lives here. She can be trusted."

"Are you sure?"

"She doesn't know anything about House Red. We're racing buddies."

"Racing?"

"Where do you think I learned to ride like that?"

Maybe it was the blood loss that was slowing my brain. "You street race. Isn't that a little dangerous... you know... for who you are?"

"My aunt always said that if I wasn't strong enough to survive my own passions, I would never be strong enough to stand up to the other Houses." She turned and headed out of the alley. I followed behind.

We climbed the steps and entered the building. I kept my hand over my shoulder, hiding the torn part of my trench and the blood soaked hoodie beneath it. Now that our ride was over the pain was coming back. It was going to need stitches at a minimum, and I wouldn't be doing myself any favors to get into any fights for the next week. Somehow, I doubted that was going to happen.

We walked up three flights of steps. The apartment building was old, but the inside was clean. Beige painted walls, sparkling recycled plastic flooring, a fresh smell.

"It was burned out during the riots, before I was born. The government paid to renovate after the Houses organized the settlement, and the residents have made it a point to keep it looking new. They take a lot of pride in proving all the idiots wrong."

"What kind is Reva?" She looked back at me, a dark expression on her face. "I'm not anti... just curious."

"Then it doesn't matter. You only have to be curious for another minute."

Reva was a troll.

She was small for her kind at only six feet, with dark green flesh that was covered in small, tough pustules filled with a yellow bodily fluid. She had a large head, a mohawk of thick black hair, and giant, heavy lobed ears covered in a hundred small rings. She was wearing a black sweater and specially made jeans, her feet bare. When she saw Jin, her toothy grin grew massive, and she wrapped her up in a hug, not even seeming to notice she was soaked.

"Jinnie. What are you doing here?" Her voice was somewhere between a train horn and a screaming cat.

"I'm sorry to show up at your door like this Reva, but my friend and I need your help."

She hadn't even noticed me until then. "You look like shit," she said, letting go of Jin and holding out her hand. "Any friend of Jinnie's is a friend of mine."

I started to let go of my shoulder to shake her hand before thinking better of it, and when I did her eyes narrowed. "What the hell happened to you?"

"Attacked by ferals," Jin said. "They came into my building. He saved my life."

"Oh my god. Don't stand out there making puddles in the hall. Come in, come in. You, take off that coat and sweater so I can get a look at the wound. Jin... get out of those wet clothes. I don't have anything your size, but you can nestle into one of my robes while I dry them."

I followed Jin into the apartment. It was a pretty standard living space. A microfiber couch, a flatscreen with the latest news glowing from it, some fake plants. A small kitchen was placed off to the side, and a bedroom and bathroom took up the rear. If it hadn't been for the caged rats on the kitchen counter, I wouldn't have been able to guess what kind of human lived here.

"Sorry, I probably don't have anything you'd want to eat." She must have noticed me eyeing the rats. "I would have gotten a few things if I'd known I was going to have guests. I've got Coke though."

"I'll be right back." Jin disappeared into the bedroom.

I worked on getting out of my clothes, but it was rough with my shoulder. I got the trench and the hoodie off easy enough, but pulling my shirt over my head was another story.

"Here, let me help you." Reva grabbed the edge of the shirt and helped me wiggle out of it. When she saw my grey skin, and the fresh stitches along my abdomen, she gasped. "You look like you find trouble a lot."

"Or trouble finds me. I'm starting to think you're right about that." I winced in pain from the sharp stinging. I looked over at it. Three deep slashes. I was lucky they hadn't reached the muscle.

"Go sit. I'll get some towels and water to clean it out."

"You do this a lot?" I asked her back as she headed for the bathroom.

She turned her head and smiled. "I am a troll."

Right.

Jin came out of the bedroom, lost in the larger female's bathrobe. She was holding her clothes, and she turned and pushed aside a sliding door to reveal the washer and dryer. She threw her stuff in, got it running, and then sat next to me. She looked different with her hair flat against her head instead of all chunked up. A little younger, a little more innocent.

"That wound doesn't look too bad, compared to what you already seem to be going through."

"It still hurts." I glanced over at the bathroom and lowered my voice. "We can't stay here. She might not know who you are, but how can we be sure they don't know who she is? They might have been watching you for weeks."

She nodded. "I know, but we had to go somewhere. I need you as healthy as you get."

"What about resources... money, intel, that kind of stuff?"

"It's a risk to expose myself when we don't know who knows what. We need a little more confidence in who our friends and enemies are before I'm going to try to access any of House Red's assets."

"Can you access them?"

"Yes, thanks to you. The necklace isn't just a pretty gem. There's a data chip inside. Once I load it into a secured workstation and put in the password, I'll be identified as Red and gain immediate control of all of it."

"It must be a lot."

She smiled. "I admit, I don't know the full breadth. But yes, I imagine it is. I have some access already, using my own code, but this will give me everything."

"Are you going to have me killed if we survive this?"

I threw it out there as bluntly as I could. I wanted to see how she would react. She kept smiling, and turned her head when Reva returned with the towels. She was probably really good at poker, too.

"Aww, you look like you got lost in a cloud. Slide over a bit."

I hadn't realized she was practically sitting on me, having moved in so we could speak quietly. She pushed herself to the other side of the couch, and Reva took the spot next to me. She patted a damp cloth on my shoulder, cleaning the dried blood away from the wound. She used another to get down into the cut a little, which hurt, and a third to dry it all off.

Then she put one against her arm, and pushed.

I could hear the pop of the pustule opening, and I tried not to look disgusted. I sat and stared ahead, while she popped two more and collected the fluid on the towel.

"Have you ever been healed by a troll before?"

"I heard trolls don't like to heal homo sapiens."

She laughed. "Yeah, a lot of us don't, but can you blame us?"

"Not at all."

The fluid that Reva was about to apply to my arm would bind to my cells, kicking them into an overdrive that pushed them to heal and multiply, fixing my shoulder without stitches in about three minutes.

In the beginning, when trolls had first started to appear, the military had taken a keen interest in the secretion's healing properties, and as trolls weren't immediately classified as people... It had left a lot of bad feelings all around that the riots had only made worse. Trolls were prized catches, and even today their puss could be bought on black markets in some cases, above the table in others. There were plenty of trolls that made a good living donating their bodily fluid, though the extraction of more than a few of the pustules at a time became incredibly painful.

"Like I said, a friend of Jinnie's is a friend of mine." She wiped the yellow ick on the gashes. It felt warm and cold and slimy, and then really, really warm. The stuff healed me so fast, I could literally see the flesh knitting back together.

"Thank you."

"I can get that one for you too, if you want." She motioned towards the stitches.

"No, that's okay. You've done more than enough for me already."

I stood up and grabbed my shirt, slipping it back over my head. My shoulder felt a lot better. It was too bad she couldn't do anything for the bruising and the sore muscles. I left the hoodie off, picking up my coat and putting it on. The familiar weight of it was comforting.

"So, Jinnie, tell me more about these ferals. Did they attack anyone else?"

I looked at Jin. Really, really good at poker. You'd never know they had killed her sister less than six hours ago. I walked over to a window and peeked out to the street below. There was no motion, and no traffic except for a couple of orcs walking down the street.

"No. They were down in the garage. I was just coming home. They came after me after I parked the bike."

"Oh shit. How'd you get away?"

"I had a gun," I said, turning around. "I lost it in the fight."

She was staring at me, trying to figure me out. I looked like death, was lurking in a garage, and carrying a weapon. It didn't sound innocent to me either.

"Jin, I really need to be getting home. Mr. Timms is going to be pissed that he hasn't had his dinner yet."

"Mr. Timms?"

"My cat."

"Oh. Okay. Let me just check on my clothes."

She jumped up, not realizing how precariously the robe was perched. It fell away as she reached her feet, giving me the full monty. I should have been the gentleman and looked away, but my eye caught the dragon tattoo again, and I was mesmerized by the intricacy of the work. I hardly even noticed the rest of her.

"Do you like it?" If she was embarrassed by her nakedness, it didn't show.

"It's amazing," I replied, still staring.

So much for honorable.

CHAPTER TWENTY-TWO

Three stars.

THE CLOTHES WERE DRY ENOUGH, and we left a few minutes later. Jin asked Reva to look after the bike for her and to make sure she kept it hidden. She also warned her to be alert for signs of any ferals wandering around.

Along with the news reports out of Connecticut, it was easy to convince her there was some kind of weird coincidence going on. She'd responded by showing off a nice 12 gauge with armor-piercing shot.

Between the bazooka and her healing factor, she would be just fine.

We took to the streets, sharing an umbrella. It was still pouring, the rain keeping a lot of people indoors or in cabs. Hopefully, the weather would keep the ferals away, too. They didn't like getting wet, because the smell made it hard for them to sneak and stalk.

She seemed satisfied to just walk for a few blocks. I had seen plenty of people lose people. I had failed to save a life on more than one occasion, and it never got easier. I didn't know exactly what she was thinking or feeling, but I could imagine some of the things. I knew what the experience felt like for me, and I was trained to be ready for it. Maybe she had been too? I didn't know. So we walked. She needed the time.

She wasn't the only one. I'd been on edge since Connecticut, and the normalcy of the activity helped me come down from my adrenaline high. It left me a little less alert, and my body even more sore than it had already been, but it was welcome. I put my hand to my mouth and coughed.

"Do you have a destination in mind?" I asked a short time later, glancing over at her. She was wearing that expressionless visage, though the slight curl in her lip told me she was pissed and scared.

"You're supposed to be protecting me. Where do you suggest?"

"I am, but I grew up near Chicago. I don't know this city that well. I recommend a hotel, not too close to anyone they might connect to you. A three-star, maybe. Not too fancy, but fancy enough they'll have to worry about control if they want to keep using ferals."

"I know a place."

She stopped walking and went to the curb, whistling and putting out her hand. It took a couple of tries, but a cab stopped at the side of the road within the minute.

The driver was an older man with a thick handlebar mustache. "Rainin' cats and dogs out there. Where to?"

"The Arcadia," Jin said, sliding across the seat so I could follow behind her.

The cab moved out at the same time I closed the door.

"The Arcadia? I've never heard of it."

"It's pretty new. I've never been there, but I've heard good things, and it isn't supposed to be too pricey."

"Good enough."

"Oh... I feel strange asking you this but... can you pay for it?"

"Don't worry about it. I was going to." I wasn't about to risk getting tracked down through her bank account, and I was pretty sure mine hadn't been compromised... yet.

"Thank you."

It was cute that she said thank you. "You're welcome."

147

My phone shook in my trench.

I fished it out. Danelle.

"Where are you?"

"A few minutes from the Lincoln tunnel. We'll be downtown in twenty minutes or so."

"Look up the Arcadia hotel. You'll be able to find me there."

"Okay. Any luck with Jin?"

I peeked over at her. She was looking the other way, out the window - giving me as much privacy as she could in the cab.

"It's a long story, but yeah. We'll fill you in when we hook up."

"I was worried about you. I'm glad you're still alive."

"Me too." I stifled a cough. "See you soon. I'm looking forward to meeting this friend of yours."

"Trust me, you're not."

She hung up.

"The cavalry," I said to Jin when she turned back around. I motioned towards the driver. "We can talk later."

She nodded, and we made the rest of the ride in silence.

CHAPTER TWENTY-THREE

Pac-man, or Donkey Kong?

THE ARCADIA HOTEL WAS A lot more posh than I had expected. Sixty stories of glass in a corkscrew shape, and a large, modern lobby bathed in sharp reds and oranges, with furniture composed of basic shapes and wrapped in white synthetic leather. The reception desk looked more like the interior of a spacecraft, with expensive translucent touch-screens and concierges dressed in a silver suits and skirts. It was an interesting place, the kind I would normally steer far away from. Hopefully that would make it a good place to hide.

"You have any suites available? Preferably something high?" I was a little iffy on going out of range of the fields, but in the end I'd decided it would hurt them more than it would hurt us.

My attendant was Jin's age, dark-skinned and lanky. He ran his fingers along the screens. "It looks like all the upper floors are booked." I guess karma had a different idea. "Room 618 is the best I can do. It doesn't have much of a view, but it's private."

His eyes tracked over to Jin. He probably thought the worst of both of us. I was way too sick and ugly to be with someone like her without money being involved.

"If that's what you've got, we'll take it." I handed him my card.

"If you'll just put your hand on the scanner, we can associate the door lock on your room to your palm-print.'"

Biometric security was pretty new to the hotel scene, and while the average Joe might have loved it for being both easy and secure, anyone who cared about their privacy would rather be robbed.

"You don't have keys?"

He smirked. "We have cards. They aren't as secure."

"I'll take the cards."

He hit a few more parts of the screen, and then reached down below the desk. He handed me the electronic room keys. "Here you go. Have a great stay. Do you have any bags you need brought up?"

"No, no bags." I almost winced as I said it, knowing it only made the whole situation look worse.

"Of course." His eyes flicked to Jin again, and I could see the smile creeping onto his face as he turned away.

I handed her one of the cards, and stuck mine in my pocket. We headed for the elevator.

"How are you holding up?" I asked. She hadn't said much since we'd left Reva's, and she'd been wearing the stoic expression almost the entire time. I was beginning to worry.

I hit the button for the elevator, and it opened right away.

"I will be fine. It's just... hard to accept that this is real. All of my life, I've had the freedom to live as I wished, and at the same time known what I might one day be expected to do. It isn't just Natsumi... I can't be the person I was anymore. For all of the money and power held by my House, all of my options are gone."

"You're talking about the racing?"

"Not just the racing. It is an example. Who I befriend, where I go, who I love... Not to mention, I have to convince everyone I'm a powerful wizard, and I'm not even sensitive."

The elevator stopped.

"This is our floor." Once we were off, I grabbed my phone and sent Dannie the room number. It was a tough gig, but I could think of worse. "You should try having one foot in the grave for a while."

She looked at me. I knew that one. Pity. Damn. "I'm sorry. I don't mean to sound ungrateful. I-"

I put up my hand to cut her off. "It isn't your place to be sorry. I'm the one being an asshole. It's been hard not to be angry at the world for where I've ended up. I hope you don't wind up feeling the same way, because it sucks most of the time."

"Not all of the time?"

Not after what Rayon said, but I wasn't going to tell her that.

The suite had a king-sized bed in a separate bedroom, a living room with a pull-out couch, and a large bathroom. It was all done up with the same modern decor as the lobby, only the walls were painted in diodes that gave off a soft glow, and allowed the guest to make it whatever color, or combination of colors, they wanted.

My phone buzzed. "My friend should be here in ten. As far as she's concerned, you're Red's niece, and nothing more. She doesn't need to know the whole truth."

Jin nodded and took a seat on the couch. She pushed her hair away from her eyes and stared at me for a few seconds, looking unsure.

"Why did you decide to become a ghost?" she asked at last. I guess she was trying to decide how much she wanted to know about me.

"I didn't really choose it. I just kind of... fell into it."

"What do you mean?"

I sat down next to her, leaning forward and putting my elbows on my knees. I coughed into my hands, and shifted against a small tightening in my gut. "My friend was a ghost. She saved my life. I wasn't a necromancer then. I wound up hearing the fields later, once I got more sick. A guy like me... career options are kind of limited."

"How long have you been sick?"

"A lot longer than I was supposed to be. If God had His way, I would have been dead years ago."

"Do you believe in God?"

I shrugged. "I don't know. I don't think about it much. Do you?"

She didn't hesitate. "No. God wouldn't have played such a cruel trick on man, letting us think we were His children, and then showing us the monsters that we truly are. For all the plots and schemes of the Houses, we aren't the ones intended to inherit this world. What happened to my aunt is proof of that."

"What do you mean?"

"The human beast desires power, and the thirst for power breeds chaos, however much we may try to pretend we control it. When the reversal first occurred, everyone was frightened, and when people are scared they are able to come together, to work towards a common goal. To form bonds to the familiar, and ostracize the unknown.

"Today, the new world is understood. We have adapted to this environment. We stay inside at night, we don't stray into the forests unarmed. The fear is eroded. Now those who know of the Houses are losing their fear of our power as well. It starts with House Red. Do you think it will end there? It is only fitting that they are using monsters."

I didn't completely agree with her, but I didn't completely disagree either. "There have always been tyrants, maniacs, outsiders. For every doctor working to save a life, there's an evil son of a bitch looking to take one. If it's us or them, let's make sure it's them."

She smiled and reached out, putting her hand on my arm. "I told you the Houses would be cautious. Like I said before, I don't want to be cautious, Phantom. Of all the Houses, Red is in the best position to be bold."

I put my hand on hers and turned towards her. "Then be bold, but not stupid. We're at a huge disadvantage right now, and we need to shore up our defense and work from the shadows until we know what we're up against."

She looked me in the eye, her expression thoughtful. I expected her to say something, but instead she excused herself and vanished into the bathroom.

I was left with the distinct feeling that there was something she wasn't telling me.

CHAPTER TWENTY-FOUR

I thought things were bad before.

"Woo! I mean I've seen some crazy digs before, but this shit is like freak central," Amos said, the moment I opened the door to let him and Dannie into our suite.

He was kind of what I expected. Overweight, a bit sloppy, with a multitude of scruffy chins and a massive face. His hair was all over the place, in a weird kind of wild afro, and he wore a heavy leather duster that I was sure covered a hidden armory.

"You must be Conor. Anybody told you that you look like shit?"

I glanced down at Danelle, and she mouthed the words 'I told you so'.

"I've heard it one or two times, yeah."

I moved aside so she could roll in. Jin was sitting on the couch, leaned back with her knees in her arms. A relaxed, defensive position. She must have heard Amos say my name. Oh well, it was out of the ordinary, but so was everything else about this job.

"You gonna invite me in?" Amos asked, following it up with a throaty guffaw. "Could use a nice soft cushion. My ass is killing me after riding in that piece of shit van of yours. And the smell... fucking thought something died in that rattle trap."

I wanted to get Danelle alone, to ask her what the hell she was thinking. I could picture her reaming me out, because it wasn't like she had a lot of choices. "So, Amos... You planning on sticking around? Dannie told me you owed her a favor."

"She told me you were working a job, a big-time job. Heh, I didn't even realize she'd found a boy-toy to run her jobs for her, and an ugly one at that. Look like you crawled out from under a rock, and then got hit by it." He paused to laugh. Nobody joined him. "Anyway, she said I'd get a share if I teamed up with you losers."

Dannie looked at me apologetically. I knew her well enough to know it was the only way she'd been able to get him to come along.

"So, yeah... about the job? What is it we're work-" His eyes landed on Jin. He stopped talking, his mouth closed, and his whole demeanor turned frigid. "What the fuck is this?"

Jin put her feet on the floor. "Do you have a problem?"

Empathic. I didn't need to be to recognize the charge between the two of them.

"Bad to worse. You brought a fucking racist?" I whispered to Dannie.

"You wanted me here, I'm here. Don't you dare question how."

I started moving to get between the two of them, but Jin put up her hand.

"I asked you if you have a problem?"

Amos was staring at her, his hand drifting towards the opening in his coat. "Dirty, filthy, pointy-eared, tree-hugging-"

It happened fast. His hand whipped under the coat, while Jin took a few quick steps forward, smacked it away from whatever it was he was reaching for, and slammed him in the kidneys with an elbow. He bent over in pain, and she kneed him in the face. He fell onto his ass and clutched at his nose.

"I think you broke it," he said, the anger drained.

Jin didn't respond, she just looked over at me and smirked.

"Okay, okay, enough of this. Amos... seriously? You want to be a racist asshole, try being a racist asshole to someone who can't kick the shit out of you. Danelle, meet Jin. Jin, Danelle. You already met the fat lump on the floor. Jin is Red's negotiator. You're lucky all she did was break your nose."

I had told Jin I was going to name her Red's niece, but between what she had done on the bike, and seeing her fight... I knew guys like Amos. He wouldn't back down and stay down without finding something about her to respect. It wasn't enough for her to beat him up once. He had to know she would beat him every single time he even thought about it. A House negotiator was part assassin, part fixer. She'd have enough autonomy to offer work on the House's behalf, and enough training to take care of the hard, delicate stuff herself.

By naming her a negotiator, I had solved that problem before it became one. I looked over at Jin. She was smiling.

"I'll get you a towel." Se walked past me to the bathroom.

"So, what the hell happened to you?" Dannie asked, trying to cut around the tension.

"You already know most of it. The parts you don't know... Remember when you told me control took out the ferals in Connecticut?"

"Yeah."

"They didn't. I mean, maybe they found some other sub-humans to shoot, but it wasn't the ones that went after me. They almost got to Jin before I did."

That was when she noticed the rips in my trench. "Oh shit, Conor. Does that hurt?" She reached up, careful not to touch the area.

"It's fine now. Jin got me some troll juice. We barely made it out alive."

"She's really Red's negotiator?"

I nodded. "Yeah. Red sent me to her because she was worried about a traitor, and she trusts her implicitly. We came to an agreement." I motioned my head over at Amos. "That was before you brought Tweedledum into the picture."

"I heard that," he said.

Jin came out of the bathroom with a damp towel. She knelt down and handed it to Amos, who glowered at her at the same time he accepted it.

"What is it you desire?" she asked the fat ghost.

He looked confused. "Huh?"

"Even ignorant fools who want to hate everything that isn't like them have desires. What is yours?"

"You don't want to know. And you don't need to. They say money can't buy happiness. I say enough money can buy as much of it as my libido can handle."

It was a disgusting thought.

"You want money? How much?"

He pulled the towel away and looked at the blood in it. Then he put his hands to his nose and pressed. I could hear it cracking, moving back into some relative semblance of place. It wasn't even close to the first time he had gotten his face busted.

"Four million. Sounds good."

She didn't hesitate. "Done. On the condition that you save your racist hate for the enemies of House Red. I don't care about you. I don't care what you think of me. Red does demand loyalty and good service. One wrong motion, one wrong word..."

"Yeah, yeah. No hard feelings. Money talks. Deal." He put out his hand.

Jin took it. Then she got to her feet and walked over to Danelle.

"Is Dannie your name, or your handle?"

"My name. My handle is Daaé."

Jin glared at me from the corner of her eye. "You must have valuable skills for Conor to have asked you to come here."

She laughed. "I think he wanted Evan and the guns more."

"Dannie..." I started to protest.

"I know, you were worried about me. I don't know if I'm any safer here, but at least I'm not twiddling my thumbs, waiting for a kill team to drop in and shoot me in the head."

"It's more than that. We need to go into the Machine."

"You do? For what?"

"You need to sign up for team Red before I can tell you."

She put her hand out to Jin. "Yeah, sure, whatever. I'm in. Conor might be a solemn asshole, but I want both of us to keep breathing. You may be our best shot."

"Our only shot," I said.

Jin took Dannie's hand. "Thank you, Miss Daaé."

"I guess you'll need your own handle for this one," Danelle said.

"We can worry about that later. Do you know anyone in this neck of the woods who can jack us in?"

"I could name half a dozen places in Chicago. I'll have to check around here. You still haven't told me what we need it for."

"Black's card. We need to know where it originated. Right now, it's our only lead to whoever arranged the job against Red. Jin is positive it wasn't Black."

Dannie pursed her lips. "Considering the outcome, I tend to agree with her. What about the stone?"

"I hid it in a hotel downtown. I'm going to make a run to get it."

"I'll come with you," Amos said. He'd moved from the floor to the couch, and was sitting there with the towel against his nose.

"I'll go alone." The last thing I wanted was to have to babysit him.

"Amos will go with you," Jin said.

I didn't like it. "Are you sure?"

"Red isn't paying him to sit on the couch."

"Don't worry, Baldie, I got your back. I have my vices, but I ain't survived the last twenty years on luck and booze and sex alone."

Another disgusting thought.

"Fine. We'll leave in a couple of hours when the traffic thins out a bit. That will give your nose a chance to stop bleeding, and time for me to grab some room service. I've been running on Coke and Twinkies for the last twenty-four hours."

"Do you think it's a good idea to wait?" Jin asked.

"If it's still there now, it will be there in two hours. To be honest, I'm kind of hoping to run into that redhead again, now that I've got some backup." I reached my hand into my pocket, picking up the dice. Warm and ready to go.

"What redhead?" Dannie asked.

"A user. She came into the Gas and Sip in Connecticut while I was there, and then turned up at Jin's place when the ferals attacked. I think she's controlling them somehow."

"And she's been in the same place you've been, at the same time you've been there twice now?"

I paused, and then shook my head. "That doesn't mean anything. We've had the same targets."

"The Gas and Sip was a target? Why would she have been there?"

I shrugged. "I don't know. She bought some cigarettes and Twinkies."

Danelle shook her head, like she couldn't believe I was so dense. "Was she on line with you? Did she talk to you?"

"Yeah, so?"

"Dammit, Conor. You're such a newbie sometimes. Take off your clothes, empty your pockets. She may be tracking you."

"How? Why? I wasn't even supposed to make it out of there alive." I started taking stuff out of my coat at the same time I complained. My phone, the dice, a lighter, my credit card and fake ID. I had been traveling light for the plane ride.

"Insurance, Baldie," Amos said. "In case you didn't stick to the plan and croak."

Shit. I still didn't think it was likely, but they were right. We couldn't take the chance.

"Just take it all off," Danelle said.

"In front of everybody?"

"Christ, Conor. We're all adults, and its not like you're anything much to look at anyway. The more eyes checking you, the better."

It was true, and I shouldn't have been embarrassed. Dannie and I had been together, and Amos had nothing to say about the shape of my body. It was Jin that was making me feel modest, even though I'd already seen enough of her. I wasn't normally such a prude, but for some reason her presence was making me very aware of how bad I looked.

Even so, I complied. I took off the trench, and Danelle set about picking through it, turning it inside out and feeling along the entire length. Jin took my pants, examining them closely, while Amos volunteered to search my shirt and boots. I was left with my underwear. It wasn't exactly clean, but it wasn't bugged either.

At least, I hadn't thought it would be bugged, until I found a small pin shaped device sticking to the elastic. "You've got to be kidding me."

I picked it away from the cloth and held it up for Dannie to look at.

She held out her hand, and I gave it to her. She brought it up to her eye. "They probably tracked the airline manifest, matched it up with car rentals, and waited to see who headed out that way. You aren't exactly inconspicuous."

I hadn't noticed anyone following me. I hadn't been looking for it either. "Then she knows we're here?"

"She knows you're here. She probably knows everywhere you've been since the convenience store."

She would have also known that I was still in Jin's apartment building. Maybe it wasn't accurate enough to know exactly where, but they had been waiting for me to come out.

"Reva," Jin whispered.

They would know we had visited her, too. We couldn't go back for her, so I hoped they would just leave her be. She had that shotgun, and she was a troll, so if they did hit her... she wouldn't go down easy.

"So we destroy that thing, right?" Amos asked.

"Not yet." I slipped my undies back on, collected the rest of my clothes, got dressed, and then returned my things to my pockets. "I'm going down to the hotel where I left the stone."

"Conor, she knows you want the stone. How much do you want a bet someone will be waiting for you to come back for it?"

"I expect that someone will, but a trap isn't much of a trap if you already know about it. Besides, I don't plan to be there alone. I'll have Amos and Evan."

"I'm coming, too," Jin said.

"I don't think that's a good idea."

She smiled at me, all sweet and innocent. "Don't forget who I am, Baron. It's time to be bold."

I wasn't sure if she meant who I had said she was, or who she really was, but it didn't matter. The bottom line was that I couldn't outright tell her what to do. Wizard or not, she was still Miss Red.

"What did you call me?"

"Baron, like Baron Saturday. Baron Samedi? The voodoo Lord of the Dead? That is who you remind me of, with your skin so tight against your bones."

She had seen me naked, and that was who I reminded her of? I had been right to be embarrassed.

Dannie laughed. "I like it. You need a new handle anyway... it's bad enough she knows your name."

"Amos was the one who spewed it out as soon as I opened the door. I didn't tell her."

"Can you two shut up?" Amos asked. "It sounds like we have a date with a hot redhead who's into dogs."

I closed my eyes and shook my head.

I thought things were bad before.

CHAPTER TWENTY-FIVE

Are we there yet?

"YOU GOING TO BE OKAY?"

I was behind the van with Danelle. Amos and Jin were already inside, digging through the trunk full of guns. Jin had found a couple of shoulder holsters and a pair of pistols to put in them, while Amos had discovered the shotgun. Not that he needed it - he'd already shown off the six handguns and two Uzis he kept strapped to his bulk beneath the duster.

"More surface area, more firepower," he'd said with a laugh.

"I'll be fine. I'll take your cards and ask the front desk for a new room. Without the tracker, they won't be able to find me. What are they going to do with me, anyway? I'm not a threat."

"Bullshit. You're easy to underestimate." She had a handgun tucked under her seat that only she and I knew about. I leaned down and kissed her on the cheek. "Just find a Machinery for us. There have to be a bunch of them around here."

"I will. Be careful, Conor... Baron."

"Aren't I always?"

"Are you ever?"

"Shut up."

I climbed into the van through the back and pulled the doors closed.

"It does smell a little in here," Jin said.

"It comes with the territory. Amos, let's get moving."

"Was hoping I was done driving this crap van. What's the address?"

"I don't know the address. It's the Golden Sunrise Hotel. It's near the bridge."

"Which bridge?"

"I don't know, it's downtown somewhere. I took a cab."

"Oh, for fuck's sake. Thanks for the highly detailed directions, Skeletor."

"It's the Bright Sun Hotel," Jin said. "It's on Gold Street."

"Christ, the elf is smarter than you are." He started the van and backed out of the double spot he had taken. It shuddered a bit when he put it into drive. "Piece of shit."

It was ten o'clock, early enough that the city hadn't been left to the denizens of the night, and late enough that there wasn't much traffic. The rain had slowed to a steady patter, replacing the pounding downfall that had soaked us earlier. I closed my eyes and tried to ignore the slight gnawing in my gut, while Amos navigated the streets with the adeptness of someone who had spent more than a few days in the urban jungle.

The treatments. I didn't know how long I could go without them at this level of alertness. I could last a couple of months if I severely limited my use of magic, and less than a day if I was really desperate. I was worried that desperate was the more likely outcome right now, and Dalton was all the way in Chicago. There had to be a black market here that could provide the medicine, but once I was bad enough, there wouldn't be much time to get a name and location.

The thoughts left me distracted, more distracted than I wanted to be. They were a bug in my mind, buzzing around and around and threatening to drive me to panic.

I could hear Amos' voice in the background the whole time, a mixed soundtrack of foul, disgusting, and rude chatter over the din of my mind. He would say something about every person we drove past. This one had nice tits, that guy was a fag, the other one looked like a child molester, or maybe a serial killer. He was like the tour guide from Hell, his running diatribe suggesting that maybe he wasn't a racist. Maybe he just hated everybody.

"Holy shit, did you see that?" he asked, turning his head to look at someone or something in the street. He put his head forward just in time to slam on the brakes and keep us from rear-ending a cab. The jerky motion almost gave me whiplash, and I held onto the two front seats to keep from being thrown into the dashboard.

"Can't you shut the fuck up and pay attention to the road?" My heart was racing, and not from his driving. I was spending too much time in my head, getting psyched out by the effect before I'd created the cause.

"Sorry, sorry." He straightened up in the seat and accelerated slowly. "I've seen a lot of shit in this town, but I didn't expect anyone to be doing *that* in public."

"What's the plan?" Jin asked, not falling for his obvious baiting. She'd been quiet the whole time, probably trying to decide if she should put a bullet in Amos' head.

"What?" I was still a little dazed.

"The plan, Baldie," Amos said.

I looked out the passenger window from my perch behind it. Some of the shops looked familiar from my first go round in the cab. We had to be getting close.

I'd been thinking about it since I decided to go back for the stone. My plan was pretty basic. Basic, and bold.

"The redhead saw us get away on the bike. I think it would have been pretty obvious to her that I wasn't carrying the stone. That means there's a good chance she would have traced my route, backtracked, and searched for it. Maybe she found it, maybe she didn't. If she didn't, she's going to wait for us to come back for it, and ambush us. If she did, she's going to take it away, and leave someone else to ambush us, because she knows we're going to have to come back for it at some point. Or, she took it and left." I glanced over at Jin. "But I have a feeling they aren't going to just leave."

She knew why I was looking at her. If they knew who she was, they were still going to want her dead. It was dangerous for her to be here. We both knew it.

"So we're walking into an ambush?" she asked.

"We aren't just walking in. They don't know that we know it's a trap. They can't know we found the bug. We can get the drop on them."

"How?"

I pointed at the cooler where Evan was resting. "My secret weapon. How far are we from the hotel?"

"Six blocks," Amos said.

"Stop the van."

It took Amos a few minutes to find a spot big enough to hold the truck. He pulled in at the same time I moved to the back and opened up the cooler.

"Hop to it, Evan," I said, holding my hand to the dead commando's bone wrist and pushing the magic into him. I felt the thread reach out and wrap itself around him, bringing his soul back from somewhere else.

"What is it now, asshole?" Evan said a moment later, his ragged face gaining movement and even a semblance of emotion. I heard Jin gasp. The driver's side door opened, and Amos oozed himself out.

Evan pulled himself to a sitting position, his bones creaking. He looked past me, to where she was standing, his half-face curling into a smile. "Well, hello."

"Get out of the cooler. It's time to play dress up."

"I was talking to the lady."

166

"Don't push me, Evan." He couldn't disobey, but that didn't mean he wasn't going to make me work for it.

"Fine." He got to his feet, twisting and stepping out of the cooler. "Could you turn around or close your eyes or something? I'm shy." He looked at Jin again. "You don't have to, baby."

I shoved the clothes into his hands and led Jin outside to where Amos was waiting, his face pale. Apparently the sight of Evan had made him sick, and now he refused to look me in the eye.

"Fucking necromancers. It's just so wrong."

"You have your strengths, I have mine." I had no idea what his strengths were. Surface area? The good news was that his disgust had quieted him down a bit, at least for the time being.

"He's taller than you," Jin said.

"Evan? A few inches. Do you think they'll notice? Most of my clothes are baggy."

"I hope not. Where did you find him?"

"Obits. He was a policeman... S.W.A.T. He's an asshole, but his tactical is flawless."

"I don't think he likes you."

"He despises me. Maybe all of them do, for bringing them back to this world, back to their old shells. I don't know. I've asked. With Evan, it's obvious. With some of the others, not so much."

I could tell she wanted to ask me more about it. It wasn't a morbid curiosity though. She was measuring me, to find out what I could do, maybe to figure out how best to use me. That's what I would have expected from Miss Red.

We were interrupted by Evan, who pushed open the back door and hopped down.

"Well, how do I look?"

He was wearing a navy hoodie, a pair of my black pants, combat boots, and my spare coat. He had pulled the hood up over his head, using it to keep his face in shadow. "I haven't done impersonation before. I might actually like this mission."

He could pass for me from behind. From the front… I could only hope they wouldn't see him from the front until it was too late.

"Fucking frightening," Amos said. He looked like he was going to be sick again.

Evan noticed, and he laughed. "Looks like fatso is afraid of dead guys." He turned his attention to Jin. "What about you, sexy?"

She didn't flinch. "I wouldn't date you, but you can cover my back."

"Oh… What a nice back I'm sure it is. I'd love to."

"We're six blocks from the hotel. We're going to play leapfrog, keeping Evan in the middle with the tracker. That way, we have both sides covered if they rush him before we even get there. Jin, you'll take point. One block down and wait. Amos, go over a block and come down, then cut across in front of her. I'll stay a block behind. Repeat the pattern until we get there. Amos, if you hear gunfire, get the hell over as fast as you can."

"I'm not known for my speed."

"Do your best."

"What's this about a tracker?" Evan asked.

"It's in the pocket of the hoodie. The target may be using it to keep an eye on me. When we get to the hotel, you're going to go into the elevator. Open the access door and pull yourself up. There may or may not be an oblong stone up there, about this big." I held my hands apart. "If it's there, grab it. Amos, you'll go in a minute after Evan and hit the front desk looking for a room. Jin, you'll hang back with me, out of sight of the building."

"Hiding?"

"Not quite."

CHAPTER TWENTY-SIX

Hugs and kisses.

WE COVERED THE SIX BLOCKS in less time than I'd anticipated, keeping spread out enough that we didn't look like we were all together, and close enough that backup was only a street away. I kept a close eye on Jin the entire time we were moving, scanning the thin volume of other pedestrians for anyone out of the ordinary, and making sure she didn't grow a tail. I barely paid any heed to Evan other than to keep the thread strong enough to pull him back in line if needed. He could take care of himself.

I didn't see anyone on the way down. It was just the normal smattering of an evening crowd, a mix of the daytime blue and white-collars heading home from a late night at the office, or dinner at a nearby restaurant, and the nighttime risk-takers, in tight luminescent skirts and jackets, dark oversized clothes, or other accoutrements intended to either attract or repel attention. There wasn't much middle ground after dark, and as we moved closer to the early morning the partiers would glisten into the foreground, the ghosts and thugs would fade into the back, and it would be up to fate and law enforcement to do their best to protect the innocent for another night.

I was a block down from the hotel, across the street in a small coffee shop that would be closing up in half an hour. Jin was sharing a small round table with me, a coffee in her delicate hands. I had my eyes half-closed, focusing on the thread of magical energy that was running from me to Evan. I was at the edge of my comfort zone for keeping him in line, and I knew it was sucking the life out of me faster than I had any desire for.

My earlier panic was threatening to resurface, and it took all of my concentration to stay sitting at the table looking somewhat normal. Still, I was proud of myself. Jin had come along, but I had managed to keep her away from the fight.

"Keep a lookout for me, will you? If anything happens, you may need to hit me pretty hard to get my attention."

"What do you mean? What are you doing?"

"Checking on Evan. He should be inside by now."

She took a sip of her coffee and nodded. I pointed my head down towards the table and closed my eyes. I took a deep breath in, pulling the energy from the thrumming of the field around us, and pushing it along the invisible line to Evan. I couldn't remote control people, but I could go along for the ride. A moment later I achieved a blurry view of the world through my zombie's damaged retina.

He was in the hotel. The woman who had been at the front desk earlier was still there, and she was yelling at him.

"Hey, mister. Mister. Someone was here earlier looking for you. They asked me to give you a message."

Evan didn't point his face directly at her. "What's the message?" His bad reproduction of my voice was comical, and likely intentional.

She moved out from behind the desk and held out a piece of paper. Evan stretched out a gloved hand and took it. He turned his back on her while she waited for a tip.

It was a pleasure meeting you in Connecticut, Mr. Smith. It was an even greater pleasure tracking you to New York. My apologies

for not introducing myself properly, but one can never be too sure these days, can they? I'm very impressed with your skill in making a mess of my employer's well-laid plans, as well as your success in escaping with the new Miss Red earlier today. After speaking with them regarding your certain talents, they have agreed that they would consider bringing you on as a contractor, a position that I can assure you would be extremely lucrative. The only requirement is that you justify my high assessment of you. My associates should be along momentarily to assist in that regard.
XOXOXOXO
- Veronica

Evan dropped the piece of paper and reached under the trench, finding one of the guns hidden beneath his arm and pulling it from the holster. He stood dead still, his head swiveling, searching for the so-called 'associate'.

Seconds passed.

Nothing happened.

Then the elevator dinged, and the doors began to open. Even with his lousy vision I could make out the massive form of the black and white werewolf crouched behind them.

It was a trap, but not quite the trap I'd been expecting. They thought he was me, and if I survived this one... they'd want to hire me?

The were moved through the doors, charging Evan on all fours. He raised the gun and fired, one round after another, while the werewolf made adjustments and corrections, taking the hits from the hollow point bullets and letting his thick bones deflect them as nothing more than deep flesh wounds. It reached him in no time, wrapping hairy, muscular arms around Evan's torso and pulling him backwards to the ground.

A look of surprise crossed the feral's muzzle when the hood fell back and Evan's half-face was revealed. The moment of shock gave my soldier a chance to throw a strong, magic-infused punch into the side of the werewolf's head, and roll it off him.

"Surprise, fucker," Evan said, rolling to his feet and reaching for his other sidearm. He had it three-quarters of the way out when the wolf slashed it from his skeletal fingers, grabbed his arm, and threw him across the lobby.

Everything got more blurry until he came to an abrupt stop against the wall, bones cracking under the force.

"Ouch." He laughed, getting back up and putting his fists out. "Come on, fuzzy. That all you got?"

Something hit him from the side, throwing him back to the ground. A second werewolf, the black one's partner, the one that I had clocked with the car door. It bit down on his head and pulled, trying to rip his skull from his spine.

"Ah, shit." Evan's arms flailed, smacking into the side of the feral, but not getting enough power behind the blows to do much damage. The were held on, tugging like a dog with a rope toy, working to claim its prize.

The massive boom that followed would have deafened normal ears. The werewolf vanished in a spray of heavy shot and blood, yelping at the sudden burst of pain. Evan wasn't spared collateral damage, having more of his rotted flesh being pulled from the bone.

"Hoooooo yeeeaahhhhh!" Amos stood at the entrance to the building, shotgun leveled at his waist and a stream of smoke rising from the barrel. He was sweaty and haggard looking, his face red from running.

He dropped the gun and turned as the black wolf snarled and launched itself at him, reaching under his duster and retrieving another firearm. Huge arms reached out for the fat ghost, and he crouched under them and got his own meat-hand on the were's head, holding it steady at the same time he brought the gun up under its chin and pulled the trigger. Blood sprayed everywhere, and the feral landed in a dead heap.

"I hate dogs," he said. Some of its blood had landed on his hand, and he leaned down to wipe it off on its fur. He looked over at Evan. "What the fuck are you just laying there for? You don't need to rest."

Apparently, the adrenaline had gotten him over his fearful distaste of the dead.

Evan started to get up. His head shifted to find the second werewolf, who was recovering from the buckshot and getting back into the fight.

I felt a sharp pain as my forehead was slammed into the table, the sudden impact bringing me back to my own consciousness.

CHAPTER TWENTY-SEVEN

Witch with a 'B'.

"WHEN I SAID HIT ME pretty hard, I didn't mean-"

"You cheated," Veronica said. She was sitting across from me, where Jin had been a few minutes before. I spun my head around, looking for her.

Gone. Like everyone else in the shop.

Shit.

"It's okay. I like cheaters. They tend to be more successful." She picked up Jin's coffee and took a sip. "Well, until they get caught, anyway."

I breathed in some of the energy, pushing it along the thread, compelling Evan to come to where I was.

"Not so fast." She put her hand on mine, and I felt the warmth of her magic flow into it. "I think its time for your little boney foot soldier to take a nap."

The thread didn't fade. It snapped. The force of it caused my gut to wrench, and I leaned over the table and coughed up half a lung.

"You have what you want," I said, once my coughing subsided. "Why are you wasting your time with me?"

She didn't speak right away, but the answer was in her eyes.

"She escaped?"

"She evaded me, yes. A problem that I was hoping you would

help me resolve. That's why I didn't just kill you while you were busy projecting."

"I'm going to help you why?"

She smiled. "Why not, Mr. Smith? Why not help me? You're in over your head. You know it, I know it. You were supposed to die in the house with Mrs. Red. You were supposed to die when you came to get the girl. You were supposed to die just now, but instead you're sitting in here having a latte while your corpse does your dirty work. You have a knack for survival. I admire that."

I laughed.

"I'm offering you an easy way out. Lots of money in the bank, my employer off your back. What did she offer you? How much of that can she even deliver on?"

None of it, right now. "I already made a deal with her."

She snorted. "How much is that worth? Please. She'll be gone, and no one will know any better."

I took a deep breath. I couldn't argue her logic. I wanted to survive this, and I wanted to take care of my family. That was why I had stolen the job, for the promise of a slightly longer, better life. What did I care if one House went away, and another came on to take its place? So they used ferals? The other Houses would pull them in line, and if they didn't, or couldn't... survival of the fittest. I would be set. The people I cared about would be set. I didn't owe anyone else anything.

"What do you need me to do?"

"She went out through the back. A couple of my boys chased her, but she killed them. Find her, convince her to come with you. That's all."

"That's all you need me to do, and it's all over? How much?"

"Ten million." She said it like it was a dime.

I pursed my lips. "You're a hard person to say 'no' to."

"I do try."

I took a deep breath. "Okay, I'll do it. I am curious about

something?"

"Yes?"

"How are you controlling the ferals?"

She laughed at me. A rich laugh that echoed in the empty shop and lasted a good twenty seconds. "That was worth the headaches you've caused me. I'm not controlling them, Mr. Smith. They're here because they want to be."

"Ferals don't work like that."

"Oh? How many have you known personally?"

They didn't think, they didn't reason. That was common knowledge. "I don't believe you."

"I don't care. Do we have a bargain?"

"Get her to come back with me, and I'm done?"

"Bring her back, and you're done. Oh, but don't think about double-crossing me, Mr. Smith. You're still a step behind. I found you here even without the tracker. I'll find you again, and next time I won't be so polite."

The coldness of her voice gave me chills. "I'll bring her back."

"Good. I'll be waiting."

"What about my fat friend?"

"He should be dead by now. I have more than just what you call 'ferals' at my disposal."

"I didn't like that asshole anyway."

I got up and headed for the back of the coffee shop. Veronica watched me from the table, looking amused.

The back of the shop opened up into a narrow alley. I had only gone a couple of feet along it when I almost tripped over the two men laying on the cement there, both with bullet holes in their foreheads.

"Jin?" I said in a loud whisper. "Jin!"

If she was hiding nearby, she wasn't coming out. I kept walking down the alley, passing a dumpster. I paused next to it and lifted the lid, checking for her inside. She wasn't there.

"Jin!" She could have run back to the van by now, but I had a feeling she hadn't. She would stay close, and try to get a shot at Veronica. She would stay bold. "Jin!"

She materialized from the shadows a dozen yards ahead of me, her gun drawing a tight bead. "Just stay there, Baron."

"What the hell, Jin?"

"Do you think I'm stupid? I couldn't wake you up before I ran. The only reason you're still alive is because she wanted something from you."

"She wants you. I told her I would bring you back."

"Not if I kill you."

"You and I had a deal." I took a couple of steps towards her.

"Just stay there. I can imagine what she offered you, and she can pay right away."

"Jin... I..." I reached into my pocket.

"Leave them."

"I can't throw them that far," I said, digging the dice out. I didn't toss them. I put them on the ground and backed away. "It's the best promise I can make."

She came forward slowly, keeping the gun trained on me. "Back up a little more."

I did. I was ten feet away from the dice when Veronica appeared in the alley behind Jin, flanked by two others in plain clothes. One of them had been working inside the coffee shop. The other we had passed on the street. I thought I was being clever. She had seen us coming from a mile away.

"I was going to bring her," I shouted.

Jin didn't know she was there. She turned and dropped to a knee, squeezing off two rounds that went wide before crying out and dropping the gun. It steamed on the wet street.

"I got tired of waiting. Oh, and I didn't believe you." Veronica looked at Jin. "Come, Miss Red. Don't make this any harder."

Jin eyed her gun, and then looked back at me. There was nothing

I could do.

"Well?" Veronica asked.

She started walking towards the wizard, defeated. The two sidekicks approached and took each of her arms, holding her tight and guiding her around the corner towards the street.

Veronica smiled at me.

"I guess this means our deal is off?"

"I'd say it's nothing personal, but necromancers are an ugly sore on the beauty of magic." Her hand raised, her lips moved, and the water lifted from the ground in front of her, condensing and shooting towards me like a bullet.

There was no way I could avoid it. I tried anyway, twisting and falling. The liquid missile slammed into my shoulder, the one that hadn't been raked by the were, piercing clean through and smashing into the wall behind me. The force spun me at least twice before I landed on the ground, my arm quickly growing warm and wet with blood. I lifted my head. She was standing there watching me, amused.

"Did that hurt? I hope so. You're like a human hemorrhoid."

I saw the dice on the ground in front of me, the black energy of the dark soul inside flowing around them like mist. I held my arm, bringing my hand inside of my trench and pulling myself to my knees. Veronica said something I couldn't make out, motioned with her own hand again, and another water bullet formed in front of her chest.

"Enjoy the afterlife."

The tiny cannonball shot towards me.

There was nothing graceful about it. I flopped over like a fish, drawing my gun as I fell. The second bullet grazed my side at the same time I was trying get the firearm in position and struggling to find enough strength.

It was a good thing I didn't need to raise my arm very far. I squeezed off every round in the clip in rapid succession, emptying it even as I crumbled against the ground. Hot casings burned into my trench while the bullets ricocheted off the pavement, sending up sprays of water, chipping away at the cement in front of my target.

Veronica laughed at me. She thought my effort was futile, that my wound had killed my aim. She raised another water missile and prepared to fling it.

She didn't know I wasn't shooting at her.

She didn't know I had activated the dice when I put them on the ground, that I had given the dark soul her name.

She didn't know I had been expecting her to cheat me, because that's what people like her did. I knew more than I was supposed to, and that made me a risk she couldn't take.

My aim was shit, but it was good enough. The vibrations rattled the dice, shaking them and lifting them into the air. They may have only turned one face, but it still counted.

I couldn't see the symbols from where I was. All I saw was the black mist waver, and then the bitch was on her back, crying out in pain and terror. The cry turned into a gurgle, and the gurgle into silence.

The barista had heard the screams, and he rounded the corner a second later. My clip was empty, my arm too damaged to quickly load another. I rolled across the alley as he opened fire, bullets clipping the ground next to me, and then the dumpster when I made it behind. I put my back to it and tried to flex my arm. It was still bleeding, and it hurt like hell, but I could move it. I started reaching for a new clip.

More gunfire echoed in the night from around the front of the building. Had Jin tried to get away, or had they heard Veronica scream and executed her? I found the bullets, managed to reload, and then rounded the dumpster. The barista had gone back the way he'd come, and I saw his body quiver from the bullets that tore through it. He toppled to the ground, and I ducked back down behind the bin.

It was quiet. I heard someone moving out near the street. I stayed behind the garbage and waited.

"Hey, Baldie! What are you hiding? Fucking baby."

Amos. I came out of my hiding place. "You're still alive?"

He laughed. "I didn't want you bringing my fat ass back from the dead."

"Where's Jin?"

"The assholes had an Escalade. She's looking for the treasure."

She wouldn't find it. Whoever had wanted it had gotten it, but it seemed they wanted her, too. Alive.

"I need to go get Evan before law enforcement shows up. Can you get the van?"

I started walking down the alley. My shoulder was killing me, and I was feeling a little light-headed. I looked over at my arm, and saw that my clothes were soaked with blood. How much had I lost? I started to feel hot, really hot.

I made it to the dice, kneeling to pick them up. I got them into my pocket before I lost my balance and started to topple over.

"I think you're gonna keel," Amos said, putting his arm under my good one and helping get me back to my feet. "We need to get you to a hospital."

"No. No hospital. One look at me, they'll never let me leave. I need to get Evan." Everything was starting to spin, and the world was fading. I wasn't ready to pass out. I pushed against Amos, but he was way too heavy to dislodge. "Let me go!"

I felt a rush of air, and then the blossoming of new pain in my shoulder. I grew numb and tingly everywhere, and my eyes forced their way closed.

I'd told him to let me go.

I hadn't expected him to actually do it.

CHAPTER TWENTY-EIGHT

Lost

FIVE YEARS EARLIER...

I DIDN'T know what time it was. I didn't know how many drinks I'd had, or even the name of the dive I was sitting in. I knew it was late, and I was drunk. I knew I didn't care.

My cell vibrated in my pocket for the fiftieth time. I didn't need to look at it to know it was Karen, wondering where the fuck I was, and what Rob had said. I knew she was worried about me. I was worried about her, too.

How was I supposed to go home, look her in the eye, and tell her that I was a dead man walking? How was making her wake up next to a corpse every day for the next two months supposed to help her, or me, or Molly?

The bar was cold and moist against my forehead. Some part of me thought I should pick up my head, but the other part had lost the will, and it was winning. The world was a dangerous place nowadays. The dead of night was the last place someone like me should be. I had a life insurance policy, I was going to die anyway. What was the point?

"Hey, shithead. It's two o'clock. Pay up, and get the fuck out of my bar."

I heard the voice, but I didn't know it was directed at me until a ham hand grabbed my hair and lifted my face from the bar. An angry mug was glaring at me from the other side.

"I said, pay up, and get out."

He let go, and my chin hit the counter. That was enough to nudge me out of my stupor, and I slid off the stool and stumbled to my feet. Where was I anyway? I couldn't remember.

I'd left work and driven to… I couldn't recall. I'd driven away, into some other part of the city, and came to a stop when I saw the sign for the bar. I'd planted myself on the stool, and cried for an hour or two while I drank. Then I just drank. Maybe I'd passed out at some point? I didn't know.

The bartender came around the bar. He didn't wait for me to find my wallet, he just reached into my back pocket and pulled it out, taking my card and scanning it.

"Don't forget the tip," I mumbled. He smiled and scanned it a second time, and then returned everything to its place.

"Good luck out there," he said, at the same time he led me to the door. "All the smart guys sobered up and left hours ago."

All the guys who gave a shit if they survived the night. I didn't say anything else, letting the guy aim me out of the door and into the street. It was dark and cold, a light drizzle coating everything in a layer of moisture. I tucked my arms for warmth and started walking towards where I thought I had parked the car.

Two blocks later, I decided I had gone in the wrong direction. The car must have been the other way. I blinked some of the wetness from my eyes, shook my head to try to get a better feel for my balance, and turned around.

I didn't see the guy who hit me. All I saw was that I had a whole group of thugs surrounding me, their white smiles standing out from their pale faces and facial hair. The first punch made me stumble. The second knocked me over.

"Oh shit," one of them said. "That was a nice shot."

I felt hands on my ass, searching for my wallet. Once it was safely in their possession, the kicks started coming.

"How many 'till he bleeds?"

"How many 'till he shits himself?"

They all laughed.

"He smells like a sewer already."

More kicks.

"That pretty face of his. I think it needs a little remodeling."

I saw the toe of a boot out of the corner of my eye, and then it was almost in my eye. Pain ran through my whole body, and I tried to get up.

"Where are you going?"

"What kind of fucking idiot walks around drunk this time of night?"

More blows to my side, my legs, another to my head. I fell over again, rolling to try to protect my face. Maybe I didn't want to live, but I didn't want dying to hurt so much.

"He's taking it pretty well," one of them remarked.

"Should have taken bets."

"How much do you assholes want to bet you walk away with all of your limbs intact?"

That voice was a new one. The blows stopped. I rolled over to see a woman in a leather jacket and blue jeans having her way with all six of them. I heard a crack when she grabbed an arm and broke it, a cry of pain as her fist found a nose, and then the pounding of feet as the rest of the posse made a break for it.

"Not such hot shit against anyone sober, are you?" she shouted after them.

I tried to keep my eyes open, to see what she was going to do, but my they were swelling closed.

"You look like shit," I heard her say. "Don't worry, I'll get you out of here."

###

I woke up in bed, a cold compress against my cheek. The smell of incense was heavy in the air, and soft, meditative chanting was flowing from the walls. Every part of my body hurt, and my left eye was still swollen closed. What the hell did I do?

I tried to sit up, and thought better of it when my ribs threatened to explode. I groaned in pain, and settled back, defeated.

"You're awake."

I angled my eyes downward, finding my savior standing next to the bed. Long, dark hair, an olive complexion, high cheekbones and a strong nose. She was beautiful in a non-standard way.

"You brought me back to your apartment?" I asked.

"I didn't know what else to do with you, and I couldn't leave you out there for the ferals, or wait to see if those little turds brought friends back with them." She sat down on the bed next to me. "My name is Danelle. You can call me Dannie if you want, or Dan, or Nell. Just don't call me easy." She smiled, to indicate she'd made a joke. It hurt too much to laugh.

"You should have left me out there," I said. Now that I was sober again, I had the clarity to remember why I had been there in the first place.

"A hot guy like you? It would be crime. I saw you in the bar. You probably don't remember. You looked miserable, and I'm the type of person whose strangely attracted to miserable people."

"A glutton for punishment?" I didn't even remember being in a bar.

"Broken home, shitty childhood. I'm the poster child for dysfunctional. But I know when I see something I like."

"Do you adopt puppies from shelters, too?" I asked. I was being a dick, but it was the mood I was in.

She didn't react to it. "What's your name?"

"Conor."

"Irish?"

"The name is, yeah."

"Okay, Conor. The way I see it, either I saved your life, or I fucked you up by not letting you kill yourself."

"Thanks for the effort, but I would have been satisfied to not wake up."

Her eyes turned a deep shade of sad.

"Why?" All of the cheeky humor was gone.

"I'm already dying. I figured I'd just speed it up a bit, and save my wife and daughter from the misery of watching me waste away."

She looked at me for a few seconds. There was no judgement in her eyes. "I couldn't just leave you there to get beaten to death."

I smiled. "It isn't your fault. You didn't know. Toss me my clothes and I'll get out of your life. No harm done."

She shook her head. "I'll tell you what, Conor. You can repay me by sleeping on it. If you still want to kill yourself in the morning, I'll drive you out to the woods and you can wait and see what gets you first. If you have second thoughts… We might be able to help one another."

CHAPTER TWENTY-NINE

That's amore.

I WOKE UP IN A round bed with red silk sheets and a mirror on the ceiling above it. The mirror showed me that I was half-covered by the sheets, and my arm had a huge wad of bandaging around it. I tried to move it, to test it out, and was greeted with enough pain that I questioned my sanity. Then I tried to move it again, gritting my teeth through the pain and forcing it to shift. A wounded ghost on a job was like a wounded gazelle on the savannah.

I turned my head to get the layout of the rest of the room. This wasn't the Arcadia hotel. The walls on either side of me were red and covered in luminescent, glittery hearts. The one in front had a large flatscreen hanging from it, thankfully turned off. There was a vending machine full of sex toys in the corner where a dresser should have been.

Where the hell was I?

I sat up and took a minute to cough up all the shit that had been settling in my lungs for however long I had been out of commission. It was only once I was through a full cycle of hacking that I thought maybe I should be more quiet. There was no guarantee I was somewhere safe. The only thing I knew for sure was that I was still alive.

I slipped out of the bed. I was in a pair of black silk boxers with red lips plastered all over them. They would have looked ridiculous on anyone. They looked even more insane on me.

There was only one door, so I went for it. I put my ear against it, and didn't hear anything. I slowly turned the handle to ease it open a crack. I looked out into a larger room with a red leather couch that had some kind of freaky, painful-looking contraption hanging next to it. Behind the couch was a massive black and white photograph of all kinds of flesh intertwined in all sorts of ways that should have been impossible and I was certain had to be illegal.

Maybe I was dead after all. Rayon had warned me about what was waiting. Eternity as the Devil's bitch?

A block of chunky black and purple hair fell into my view.

"You're up."

My heart started racing, and I stumbled backwards, startled. I hadn't even heard her coming.

She pushed the door open and came in, holding a stack of clothes in her arms and wearing a smile on her face. "How are you feeling?"

"Confused," I said, backing up until I could sit on the edge of the bed. "Where are we?"

"Brooklyn. The Greens."

"I don't know it."

"Really? I thought you were up on your history?"

"I guess I missed that class."

She put the clothes next to me. "These are for you. I got them at the Salvation Army on our way here."

I picked up the top piece, a dark green hoodie that smelled like mothballs. "Who died in this?"

"Beggars can't be choosers. Before the reversal, the Greens was a public housing block, a pretty rough neighborhood. Then came the leathers, the riots, the First House... Thanks to them, Governor Rojas moved the old residents to more gentrified areas and the property was given over to the new humans to do whatever they wanted with it. Kind of like a reservation, only for orcs and goblins and dwarves and any other homo nuevo that wanted to call the place home. They had to come up with some way to make a living, legal or not, and so they settled on vice. Gambling, prostitution, drugs, and other things."

The decor was starting to make sense. "Other things?"

"There are a lot of things in this world that get different people excited. The Greens tries to cater to as many of them as they can. It looks bad on the surface, but they keep a pretty tight control on it. Anyway, Danelle didn't feel comfortable with you at the Arcadia. They would have known you had been there, and she figured once they learned you'd killed the redhead they would come knocking. This is a good place for someone to disappear, because everyone here has something to hide."

She seemed to know a lot about it.

"You've been here before?"

"Motorcycle racing. They have a pretty hardcore course. That's all I ever came for." Her face turned red and she looked down. It was cute that she was embarrassed.

"You don't have any other vices?"

Her head shifted again, and her eyes caught mine. "I didn't say that."

"I get why we came here to hide out. How did we end up in the love shack?" I stood up again and started getting dressed. I did okay with my pants, but my shoulder really didn't want to go up high enough to pull on a shirt.

"People ask fewer questions when sex is involved. Let me help you with that."

She took the shirt from my hands and repositioned it so I could push my left arm in below my chest. Then she lifted it up and over my head while I lowered myself closer to her. By the time she pulled it down to my waist, our faces were only inches apart.

"Thanks." The last time we had been this close I hadn't been able to see her eyes. They were dark, with flecks of maroon scattered throughout.

She nodded and reached around me to grab the hoodie. "It's the least I can do. You already saved my life twice, and you got shot for me. Put your arms out."

I repeated the motion, and she helped me finish dressing.

"I lost the stone, and I almost got you killed. Amos saved your life, not me."

She put her hand to my face. It was soft and cool. Such a simple act of kindness, but I appreciated it more than I was going to say. "We'll get the artifact back. Danelle and Amos are out right now, trying to raise enough money to book time in the Machine."

That must have been the other reason she had chosen the Greens. I knew it wasn't for the unique vending machines. "What do you mean raising money? The payment I got for this job was guaranteed."

"Danelle said you haven't received it yet. They were going to pawn some of the guns."

Mr. Clean told me it would take a couple of days. I was hoping information traveling at the speed of light might have moved things along a little faster.

"Ouch. It's a small price to pay, I guess." I reached out with my good hand and put it on her shoulder. "Back in the alley... did you really think I was going to renege on our deal?"

"To save your own life? You told me you were afraid of death."

"I am, and I've done a lot of things to keep myself alive... some of which I'm not proud of. I do have a few morals left in me, though."

She leaned forward and kissed me on the cheek. "My apologies, Baron. I won't doubt you again."

"Is my trench around here somewhere?" It hadn't been in the pile with everything else.

"Unlike you, that thing was beyond repair. Torn, bloody, dirty, and it smelled worse than you look. We tossed it over the bridge on the way across."

Damn. I liked that coat. "What about my stuff?"

"There's a safe in the bathroom. The combination is 3223."

It could stay there for now. "Okay."

There was an awkward moment of silence, like we had both just realized where we were standing.

"Believe it or not, this is one of the tame rooms."

I laughed. "How many of the others have you seen?"

Her face turned red again, and she looked away. "I'm not like that."

Shit. "I'm sorry, I didn't mean to offend you. I was just joking. Trying to ease some of the tension."

She turned back towards me and nodded. "Are you hungry?"

"Starving." I hadn't realized until she mentioned it. "Do they have room service in this dive?"

"They do, but the menu isn't quite what you would expect."

I bit my lip. I should have known. "I can wait."

She reached out and took my hand in hers. "No, you can't. You haven't eaten a decent meal in days. There's a sushi place right across the street. It's a hole in the wall, but the food is fantastic."

I let her pull me towards the door.

CHAPTER THIRTY

Good fish.

I DIDN'T GET TO SEE much of the Greens on the way from the 'More-a than Amore' hotel to 'Secret Sushi'. It literally was across the street, a wide thoroughfare that was closed to cars, and open to every kind of freak and thrill-seeker I could have imagined. It was loud and bright and colorful, like a carnival, and packed with every sort of human both old and new. It appeared to be a melting pot of culture, where every bias could be put aside and everyone was free to enjoy whatever they had come to enjoy.

Plenty of armed guards made sure it stayed that way.

They didn't stand out, but I spotted them right away, leaning against the buildings, hidden in black body armor and shadows. They held heavy automatic rifles, and seemed to be immune to the chaotic energy of the place. Jin had said they kept a tight control. She hadn't been kidding.

The food at Secret Sushi was as good as she had claimed. The atmosphere was even better. Each table was cordoned off by soundproof walls, completely enclosed save for a small opening against the back where a thin conveyor belt carried food and drink along. You took what you wanted and scanned it on the table to have it added to your bill, and you didn't have to interact with anyone. You could pay with cash or bitcoin, or credit if you really

191

wanted to. No annoying neighbors, no waitresses, nothing. We'd had to pay the hostess at the front to send Dannie and Amos our way if we were still here when they got back.

"My aunt used to meet me here after races," Jin said. "It was the only place outside of our holdings that she trusted to be private, and it was convenient for both of us to be here at the same time, for different reasons."

"Why would she be here? The Greens doesn't seem like the kind of place the head of a House would frequent."

"You know who my aunt was?"

I nodded.

"There's a hospital here. It's where Parity tests a lot of the new technology, because the laws are more... lenient, here. They can move to human trials a lot faster, bring the new tech to market faster, and save more lives."

"And make more money."

"That is part of it."

"Okay, but here's what I don't get. Your aunt was married. What about you uncle, Kai? Doesn't he own Parity Limited?"

She popped a slice of tuna roll in her mouth, closing her eyes and appreciating the flavor. I took a drink of water while she chewed and swallowed.

"Poor Kai. He was married to Auntie when the reversal happened. She became Mrs. Red, but he wasn't even sensitive. He's ninety-three years old, and he has a team of technicians working around the clock to keep him alive."

"What does that mean for you, and for Parity?"

"It doesn't mean anything for Parity. They have a CEO, Matsuhiro Liu. He knows there is an heir, but he doesn't know who, and won't until I confirm myself. Like I said, nobody was supposed to know about me. Outside of that... the employees don't know or care who cuts their paychecks."

She had answered the second part, and tried to dodge the first.

"What does it mean for you?"

She looked down at her roll. "With Auntie and Natsumi gone, Uncle Kai is all the blood family I have left. It means I will be left to manage the entire House alone."

"Sounds like a tough situation. What happened to your parents?"

"Killed in a plane crash, ten years ago."

"Intentional?"

She looked at me. "The official report says it was pilot error."

"You don't believe that."

"Do you?"

No, I didn't. I shook my head. "You said nobody was supposed to know about you, but someone obviously does. Can you think of who, or how? I mean, if someone killed your parents, they must have known there was a connection there."

She looked down and speared another piece of her roll, chewed and swallowed, and then poured a new cup of green tea. She looked over at the new items rolling by on the conveyor belt. She looked everywhere but at me.

She was still looking away when she spoke.

"I was fourteen when they died. Natsumi was only ten. We would spend a month each year with them, on a private island owned by my aunt. The steps she went through to get us there without anyone knowing... to have us there with our parents. They loved us, I know, even though we barely knew each other. Natsumi should have been with them, but they insisted that I not grow up alone. They sent her to live in New York with me."

I used the chopsticks to pick up a piece of salmon. I couldn't imagine the childhood Jin had experienced. It was anything but normal, yet she seemed strong, and sensitive, and that her head was in the right place. "So you're saying it would have been impossible for anyone to know about you?"

"It should have been. It is clear that someone does. I wish I knew how."

She still wasn't looking at me. It made me wonder again if there was something she wasn't saying.

"If there are answers, we'll find them. Dannie is a total bad-ass in the Machine."

We spent a few more minutes eating and drinking in silence.

"What about you, Conor?" she asked, sounding a little timid. "Tell me about your family."

I looked at her, surprised. "No offense, Miss Red, but I'm a ghost. An employee. You aren't supposed to even know my name, and anything I tell you... you could use that against me."

She looked hurt, and I felt like an asshole for causing it. "I wouldn't do that."

"Not today you wouldn't. Maybe not tomorrow. Give it time. I've been a ghost for five years now. I've stolen, I've killed, I've hurt people and left their lives in ruin. They've all been involved with the Houses, so I don't consider them innocents... Still, most of the time, I don't even know why. It's nobody I ever thought I would be. It's nobody I ever wanted to be. It's the life I found myself in, when my other one fell to shit. When I got sick. It's the only way I found to live with myself when I wasn't sure I wanted to live at all, but I knew for certain that I didn't want to die."

She started crying as I was speaking. It wasn't because I had rejected her conversation. She was reading me, seeing my pain and anger and guilt. She was feeling it, and feeling for me. Empathic. She slid around to my side of the table and put her arm over my shoulders.

"You don't know what you'll have to do to protect the ones you love. To take care of your House. You don't know the decisions you'll have to make. I'm a ghost. I might not be a threat to you today, but what about in the future? Who knows what jobs I'll work, or who I'll do them for? Who knows what alliances you'll make? That's the life we've fallen into, the world we belong to that's supposed to keep the rest running smoothly. You know... the only thing that keeps me sane is when I sink money into my ex-wife's account, and I know I'm doing something to take care of them. It's the least I can do, after I failed them in the worst way a man can fail his family."

Damn it. I didn't want to talk about it, and I found myself letting out every painful guilty thought I fought so hard to bury all of the time. She was careful with my wounded shoulder when she pulled me close, and held me while my own tears fell.

I was thankful for the soundproof walls. I was glad Dannie wasn't here. Whatever the new Red was, she was reaching parts of my soul that I had tried really hard to kill. Part of me hated her for it, and part of me found itself feeling a little too much.

"You were right about the food," I said after a minute. I turned my head, my teary eyes finding hers only a few inches away. "We should go back to the hotel."

"The hotel?" She was staring into my eyes, unblinking, her expression soft.

"To wait for Amos and Dannie. They missed out on a good meal."

Her face turned red, and she pulled away, looking down and smiling.

"It is good fish," she said.

CHAPTER THIRTY-ONE

Ghosts in the Machine.

"BALDIE!" AMOS' BELLOW ECHOED IN the hotel room, and he waddled over to greet me when Jin and I got back.

"You're happy to see me?" I couldn't see past his bulk, but I could hear the wheels on Danelle's chair gliding over the carpet behind him.

"I threatened to cut something very dear to him off if anything happened to you," Jin said behind me.

"I wasn't worried. The wound was clean. Did you get to go outside? Holy shit, some of the girls here... biggest-"

"Amos!" Danelle snapped, at the same time her chair rolled over his foot. He shut his mouth.

"You've never been to the Greens before?"

"Oh, I have. Try to get here whenever I'm in the Northeast. Damn shame it's run by dir- hooooo! Fucking amazes me every fucking time."

I knelt down and wrapped my good arm around Danelle. "It's good to see you."

"We figured you'd be back soon, and I grabbed a dog from a vendor down the street. I'm glad you're up. You worried the shit out of me. How's the arm?"

I stood up and flexed it. The motion hurt, but I needed to get back into fighting shape. "I'll be fine. Like Amos said, the wound was clean."

"I got you something while we were out. I left it in the bedroom."

"I already have a good supply of sex toys."

She smacked me on the arm. "Don't be an asshole."

"Did you get some time in the Machine?" Jin asked.

Amos reached into the inside pocket of his duster. "Ta-da!" He was holding two credit-card shaped pieces of gold plastic. "Two hours each. We had to pawn half the armory to get it done."

Danelle sighed. "We had to do the golden tickets. They were booked for the next two weeks." The gold cards meant no reservations, and no waiting.

"I didn't know the Machine was getting that popular."

"In a place like this it is. According to the owner, the sovereignty of the Greens means they don't have to lock down any mods. If I had known that beforehand, I would have brought you somewhere else."

"Do you think you can get what you need in two hours?"

Danelle shrugged. "Let's hope so. We're going to be out of guns otherwise."

That reminded me. "What happened to Evan?"

Amos made a sound like he was puking. "Ugh. I'm putting carrying a half-decayed corpse at the very top of my list of the most disgusting things I've ever done. Number two is -"

"I don't want to know what number two is," I said, cutting him off.

He started laughing. "Fine. Trust me when I say it was really fucking gross. Anyway, he's back in his cooler in the van. Head's hanging a bit cockeyed after the werewolf tried to pull it off."

I could only hope the damage wasn't too bad; bodies like his were hard to find. "Thanks for collecting him, and for getting me loaded up and out of there."

"Like I said, she threatened to cut my balls off if anything happened to you. After what she did to my nose, I didn't doubt it." He ran his hand along his face. "Beautiful mug like mine. Damn shame."

I looked back at Jin and mouthed a thank you. She smiled in return.

"I think we've lost enough time. Let me go grab my stuff and we can head back to the Machinery. Every minute we waste gives whoever is behind this shit another minute to solidify their position."

I moved past them, hitting the bedroom first. I wasn't that surprised to find a black wool trench coat laid out on the bed. It was an oldie but a goodie, maybe a little too heavy to be practical and not the best suited for rain, but I didn't care about that. It had two deep front pockets, and two deep inner pockets, and was big enough that it would hide any kind of weapon I wanted to stash under it. I could always upgrade when I had a chance to do some real shopping.

I put the coat on and slipped my hood up, and then walked across to the attached bathroom to check myself in the mirror. The hood was casting a nice shadow, and the trench did what I wanted it to do. I found the safe and put in the code. All of my stuff was organized in the front, and I withdrew it and stuck it in my various pockets. Everything but the cell... the battery was dead, and the only person I ever called was already here. I noticed Jin's necklace was sitting all the way in the back, and I wondered if I should pocket that, too. Some part of me didn't feel like this safe was all that safe.

I stared at it for a few seconds, and then took it.

"I'm ready to rock," I said, joining the others in the living room. "Thanks for the coat, Dannie. It's perfect."

"You needed it. You looked like a stiff wind would knock you right over."

"Here, take this." Amos offered me a shoulder holster with one of the guns resting in it. "Place like this... you never know."

"Are you kidding me? There are armed guards everywhere."

"Safe enough in the streets. Can't say the same for the Machinery. Get a big enough crowd of assholes, you never know what could happen."

I shrugged off the trench and took the offered gun, slipping it on and burying it beneath the wool again. "Thanks."

"No problemo."

We headed out of the hotel again, with Amos in the lead. The big man was useful for clearing a path for us to move through, his massive girth threatening to knock aside anyone who was careless enough to get in our way. He brought us straight through the gathered crowds, past barely dressed men and women both showing off their assets, past goblins hawking baubles and necklaces, and dwarves playing up their mythos, dressed like they had fallen out of the Lonely Mountain to sell handmade axes and daggers. There was even a pair of elven magic users here, a pyro and an aqua who were wowing the crowd by dancing through rings of fire and water, crisscrossing them, or pulling them into one another to bathe themselves in mist and steam.

All the while, my eyes stayed on the guards. There was at least a pair at every corner, leaning back and taking it all in. From the size, most of them had to be ogres, or maybe trolls. From the armament, they could have annexed the rest of Brooklyn from the United States before morning if they were so inclined.

"When we get there, just stay quiet and let me set everything up," Danelle said. "Tony is an okay guy, but he doesn't have much patience for newbies."

"I've been in the Machine once before."

Danelle looked up at me and rolled her eyes. "You're running a stock avatar with no mods."

"I don't know what that means."

199

"Exactly."

We walked another block and turned right. The Machinery was up the street. It was easy enough to find, with massive LED lettering beaming out past mirrored windows and a huge installation of gears, pulleys, and winches taking up a hundred feet of walkway in front of it.

The Machine was created ten years ago by a technomancer named Aldred Jones. He had this idea that it would be an awesome business and great fun to create a world that couldn't exist anywhere but inside a computer. A world that looked, felt, tasted and smelled like it could be real, but had no solid laws, no solid rules, was completely anonymous, and no one could ever actually get hurt.

The first iteration was a disaster.

Not because the interest wasn't there, but the whole idea of lawlessness worked a lot better on paper than it did in reality. When anyone could do anything without consequence, it quickly became a race to see who could come up with the grandest scheme of depravity. From what Dannie had told me, V1.0 got shut down when someone forced all of the avatars to do some pretty nasty things with one another, and locked down the active accounts so that nobody could get out. The only reason Aldred had escaped prison was because nobody knew who he was, or where to find him.

Version two had a lot more inter-avatar safeguards in place, and maintained a basic ruleset that kept that bit of history from repeating itself:

1. Keep your shit in its zone. Penalties for acting out-of-zone, or 'oozy', were the harshest penalties in the Machine. Banned for a year, all of your in-Machine credits lost, and your name on the Slime List.

2. If you died in-zone in the Machine you got kicked off, and

you couldn't come back for a week.

3. If you killed someone in-zone, with the exception of the war zone, in the Machine, and another machinist or the bots got you, you were kicked off and couldn't come back for a month.

That was it on the inside. Three simple rules. On the outside, it was a little different. The Machine was under constant scrutiny from governments around the world, and while the Houses had seen to it that it was never outright banned from use, it was typically subject to any number of regulations, with certain activities and mods illegal to users depending on their node of origin.

That was what Dannie had suggested made the Greens so popular, and so expensive. Here, anything and everything was allowed.

She had owned an account ID for years, but she'd gone into the Machine only rarely, using the anonymity to meet with other ghosts, make some connections, and practice her stealth and combat in the war zone.

That was before she lost her legs.

Since then, she went in as often as our finances would allow. She could walk in the Machine. She could run, jump, kick, dance… everything she'd lost was returned, if only for the hour or two that she could afford each week.

Dannie had told me stories about Ivan Ilyn, a Russian billionaire who had been diagnosed with ALS, and now lived in the Machine full-time. He was strong and healthy inside, even while his body wasted away to nothing outside.

We passed through the sliding glass doors into the main lobby. It was massive, taking up the entire breadth of the ground floor, and broken up only by support beams, elevator shafts, and a small desk near the center. The outer shell was a single massive wall of video screens, where thousands of streams ran from the inside of the

Machine, and hundreds of onlookers loitered in voyeuristic fascination, their eyes shifting from one feed to the next.

Most of the action was occurring in the war zone, where avatars crouched behind blasted out shells of buildings, or charged through bullet-ridden streets. They were mainly human, though a good portion had mods to give them chameleon skin, or a cannon for an arm, or other craziness like that.

There was one machinist, recognizable only by his ID number, who seemed to have a following in the building. He was a beast of an ogre, in electric blue combat armor and carrying only a glowing chainsaw. He ran through the debris, taking massive leaps ahead and somehow avoiding all of the incoming gunfire his armor was attracting. He landed on a platform twenty feet up, where a sniper was scrambling to get a bead on him.

The chainsaw took care of that.

Danelle followed my eyes to the action. "14596. He's famous in this circle. He calls himself Abe."

"He's been around a long time." The IDs were sequential. The only person in the Machine who wasn't anonymous was '1', though most believed he had a few accounts.

"Or she," Dannie said. There was no way to know.

We kept moving, until Danelle rolled up to the desk. "Hey, Tony."

"Back again already?" the goblin asked. He cracked a wide smile and held out his hand.

Amos dug the golden tickets out of his coat pocket and passed them on. Tony looked them over and then glanced down behind the desk. "Room 1214 is open. Who's going up?"

Dannie pointed at me. "The two of us. Can you run a feed to a private viewing room?"

He shook his head. "All the viewing rooms are full. It's nuts in here tonight. I can run the feed to the hall?"

"No. Just keep it closed."

"You got it. Follow me."

He turned and headed straight back for the elevators.

"We'll be back soon," I said.

"Good luck," Jin replied.

Amos didn't even notice. He was staring at a feed on the far wall, his eyes bulging and his tongue hanging slightly from an open mouth.

I trailed behind Danelle and Tony, putting my hand to my mouth to cough a couple of times on the way. My stomach gurgled and churned, and I wondered if the sushi had been a good idea after all. Now that I'd been awake for a while, it seemed my system was getting moving again, reminding me of the truth of my conditioning.

"So, what kind of mods you got?" Tony asked once we were in the elevator and on the way up.

I hadn't realized he was talking to me. I opened my mouth, and was saved by Danelle.

"I'm having him shadow me. He's kind of a newbie. I've got reversal, marksman, agility, ghost, and some other odds and ends."

"Nice." Tony laughed and put his attention on me. "Fresh meat, huh?" His beady eyes looked me over. "You look like you'd be happier to spend more time in the Machine."

"Make it a quarter of the price, and I'd consider it."

He rolled his eyes. "Please. We just increased the prices, and we're still filling to ninety five percent every night. Guess you're just stuck being you."

I was going to say something unfriendly, but Danelle put up her hand to shut me up. It wouldn't help anything to start with the man in charge of the node.

"So where'd you get reversal from?" Tony asked. "That one's pretty rare."

Danelle looked at me, and I could tell she wasn't sure if she should answer or not.

I raised my eyebrows. "Yeah, D... You told me that one's pretty rare."

"Shut up. A guy I met inside was selling his, said he needed to raise more cash to buy time."

And she gave me a hard time about sending money to my daughter?

"How much?"

"Do we have to do this now?"

"How much?"

"Fifty."

I laughed. "You were getting me all worked up over fifty dollars?"

Tony looked at me with a strange smirk on his green face, and I stopped laughing.

"There are a lot more zeroes attached to that fifty, aren't there?"

Danelle was silent. The elevator reached the twelfth floor. She rolled out ahead of us.

"D..."

"Later. Please."

I let it go. What was done was done. I would save it for later when I needed something, or the next time she got pissed about Karen and Molly.

Tony got ahead of her and put his fingerprint to the sensor on the door to 1214. It clicked and swung open, and he led us in.

Aldred Jones was a technomancer, but there was a different kind of magic written into the code that ran the Machine: a billion or so lines of brilliance. The special sauce was in the equipment that immersed the 'machinist' into the world.

Visually, it was nothing more than a really comfy recliner and a motorcycle helmet. Except, the helmet wasn't just a helmet. It was infused with magic in the form of a pattern like a circuit that rested at the base of the neck right above the spine.

When you put the helmet on, the magic-powered circuit

connected with the latent field energy that humans of every kind had trickling through their systems, and essentially hot-wired it, sending it signals that were able to fool the brain into thinking it was running, falling, lifting a heavy object, having sex, whatever. Ultra-high resolution screens filled the field of vision to trick the brain even further, and the end result was that you felt like you were really in some new three dimensional space.

I followed Danelle over to the left-hand chair, and gave her my arm so she could swing herself into it. Then I flopped over onto my own rig. Tony hit a couple of switches on each, a soft hum the only indication the system was running.

"Interfaces." He tapped the helmets resting on the arm of the chair. I picked mine up and slipped it over my head. Foam moved away to let my skull through, then expanded back out to cut off the light from below. It was a lot lighter than I had expected; a newer, better, more breathable version of the one I had used during my only other excursion in the Machine. It sat comfortable and snug, supported by the shape of the chair around it. The screen wasn't on, leaving me in pitch black.

"The timer starts as soon as I put the tickets in," I heard Tony's muffled voice say. "If you want to know how much time you have left, check your watch. Which zone do you want to start in?"

"Free," Dannie said. "Near the Jungle."

I was glad she knew where we were supposed to start.

"You got it. Three...two...one..."

CHAPTER THIRTY-TWO

Machine head.

I FELT A SLIGHT TINGLE in my neck, and the high res screen blew up in a solid white light. The sound of running water filled my ears, and then all at once it started fading, the white replaced with a blur of color, the water overcome by the sound of… engines?

"This doesn't look like a jungle," I said.

We were standing on a sidewalk. Cars raced past us in the street. Most were the same brands and models that existed on the outside, but there were a few that stood out. One had paint that seemed to ooze and flow and morph the shape of the vehicle as it cruised down the street, while others sported more complete mods that turned the car into a hovercraft or even a flying pink Cadillac. They were the attention getters, and they captured mine, leaving me staring.

"The Jungle is a club." Danelle grabbed my arm, breaking me out of my trance.

I started to look down to where her face usually sat. I had to adjust my angle to look her in the eye. Her purple eye. She looked different here. It was her, but not her. It distracted me more than the cars had. "Dannie, I…"

"Shhh. No names, remember? I'm Daaé here. You're Baron. Don't forget."

"Right. You said the Jungle is a club? What kind of club?"

She turned me to the left. We were standing in front of a large, square building. It had a large neon sign arcing across a vine covered entrance, where a huge man-eating plant snapped at the avatars as they tried to enter. It took good timing to smack it on the head and force it to back away, and if you didn't make it... You were done for the week.

"Just a regular club with a fun theme. It's run by machinist number forty-two. It's popular here because it's a trade zone. It's also a ghost hangout. Come on."

She started tugging me towards the entrance, but I pulled back. "Hold on. You told Tony I was shadowing you. What does that mean?"

She sighed at my inexperience. "Okay, so the Machine is like an alternate reality, right?"

"I guess."

"Right. It's also like one massive game. You can choose whether or not you want to play, but the basic idea is that you get in-Machine credits for different things, including just spending time here. The credits can be spent on mods, vehicles, even virtual property."

"I thought you said the Machine only has three rules?"

"Damn it, Co...Baron, it has three basic rules. The game part is opt-in, get it?"

I nodded. "Okay, I get it. What does that have to do with us?"

"I'm playing the game. Shadowing means whatever you do to earn credits, they go to my account. That's the benefit to me. The benefit to you is that you get to share all of my mods."

I didn't care about earning credits for myself, so whatever. "How do you earn credits, besides just being here?" I turned my head and followed a white streak of light in the sky - some machinist shooting by riding a jet pack.

"Mainly through admin organized events with credit pools for the winners. Item hunts, death matches, missile races, that kind of thing."

"Did you say missile races?"

"Yes. And yes, you have to ride the missile."

"This place is fucked up."

"More fucked up than the real thing?"

I put up my hands in submission.

"You can also get points for bounty hunting machinists who are tagged for killing someone else against the rules, or for successful self-defense. They want to reward people for not being pansies."

"How does it feel?"

She tilted her head like a dog. "What?"

"To be able to walk? To have your legs?"

She didn't need to say anything for me to see what it meant to her. I decided right there that I wasn't going to use the reversal mod fiasco against her.

"I know why Ivan spends all his time here."

"Would you, if you could?"

She took a deep breath and shook her head. "No. Somebody has to watch out for your stupid ass."

"Thanks."

"Can we go in now?"

"Yeah."

We walked up to the entrance. Danelle leaned in towards me. "Want to see why reversal is awesome?"

"Sure."

"When the plant attacks you, just say 'mod reverse'."

"I need to say 'mod reverse'?"

"I know it sounds a little silly, but just try it. It isn't any different from vocalizing the magic."

Except I didn't have to add stupid prefixes to the magic. I went ahead of her, approaching the plant without worry. I trusted her that the mod was awesome, even if I didn't know why or how.

The massive red bulb of a head slithered back and forth as I approached. I kept my own head straight, watching it out of the corner of my eye. The moment it darted towards me, I said the special words, and it bounced back with a huge chunk out of its front. A second later, it vanished.

"Hey, hey, hey, what the fuck?" A dwarf dropped from up in the neon sign, landing in front of me. "You can't null Audrey Three."

I shrugged. "I was just trying out my mod."

"I can see you were trying out your fucking mod you damn nitwit newbie. You said it like a damn tourist. You must be one of of those rich assholes who just buys half the stuff in the game. You guys screw it up for everybody."

I didn't know what to say, but Danelle was at my side a second later. "Shit, Oscar, I'm sorry. Will a hundred credits make it better?"

I could tell by her voice she knew this was going to happen. She was just screwing with me.

"Daaé? This your new toy or what?"

"A friend. He's a virgin."

"Obviously. Yeah, a hundred and we're even. Just for you."

They shook hands, and I guess the exchange was made. She took my arm and pulled me inside.

"Why did you do that?"

"I needed to teach you about the mods. You remember all the ones I mentioned in the elevator?"

"Reversal, agility, ghost... yeah."

"You can use each one once an hour if you need to. Hopefully you won't, but I wanted you to be prepared."

We reached the inside of the club. Like Dannie had said, it was themed to look like a jungle, with vines hanging everywhere, monkeys swinging, birds flying, and snakes slithering. They all moved in a set pattern that I picked up inside of ten seconds, varying only to keep clear of the hundreds of avatars that sat at large tree trunks, stood in dark corners, or lined up at the bar.

"You can get drunk here?" I was surprised by the orc pouring thick, glowing liquids into frosty cylinders.

"Why not? You can do anything here you can do in real life, except die permanently. Get drunk, have an orgasm, even give birth."

"No shit. Why the hell would anyone want to do that?"

Dannie laughed. "Lose a bet, on a dare... You never told Karen you wished you knew what it was like?"

I hadn't, but I knew people who had. "Point made. Are we here for anyone in particular?"

She pointed ahead, to where a young man with long black hair was sitting by himself. "His name is Azeban. If anyone knows anything about Black, it's him."

"Relative?" It was hard not to notice the similar hair and cheekbones. Of course, he could have been anybody outside the Machine. Hell, he could have been Mr. Black.

"Not quite. We hooked up a couple of times."

I looked at her.

"Don't you dare judge me, or get jealous, or any of that shit."

"I'm not. To be honest, I'm happy for you, if it gives you a chance to work off some steam. It's the safest kind of sex you can have, right? No VD, no STD..."

"No impotence either," she said quietly. I hadn't even been thinking about that.

"I'm not in the market for that kind of fun."

It was easy enough to lose interest when it stopped being a possibility.

"You never know."

We walked together to Azeban's table. He didn't move the entire time we approached. He didn't even blink. When we sat down with him, he turned his head towards Danelle.

"Daaé." A pause. "One moment."

We waited ten seconds. Then he smiled and stretched his shoulders.

"My apologies, Miss Daaé. I was doing a little business offline. Who's your handsome friend?"

Handsome? I looked over at Dannie, and she shook her head and motioned for me to touch my face. I cupped my chin, and was surprised to feel the two days' worth of stubble pricking my hand.

"This is Baron. I'm helping him with a job. I was hoping maybe you could help him, too."

"Perhaps. What do you have to offer?"

"Nothing right now. Future favors?"

Azeban laughed. His voice was rich and delicate. "Oh, come now, Daaé. You are fantastic in bed, but I have a reputation. I can't just give away information that I work so hard to collect."

"Cut the shit, Az. You wouldn't be here if you weren't looking to make deals. It's what you do. Anyway, my friend Baron here is about to come into his own, if you know what I mean. A small deal today goes a long way tomorrow."

He looked at me. "Come into your own?" He pursed his lips. "An investment, then. A bit of risk. How many credits do you have?"

"Four thousand." Her voice was strained. She didn't want to tell.

"Well, I don't want to leave you penniless. Thirty-five hundred, plus a small favor in the future."

"Wait," I said. "What if you don't know the answer to my questions?"

"She wouldn't have brought you to me if she didn't think I had any answers."

"Done." Dannie held out her hand. Azeban took it and brought it to his lips.

"Maybe later?" he mouthed.

"Not tonight," she mouthed back.

Azeban leaned back in his seat. "Ask away, Baron."

"Mr. Black paid two million to do a job. Except, the job didn't come from Mr. Black, only the payment did. How could that be?"

He put his hand to his chin, and then looked at Danelle. "How did you get caught up in this?"

"So you know about it?"

He leaned forward again, and put his hand on top of Danelle's. "Take your credits back. I won't help you."

"Az? What the hell?"

He pushed his chair back and stood. "I'm sorry Daaé." He looked at me. "A little free advice. You should be hiding in the deepest, darkest hole you can find. House Red is finished. They took something that didn't belong to them, and they're paying the price. Forget whatever House politic bullshit they're trying to sell you. Sometimes the simplest reason is the only one."

I got to my feet. "What are you talking about?"

"Tarakona. That's what he calls himself. He's not a ghost. He's not a House. He's the future, and he knows where you are." He waved goodbye as he vanished from existence.

"That doesn't sound good."

"We have to get out of here, back to Jin and Amos," Dannie said. "If he's compromised the Machine somehow... Just say 'exit the Machine' to get out."

"Exit the Machine."

I looked around. I was still in the Jungle.

"Exit the Machine."

"Going somewhere?"

The voice came from behind me. I turned around.

Veronica was standing there, smiling at me.

"I killed you."

The face was stoic. "No, you killed my sister, but I thought confronting you in her skin would make a nice statement. We've been waiting for you to turn up again. Did you know necromancers have a fairly unique brain chemistry? Our man on the admin team picked it up as soon as you jacked in. From what he tells me, you still have an hour and…" He looked upward, like he was getting messages from God, which I guess in a way he was. "…forty-five minutes left on your clock." The avatar morphed from a female redhead to a male one. "Our team will be at the Greens within the hour."

CHAPTER THIRTY-THREE

Dumb ways to die.

I GLANCED OVER AT DANNIE, and then charged the bastard.

He let me hit him, toppling over with my arms around his waist, laughing the entire time. We hit the ground together, and I started pummeling his face with my fists.

He kept laughing.

"Keep on hitting me. I'm not going to fight you."

I felt a hand on my shoulder.

"Baron, let's go. There are plenty of ways to die in the Machine, and that directive can't be overridden by anyone except Aldred himself."

I stopped punching and looked down at the bastard. He stopped laughing when Danelle threw the logic on my fire. There were three ways out of the Machine. Saying 'exit the Machine', running out of time on the clock, and dying. We'd been cut off from the first, and had way too much of the second.

I hopped off him. "Okay, how?"

She grabbed my hand. "Oscar probably got Audrey booted back in by now."

Let the plant eat me. Simple.

Veronica's brother was still on the floor. A pair of massive arms appeared from behind me and squeezed tight. A second ogre grabbed Danelle.

"What do you want us to do with them?" my guy asked.

"Nothing," he replied, getting to his feet. "Just don't let go."

"Don't let go?"

He reared back and threw a heavy punch, getting me squarely in the ribs. I held my face calm against the pain, not willing to give him the satisfaction.

"I thought you said you weren't going to fight?"

"This isn't fighting. This is restitution." He punched me again.

"You know what Veronica's problem was? She was overconfident. She thought there was no way she could lose." I tightened my muscles as another punch hit the other side of my ribs. "You think because you managed to get some ferals working for you, or one of the Machine's admins, that makes you untouchable? It didn't make her untouchable. I touched her, and she liked it."

I was being an asshole. I was trying to piss him off, to get him to punch me harder, hopefully too hard.

It didn't work. He stopped hitting me and backed off. "Some ferals? You have no idea." He shook his head. "Know your enemy. That's the first rule of warfare. You don't know jack shit." He looked at his watch again. "Forty minutes. Would you like a beverage? I've heard the cocktails here are to die for."

The goons holding us chuckled at his humor.

"Fuck you," Dannie said. She was struggling against the ogre, trying to break free.

He sauntered over to her. "Who are you, I wonder? The necromancer's partner. You-"

"Mod ghost," Dannie whispered. Immediately, her form became translucent, and she slipped right through the arms of the ogre. She started running, not towards the exit but further into the club.

"Mod solid." Our captor aimed his hand at her. A web of energy spiked out from it, striking her in the back. She lost her translucency, slamming right into an avatar with a bubbling green concoction in his hand. They both crashed to the floor.

"Mod-"

A leathery ham-hand fell over my mouth. "I don't think so."

The other one chased after Dannie, but she rolled off the guy she'd collided with and bounced up. She threw a fist into the face of another avatar, a blonde with a huge chest, hanging to the arm of a slimy looking guy in a long, dark coat. The odds were good that in a place like this, an avatar like that would be packing.

"What the fuck?" he said, reaching under his coat.

Danelle punched the blonde again, and then grabbed her shoulders and threw her at the ogre. He caught her at the same time her escort got his gun clear of his coat.

I heard a gunshot. A dark hole appeared in the forehead of the slimy guy, and he fell backwards. The machinist was kicked out, booted from the Machine for a week for being dumb enough to get shot. His avatar lingered on the ground in its death position, an artifact that would hang around for another hour or two.

At once, a dozen more avatars pulled a dozen more weapons from various places on their bodies. The ogre dropped me to the ground as the entire place erupted in gunfire. Veronica's brother crouched next to us, a smoking Magnum in his hand. I could hear the bullets passing overhead, and thumping into the tables around us.

"That little bitch," he said.

I was held tight, and couldn't see where she was. I started squirming, fighting back against the ogre, but he was way too strong. My captor leaned up and fired a couple more times, then ducked down when another volley followed.

"Illicit kills detected. Targets acquired."

Three robots entered the Jungle. They were each a single solid piece of metallic silver, with long limbs and blank faces. They raised their hands in unison, a red glow forming in the palms. They were aimed at the asshole crouched next to me.

He had seen them, and he cursed and dove aside at the same time three tight red laser beams blasted the spot where he had just been, leaving scorch marks in the ground.

He returned fire, blasting at the bots with his hand cannon. The bullets sparked on their metallic torsos, skipping off without causing damage. Their bodies twisted to fire back.

The ground shook, and the bots vanished. An armor-plated black van crashed through the entrance to the Jungle, crushing them underneath. It came to a stop a dozen feet in and the doors slid aside. Seven or eight avatars piled out, dressed in black combat fatigues and carrying heavy weaponry. They didn't strafe the crowd, instead using the van as cover and firing single, sighted shots at targets I couldn't see.

Was one of them Danelle? I had no idea. Maybe she'd gotten herself shot, and I would be out of there any second. I struggled against the ogre. I needed to get loose so I could see what was happening.

Veronica's brother returned to his spot, tapped the ogre on the shoulder, and pointed back to the van. "Let's go."

The ogre pulled me to my feet, giving me a chance to survey the scene. The entire place had been trashed, with broken glasses and bullet-ridden tables and chairs thrown all over place, empty avatars scattered everywhere in all kinds of bloodless death poses. There was a line of tipped tables at the far end, where the remaining shooters were staying under cover, rising up to take pot shots at the armored group at the van. Since they were with the aggressors, my guess was that taking them out wouldn't cause a penalty, and would have some kind of value for the machinists participating in the gamification.

I scanned the bodies, searching for Danelle, at the same time the ogre dragged me away. The squad laid down cover fire, keeping us from getting shot and preventing me from being killed.

Then I heard a shout, and saw a flash of red. Another team of bots streamed into the building, their lasers finding two of the soldiers and turning them to dust. They turned on the bots, raising grenade launchers and firing back, explosions coating the metal creations in smoke and dust.

The attack left them distracted. The avatars lined up behind the table rose and opened fire, bullets pinging off the armored van, skipping off the ground around the ogre's feet, and then finding their way into the ogre. The pain and shock made him let go of my mouth, and I didn't waste any time.

"Mod ghost." I felt an electric tingle, and saw my body begin to fade. I stepped right out of the ogre's arms at the same time someone turned their grenade launcher on the defense. The area behind the tables exploded, three bodies were thrown aside, and the bullets stopped coming. "End mod."

I turned solid again, and ran towards the center of the room, waving my arms. Neither side shot at me. The attackers wanted me alive, and the defense knew I had been a captive and didn't want to risk hitting me. Shit.

I scanned the floor, looking for a gun. All I had to do was shoot myself, and I'd be out of this crazy-ass place.

Instead I found Danelle's avatar, half-buried by the busty blonde. She had four bloodless holes in her chest.

My heart had been pounding the entire time. Now it found a new level of panic. Why the fuck was I still here?

I could imagine the ugliest reasons, but I wasn't willing to accept any of them. The simplest reason was probably the right one, that's what Azeban had suggested.

She couldn't get me out. I had to do it myself. She would be stranded in the setup until I could move her back to her wheelchair.

I found a gun laying on the ground nearby. I dove for it, sliding across the floor between two dead avatars and getting my right hand around the butt. I was bringing it to my mouth when a bullet smashed into my hand, tearing it from my grip and breaking my fingers. I ignored the pain and looked around for a new weapon. Another gunshot, and my left hand exploded in agony. They didn't have to kill me to keep me from shooting myself.

"Give it up, necro," Veronica's brother shouted. "Even if you manage to get out of here, we're still going to find you, we're still going to kill you. You picked the wrong side."

Maybe I had, but I was committed to it. There was an emergency exit on my left. I ran for it.

I could hear boots behind me. I saw two of the armored soldiers out of the corner of my eye, firing on the defense and headed my way. They were running impossibly fast, gaining in a hurry, trying to cut me off before I made the door.

Dannie had listed some of her mods. I tried to remember them. Reversal, ghost... what were the others? Fuck. Reversal, ghost... The soldiers were almost on me.

Reversal, ghost... It hit me. "Mod agility," I said.

Everything slowed down. One of the soldiers dove to tackle me, but it was like he was running in slow motion. I ducked aside and kicked out, catching his head with my foot, breaking his neck. The other was still running towards me, and I kicked his kneecap, forcing his leg in the wrong direction and hearing the deep, retarded crack. I kept going for the door, making it out before either had crumpled in a heap behind me.

I was outside, on a side street adjacent to the club. I saw more bots run past, headed to the scene of the fighting. Traffic had slowed here, trying to stay out of the way of the battle.

I didn't dare ease up. I ran down the street, even though I had no idea where I was going. I'd only been in the Machine once before, for only an hour. I'd spent the entire time in a room, just getting used to the sensations of being whole again, of not feeling the need to cough, or the tightness in my stomach.

It sounds stupid, but I hated it. That's why I'd never gone back.

It felt like such a cop out to hide from life here, though I would never have told Dannie that, and I didn't judge her for coming back to this place to be complete again.

It just wasn't for me.

Now I was stuck here, and I wanted to get out and couldn't. I needed to kill myself, but how? I didn't even know half of the unwritten rules of this place. All I knew was that the bad guys were on my ass, and they wanted to stop me from leaving.

I kept running. I felt a pulsing in my body as the agility mod ran out, and everything went back to normal speed. I checked the watch. An hour and a half. Thirty minutes to get out.

I heard the roar of an engine, and saw a nice-sized truck headed my way. I took a deep breath, and threw myself in front of it.

A horn, skidding tires, an avatar cursing at me. The breeze of the truck blasted my side, but the vehicle itself got around me. In the real world, there was no way something that size could maneuver like that. Damn.

I raced down a standard city street, avatars wandering the sidewalks around me, tall buildings rising up on either side. Most were nondescript bastions of steel and glass, but a few had their own personal touches, in-Machine real estate, owned by anonymous machinists. I thought about throwing myself off one, but the boring ones didn't look like they even had doors. They were just facades to lend atmosphere, flat canvasses like a movie set.

There was nothing to do but run. I knew the armored van was going to come for me. I waited for it to pull up alongside any minute, for the doors to open and for them to pluck me from the street. I moved as fast as I could, my feet pounding the ground, pushing my way past the other machinists and feeling the seconds ticking away. I was getting tired, my hands hurt, my throat was dry, and my heart was starting to throb from beating so fast for so long. I'd never heard of someone dying for real from the Machine, but it felt convincing enough.

I crested a hill, and my salvation appeared in front of me. A massive structure of steel hanging across a churning body of water. A bridge. All I had to do was throw myself off, and I'd be out.

Seeing it gave me a second wind. I picked up the pace, pushing harder to reach it before the goon squad showed up. I was half a mile away. I could run that in no time.

The van didn't come from behind me. It appeared in front of me, rocketing from a cross-street and skidding to a stop, blocking the bridge. The doors slid open and Veronica's brother got out, flanked by two remaining soldiers. They held something in their hands, some kind of weapon, or...

One of them fired. I saw the shot coming at me, and it broke apart and spread wide into a weighted net. If I hadn't used the agility mod already, it would have been easy to escape. Now, there was no way I could avoid it. I was caught. Done. I could only hope Dannie had somehow gotten to her chair and made it to Jin and Amos.

I didn't want these assholes to win.

A horn echoed right behind me, a car appearing as if out of thin air. I barely had enough time to turn my head before it hit me. I barely had enough time to see the driver.

Azeban.

He gave me a curt wave and plowed into me, and even as I flew up over the hood I could tell he was still accelerating, the car destined to reduce the three assholes in the van to nothing more than pieces.

I don't know why he helped me. I wondered who he even was. I wish I could have gotten the satisfaction of witnessing the collision, but I hit the ground hard, and everything went black.

CHAPTER THIRTY-FOUR

Who lives forever, anyway?

I STILL COULDN'T SEE ANYTHING, but I knew I was out of the Machine. I could feel the weight of the helmet over my head, and the noiseless din of the real world. My heart was still going too fast, but it was nothing compared to what I had felt inside.

"Dannie?"

I reached up and gripped both sides of the helmet, lifting it off my head. I looked over at the chair next to me. She was still there, her helmet still on.

That was strange.

"Dannie?"

I slid off the chair and put my helmet down on it. She had died in the Machine, hadn't she? Maybe that hadn't been her? It was possible she had a mod to make her look like someone else, and make someone else look like her. Could it be that Azeban had known about it, and that's why he had saved me?

I needed to wake her up. Was it as simple as just taking the cap off? It seemed like it should be. I leaned over her and put my hands on it.

That was when I saw the blood.

"Let go of the fucking helmet and turn around," Tony said.

I was panicking for real now, and fearing the worst. I wanted to take the helmet off, to make sure she was okay. I took a deep breath, and turned around.

The goblin was holding the gun that Amos had given me. "Don't you try anything."

He was shaking, nervous.

"What did you do?"

He looked past me, at Danelle. I could see it in his eyes.

"What the fuck did you do?" I screamed, moving towards him.

"Don't move," he yelled back, pushing the gun forward. "I told her not to move. I told her to just sit there. She didn't fucking listen. She thought she was so tough." His voice was cracking as he spoke. "One of the admins called me. They said to keep an eye on you. If you woke up, not to let you leave. Twenty thousand, to not let you leave."

I turned around again, and reached for the helmet.

"Don't."

I lifted it up.

"Twenty thousand, just don't let you leave. All she had to do was sit there. Why wouldn't she just sit there?"

Tony was a good shot. The bullet had gone into her head, right between the eyes. It was armor piercing, I bet it was buried in the soundproofing behind us somewhere.

I looked into her eyes. Her dead eyes. My entire body went numb.

"Turn around." His voice was desperate. He was scared.

He was right to be.

I turned, throwing the long coat out around me and shifting to the side. The goblin was a good shot against someone with no legs. The bullet made a nice hole in my new-to-you trench, but it didn't even come close to hitting me.

One hand took the gun, the other wrapped around his narrow throat. I didn't think about the consequences, and I didn't care. I heard the fields, and I took the power in.

"Please. I'm sorry. Please, please, it was an accident." He was begging for his life. I watched his neck begin to turn grey, and then black.

"She has no fucking legs," I screamed into his pathetic face. "She couldn't hurt you." She probably called him to help wake me up, or to get her to her chair.

"Please." His voice was getting more raspy. The flesh was flaking away beneath my hand, the disease spreading.

My anger went quiet. "Stop whining. It's too late."

I let him go.

He fell to the ground, coughing and choking. I returned the gun to my holster, and went back to Dannie. This was wrong. This was all so wrong. I was the one who was dying. I was the one who should have been dead. If I had died five years ago like I wanted to, she could never have saved me. She'd still have her legs, and her life.

Tony died behind me, but I didn't even notice. I leaned over Dannie, the anger washing away and the pain filling the space. My eyes filled with tears, and I leaned over and put my forehead to hers. I gave myself a minute to cry, to bawl. Then I gave myself a minute to tear apart the small room, ripping at the chairs and the wires. I took my helmet and threw it at the window. It was hardened, and it just bounced off.

"No, no, no, no, no, no, no." I stroked her hair. "I love you. I'm sorry."

This was all my fault. From beginning to end, I had caused this. I had been delusional to think I could handle the job, insane to think it wasn't a trap from the start.

"I'm sorry, Dannie. Fuck. I'm so sorry."

I'd blown it, and she had died sitting in a chair.

For twenty thousand dollars.

Getting killed was a risk every ghost took. If you ran as a team, or if you had a partner, having to watch them die bore the same risk. It was part of the job description, and you had to come to terms with it if you wanted to survive and succeed. It was just part of the business, and anyone who had ever had the same career would have told me not to make it personal.

Fuck that. It was personal.

I wiped my eyes on the trench and checked my watch. I had twenty minutes to get Jin out of the Greens, before this Tarakona's kill team showed up to finish this thing. I would have loved to take them all on at once, but I couldn't get my revenge if I was dead. Instead, I leaned over and scooped Dannie up, holding her corpse across my shoulder and heading for the door. It hurt like hell to use my arm like this, but she wasn't very heavy, and I was too pissed to care.

I got the door to the room open and ducked out into the hallway, sweeping left and right with the gun. It was clear. I walked fast towards the elevator, doing my best to keep my mind focused. I was guilty, sad, frightened, angry... more angry than anything else.

The elevator was waiting. I got in and directed it back down to the lobby. It occurred to me the guards wouldn't react too well to me carrying around a dead body and brandishing a weapon. I put Danelle down and returned the gun to its holster, and then removed the hoodie and put it on her, using it to cover her head. Then I picked her back up and re-slung her. She was drunk, I was taking her back to our hotel... It was as good an excuse as any.

I kept to the corner of the elevator as it hit the lobby and the doors slid open. I was glad I did. The place had been nearly emptied, with the exception of six of the armored leathers, who had Jin and Amos cuffed near the front desk. Amos was cursing and complaining about the whole thing being bullshit, and in this case I was grateful for his big mouth. They hadn't noticed the elevator's arrival.

I didn't have much time. I found the dice in my pocket, brought them up to my lips and whispered into them. "Six souls, leather and strong. A good meal."

I felt them grow warm to the suggestion. I don't think I ever enjoyed feeding them more.

I peeked around the corner, and ducked my head back before I could be spotted. The doors started to close, but I slammed my fist onto the open button. I didn't look into the lobby again. I didn't need to. I knew where the desk was. I stood in the corner and threw the dice backwards out of the opening. Then I pulled the gun.

I counted. One... two... three... I swung across the open doorway. I couldn't see my roll, but I saw the effects. Fire, and Daggers. It had to be. The guards were standing still, their weapons dropped from paralyzed fingers, their eyes wide with fear and confusion. I didn't shoot at them, not yet. The paralysis would spread, inward until it reached their hearts.

Then they would die.

The problem was that I couldn't collect the dice until they did. If the second cast had been Daggers, that could mean a couple of minutes. If we were ready to go before then, I'd have to shoot them anyway.

I walked out of the elevator. Jin and Amos saw me, and they looked relieved. They couldn't have known Dannie was dead. They would have thought I was just carrying her.

"What did you do?" the lead guard whined at me as I approached. He wouldn't be able to speak for much longer. The cuffs were fingerprint activated. I grabbed his hand and lifted it.

"Come on. We need to get out of here." I looked at Jin. "There's a kill team incoming."

"What happened?"

"Yeah," Amos said. "These assholes came up to us and said we were under arrest for illegal use of the Machine. We were just fucking standing here. Seriously. You're gonna make up some bullshit, at least make it somewhat believable. Just like these fucking dirty pricks. Too stupid to even lie right."

He moved so I could put the cuffs against the orc's finger. They unclasped and dropped to the ground. Jin followed after, and then Amos clocked the leather in the head. Helmet or not, he dropped like a sack of crap.

"They cleared out the rest of the people in the building," Jin said. "It was only five or six minutes after you went up. Tony got a call, and then the guards came over. All the feeds went off."

"They have an admin helping them. Said they made me as soon as I booted in, thanks to being the only necro on the grid. He probably told them the Machine was compromised. They almost had me inside, but a friend of Dannie's helped me get out." I wished I knew why. It had to be for a better reason than because they had messed around a couple of times.

Amos ran a fat hand through his hair. "This is totally fucked up. Hey, Dannie, you okay? It's not like you to be so quiet."

I looked at him.

He looked at me.

I saw the muscles in his jaw clench.

"Mother fuckers." He kicked the guard in the head again, and then turned to the others. He lifted the firepower from two of them, and then knocked them down. He tossed one of the guns to Jin.

"Baron? Danelle… she…" She had tears in her eyes.

"Not now. We need to get out."

We were ready to go. The dice weren't. The guards we hadn't dropped fell on their own, deep moans pouring from their mouths. If they could have moved, they might have screamed or begged or something.

"Waiting for an invitation?" Amos asked.

"Hold on." I walked back to where the dice were laying. I had been right. Fire and Daggers.

"What? Shit, Co… Baron we need to get the fuck out of here."

"We have to wait." I looked at my watch. "Ten seconds. We can wait ten seconds." It would have taken longer than that to get the helmets off to shoot them in the head.

The black energy started drifting from the dice, towards the targets. I felt the coldness of it, and it brought me satisfaction. Dannie had always loved the dice, the mystery of their creation and the power of the creature that embodied them.

I didn't love them, I was afraid of them. I had been since they'd called out to me. It wasn't something I liked to think about. It wasn't something I liked to admit.

I hadn't found the dice, the dice had found me.

The energy wrapped around each of the leathers in turn, collecting their souls and dragging them back into the small bone cubes. Jin watched with familiar fascination. Amos turned completely white, and looked away. A moment later, it was done.

I scooped them up and put them back in my pocket.

"Where did you leave the van?"

"At the Amore. I didn't think we'd get into this much shit an hour after you finished your beauty sleep, which, by the way, didn't help you at all."

"Just give me the keys and take Dannie."

He only considered being horrified to take her dead body for a split second before he reached into his pocket and found the keys. I cradled her in front of me, leaned down and kissed her cold cheek, and passed her over.

"Get somewhere safe. I'll be back in five minutes."

"Yeah right. In case you hadn't noticed Einstein, there is nowhere safe."

I turned towards the front door. There were a pair of guards standing outside, facing the other way and keeping the crowds back. They hadn't heard any commotion from inside, and none of the assholes in here had time to call for help.

"There has to be an emergency exit."

"They'll have guards there, too," Jin said.

"I know, but not as many onlookers." I turned around, finding the glowing exit sign near the back corner. "Amos, you have a knife?"

He shifted Danelle on his shoulder and leaned down, pulling a four inch shiv from his boot. He handed it to me.

"Five minutes. If they notice the guards are down, hide behind the desk and keep them pinned."

I took off towards the door at a full run.

CHAPTER THIRTY-FIVE

Three little pigs.

I WOULDN'T HAVE BEEN ABLE to tickle an orc in a straight-out fight. Slipping through a door without being noticed? That I could do.

I jumped on the leather's back and jabbed the shiv into his neck, riding him to the ground and doing my best to keep his fall quiet. Fortunately, he was the only guard out in the alley, positioned to keep people out, not to keep us in.

I needed to get over a couple of blocks and up another without being completely obvious. The hardest part was going to be getting out of the alley unnoticed. Looking towards the mouth, I could see some of the onlookers that were bleeding over from the front of the Machinery, waiting to see when they would be allowed back in.

I had given myself five minutes to get the van and get back. That wasn't much time, and I was starting to feel the drain of the power I'd used on Tony. There was no choice but to make a run for it. I exchanged the knife for my gun, keeping my arm under the trench, and walked towards the crowd.

There was a dumpster near the end of the alley, and I ducked behind it for a few seconds, surveying the scene. There were a couple hundred assorted people standing behind the line the guards had made. Some were just standing there waiting, while others had found ways to entertain themselves: messing with their phones, messing with each other, or whatever.

Nobody was looking at the alley, and I slipped out along the wall off the adjacent building, walked a couple dozen feet, and then started to run.

The machinists were interested in the Machinery. There were plenty of other residents and visitors to the Greens that didn't give a shit about that kind of thing, and were still crowding the streets and going about their business as if nothing was wrong. I would have loved to blend in and take my time navigating through them to the hotel, but Amos and Jin were counting on me. I kept running, knowing it made me suspicious as hell, and winding up not very surprised when I blew past a guard leaning against the dark, inner side of a building, and drawing his unwelcome attention.

"Hey buddy," he shouted.

I didn't slow, but I did change direction, moving into the crowd. I twisted and shoved my way through, ignoring the curses behind me.

"Fucking stop, asshole."

He was chasing me. I cut diagonally across the street, and then up the block to the Amore. I was halfway across when another guard popped out in front of me, his assault rifle raised, the scope against his eye.

"Stop!"

I fell to my knees and let my hand come out from under the trench. My shots were wild, but they served to force him to lower his own weapon and take evasive action. I hopped back up, my knees skinned and bleeding, and kept running towards him. By the time he recovered I was in his face, and I smashed him in the jaw with the butt of my gun. He spun to the ground with a grunt.

A shot echoed in the night, and chips of cement broke free of the building next to me, leaving me wishing I could run just a little bit faster. I reached the corner and saw the sign for the hotel, all done in pink script with the 'a' in 'More-a' shaped either like a heart, or a vagina. The ramp into the parking garage was on the far right side of the building, open and inviting.

I turned back and took a couple of potshots at the guard following me. He didn't flinch at the bullets, sending his own volley back at me, the spray whizzing past and tearing up the ground on my left. I zigged that way, trying to catch him in between adjustments of aim, and was rewarded with a shot that grazed my calf and almost knocked me down.

The parking garage was looming. I turned and emptied my clip, two of the shots smashing into his body armor, the armor piercing rounds digging far enough through that he cried out and toppled to the ground. I half-ran, half-limped down the steps. Where the hell was the van?

The garage had three levels, but Amos was Amos, and he had parked in a handicapped spot near the elevator. I fumbled with the keys for a second, my entire body shaking from the shock and adrenaline, before getting the rear door open and climbing inside. I threw open Evan's cooler and reached down.

"Come on, Evan. I need you." I sent the power into him, and then drew back my hand to cough.

"Damn. What now, asshole?" His head was at a bit of an odd angle, but he didn't seem to notice. "You look like shit."

"Get up and get armed. Don't give me any shit, I'm not in the mood. Dannie is dead."

For once, he didn't offer any lip. He got up out of the cooler and went over to the trunk and flung it open.

"Where the fuck are the guns?"

I looked over. They had understated how much they had needed to sell. The sawed-off was in there, along with a couple of .38s. Not the kind of firepower he was used to.

"Make do." I punched the top of the van. "On the roof."

I got behind the wheel and started it up, backing out of the spot at the same time Evan grabbed the shotgun and one of the pistols.

"You have got to be kidding me."

The noise of the gunfire in the garage made my ears hurt. Bullets pinged into the side of the van, puncturing the metal and thumping into Evan.

I skidded to a stop. "You want better guns? Go take those fuckers out!"

"Fine. Give me a ride." He jumped out of the van and moved to the front, hopping onto the snub nose. I peeled out, turning the wheel and heading straight for our attackers, a new pair of guards.

The din continued. Bullets peppered Evan and the windshield, breaking it to pieces. I ducked behind the wheel, keeping it straight.

"Brakes," Evan said.

I slammed on them. He threw himself forward, letting his body roll with the momentum and coming up right in front of the leathers. He shoved the shotgun right into one's chest and fired, blowing through the armor. The other shot him point-blank, but he couldn't feel a thing. He brought the .38 up under the guard's chin and blew his brain into his helmet.

I drove up slowly. He grabbed the two assault rifles and the extra clips they were carrying, and climbed into the van through the blasted windshield. He had bullets planted in his skull, and his clothes were shredded to almost nothing.

"It's about time I got some action." He lifted a finger to one of the slugs in his head. "Better than a fucking tattoo."

I floored it, ripping out of the garage and blasting the horn, scattering the onlookers. "More action incoming. We're going in the front door."

"Hell yeah."

I went up another block and over, drawing fire from a pair of guards on the way by, the van gaining a few more holes. Then I skidded around a turn and got us pointed directly at the Machinery.

The bystanders had scattered, and the guards were facing the other way. I could see their muzzle flashes, and hear the return fire from Amos and Jin inside.

I hit the accelerator, racing down the street, my hand glued to the horn to try to get the innocents out of the damn way. Evan leaned forward, resting one of the rifles on the dash and putting his dead eye against the scope. He hit the trigger once, and one of the guards dropped.

I swung the wheel as we approached the Rube Goldberg that rested in front of the building, jumping onto the grass next to it and staying as tight to the entrance as I could. Evan squeezed off another round, and a second guard lost his feet.

I nailed the breaks and spun the wheel, sending the van skidding to the left with a squeal of tires. Evan planted his hand in the dash and held on while I brought us back around towards the lobby at an angle. The glass wall loomed in front of us, and then I collided with it, ducking down and feeling the glass rain in. I spun the wheel wildly again, forcing the van to spin on the smooth floor of the Machinery, and come to a heavy rest with the ass facing the front desk.

There were four guards spread out behind cover inside, and they opened up on the van again. I ducked down and held my head while Evan opened the passenger door and jumped out, returning fire. A few seconds later it was quiet.

"Hey sexy, your ride is here," Evan said.

The back doors opened, and Amos climbed up, Danelle still in his arms. "And I thought this thing was a piece of shit before."

Jin hopped in behind him. "Baron, are you okay?"

"They only shot me once. Evan, in the van."

My corpse soldier grabbed another rifle and tossed it in, then slid into the passenger seat again. I started us moving, driving over the decimated glass and hoping the tires would stay intact. They were reinforced, and they got us over and out.

I was going to go back the way we'd come, but as I maneuvered to go around the installation I saw a another car incoming, a black Hummer with tinted windows. I hit the brakes and started backing up so I could go around to the right. The Hummer stopped and the doors opened, three men stepping out.

I didn't recognize any of them. They were well-built, tall, angular, and unarmed, dressed in grey suits with white ties. What were they doing? I stopped the van and started turning the wheel, putting my foot down on the gas and cornering as best I could.

One second, the three men were walking towards us. The next, they were gone. Not visibly gone, but replaced with the biggest, meanest looking weres I'd ever seen. They ran towards us on all fours, approaching ridiculously fast.

What the fuck? Werewolves didn't shift. They got the virus, they got primitive and hairy, and that was it. At least, that was what they taught us, and that was all I had ever seen before.

I put my foot all the way to floor, and we started moving down the street, away from the incoming monsters.

Everything shook when the first one slammed into the side of the van, putting a solid dent in the side and sending it rocking and rolling, threatening to tip. The second bounced up onto the hood, and I got a great look at the inside of its massive jaws right before Evan put a bullet in its head. It fell away without a sound, rolling to a stop next to us. I saw it shake. A point-blank shot, and it was still alive.

Where was the third? I looked out the window, and checked the mirror for it, but I didn't see it. The van was struggling to accelerate now, the damage complete enough that I was amazed we were still moving. These things were fast, there was no way it hadn't caught up.

A claw tore into the roof near the back, and then another. Massive muscles started peeling the top of the van away, at the same time Evan and Amos both opened fire into it. I heard the wet slaps of the bullets finding flesh, but the were didn't seem impressed. It jumped down through the opening it had made, the motion itself threatening to throw the car off its track. It elbowed Amos, knocking him aside, and reached out for Jin.

"Eat lead, asshole," Evan said, sticking his rifle in its face.

Its head snapped around, grabbing the end of the gun in its teeth and pulling it from his grip. Then it lashed out with its other hand, raking claws though Evan's left arm. It dropped to the ground.

"Damn. I liked that arm." He took three steps forward and threw his weight into the creature, magic-powered muscles pushing against inhumanly strong ones. He got the thing off-balance, and they crashed into the back doors together, their combined force and weight too much for the locking mechanism. The doors swung open, and they both fell out, tumbling to the ground still entwined.

I kept my foot to the floor, and the van picked up speed. The good thing about the Greens is that it was small, and the leathers inside had no jurisdiction to do jack shit outside of the borders. I powered through the checkpoint, blasting the barrier arm to splinters, and drove out into greater Brooklyn.

I could feel my link to Evan fading as I moved away. He'd always been an asshole, but in the end he'd come through.

I was going to miss him.

CHAPTER THIRTY-SIX

Referee.

THE VAN MADE IT ABOUT ten miles before the damage became too much, and I pulled it into a dark alley and let it rattle to a stop. It breathed a heavy sigh of relief, the engine shutting down for the last time.

The familiar whine of the secondary motor that kept the coolers chilled was the only sound remaining.

"Conor?" Jin said. We'd driven the distance in tense quiet, hunkered down, guns ready, expecting the creatures that attacked us to catch up at any moment. Now she broke the not-quite-silence.

I looked over at the empty passenger seat.

"Are either of you hurt?"

"I took an elbow to the cheek that's going to leave a nice beauty mark, and my ego's been in better shape. What the fuck was that?"

I shifted in the seat so I could look back at Jin. "Dannie died for you, Miss Red. I'd be a lot more comfortable with our agreement if you would at least give me a quarter of a clue why. And don't give me the line about the Houses again. Now that I've seen it, I know it's more personal than that."

"Whoa, wait..." Amos had his small eyes on Jin. "What do you mean Miss Red. Like, fucking Red, Red?"

Jin's eyes darted between us. I had spilled the secret, but I had only kept it to keep Dannie safe. I didn't give a shit if she had Amos killed somewhere down the line - assuming he survived this thing in the first place.

"If you're Red, why the fuck didn't you rain some kind of armageddon on those assholes? Christ, even a fucking shield or something would have helped."

"Amos-" I tried to shut him up, but I hadn't gotten the impression he was the type to start ranting and go quietly.

"No. Fuck that." He loomed over Jin. She didn't back away. "You have magic like... holy shit I don't even know the type of shit you can do. Then you just sit there and wait for me to save your ass, like I even want to help a dirty fucking elf in the first place..."

"Amos-" I tried again.

"...I was only doing this shit as a favor to Dannie, because she promised I'd get a nice fat credit to my bank account when it was over. She didn't say shit about a drama queen wizard who refused to use her damn magic to help her hired hands. You get your kicks watching us die? You think its exciting Dannie's a fucking corpse right now? What kind of bullshit game are you playing?"

"Amos!" I went into the back and put my hand on his wrist. "One more fucking word, and there will be two corpses in this van."

He shut up, looking down at my boney grey fingers wrapped around him. His face had been red with anger, but now it paled. I glanced over at Jin.

She was crying.

Great.

Nobody spoke. I took a few deep breaths, fighting back against the urge to cough and trying to calm my nerves. It was my best friend that was laying dead on the floor next to me. The person I had spent almost all of my waking life with over the last five years. Why did I have to be the one to hold everything together?

"We need to get out of here, try to find someplace safe to lay low and figure out our next move. The van is shot. Amos, I need you to keep an eye out in case whatever those damn things were show up around here. I'm going to go steal us a new ride."

I put my hands on both of them. "Right now, I don't care who you are, Jin. You want to stay alive, you do what I ask. Amos, close your mouth, and keep it that way. You don't know a damn thing, and you aren't going to learn with your lips constantly moving. She was my best friend. Get it?"

Jin nodded, biting her lip and blinking away the tears. Amos didn't react at all, which I took as acquiescence.

"Stay alert, I'll be right back. In the meantime, put Dannie in the cooler. Evan isn't going to need it anymore."

CHAPTER THIRTY-SEVEN

Here's to yesterday.

IT WASN'T THAT HARD TO find a car in Brooklyn, and hot-wiring and
lock-picking older models was like 'Thievery 101'. I was back at
the van within ten minutes, driving a late 80s model Chevy Impala
- an ugly beast of a car that had been fairly well maintained by its
current owner. I had been fortunate that the rumble of its engine
hadn't gained the attention of the residents living in the apartment
building I stole it from. They were used to late night noises, and at
least a car engine wasn't threatening.

"We aren't going to be able to keep Dannie cold," Amos said,
lifting her up over his shoulder and bringing her to the trunk of the
car. He was much more quiet and agreeable since I'd touched him.
"She's gonna start to smell."

It was only about forty-five degrees outside. "We can get some
ice at a gas station, it'll take a while to melt. We'll need to keep the
heat off in the car."

"Not a problem for me, I got plenty of blubber to keep me warm.
What about our princess?"

Jin was standing on the corner, keeping lookout while we
unloaded the van. She didn't seem cold from here.

"She'll be fine. You already saw she's tougher than she looks."

He licked his lips. "Come on, Baldie. We were knee deep in shit and she didn't lift a finger to help us. We're supposed to be keeping her alive for fuck's sake."

"Are you really as dumb as you sound, or do you just like to act it?Why do you think the head of a House would need anyone to protect them?"

He looked back at her again, and then at me. "You're saying…"

I nodded.

"No shit?"

"No shit."

"Ah, fuck." He pulled his bulk into the van and picked up one of the assault rifles from the ground. He held it to his shoulder and looked through the sight. "At least we got some artillery out of it."

"Three extra clips. What is that, a hundred, hundred-fifty rounds?"

"More or less."

"Amos, I wanted to ask you. How did you know Dannie, anyway?"

He tossed the rifle to me so I could put it in the back seat of the car.

"I knew Dannie from the time she was this high." He put his hand to his knee. "Scrawny little thing, but she always had that spunk. She wasn't afraid of squat." A sad smile. "I was different too, back then. Used to work for Black, directly for Black. Oh, not in the early days when I was young. Started out as a ghost, doing protection. Made a name for myself keeping people safe. Did, I don't know, fifteen, sixteen jobs in a row for Black. Didn't know what I was guarding, didn't care. Nobody got past me. Nobody.

"Didn't even know Black had a kid until she was five. Get a call one day, telling me to look out for her, teach her guns and shit. How to fight. Black's kid and she needs to fight? I do what I'm told, you know?"

"No offense, but Dannie never mentioned you."

He laughed. "She wouldn't. Shit, she was pissed when Black

kicked her out of the house, told her to go figure it out for herself. No magic, no family. That's how it is with Black. Anyway, she didn't want anything to do with the House once she wasn't part of it. Ain't seen her for... I don't know... twelve, thirteen years before she called me. She was desperate. Worried about you." His eyes filled with tears. "Between you and me, I don't give a fuck about the money. I made enough with Black I never have to worry. She was like my kid. Taught her everything I know."

I stared at Amos for longer than I should have. In five years, Danelle had never said a kind word about Black or anyone in the House. She'd barely said a word about her childhood at all. Then I had taken a job from Black. Then I had fucked it up. She had gone to the only person she knew would help her without question, in order to help me.

I thanked her by getting her killed.

"So you can say she was your best friend, Baldie, and I'll give you that. She was the closest thing I ever had to a family." He laughed weakly. "I guess that makes us brothers or something. Or your fucked up uncle. I won't lie. I'm dirty, and disgusting. I ain't got shit for manners, and I fucking hate elves. I hate all the so-called 'new humans'. They say it's the way it's really supposed to be, but I think that's bullshit. That ain't why I went off on the princess, though. Now you know why."

He grabbed the other rifle and tossed it to me. I caught it and dropped it in the car. I had one more thing to do before we could go.

"We'll kill the bastards who caused this." I pointed back towards Jin. "She knows more than she's told me. That's going to change."

He hopped down from the van, his legs somehow supporting his mass. He opened the driver's side door and slipped in behind the wheel. "At least we upgraded our ride."

Maybe he thought it was an upgrade. I'd lost Evan to the kill team. Now I was going to lose Kerry to attrition. I thought about waking her up to say goodbye, but I'd be doing that for me, not for her. Instead, I found the jug of gasoline near the wheel well and started splashing it all over everything.

I opened her cooler and looked down at her. She had been less macabre looking than Evan, with most of her damage on her hand and arms. Mr. Timms was resting at her feet. I couldn't take Danelle and not take her cat. I lifted him from the cooler and held him under my arm.

"Thanks for everything, K. I'm sorry I can't give you a proper burial."

There was a book of matches in the glove compartment. I took it out and lit one, and then threw it in the cooler. Then I left the van behind, putting Timmsie in the trunk and getting into the Impala on the passenger side. Amos eased it up to where Jin was waiting on the corner.

"Care for a ride, Miss Red?"

She smiled, opened the door behind me, and climbed in.

"Where are we going?"

"Right now? Westchester. After that? Well... that depends on you."

CHAPTER THIRTY-EIGHT

Touched.

WE DROVE UP TO WESTCHESTER, stopping at three gas stations to gather enough ice to keep Dannie cold, and enough coffee to keep us warm. We didn't speak much during the trip, and Amos turned on the radio fifteen minutes in so that the silence wouldn't be too awkward. At some point, I fell asleep.

When I woke up, we were driving slowly down a residential street. The radio was off, and Amos was scanning the rows of houses, looking for one that wasn't currently occupied. I held back a cough and checked on Jin. She was laying across the back seat, asleep. The tiniest bit of drool was pooled at the corner of her mouth. It reminded me of Karen.

"How'd you get through the gate?" I asked, keeping my voice low.

"Don't need to be a surgeon to get into a community. Just kept trying all zeros until one of them opened up."

Of course. I winced when a shot of pain jolted from my stomach up through my chest. I put my fingers on my wrist to check my heartbeat. Then I put my hand on my head. I was cold, and slowing down. Symptoms of the treatment beginning to wane. I'd been using too much, too often. At this rate, I'd be lucky to last the week.

"That one looks good." He pointed ahead to a four bedroom colonial with a 'For Sale' sign out in front.

Amos brought the car into the driveway and we got out, carrying two of the rifles but leaving everything else. We went in through the back, keeping the lights off. If anybody woke up and looked outside, they would think somebody had used to the driveway to park while they visited a neighbor. There was no outward sign we were in the house at all, and the gate probably made them feel more secure than they really were.

"What a fucking day," Amos said once we were inside. "Looks like they have this place set up for modeling, so I'm gonna go upstairs and try out the bed."

He didn't wait for a response, or permission. He disappeared through a doorway, and a moment later his heavy footfalls shook the ceiling above us, leaving Jin and me alone in the kitchen. Before, I would have thought he was just being an asshole. Now, I knew he was giving me space to deal with Miss Red.

"Let's talk." I pointed to the living room, where a thick leather couch was waiting.

She sat, I stood. There was just enough light filtering in through the window for me to see her face. She looked tired and defeated. Not like when she had been asking me to be bold.

"Conor, before you say anything… I'm sorry about Danelle. I never wanted this to happen. I hope you believe that."

Her apology was sincere.

It also wasn't good enough.

"Tell me about Tarakona."

Her face blanched at the name, and she started to tremble. "Where did you hear that word?"

"Inside the Machine. A friend of Dannie's dropped it, along with the suggestion to hide in the deepest, darkest hole I could find. Where did *you* hear that word?"

She took a deep breath. I got another sharp pain and bent over to cough. It was a rough one, lasting a minute or so and leaving me winded.

"Are you okay?" she asked, her concern visible, her other fear momentarily forgotten.

"Just answer the question." I took a deep breath and held it. Why did I have to touch the damn goblin? I'd let my anger get the best of me.

"Conor... I..."

"Whatever is happening here, Jin, it's not a straight up power play. I think you already know that. When I look at you, I don't see a cold-hearted bitch who thinks watching ghosts die is fun. What I see is a young woman who's in deep shit and doesn't know how to get out of it. You can either be the person that Amos thinks you are, or you can be the person I think you are. You don't get to be both."

She looked out the window. The light caught her face, and I saw a tear in her eye. "I already told you about my aunt, and the situation she was in. No children, no users to carry on the family name and to maintain the House. Without a wizard at our head we're doomed to be consumed by the others, if not through violence, then by attrition. Either way, House Red falls." She looked at the ground and laughed. "An empath can't pass as a wizard."

"I don't understand."

She licked her lips. "Did you know that Mr. Black and Mrs. Red were having an affair?"

The statement shocked me, but that was the only power it had. "What does that have to do with anything?"

"It has to do with everything. Black knew that our House was in trouble. He helped my aunt find a way to get out of it."

"A way out. The stone?"

"Black spends millions of dollars on historical research and archaeological digs. There is a race among the Houses to find as many of the old artifacts as possible, with the hope that they will discover something to give them an edge. So many of these things... they were inert for thousands of years, longer than most written history. Anyway, his people were at a dig on Moutohora Island, near New Zealand. From what my aunt told me, they found the stone there."

"So they took the stone to Black, and Black gave it to Red?"

"Yes."

"What does this have to do with Tarakona?"

"That first night after they found it, the archaeology team is camped out, with armed guards keeping watch, and a team en route to take the stone and bring it back to Black so he could test its properties. When they get to the site, they find all of the guards and all of the archaeologists dead except for one. He told them that they were attacked by the biggest wolves he had ever seen. He had taken the stone and hidden under a tarp in one of the dig pits. He thought the smell of the dirt disguised his scent enough that they didn't know he was there.

"The team took the archaeologist and the stone off the island. Black gave my aunt the artifact, and told her the story of what had happened. In the beginning, they believed the attack on the camp was random, carried out by a wild pack of dire wolves. Except..."

Her voice trailed off, and she looked towards the front window. I could see the pain dance across her face.

"I lied to you about my parents. They didn't die in a plane crash. They were at home in Japan when they were attacked. When their bodies were discovered... they had been torn apart, the same way the scientists had, and the word 'Tarakona' was written in their blood on the wall next to them."

It was the second time she had surprised me in a less than a minute. That's what she'd been keeping from me. She had known from square one who was after her.

"Why didn't you tell me the truth? Why keep that from me, and send me on a wild goose chase to figure out who was behind your aunt's death? Damn it, Jin, Dannie never had to go in the fucking Machine." She'd still be alive, here with us now.

"Don't you think I know that?" She shook her head. "I didn't know it was Tarakona, not for certain. He isn't House Red's only enemy. I was afraid that it was. That their death was related to my aunt's. That the same person killed them, and Natsumi. But I don't know who he is, Conor. I don't know what he wants."

For whatever reason, Tarakona wanted the stone, and he organized this whole thing in order to claim it. He even used Black's money to pay for the fake job, which I doubted was a coincidence. I could only assume he'd done it to throw it in Black's face.

"I don't know who he is either, but I know what he wants. The stone, and you. He has the stone. Why does he want you?"

"I don't know."

I looked at her, searching for any hint of deception. "Are you sure?"

"Conor, I don't know. What I can tell you is that my aunt never had armed guards in her home before my parents were killed. She was a powerful wizard on her own, she didn't need them. Then they died, and she changed. She began to worry about the safety of the people around her, the people she cared about, as though she had no way to protect any of us. It's the same reason I had a panic room in my closet. She was always afraid they would come for Natsumi and me. I don't think she ever expected that he would get to her directly."

He had gotten to her through the guards, who had only been hired because of her fear. She had known them, and trusted them enough to let her guard down. Whoever Tarakona was, he was playing the long game to perfection.

Or at least he had been, until I had made the mistake of getting involved.

"Dannie's contact in the Machine, he called Tarakona 'the

future'. It didn't make any sense to me, until those things attacked us. There's plenty of mythology that says werewolves can change forms, but I've never heard of it actually happening before."

"You think he created them somehow?"

"Could he? I don't know, but he does have some measure of control over ferals, and those things took a dozen bullets and didn't even flinch. I don't think he's a full-frequency wizard, but he has some kind of power. In any case, knowing that this Tarakona is behind your aunt's death only gets us so far. There are still a lot of questions we need answered. How did he even know about you in the first place? How does he have enough clout to get a Machine admin to help him? Where the hell can I find him so I can shake his hand?" I sat down on the couch next to her. "As far as I'm concerned, he killed Dannie, just as surely as if he'd pulled the trigger himself. I don't give a fuck who he is. You want bold? I can do better than that."

"How? We don't even know where to find him."

"No. I think I know someone who does." I wasn't sure if I would be able to get in touch with him, but I was going to try.

I was going to suggest getting some rest, until my stomach convulsed and I turned away from her, leaning over and casting bile all over the floor. I clutched at my chest as I heaved, coughing and vomiting until my mouth began dripping blood all over the new carpet.

"Conor?" I felt her hand on my back. She started rubbing it.

"I'll be all right. It's been a tough couple of days. I just need to get some rest, and it'll pass. It's all part of the pleasure of being me."

I coughed a few more times.

"You're going to get worse before you ever get better. I know how necromancers are made."

There was nothing I could do about it. "Unless you happen to have my meds in your pocket, there's no way to avoid it. This so-called life doesn't come cheap or easy."

My head was aimed at the floor, my eyes on the disgusting mess of phlegm and blood I had left there. I felt her shift behind me, and then she took my hand. She put something in it.

"Did you know that Parity Limited makes anti-cancer medication?"

I looked in my hand. A vial. I held it up so I could see through the bottom. Two round balls sat there. "Is this?"

"Yes. I'm sorry I could only get you two."

I shifted so I could see her face. "How?"

"While you were sleeping. I went to our hospital in the Greens. I have access. It was easy enough to grab a lab coat and convince the techs I worked there, especially since I was in a restricted area. I questioned them about the treatments. They're banned, you know. They didn't pass field trials. Ninety-five percent of the people who took them turned."

"Turned? Into what?"

"You don't want to know. You aren't in the ninety-five percent."

Shit. Did Dannie know what a risk she had taken to introduce me to the drugs? Had Dalton? Why the hell didn't anyone tell me? At least now I knew why I had to pay up front.

"They had a few hundred before a break-in last month. This was all they had left. Two capsules dropped on the floor."

"A break-in? More like an inside job, maybe a ghost hit. These things go for thousands on the market, even if they might be killing most of the people who buy them. How did you get them to give them to you?"

"I'm Miss Red."

"You told them?"

"No. I put my access codes into the terminal to sign them out."

My eyes went back to the meds. They would keep me alive, but at what cost? There was no way to know if the hospital network had been secure. "What happened to not trusting anybody?"

"I know. I had to. I couldn't let you die. You saved my life, and no matter what that racist asshole thinks, I don't like seeing anyone die."

I started coughing again. Now she was going to save my life.

"I know he's a bigot, and he doesn't know when to shut his mouth, but try to cut him a little slack. He told me he knew Dannie since she was a kid. He feels like he lost his daughter."

She bit down on her lip. "I didn't know."

"I know." I put my free hand on hers. "Now you do."

Our eyes met, and we sat like that for a dozen heartbeats. The moment was interrupted by another round of hacking. I held the vial up again. This was as good a time as any.

"Did they give you an injector, too?"

"Yes. I put it in Danelle's bag."

"Can you go and get it? Unless you want me to ask Amos to do it?"

"I'll do it. Take off your shirt." She got up and disappeared, going back outside to the car and retrieving the injector.

I tried to act confident while I took off the trench and my shirt. The aim had to be perfect, or either the treatment wouldn't last, or I would die. It had taken me multiple visits to fully trust Dalton with the procedure, and he knew what he was doing.

Jin came back with the gun in a black plastic box.

"It needs compressed air."

"It's already loaded." She took it out and opened the back to show me. "I had them show me how it all worked. I told them I was following up on an alternate treatment path that was based on the initial research. They were exited about the chance to revisit the work."

I was impressed. It was a tight lie.

"We don't have anything to stitch it with when we're done," Jin said.

"We'll have to cauterize. Go wash your hands as best you can."

She took off her jacket and padded down a hallway to where I assumed the bathroom was. She was gone for a good five minutes, doing as thorough a cleaning job as possible. She brought a few damp hand towels back with her.

"For the blood."

She took up a position on her knees at my side, while I shifted so I was laying across the couch, my wound exposed.

She picked up the vial and uncapped it, and dumped one of the balls into her hand. She opened the door of the injector and stuck it in.

"Are you ready, Conor?"

I felt my stomach clench. I would never be ready. I nodded and closed my eyes. She put the needle up to the wound.

"How far does it need to go?"

"Far enough, but not too far."

She pressed down, sinking the needle into my skin. My hands gripped the cushions, and I stifled every desire to scream. Once the needle was buried, she put her finger to the trigger.

"Hold on." I tried to remember the angle of the gun. It was different from this position, looking down on it like this. I reached up and took her hand in mind, shifting her target ever so slightly. She looked up at me, our eyes meeting.

"What if we do it wrong?"

"I'll die. Let's not do it wrong." I kept my hand on hers and took a deep breath. "Pull the trigger."

She did. The capsule fired into me, and I held my breath, waiting to feel more than the normal pain. When a minute passed and I was still alive, I squeezed her hand on top of the injector.

"Nothing to worry about."

"How do we close it?"

I looked down. Blood was running out through the wide hole the needle had made. I reached down, grabbed one of the towels, and put pressure on the wound.

"There's a knife in my boot. Take it out and bring it to the kitchen. Heat up the tip on the stove."

She nodded, found the shiv I had taken from Amos, and carried it away. The seconds passed as hours, my stomach beginning to throb and my head starting to spin. Maybe the aim had been off after all.

I gritted through and thought of Danelle, of the last time I had seen her in the Machine. The anger carried me along.

Jin ran back with the knife, the tip a soft red from the heat. I pulled the towel away. "Put it against the incision."

She dropped to her knees and pressed it against my flesh. It hurt more than anything I'd ever experienced. It was searing agony, and for the first time made me question if being alive was worth it.

Then I remembered what Rayon had said.

Jin took the knife away and used the other towel to wipe away the remaining blood, doing her best to clean it from my stomach and from the couch. I just laid there, trying to fight through the pain. I turned my thoughts to Tarakona, and Veronica's brother, whoever the hell he was.

I'd never had an extra dose before. It meant I could do whatever the fuck I wanted to those two. It helped me through the pain.

"Conor?" Jin took my hand in hers and brought it to her lips, kissing it gently. "Conor?"

I didn't realize I looked dead. "I'm still here."

I opened my eyes. She had moved up so she was kneeling next to my head. She stroked my bald scalp with her free hand. I gave her a weak smile and closed my eyes again. Her hand in mine, the touch on my skull, it was a simple comfort I didn't realize I missed until I had it again.

Exhaustion took me.

CHAPTER THIRTY-NINE

Mission impossible.

FOUR YEARS EARLIER...

"ARE YOU ready?"

We were standing outside the Four Seasons Hotel in Chicago, in the back near the loading docks. We were pressed tight against the stone wall, covered in shadows, dressed in blacks.

I took a deep breath, trying to calm the rapid beating of my heart, and come to grips with what I was doing, and why I was doing it.

Danelle held my wrist in her hand and looked me in the eye. "Remember, get in, get out, don't get caught."

I nodded. Dannie looked totally different worked up for a job. Skintight black leggings and a long lycra turtleneck that covered ninety-percent of her body in darkness. Thin, tight, microfiber black gloves and a skull cap that held her hair close to her head did the other five that wasn't exposed. She also had on a black nylon jacket with her holstered guns underneath, and tall, soft-soled boots with a couple of painted knives hiding inside. Don't get caught. If she did, she'd spend the rest of her life in prison.

I was looking a little more casual. A black suit with a black shirt and black tie. I needed to be able to fit in, to be able to be seen. I was wearing a wig of curly black hair to cover my recent baldness. I wasn't carrying any weapons.

"Let's go."

She squeezed my arm and I followed her at a run, along the wall to the back door near the dock. The security guard that had just been standing near it had ducked inside to take a piss or something - the queue we had been waiting for.

She didn't even try to open the door. There was a small black pad next to it that required an RF key. Instead, I pulled a plain grey card with a small digital readout from my pocket, and put it up next to the reader. I didn't know how the thing worked, and didn't care. It took three seconds for it to decode the guard's signal and echo it back, unlocking the door. I had to fight myself not to look up the whole time. There was a camera hanging right above the door, aimed down on us. If Dannie's timing had been even a little off... we were done.

I trusted her. After that first night, I'd decided I wasn't quite so ready to die. She'd given me a couple of days to cry and rant and talk it out, and then she'd told me about her friend Dalton, and the treatments he could offer. She named the price, told me what I'd have to do to earn that kind of money that fast, and a year's worth of training later - here we were.

She was holding a separate device up to the camera, and she kept it there as I pulled the door open and slipped inside, then reached back and tapped her hand. She swung herself through and pocketed the device again. If anyone had been watching the feed, they would have only seen two frames of blur, and nothing else out of the ordinary.

The guard was still in the can, and the rest of the workers were done for the night. The only thing we had to worry about were cameras, and they rotated on set schedules, leaving small blind spots at timed intervals. Dannie and I kept pace with them and each other, ducking out of the way as the lenses tracked past, and getting to the service elevator before Mr. Security finished his nightly crap.

It wasn't like we had just walked up to the hotel. Two months of planning had gone into the job for House Blue. We'd paid a guy to hack into the cameras and watch the guard. We'd paid a guy for the little devices that had gotten us in. We'd paid a guy for full schematics to the thirty-second floor. The cost of doing business, according to Danelle. We'd lost half our take before we'd even started.

What we lost in profit, we gained in safety. The information reduced our risk of getting caught, and as far as Dannie was concerned this work was as easy as it came. Perfect to get me started on the life of a ghost. It also paid better because it was a two man job.

We reached the thirty-second floor in silence. Just before the doors opened, Dannie leaned up and kissed me on the cheek. "Good luck."

I nodded, ducking out when the doors moved aside and stepping out into the hallway. Most people were asleep by now.

Danelle didn't join me. She took the freight up to the roof. Two person job. Her part was separate from mine. I felt a pang of concern for her, mixed with a measure of excitement. I was on my own.

I walked down the hallway, unconcerned about being seen. My part was the easy part. As I approached room 3270, I reached into my pocket and found a small scalpel and a pair of glasses. I put the glasses on and palmed the scalpel, also removing my cell from another pocket and looking down at it, like I had received an important message that required me to stand there and stare at it. I shifted the scalpel in my grip at the same time I glanced through the specs towards the door.

Upscale hotel room security meant a magnetically locked deadbolt and either a card or fingerprint based access mechanism.

The whole thing ran on electricity, with a battery-powered failover buried inside the wall. It was unbeatable against conventional attacks; the doors couldn't be brute-forced without a battering ram, and if the fingerprint security had been used only the finger or a remote signal from security could open it up. The downside was that it was all electronic. And while the wall offered enough shielding that a hand-held E.M.P. couldn't bring it down, it still required delivery from one power source or another.

In other words, wires.

Wires could be cut.

The glasses were black market, finely-tuned for infrared, and they could pick up even the small amount of voltage that was moving to the lock, giving me a clear path of the electrical signals. The wires were bundled tight, and hitting the wrong one would put the whole thing on lockdown and send an alarm signal back to base. This would have been a tough job for a lot of people, but I had a lot of practice cutting tiny wires from a packed group. It wasn't much different than repairing muscle and nerves.

I had to pause for a minute and stay on the phone, as a couple came wandering past. They were in their fifties, dressed for an evening at the theatre or a fancy restaurant. They hung all over one another, laughing loudly and making drunk asses of themselves. They probably didn't even notice me standing there.

Once they were gone, I put the phone away, turned, and powered up the laser scalpel. It dug into the wall without issue, through the E.M.P. shielding to the wires behind. It took only a couple of minute flicks of the wrist to sever each of the connecting wires. There was no sound to indicate the door was open, but when I took the handle and gently pushed, it moved without a fight.

I slipped inside and eased it back closed. My heart was racing and my body coursing with adrenaline in an even mix of fear and excitement. I looked around with the glasses still on, checking for bodies inside the blackness of the room. It was supposed to be empty, but there was someone in the bed. Shit.

I stood motionless, waiting to see if they would cry out, ask who was there, invite me to join them, or anything else to indicate they were awake. I heard a soft gurgle, followed by another. Sleeping.

My part of the job was to steal a necklace, a blue diamond. I didn't know what was important about it, and didn't care. All I knew was that House Blue wanted it, and they had offered to pay Miss Daaé and an accomplice quite well to retrieve it and take care of the thief. The diamond was in the room somewhere.

The thief was on the roof.

We'd known he would be there, because Blue knew who he was. Not another House, but a former employee who thought he would be safe outside the reach of the magical fields. A man who knew enough to be stupid, but not enough to keep himself alive. He'd be on the phone, trying to make deals. He'd gotten himself a raw one.

He was Danelle's problem.

I gave my eyes a minute to adjust to the dim light that was filtering in past the heavy drapes, and then crept slowly towards the bed. It would have made sense that the diamond would be in the safe, but I discounted that as soon as I had been able to see the person on the bed.

A woman. Young, naked. The clothes laying next to the bed suggested a prostitute.

The diamond was hanging from her neck.

He had probably bought her so he could bring her up and do her with the rock around her neck… a double-fuck, you could call it. I needed to get it away from her, without her raising a fuss. The easy part had gotten a little more complicated.

I stood right next to her, considering. My eyes wandered to the nightstand, where a half-empty bottle of Jack Daniels was resting. Drunk? Maybe it wouldn't be so bad.

I didn't just lean over her to undo the clasp. Instead, I shrugged off the suit jacket and went around to the other side of the bed. I laid down next to her and waited for her to move.

She didn't.

I turned on my side and draped my arm over her, putting my hand on her breast and again waiting for a reaction.

Nothing.

I put my face against the back of her head, and nuzzled her neck. She gasped and squirmed slightly, but she didn't cry out in fear or say anything, and a moment later the light snoring resumed.

Satisfied, I took my hands off her and ran them down her neck until I found the clasp for the necklace. I opened it without a problem, and then carefully extracted it from her. I half-expected her to wake up once the weight of the diamond was off her chest, but she just shifted slightly and continued sleeping off the Jack. I let myself smile as I got away from the bed, grabbed my jacket, and pocketed the rock.

She was still asleep when I closed the door and walked calmly to the main hotel elevator. You didn't need a card or a print to get down, only to go up.

I met Danelle half an hour later. She opened the rear door of the van and hopped in, closing it and sighing. "I hope you had an easier time than I did."

I was sitting in the passenger seat, and I turned to look at her. She wasn't injured, but she had blood on her cheek and stains on her arm.

"What happened?"

"They didn't tell me the asshole knew how to fight. He turned on me when I put the knife to his throat, managed to knock me back. I had to stab him in the neck, and he bled all over me. A fucking mess."

"You killed him?" I hadn't killed anyone yet. I knew one day I would have to, but I wasn't looking forward to it. It was enough of an adjustment just to hear Dannie talk about it so casually.

"Yeah. Did you get the rock?"

I held it up so that it caught some of the light from the street. "Piece of cake. He left it on a whore, and the whore drunk on his bed."

She laughed. "Grab my phone from the dash, will you? Let's call this in."

The phone was the only thing in the glove compartment. I passed it back, and she dialed the number. I heard a slight click. It was the only indication anyone had picked up.

"Done deal," she said. A deep voice mumbled something. "Got it." She hung up. "He said we can toss the diamond, it's a fake."

"What?"

"Don't look at me like that, I didn't know."

I took the blue diamond and brought it really close to my face. "I risked my life for a fake?"

She came forward to the driver seat. A set of keys appeared in her hand, and she got us moving. "Get used to shit that doesn't make any sense. That's how the Houses work. Teaching someone a lesson for stealing a fake diamond is worth it to them, even if that means a ghost gets screwed. We got our money, which means your treatment is paid for next month. Better yet, you aren't a virgin anymore. Welcome to the profession." She turned her head and smiled at me. "It's time to celebrate."

We went back to our place so she could shower and change, and then we headed out, spending the next three hours in a dive downtown. It was the kind of place that only the most brazen or stupid would hang out at into the early morning. The kind of place where I had been jumped almost a year ago to the day. I almost wished I could find those assholes, to give them a little taste of what I'd learned in the months that had followed. Firearms training, martial arts, and magic. Fucking death magic. Necromancy. It scared the shit out of me, and I pissed myself the first time I brought a dead thing back to life, but damn I wanted to see their faces when I touched one of them, drained the life from the body, and brought them back under my control. I wanted to see them piss themselves.

I explained all that to Dannie on the ride home, stammering and slurring every word of it in a drunken daze of excitement. I felt more alive than I had since before the biopsy. I felt like I was in control, that my future was my own, and that I could do right by Karen and Molly by earning enough to provide something for them.

By the time Dannie opened the door to our small house, all of the drink and the excitement and the adrenaline had gotten to me. She was half holding me up, drunk enough herself, and leading me to my bedroom across from hers. When we got there, I started thanking her for everything she'd done for me, and telling her how she'd saved my life. I cried while I told her how I would have died without her, and how I loved her for being there for me. Even more, I was aroused for the first time in months, despite the drink. So I kissed her. Then she kissed me back. Our hands found parts of each other above our clothes, and then our hands found each other's clothes to remove them, and an indelible and unfortunate memory was made.

CHAPTER FORTY

Chowdah.

"You don't get it, do you, Baldie? There is no fucking way in hell that is going to happen."

"Come on, Amos. This is for Dannie."

Amos wiped his brow. "You're making me regret I told you anything about it."

It was nine o'clock, the morning after. I'd only gotten about three hours of sleep after Jin had helped me with the meds, and had woken up with her head resting on my chest, and her breath tickling my skin. I'd sat and stared at the wilting chunks of black and purple hair before gently shaking her awake. There was something about her that was scaring me, and moving into a dangerous place in my mind.

The good news was that I felt a lot better.

A cold shower and a change of clothes from my shitty suitcase had refreshed my spirits, and helped me focus on moving forward, not looking back.

"He's the only one who might know who this Tarakona asshole is." It was the third or fourth time we had circled back around in the argument. Each time, the fight got a little more intense. "What the fuck are you so afraid of?"

We had traded the stolen Impala for another rental car, courtesy of Amos. It was a big Cadillac, the newest, fanciest model that could be rented, the car of the fat ghost's dreams. He had picked it up while we were asleep, somehow getting his bulk down the stairs and out the door without making a sound. He'd explained the math that had allowed him to do the switch alone when we had gotten underway, leaving the gated community and heading north. It was impressive.

Now we were standing behind the car, in a parking lot across from a Walmart. The weather was still shit, leaving us cast in a gloomy gray.

"You think because I worked for Mr. Black, that means I shouldn't be afraid of him? Just the fucking opposite. Eighteen years, I never met him face to face. Talked to him on the phone twice. Got my orders from his negotiator sometimes, but most times from fixers."

"He trusted you with Dannie. That has to count for something."

"Means he'd kill me quick instead of slow… maybe. I want to get even for Dannie too, but pulling Black into this shit, that's a bad idea."

Jin put her hand on my better shoulder. "Just forget it, Baron. We'll find another way."

I couldn't believe it. The man who had grabbed a werewolf by the head and shoved a gun into its throat was afraid to make a phone call? I reached over and unlatched the trunk, swinging it open and pushing the remaining ice from Dannie's face.

"Look at her."

Amos looked at me.

"Fucking look at her, Amos. Tell Dannie you're too afraid to call in some favors and find out where Black is. Tell her that its better that you die, and that I die, and that the guy who's recruiting ferals to his cause gets what he wants. Forget about House Red, and just think about that. Tell her you could have done something to stop it, but you were too much of a baby."

263

His eyes moved reluctantly to her face, pale and peaceful, save for the hole in her forehead. "Fuck you, Conor. You don't know you can stop him. He's got at least three of those monsters, and you have what? The corpse of a woman with no legs?"

"And a pair of balls, which is more than you've got right now. We're going to die anyway if we do nothing, we might as well double-down."

He slammed the trunk closed, the anger fading from his face. "I never should have answered the phone. I'll be right back. I'm gonna go get more ice."

"He'll do it," Jin said while he walked away. "But he isn't going to be happy about it."

"I don't give a shit if he's happy. I need to talk to Black, get his side of the story. If what you said about Black and Red is true, there's no way Tarakona hits her and he's twiddling his thumbs on the sidelines."

Of course, that didn't mean he hadn't helped him do it. Jin didn't know what the status of their relationship was at the time of her aunt's death. Mrs. Red had insisted that Black wasn't responsible, which led me to believe it couldn't have been that bad.

"You can't be sure he'll help us."

"No, but I don't think anyone else will."

Amos came back fifteen minutes later, cradling two huge bags of ice in his arms. I opened the trunk for him and he put them in, making sure not to look at Danelle when he did.

"I know a guy, fixer calls himself Larry. Works for Black. Lives in Boston." He swung the trunk closed and walked around to the driver's side without making eye contact.

We joined him in the car. Jin sat in the back with one of the rifles across her lap, while I took shotgun with another between my legs. None of us felt safe, even in the rented car. It was doubtful they knew who Amos was. It wasn't impossible.

"You think he'll hook you up with Black?" I asked.

"No fucking way. Not without a little persuasion."

We pulled out of the lot. It was a three hour drive to Boston from here, back on I-95. Back past Connecticut.

"What kind of persuasion are we talking about? Money?"

Amos looked over at me. "Pain."

We drove in silence for five or six minutes, and then Amos started yapping about all sorts of nothing. The trees on the side of the road, the drivers around him who did all sorts of stupid things and were generally complete incompetent assholes, the storefronts and the kind of people that went to each kind of business. What was a front, what wasn't a front, and finally just general, racist laden overviews of the different towns we blew past once we were on I-95.

More than once I was tempted to shut him up, and I kept glancing back at Jin to see how she was reacting to his bullshit. She was unaffected. Now that she knew why he was so pissed, she took all of his venom in stride, letting him spew it and work off his emotions in his own way.

Maybe there was something to be said for a House without a wizard at its head. When you couldn't depend on nuclear magic to bring people in line, you needed to be a bit more understanding and diplomatic, a better mix of strong and vulnerable, commanding and open.

I couldn't help but wonder if it was intentional. She'd been trained to take over a House. Was she authentic, or was all of her outward personality an act, a masterful performance intended to perfectly manipulate? I wish I could say I knew.

If it was an act, was I falling for it?

Was I falling for her?

Shit.

CHAPTER FORTY-ONE

Six of one, a half-dozen...

WE MADE IT TO BOSTON without trouble, riding through the city around one in the afternoon. The clouds had given way to an hour of sun, and then fought back against the brightness and carried out their revenge with intermittent downpours and a stiff wind. It was nasty weather.

A good day for nasty business.

Amos made it clear that the fixer wouldn't be cooperative. He also made it clear he was pretty sure Black was going to kill him for what he was about to do. He questioned his own sanity a few times, and went through with it anyway.

"Larry lives up there," he said, pointing up from the windshield of the Caddy to the top of an older apartment building. "Eighth floor walkup. Eight fucking flights of stairs. Pain in the ass, always going so high. My knees can't take much more of this shit."

"How do you know he's up there?"

"He's a fixer. Usually works at night. Means he'll be home catching some z's."

He pulled the car into a spot a few blocks away. We grabbed whatever we could conceal, and put the rest in the trunk. Then he went over the plan while we walked back to the building.

"Walk around to the alley and wait there. He'll come out his window, try to get away from me down the fire escape. Stay hidden, jump him when he gets to the ground floor." He held his arms out wide. "Or I could just off him, and you could suck him back and make him make the call?"

I shook my head. "It'll take too much time and energy. The best corpses are at least a week old."

"Suit yourself. Like I said, he'll come down. You grab him. Watch your ass though, asshole's an illusionist."

"How am I going to know it's really him coming down the fire escape?"

"Shoot him in the leg or something. If it bleeds, it's him."

We went to the front of the building. Amos vanished inside. Jin and I moved to the alley, and waited together behind a trash bin.

"I've been spending too much time crouched behind these things the last couple of days."

Jin laughed. "I would think ghosts spend a lot of time in dark alleys."

"Not really. Thugs and ferals hang out in alleys. Ghosts plan, prepare."

"Then I would say that what we're about to do is more like being a thug."

"Then I would agree. I guess the setting is apropos."

"How is your stomach?"

I shifted my hand and touched the wound beneath the shirt. It was still tender as anything, but as long as it didn't get infected I would survive. I still couldn't be sure if the shot had been good. I wouldn't know that until it wore off.

"As good as I could hope for."

She put her hand on mine. "I'm glad I could help."

I didn't react. I didn't say anything. I kept my eyes on the fire escape.

The window exploded outward in a rain of glass.

It was followed by a thin guy in a black bathrobe and slippers, who swung out and onto the fire escape.

"There's our guy." Jin started to stand. I put my hand on her shoulder.

"Hang on, let him get a little closer."

He looked back while he descended the iron steps, not making a sound in the soft slippers. He was halfway down when Amos' head appeared in the window.

"That ain't him. Fucker got past me, get around front."

The guy on the escape didn't react to Amos' voice. Shit. I stood and started for the front of the building.

"Wait. What if Amos was the illusion?"

"If he was, then where the hell is the real Amos?"

Jin raised her rifle and stepped out from cover. She sighted and fired, a single shot that passed through the illusion's leg.

"What if you had been wrong?"

"Then he would have been easier to catch."

I couldn't help but laugh at that, at the same time I sprinted for the front, with Jin right behind. We turned the corner at the same time Amos rumbled through the entrance.

"Amos?" Jin asked.

The ghost raised his gun.

"Not Amos." I tackled Jin, knocking her into the street behind a parked car. Two shots pinged off the sheet metal.

It was the middle of the day, and a firefight was going to draw all the wrong kind of attention. I peeked up over the corner of the car in time to see Amos vanish, replaced by the guy in the bathrobe.

A horn sounded, and I saw the grill of an eighteen wheeler bearing down on our hiding spot.

My heart skipped a beat, and I grabbed Jin's arm before my brain caught up to my eyes and told me it wasn't real. The illusion vanished right as it should have hit me. It did what it was supposed to, distracting us while our target ran away.

The real Amos almost fell onto the sidewalk when he pushed through the front doors. His face was red and covered in sweat, and he bent at the knees to try to catch his breath.

"Come on," I said to Jin, running over to him. "What the fuck, Amos? You said fire escape."

"Son of a bitch. Knew I was coming or some shit. Had an illusion already waiting when I busted in his door. Slipped right out behind me, the little shit."

I looked down the street. "Amos, he went that way. Why don't you go after him? Jin, stay here."

"What do I look like, Usain Bolt? Where the fuck are you going?"

Back down the alley.

He was dropping from the fire escape when I came back around the corner.

"Hey, Larry."

I startled him. He turned and looked at me, his eyes wide. He split into half a dozen Larrys.

"Who the hell are you?" they all asked. "What do you want from me? Do you know who I work for?"

He was tall and thin, with a ring of grey hair around a bald scalp. He had a sharp nose and wire-rimmed glasses. He looked like an insurance salesman or an accountant. Not a fixer.

"I know who you work for." I reached up and lowered my hood, so he could see my bald head and ravaged skin. It was enough to tell him what he was dealing with.

"A necro?" He stared at me. I heard a squeak, and the dumpster started rolling towards me.

"I'm dying, not an idiot." The illusion passed through. "I'm not going to hurt you."

He laughed. "I'm not an idiot either. Necros don't drop by for tea and crumpets." He started running towards me, the six Larrys doubling to twelve. They all mixed together.

I could only stop one.

A line of bullets tore up the cement between him and me. I glanced up to where Jin was standing on the fire escape, outside Larry's apartment.

"My associate suggests you stay there."

The doppelgängers vanished.

"Fine. What kind of tea do you like?"

I brought Larry back into the building through the front. Amos was waiting there, and he laughed when he saw the fixer.

"Think you're slick? Make me fucking run like that."

"What was I supposed to do? Fixers go to ghosts, ghosts don't come to fixers. Mr. Black is going to have your ass for this."

"Ah, stow it, Larry. We ain't gonna hurt you, although if it can get us Black's attention, we might reconsider."

We went into the apartment building and started up the stairs. It didn't take long for Amos to fall behind, the chase having taken away what little stamina he had. I met Jin at the entrance to Larry's place.

"Thanks for the cover."

The fixer's apartment was a model of minimalism. The living area sported only a folding aluminum table, a matching chair, and a laptop trailing a plug to a wall that hadn't been painted in at least thirty years. There was no television, no couch, not even any lamps.

"Nice place," I said.

"I'm only here to sleep and organize jobs. What do I need a bunch of sentimental garbage for?"

I thought my life was sad. At least I missed my sentimental garbage. Molly's teddy bear, my Tesla...

"Jesus Christ, are you kidding me?" Amos burst into the room, his eyes scanning the landscape. "Would it kill you to at least get a couch?"

Larry shook his head. "Look, I don't know what you guys think you're going to accomplish by jumping me. I'm just a fixer. You want Black, you need to talk to his negotiator."

"We're talking to you," Amos said. "I know you have Pelfrey's number."

"That was fifteen years ago. Pelfrey isn't in charge anymore. He got killed during a deal."

"No shit? Who's in charge now?"

"Adams."

Amos slapped his hand to his forehead. "Fucking Adams? Are you shitting me?"

"No joke. Mr. Black was impressed with the way he handled that business with Gold. You remember that?"

"Yeah, I remember."

"There you go. I can't call Adams, Amos. I just can't. He isn't Pelfrey. He'll kill me if I contact him without being asked. Literally kill me."

Amos nodded. "Jin, may I please borrow that for a moment?" He reached out for the assault rifle. Jin handed it to him.

The shot grazed Larry's calf, and sunk into the floor behind him. "I'll kill you if you don't, you little shit. Who the fuck do you think you're talking to here?"

Larry didn't react to the wound, he just raised his head, defiant. He was probably scared, but he was also a fixer. He was used to dealing with tough guys. "I know who I'm talking to. I know you Amos. Geez, you know where I live, I know you so well. And you know me well enough to know that nothing you do to me can be worse than what Adams can do. Have you ever been water boarded by an aquamancer?"

Amos shouldered the rifle and started aiming. "Next shot goes through your balls."

Larry didn't respond. He just stood there and waited.

"I told you what it would take," Amos said, lowering the rifle and looking at me. "It's your turn."

I didn't want to touch him. I wasn't sure the meds had taken well, and the idea of winding up drained again and needing the second capsule wasn't pleasant. Even so, I approached Larry and put my hand on his wrist.

"Don't make me do this."

He looked down. "Even that can't be as bad as some of the shit I've heard that Adams has done. Why Black picked him... I have no idea."

I could hear the fields in the background, the pulsing and chirping. I looked into Larry's eyes, and started to draw the power. "You're sure you won't reconsider?"

He shook his head.

I took a deep breath and blew it out. I really didn't want to do it. "I don't suppose the name 'Tarakona' means anything to you?"

Larry kept staring at me. Then he glanced over at Amos. "Let go of my wrist."

Had that actually worked?

"Don't even think about trying anything," Amos said, bringing the rifle back up.

I let go of his wrist.

He put his hands up, and then slowly reached under his bathrobe, to the chest pocket of his silk pajamas. He pulled out his cell, tapped the screen a few times, and put it up to his face.

"Hey Adams, it's Larry... Yeah, yeah, I know, I know. What, do you think I have a death wish? I can explain. If you give me a second... Thanks. You remember what you told me... I think it was, what, three years ago now? Something like that... No, not that. No, no, no. Tarakona."

Everything around us paused. It was as if the name had stolen all of existence from the room.

Larry's eyebrows went up.

"Yeah, that's what I said. Tarakona... Okay."

He lowered the phone and breathed out, his relief obvious. "He's going to call back."

One second, I was standing in the sparse apartment with Larry, Jin, and Amos.

The next, I was somewhere else, standing face to face with a stoic Native American man. I didn't need to ask who he was.

Mr. Black.

CHAPTER FORTY-TWO

As for getting even.

HE WAS TALL, WITH BLACK hair that fell to his shoulders, a strong jaw and a solid build. He had a wide mouth and a proud nose, his eyes sunken in so that he looked like a raptor, staring down at a distasteful meal.

I was feeling a little dizzy, having just been carried to somewhere else on the wings of some insane magic. He seemed to expect it, and he stood still and silent while I caught my breath and got my bearings.

I assumed I was in a house. The floor was a pink marble, the walls papered in silks and mostly hidden by huge, gold-framed artwork. Two stone columns rose up behind Black, and between them rested a block of stone. It was a statue. A half-carved statue. The left side was still uneven rock. The right side was carved into faces and torsos of Native American men and women. At the top was a depiction of Black, sitting on a horse and looking down at the rest.

"My family."

It was the first thing he said to me. I scanned all of the faces. Of course, Dannie's wasn't there.

"Mr. Black, I…"

I wasn't sure what to do, or say. The way he had plucked me

from Boston and brought me here... he could kill me whenever and however he wanted to. I think he could do whatever the hell he wanted with anybody. I was suddenly glad there were other wizards around, other Houses, to keep power like this in check.

"Conor."

He knew my name. Shit.

"You know who I am?"

He smiled. It was a massive smile, and in a moment his appearance went from evil overlord to wise grandfather. "I know more than you're likely comfortable with. You know why I brought you here?"

I nodded. "Tarakona."

"Yes."

"Do you know him?"

"No. I know of him. I know what he has done. To Mei, and her family. To Danelle."

How did he know about Dannie?

"She was family, once. I could always feel her, the part of her that came from me. I didn't expect that feeling to vanish so soon."

"Neither did I."

We looked at one another in an awkward silence, leaving me feeling like an ant sitting below a massive boot. Then he reached out and put his hand on my shoulder. It took everything in me to not flinch.

"Walk with me, Conor."

He turned me around, away from the statue, leading me through a pair of large doors in the back of the room. I noticed the sounds of the fields then, so strong it was as though we were standing below a waterfall. Black's hand guided me forward. Through the doors into a large hallway. Unlike Red's house, there was nobody else here.

"Danelle always hated me for sending her away."

He paused, waiting for me to say something. What was I

supposed to say?

"Yes."

I saw his eyes glance over at me for just a moment. Was he testing me, to see how I would react? Did he expect me to make up an excuse for her? Or to lie to him if I thought it would incur his wrath? He could crush me for any little thing. It was safer to be honest.

"She was right to. I never wanted to remove her from the House. I always hoped that when she was older, she would come to understand why I did it. Do you?"

"No."

"Being a wizard isn't a gift, is it?"

I looked down at the floor. I had never thought about it. "I don't know. The magic keeps me alive."

"It does, doesn't it? At what cost? What is the price?"

I remembered what I had said to Jin, about being someone I never thought I would be. Was that because of the magic, or because of who I was? Were those things exclusive to one another?

"I can tell that it has been more than you expected. Now think about it from my point of view. For whatever reason, when the reversal occurred I was given an ability to do miraculous things. In the beginning, I saw so much potential in that ability. So much freedom. So many things that I could accomplish. I thought I could change the world."

"The Houses did change the world. You settled the riots, the wars..."

"For every inch of power I gained, I lost an equal amount of freedom. All of us did. Yes, we tried to save lives, we tried to help people adjust, and in many ways we succeeded. While we were doing it, we imprisoned ourselves. We took on a responsibility for the world, without understanding the true breadth of that responsibility. In time we changed, some in ways that made us better. Some in ways that made us worse."

We reached a fork in the corridor, and he directed me to the left.

"In the end, we all want the same thing. It just holds a different meaning for each of us."

"Freedom?"

"Yes."

"I don't follow how this relates to Dannie?"

"She was supposed to be my freedom. I poured millions of dollars into research on how our biology affects our ability to use the fields. After Danelle's mother conceived, the fertilized egg was removed, and all of that research was put to the test. When she was born, I expected that I would be able to give the House over to her. She would be raised into the role, and she would never feel the same desire for freedom, because she would have never had the taste of it."

"Sounds selfish." It came out of my mouth before I could stop it. I stopped walking, waiting for him to turn me to ash. Wasn't Jin in the same predicament? Raised to be the head of a House? She had known freedom, had tasted it, and already feared for its loss.

"It is selfish. I think I've earned the right."

The corridor ended at an elevator. There was still no one else around. The doors opened as we approached. Black didn't have to touch anything or say anything to make it happen. We got in.

"When she turned out to be... normal... It was a bittersweet occasion. My imprisonment would continue, but she would always be free."

"She wasn't free. She was never free. She was trapped in your shadow."

He turned his head to look at me. His expression changed. Not anger. Sadness.

"That was never my intention. I know she hated me, but I loved her all the same. I could never tell her that I cared for her. If the other Houses had known... it was safer for her to despise her father."

"You're saying you were trying to protect her?"

"Yes."

"That's bullshit."

"Excuse me?"

I felt my heart start to race. I was getting a little too honest. I licked my lips and looked him in the eye. "I said that's bullshit. You just sucked me how many miles away from where I was standing in the blink of an eye? And you're telling me she wouldn't have been safe with you, or with her brothers and sisters? You think that life would have been more dangerous than being a ghost? You're deluding yourself. She always knew you were embarrassed by your failure. She always knew you were embarrassed by her."

He didn't say anything. The elevator reached wherever it was going, but the doors didn't open. Maybe he was deciding whether or not to let me live. He'd gotten me pissed. I didn't care. Dannie wasn't here to defend herself, to make her case. I was going to do it, no matter what.

Finally, he reacted. Nothing could have prepared me for it.

He smiled, and put his arm around my shoulders.

"Do you know the last time anyone spoke to me from their heart and soul? I can't even remember."

The doors slid open, and we stepped out into what looked like a museum. There were all kinds of artifacts resting in all kinds of glass enclosures, artfully lit from above.

"You don't fear me," he said.

"Today is your day to be wrong, Mr. Black. You scare the shit out of me. I'm already dying, and I lost my best friend. Self-preservation isn't that high on my agenda right now. Getting even, on the other hand…"

"She was fortunate to find a friend like you. You aren't completely right about me, but I will admit you aren't completely wrong. Having this power, it doesn't make me inhuman. It doesn't enable me to make all the right decisions, or have no regrets. I did what I thought was best for both Danelle and myself. Her loss is tragic for both of us."

He guided me through the exhibit, past all kinds of spears and wands and bricks, past chunks of cave walls covered in runes, and ancient tomes held delicately in a strange gel. He took me all the way to the back corner, to one specific enclosure. One specific artifact.

"As for getting even..."

CHAPTER FORTY-THREE

Fade to black.

IT WAS A MASK, AS ancient as the dice in my pocket. It was tattered and worn, the face composed of hundreds of chips of bone, the surface layered and uneven, glued together by who knows what. The mouth and eyes were a black nothingness. Not an open space, but a midnight sinkhole that seemed to capture everything that fell into them. It was frightening in the way the dice were frightening.

It called out to me.

I could feel it in my soul. It was related to the dice, connected to them, born of the same source over forty-thousand years ago, and now reunited for the first time since.

Mr. Black moved his pinkie, and the glass lifted away on its own, floating in the air above the display. "Take it."

I stared at it. I knew I shouldn't. I knew I had no choice. He wouldn't have brought me to it, he wouldn't be giving it to me, if he didn't think it would help me with Tarakona. It didn't matter what it did, or what the cost was.

"Mei Sakura was a good woman, and my lover. Danelle was a gift to the world, and part of me whether she knew it or not. Whether she wished she wasn't or not. I found this mask in Haiti. I don't know what it does, but I know it has power. I can feel it. I also can't use it. There's only one frequency I can't draw from, only one magic I can't command."

Death magic.

"Take it."

I reached out, nervous and slow. I could feel the energy of it reaching back, tickling my fingertips, urging me to keep going. I looked at Mr. Black, and then back at the mask.

What the hell, I was dead anyway.

I stepped forward and snatched it up. Something told me to put it to my face, so I did.

It didn't have a strap or anything to hold it in place. Instead, I could feel it growing around me, branches of bone spreading and twisting, looping and wrapping over one another and my head. There was no weight to the thing, and despite the non-existent opening for the eyes and nose and mouth, I found that could still see, still breathe, and still talk just fine.

"Well?" Mr. Black asked, expectant.

I could sense the power all around my head. There was a malevolent ease to it, a subtle darkness I couldn't quite capture, but could sense in the back of my mind. It was disconcerting, but like the dice, if it would help me, it was doable.

Now all I had to do was figure out how it worked.

"I can feel the power. I don't know what to do with it."

You know what to do.

The voice sounded from inside my head. It was like a whisper, framed in a cacophony of souls crying out in damnation.

You must take it.

I put my hands to my head, to get the mask off. My fingers ran along it, searching for a break in the seam, a place to grip to lift it away.

Why so scared?

"Conor?" Mr. Black stepped back, away from me. He looked ready to blast me to pieces.

You know me.

You know yourself.

We're the same.

My vision darkened. Instead of Mr. Black, I saw the two ogres at the Paramour Hotel, howling in pain while the dark soul of the dice waited for them to die.

I've been waiting.

A mirror appeared on the wall behind them, splattered in their blood. I looked up into it. My face wasn't my face. My body wasn't my body. It was Rodge. I was Rodge. Ten feet tall and all muscle. I felt the strength of him, the raw power.

Do you like me?

Do you like you?

I've been waiting to trade.

The power of a soul, for the power of a soul.

The bargain. The deal. Offered this once, or lost forever.

I tried to close my eyes, to regain darkness in order to think. The mask, the dice, the spirit. Had it created the artifacts, before it had died? Had it created them after? Did it matter?

Make our choice, necromancer. Yes, or no?

The offer was tempting. Impossible to resist. I tried to pretend I could, or that I even had to consider it. It wasn't the answer to all my problems, and I wasn't completely sure what I was agreeing to. Being able to use the power of the souls the dice collected... it was a deal with a devil that I didn't know. What did I have to lose? I was going to die anyway.

"Yes."

I don't know if I said it out loud, or only in my head.

The bargain is made. We are bonded to death. You will serve me, and I will serve you.

The power of a soul, for the power of a soul.

I still had my fingers on the mask, trying to pull it away. The deal made, it contracted in on itself, the roots shrinking down until it was once again just enough to cover my face. I held it in my hand and looked down at it. I saw a flicker of motion in the eyes. The presence, the voice, was gone.

"Conor?" Mr. Black asked again. He was motionless. He didn't even blink.

My eyes shifted back and forth, between him and the mask. Had he given it to me of his own volition, or had the gift been arranged by a different kind of power?

"You were right. It does have power. It will help."

"Good. I want to be sure you understand me, Conor. I'm grateful to you for taking care of Danelle, for being her friend. I'm just as grateful to you for helping Mei's niece. Yes, I know about her. I don't know what fates aligned to involve you in this, but I am thankful that you are." His eyes narrowed, and his whole expression grew dark. "That doesn't make us friends, and we certainly aren't peers. I will help you deal with Tarakona in any way I can, save direct intervention. I can't risk attracting the attention of the other Houses, or having them think I am making a strong move that could be misinterpreted. It would be bad for everyone."

I knew by everyone, he didn't just mean the Houses. He reached into a pocket and threw me a cell phone.

"If you need anything, pick up the phone. It will call my negotiator, Adams. He will be instructed to assist you. Once this business is done, don't try to contact me again. Don't think that because I respect you and your honesty, that because you were a good friend to Danelle, that I care for you one bit. Death magic is a stain, and you have already outlived your welcome on my Earth."

I felt a shiver run down the base of my spine. His Earth?

"Mr. Black, I need to know where Tarakona is, or at least how to find him. You can send me back to Boston, and the mask will come in handy, but I called to see if you could help lead me to the bastard."

Black shook his head. "No. Not directly. Ten years ago he had

Mei's sister killed, and left his mark so that she would know who was responsible. Even after all of this time, we've been unable to identify him. Even as he carries out his so-called revenge, he remains behind the scenes, directing his puppets from the shadows. Puppets have strings, and strings can be traced back to their origin."

They could also be cut.

He reached into his pocket again, and withdrew a piece of paper. I watched wisps of smoke rise from it, and then he handed it to me. An address was burned into it in a neat script.

"That is the address of an office building outside Boston. It's one of the many server farms that help power the Machine. You'll find a woman there, her name is Prithi Sharma. She's the admin who trapped you inside."

"How do you know that?"

"Tarakona isn't the only one with people in his pocket. I have a contact at the same facility, who traced the code commit back to her. Pay her a visit, find out who she knows. Connect the dots."

I shoved the paper in the pocket of my trench. "Just one more thing?" I asked, putting my hand to my forehead. "We were attacked by werewolves, but they weren't normal. They changed from human to were right in front of me. I watched one take a bullet point-blank to the head and get back to its feet."

"Skinwalkers. I always suspected, but had no proof. The Navajo have legends of men who can turn into animals, that can only be killed by speaking their name."

"I have to know their name to kill them?"

"Legends are just that, in many cases an exaggeration. You don't need a stake to kill a vampire, or silver to kill a werewolf. It is likely they have a powerful healing factor, allowing them to take a beating, and a bullet or two. There's nothing in this world that's invincible."

I reached into my pocket and took hold of the dice. "Where the hell did they come from? Is it possible Tarakona created them somehow?"

"As I said, even after all these years he is a mystery to me. Consider that anything is possible. I've given you what help I can. I'm depending on you to solve Tarakona. I'm depending on you to save Mei's legacy, and keep House Red alive. I'm depending on you to avenge the death of my daughter."

He stepped towards me, reaching out and putting his hand on my shoulder. Just like before, he delivered me from one place to another in a split second, leaving me a little dizzy and disoriented. I blinked a few times, and felt my breath catch in my throat.

Larry was on the floor, his insides ripped out, his blood splattered around him.

CHAPTER FORTY-FOUR

Souvenir.

I GRIPPED THE DICE TIGHT in my fist, and started backing towards a corner.

"Jin? Amos?"

I didn't dare say it too loud. There was no way to know if I was alone, and the damage to Larry looked like it had come from a werewolf. Or a skinwalker.

Nobody answered. Had Mr. Black known about the carnage here? Had he seen it when he dropped me off? I didn't think it mattered to him. As far as he was concerned, figuring out this mess was my responsibility. If I failed... it was clear he didn't think Tarakona could touch him. The way he teleported me, I had to agree.

"Jin? Amos?"

I said it a little louder.

Nobody answered.

Shit.

I moved forward, headed towards the short corner where the rest of Larry's apartment waited. I kept my fist to my mouth, ready to activate the dice. I held the mask in my other hand, and considered whether or not I should put it on. I had accepted the deal. That didn't mean I wasn't nervous about using it.

286

I reached the corner. The bedroom door was open, and I leaned in.

The muzzle of the rifle came first, appearing on the other side of the bed. Amos' head followed after. His hair was soaked with sweat, mixing with blood on his forehead.

"Amos?"

"Baldie." He coughed, a heavy cough. It sounded like his lungs were filled with fluid.

He pushed himself to his feet. His duster was torn, and so was his shirt under it. There was a strange absence of blood.

"What the fuck happened?"

"One of those bitch-ass monsters showed up. Opened fire, but not before it gutted Larry. Fucking threw me clear across the room, go check the wall, plaster's all cracked. Took Jin and left. Managed to crawl in here, get a defensive position for when it came back to finish me off. It didn't come back." He put his hand to the tattered remains of his shirt. "Good thing for me, at least some of this tub is kevlar. Left scratches in it."

That meant Tarakona had the two things he wanted most. Where was he going to take them?

"Have a nice chat with Black? I see he gave you a souvenir."

I was still holding the mask in my hand. "You knew he came for me?"

"Heard he does that sometimes, usually to people he wants to punish himself. Jin was worried about you. I wasn't. Not the way Larry reacted to the name. Larry was about to get me a drink when shithead burst in. How the fuck did they find us?"

"Maybe they never lost us." It was possible they had been tailing us the whole time, watching to see what we would do before they made a move.

"Christ." He walked around the bed. "What's our next move, after I get my drink?"

I found the paper in my pocket. "Black gave me an address. The

Machine admin who fucked Dannie and me over works there. We need to go pay her a visit, get her to tell us what she knows. We need to do it fast. Tarakona wants Jin alive for something, that doesn't mean he wants her alive for long. If he makes skinwalkers, and runs with ferals, who knows what kind of other crazy ritual bullshit he's into."

We moved back out into the living room. I looked down at Larry's corpse, and then over at the wall. There was a massive dent in it.

"Sounds like a plan, I'm just gonna get my-" He stopped talking, and raised the rifle. "Get back in the bedroom."

I didn't question him. We started backing away, ducking into the bedroom at the same time someone kicked in the door, and the flames of a pyromancer filled the room.

"Behind the bed," Amos said.

I started towards it when I saw a face appear in the window. "Amos!"

He turned and opened fire, rounds shredding the glass and digging into the person behind it. The gunfire was going to draw attention from the others in the room. I took the mask, and put it to my face.

It was warm. I felt the tendrils of bone growing out and wrapping themselves around me. I heard the malicious chuckling within the cries of souls.

"What the-" I heard Amos say.

The dice were warm in my hand. I put them to my lips. How many had come in the front? At least three.

We know. We hunger.

I threw them out the door. I could hear the laughter grow more distant. I could feel the connection between the mask and the dice.

Tooth, and Fire. Three of the attackers cried out, including the pyro. I could sense the spirit's elation, his anticipation of their deaths.

I moved out into the room.

The pyro was on his back, his bare arms covered in deep bruises, his face dotted with oozing sores. He turned his head to look towards me, mouth twisted in agony.

A fourth assailant appeared in the doorway. He swung his handgun my way, and hesitated when he saw the mask. I used it to my advantage, stepping into him and hitting him hard in the gut. When he doubled-over, I slammed him hard in side of the head with both fists, knocking him to the ground.

A tasty treat. The bargain is made.

The power of a soul for the power of a soul.

"Baron, we need to get the fuck out of here," Amos bellowed from the bedroom. "Got four more coming up the fire escape, who knows how many through the front." He sent off a round of fire that only lasted a couple of seconds. "Shit! And I'm out of fucking ammo!"

I heard the voices of the souls in my head. They were clearer now, their cries identifiable. The two ogres, the vampire, the orcs from the Greens, the pyro and his buddies. Every soul the dice had taken in the last forty-eight hours.

"The pyro."

A good selection. A strong soul.

I felt his energy, his life pour into me. So strong, so healthy. It was almost enough to make me cry. His power was mine now. I could hear sounds I had never heard before, fields I had never been able to recognize or understand.

Amos came out of the bedroom. "You fucker."

He started charging.

"Amos, wait. It's me. Baron. Stop." I held my hand up.

He stopped coming, looking confused as hell.

"Grab the guns. As many as you can." We were going to need them. I bent down and found the pyro's sidearm, pulling it from the back of his pants.

Amos started lifting weapons from the others. I tapped into the fields, and brought the magic into me. Magic I had never held before.

Fire magic.

I walked over to the window. I brought the gun up, and fired straight out, hitting the side of the building across the street.

The bullet didn't matter. The muzzle flash did. I caught it in the power and redirected it, spreading it wide, multiplying it, and sending it down the fire escape. I heard shouts of warning, and then screams of pain.

You like it, yes?

My heart was pounding. My healthy, strong heart.

"Yes."

It was like a drug. It scared me and thrilled me at the same time.

"This way is clear," I said, looking out the window. Our attackers were spread across the fire escape, their bodies smoldering.

Amos trundled over, laden with the weapons he'd lifted from the dead ghosts. "Holy fucking shit."

"Wait."

There was no telling if there were more coming up the other way. I fired the gun again, catching the flames and sending them out into the hallway, burying them into the walls of the apartment, and setting the whole place on fire.

"Let's go."

Amos barely fit his fat ass through the window, twisting and cursing while he shifted his bulk around. I slipped through after, still in amazed shock to feel healthy and whole. We started descending. A couple of the bad guys were down and not out, their bodies quivering in pain, soft gasps escaping between their lips. Amos took pity on them with a bullet each.

"Sent a whole damn army, when it could have just tore us to shreds with those claws. All it wanted was Jin."

"Did it say anything to her?"

"No. Shithead was in and out in fifteen seconds."

It didn't care about us. We weren't even enough of a threat to be worth dealing with personally.

We reached the ground. There was no sign of any more assholes incoming. I guess Tarakona had thought ten would be enough. I was glad to prove him wrong.

"You stuck like that?" Amos asked, looking me over again.

"I don't know. It didn't come with a manual."

I could still feel the presence of the spirit, its soft laughter persistent atop the screams of the souls, and the sounds of the magic fields. It was enjoying the reaping, the death and chaos and destruction.

"How long?" I tried to ask it. I didn't mind staying this way for as long as I could. I hadn't realized how shitty I truly felt most of the time, until the power of the mask and the pyromancer's soul had taken the illness away.

Until it is gone.

It was a cryptic answer. It was all the answer I was going to get. I couldn't tell how much power remained, which meant it was going to be as much of a crapshoot as the dice.

"How long what?" Amos asked.

"I wasn't talking to you."

He raised an eyebrow at me, and shook his head.

"That is one fucked up souvenir."

CHAPTER FORTY-FIVE

Open wounds.

THE EFFECTS OF THE MASK wore off an hour later. There was no warning, no clue. One minute I felt strong and healthy, and could hear the rhythm of the fire magic.

The next I was coughing.

It was a jolt to my system, and it sucked. It was as though the years in between my diagnosis and that moment vanished all at once, and I was left in the same mental place as I had been when I decided to get wasted instead of going home to my family. The familiar hurt returned. A new one came along for the ride.

I had enjoyed the power the mask had afforded me. Now I wasn't convinced it was worth it. I should have expected there would be an untold price.

"You okay?" Amos took hold of a bottle of Coke resting in the center console. "Have a drink."

I waved it away. My stomach was clenched again, and I felt nauseous. "Are we there yet?"

"Eleven miles left. You need another break?"

"No. We've wasted enough time already."

We had stopped once to gas up. Amos grabbed the snacks and sodas while I went to use the restroom. I stood in front of the mirror and examined the completeness of the mask's power.

It was okay being on the inside looking out. Trying to look back in had thrown me into a panic, and I grabbed at the mask and tried to tug it off. I pleaded with the spirit to release it, to take back the power that was left, and let me get it off my face.

I was ignored.

Amos found me sitting on the floor, crying. For what I had lost. For what I would lose again. For Dannie, Karen, Molly, and even Jin, because I didn't know what Tarakona might be doing with her. Most of all I cried for myself. Then I derided myself for crying in the first place. He didn't judge. He just helped me up and brought me back to the car.

When the power had run its course and I was finally able to remove the mask, he still didn't say a word. He didn't even glance over when I put it on my lap and stared down at it.

"Black told me he cared about Danelle." I turned my head to look out the window.

"Maybe like she was his property. Don't know if he remembers what it's like to have feelings."

"I'm remembering too well. I've been sick for so long... The mask gave me a taste of what I used to take for granted, and now I can't shake it."

Amos was silent for a minute, leaving me alone with the sound of the road.

"Her name was Julie," he said. "Knew her for years, ever since High School. She was kind of plain, greasy hair, a lot of acne... but she had the biggest tits..." He smiled at that. "She was also just the sweetest thing. Loved everybody, so friendly. Me and her, we started going out. Three months and I was ready to marry her, settle down, have some kids, get a job at McDonald's or some shit. Whatever, I didn't need anything fancy as long as I had her."

The thought of Amos with kids of his own was a frightening one. "I take it things didn't go as planned?"

"They did for a while. Got married by a justice, moved in

together. I got a job at Dunkin' Donuts instead. Sex was great, everything was perfect." He paused. "Course, you know that's when the bad shit happened. Come home late one night, door to the apartment is open. Dad was a cop, until he started ghosting, so I always carried a piece. I take it out. Calling her name. No answer. My heart is pounding like a stud on a bitch in heat.

"Go into the bedroom. Julie is there. Nothing on. Blood all over the sheets. Raped. Murdered. Should have taught her to shoot." He took a heavy breath out and slammed his fist on the steering wheel. "Used to believe in God. Used to follow His word. After that, I made two promises. Never let another woman die on my watch, and do everything in this fucking world I can to forget about the pain and the guilt. You know what?"

He waited for me to ask.

"What?"

"Dannie died on my watch, and I ain't never forgot the pain or the guilt no matter what I've done or who I fucked. Some shit you just can't control. Let it rip and hope for the best. Pain is life, and life is pain. If it didn't hurt, you didn't care, and if you didn't care, you're already dead, like one of your little soldiers. You want to be alive, then fucking be alive. Embrace it, use it, let it motivate you. Fuck feeling sorry for yourself because you got sick. Julie wasn't sick. She's still just as dead."

I looked over at him. He took a huge inward snort of air and heaved another sigh. I didn't really know what to say. He was right. It hurt to get a taste of what I'd lost, but only because I spent so much time dying instead of living.

I took a deep breath and put the mask inside one of the big inner pockets of the old coat. Let whatever fucked up spirit was hanging out in it use me to get its kicks. I wanted the power. I needed the power. Jin and Dannie were counting on me.

"Feel better now?"

"Amos, I'm sor-"

"Don't. Don't fucking apologize. I got to live with my pain, just like you got to live with yours. We do the best we can with the shit hands we're dealt. That's it. We find this Prithi chick, and then we find Tarakona. Stay focused. Worry about everything else after."

We rode in silence for a few minutes. I spent the time staring out the window, watching the other cars whiz by. We were moving fast.

"If we survive this… Do you think Mr. Black is going to have me killed? I've seen his face."

"No, you didn't. You saw who he wanted you to see. Anyways, he'll give you a pass this one time for Dannie. Cross him again…"

I knew what he meant. "What about Red?"

"Jin? Don't know. Way she is around you… Think she'd rather fuck you than kill you."

That statement made it harder to focus. "What?"

"You telling me you didn't notice?" He started laughing.

"You know I'm impotent, right? Comes with being half-dead." I remembered how she had acted in Secret Sushi, and waking up with her head on my chest.

"Don't matter. You're her knight in rusted armor. She totally wants you to-"

"Amos."

He shut himself up on the first try, for a minute anyway.

"Damn shame for you that you can't perform. She may be an elf and all, but man if I had a shot at that a-"

"Amos!"

"Yeah, anyways, she keeps giving you those big anime doe eyes. Course, you'd have to be an idiot to start anything with her. Miss Red and a fucking necro? Talk about nuclear winter."

I closed my eyes and took a few deep breaths. The idea of spending more time with her was appealing on a lot of levels, and terrifying on a whole lot more. It didn't matter. It was impossible, and we both knew it.

"That doesn't mean she won't have me killed."

"Nope."

CHAPTER FORTY-SIX

My name is mud.

AMOS STEERED US OFF THE highway, while I used the phone Black had given me to go online and pull up a satellite view of the address. It turned out to be a small industrial complex just outside of Acton, a more rural suburb that seemed like an odd place for there to be any kind of corporate infrastructure. According to the satellite, there were three large two story buildings and a couple of parking garages nestled between the trees and hills. Our target was the one on the left. According to Google, it was owned by Parity Limited.

What the fuck?

This whole thing was getting crazier by the minute. I knew the Houses had an interest in the Machine. I didn't know they had control of it. Did House Red own the Machine, or just the building? It couldn't be a coincidence. Tarakona had gotten to someone in House Red, someone with an awful lot of clout. Red's real negotiator, maybe? I wish I'd asked Jin who that was. Now it was too late.

"You got a plan?"

We were still a couple of miles out. It was early afternoon and gray.

"We need to get inside. I'm willing to bet that won't be as easy as walking in. They're going to have some kind of security."

"Machine server farm? They're gonna have users to back up the armed security. Think you can necro them all?"

"No. The dice will do six targets at once, max. We can't go in there guns blazing when we don't know what we're up against. I don't want to kill a bunch of innocent people."

"We can say we're here to see Prithi? Some kind of nerd business or something."

"Look at us. I don't think we can convince anyone we're into the corporate scene."

"Wait for her to get off work?"

"We don't know what she looks like. And you're assuming she's a girl because of the name. Anyway, we can't wait. Every minute that goes by raises the likelihood that Jin is dead. You may not need the money, but I still do."

"Shit. Okay, what then?"

I knew what. I just didn't like it at all. I wanted some other way, and couldn't think of anything. "We need to hope someone is leaving work early today."

"Steal their badge? What if they're using fingerprint? Anyways, the building is big but it's all servers. This ain't some massive corporate headquarters where you just blend right in. You'd have to-" He stopped talking. His face started to flush. "Look, I'm guilty of a lot of shit, but no."

"There's no other way."

"Fuck that, there has to be."

"There isn't. I've tried to think of one. Everything else is too much of a risk. Maybe I would have taken it before. There's no reason to now. One person, that's all. The building is owned by Parity, and it houses people who work the Machine. These aren't innocents. They signed up to do this job. They put themselves into the shit storm. They could have gone to work for Facebook or something."

"Trying to rationalize killing someone?"

"Someone in there got Dannie killed, and Tarakona has already wasted forty plus innocents in this little Jihad. All we need is one, and we can stop him from killing more."

Yeah, I was trying to rationalize. I had taken an oath once to do my best to save lives. The fact that I was suggesting taking one... it left a sick taste in my mouth. It showed me what I had become, and how far I would go.

Thanks, Grandma Sophie.

Amos covered another mile without a word. "This is on you. I'm waiting in the car. Only reason I don't turn around is because of Dannie. Gonna feel dirtier than lesbian mud wrestling for this."

"So am I. If you have a better idea, give it to me now."

He kept driving.

Of course, we had to pass through a manned gate to get into the industrial complex. It was a good thing Amos was an amazing straight faced liar. He convinced the guard that we were stopping by to check on the coolant systems for the center building, some place called Raven Microsystems. He went on and on about how he was the owner of the HVAC company and that he had gotten an emergency call and left the golf course to handle this himself. He then rattled off a half-dozen possible causes of the coolant leak before the guard waved him through, despite not being on the list of expected visitors.

Hell, I would have let him in.

"I'm standing in the corner of the ring, up to my ankles," he said, keeping with his mud wrestling analogy. "Chick on the other side is hot and athletic. Not a BBW like me."

"Are you sure you aren't okay with this, because you sound like you're enjoying yourself a little too much?" I pointed ahead. "Stay near the reserved spots. The assholes in the front are more likely to have better access."

He sighed and drove slowly towards the front of the garage. I could only hope we wouldn't have to wait too long for someone to bail early.

I could see the building once we reached the front of the garage. Nondescript would have been an exciting way to describe it. Two stories, simple white stone, with a pair of glass double-doors leading into a bland lobby and no windows anywhere else. The only indication it was owned by Parity was the butterfly and DNA logo etched onto the door.

"Those cameras are going to be a bit of a bitch." They were hanging from every support on the garage. The good news was that they were in a fixed position.

"Stay low," Amos replied. "I ain't gonna stop. Too suspicious. I think I heard the bell ring. Time to get messy."

I unlocked my door and took off my belt. He turned the front corner of the garage and slowed down a little. I pushed my door open enough to fall out, shoving it closed even as I hit the ground on my knees, scraping up my pants. I stayed on them, hiding from the cameras by positioning myself between the cars.

Amos kept driving, headed for the visitor's spots on the other end. If the guard had been watching the camera that picked up my move, I would know it in a few seconds.

Nobody came running, no alarms went off. I stayed crouched, pressing myself against the side of a Porsche and watching the front of the building. I started moving through my stretching routine, yodeling at a whisper and cracking my fingers.

For the first time, I felt stupid for doing it, not relaxed. I was about to kill someone. I stopped.

Ten minutes passed. Then twenty. It was getting hard to stay crouched, and I had gotten a couple of panics when two other cars had driven past and a couple of people had headed towards the other buildings. I was lucky they hadn't seen me.

Finally, a guy in a gray suit came out of the Parity building. He was an older man, with thick white hair and good skin. He picked up his phone while he headed towards the lot. A few steps later, the lights on the car two spots over flashed.

I checked to make sure no one was coming, and then moved slowly around the back of the Porsche, rolling across the space between vehicles, and getting myself into position. I found the dice in my pocket.

They were cold.

Shit.

I reached into the inner pocket and pulled out the mask, sticking it against my face. It wrapped around, leaving me feeling more secure with my identity concealed.

"A soul, a good soul," I whispered.

He is old and weak.

Damn it.

"I want him. You owe me."

It is not his time.

"What does that mean? You take them when you want. When we want."

Not before their time.

I was crouched behind a car in a parking lot, arguing with myself. The guy in the suit was getting closer. He would be able to hear me in a second.

"Give me a fucking break. How many souls have I fed you over the years? How many have I offered, and gotten nothing back in return."

Silence.

"Please. There has to be some kind of bargain." I didn't know any other way in. Prithi was our only lead.

One that I choose, for one that you choose.

I balked at that. It could choose anyone. Jin, me … fuck. I didn't know what to do. He was getting closer. I could hear him talking.

"We've got her in one of the offices, just waiting for you to send someone to pick her up… I couldn't just kill her in front of all her co-workers… Yeah, she's kind of stupid, thinking she could do something like that and stay alive, she doesn't seem to know how these things work."

He reached the door of his car, a Range Rover. I was crouched behind it. His conversation made my decision easier.

"Fine. Bargain made. I choose this asshole."

The bargain is made.

The dice grew warm in my hand. I rolled them under the Range Rover. They popped out at his feet.

"I'm on my way. Be there in thirty." He lowered the phone and looked down. "What's this?"

Fire, and Fire.

Was it random good luck, or had it given me exactly what I needed?

The man in the suit dropped in a paralyzed heap. The dark energy pulled its soul in, and I heard his screaming voice in my mind.

"Him," I said.

The power of a soul for the power of a soul.

I felt myself grow healthy again, though I could also feel the age of the man in my muscles and movements. I crept around the corner, took his keys from the ground next to him, and opened the back door to the car. I stood up, secure that I looked like him, and lifted his body up and in. Then I headed back towards the building like I forgot something.

He was talking about killing someone. It made my decision and action a lot easier to take. It allowed me not to feel sorry or guilty. What the hell had he been talking about?

I moved through the doors, into the lobby. A woman was sitting behind the reception desk. She was pretty, and she had a confident look about her. I was guessing she was a user. A uniformed guard stood next to her.

"Forgot my wallet." I heard the guy's voice come out.

"I can have Rose bring it to you, Mr. Campbell," the receptionist said.

"No, thank you, Claire." Her name was on a small placard on the desk. "I'll get it."

I kept walking, to a solid wood door with gold inlays. It had a retina scanner next to it. I leaned in, let the laser pass over my right eye, and smirked when the door clicked open.

I was in.

CHAPTER FORTY-SEVEN

The greatest escape.

THE PLACE WAS NOTHING OUT of the ordinary. Lines of offices along the windows, cubicles in the center. There were maybe three dozen people inside, most sitting at their desks pounding away at keyboards, or watching data stream through monitors. I skirted the edge, looking for Mr. Campbell's office. My office.

On the way, I crossed a schematic of the building. It was constructed like an iceberg, with the small office topside, and multiple floors of servers buried underneath, using the cold ground and circulating the rainwater that fell into it to help keep the system cool. There had to be a dozen levels, thousands of servers. How much of the Machine did this one building actually represent?

I passed three people while I was walking. I was going to say hello, but by the way they cast their eyes down when I approached, I decided Mr. Campbell wasn't too friendly to the lower class. Instead, I moved past them, bumping their shoulders without an excuse me. I was feeling better about offing the guy by the second.

My office was next to the corner, which belonged to Desmond Carlyle, VP of Operations, Acton. The door to mine was open. The door to his, closed. I leaned over so I could see in the window. There was only one person in the room, and I doubted their name was Desmond.

She was eighteen, or twenty-two at most. She had long, shiny black hair that fell in a wave to her shoulders, dark skin, and a thin, delicate face with long eyelashes and deep eyes. She was wearing a colorful thin silk blouse buffered by a white tank and cropped cargos.

She was shivering, and crying.

Prithi Sharma, if I had to guess.

I reached for the door.

"Colin. I thought you were headed out?"

I turned around. Mr. Carlyle, I presumed. Another older guy in jeans and a polo shirt. He was holding a glass of water.

"They told me to bring her," I said, quietly enough that no one else would hear.

His smile faded, and he looked concerned. "I thought they were sending a patrol car, so we could avoid a scene."

Real police, or fake police?

"There's no time. There have been some complications."

I could see his tongue moving behind his lower lip. "That damn necromancer? Tarakona is going to have someone's ass."

"Tell me about it. I need to get her out of here and buried before that asshole can get to her. Can you cover for me?"

"I'll think of something. You think he'll be able to trace the lock back to this farm?"

"I would say no, but he's done a great job fucking things up so far. They don't want to take any chances, not when we're so close." To what, I didn't know. It sounded good.

"Okay. Go on in and grab her. Give me a few minutes to gather everyone up so I can make a speech about... something. I'll figure it out." He clapped me on the shoulder, and handed me the water.

"Thanks." I opened the door, and ducked inside, closing it behind me.

Prithi looked at me without saying anything. I took a breath in and tried not to get embarrassed. She had wet herself. This was the bitch who had screwed us?

"Mr. Campell, please, please, please don't do this. I only did what Mr. Carlyle asked. I did what he told me to do, that's all."

I knelt down in front of her, and handed her the water. "Have a drink."

She threw it in my face. "I'm not stupid. He went to get it. I know it's drugged. Mr. Campbell, he's setting me up. He's blaming me for altering the Machine. He made me do it."

I believed her. I needed to get her out of here, and then we could talk.

"I'm sorry, Prithi. Someone has to take the blame."

"No," she shouted. "Help-"

I put my hand over her mouth. We didn't have time for this. "Be quiet, damn it. I'm not fucking Campbell. You want to get out of this building alive, start pretending you drank that water." If I had to guess it would have been a sedative, to make her more cooperative.

"What?" she asked below my hand. I took it away.

"I said, I'm not Campbell. Those assholes took my boss, and killed my best friend. You're going to help me find them."

She started to speak. I put my hand back on her mouth.

"Listen to me. You're saying Carlyle told you to lock me in the Machine?"

When I said 'me', she got a better understanding. She nodded.

"Who told him to do it?" I took my hand away.

"I just work on the Machine. I don't know anything about what the execs do."

"Right. You work on the Machine. That means you're good with computers." I turned my head. Carlyle's laptop was resting on his desk. "If we take that, can you get into it?"

"I... I can't... I mean... my job."

"You don't have a job here anymore. The only way you get to live past today is to come with me, and break into that laptop."

"It... It's not enough. You need his phone. They may have called him, not e-mailed. You can't risk it."

She was right. I went over and peeked out the window. Carlyle had everyone gathered up in the back corner, and they were clapping while he spoke.

"Fuck. Okay." How was I going to get it from his pocket? Be bold. "Grab the laptop and anything else you think might be handy, and wait near the door. I'll come back and get you."

"Where are you going?"

"I have to get the phone."

I left the office and headed towards Carlyle. I kept my posture confident but concerned. He was talking about profit sharing and quarterly results. He saw me coming. I was damp from the water.

"Excuse me one second."

He took a few steps towards me and wrapped his arm over my shoulders, huddling me close. "What's up?"

The initial contact was the best chance. I brushed my hand over his pockets, finding the cell in the front of his pants. I was quick and precise as I lifted it.

"She wouldn't drink it. Do we have more?"

"That little bitch. No. Just drag her out if you have to. I'll make something up. At the end of the day, all these people care about is their paychecks, not if one of their nerd peers goes psycho."

"Okay. Two more minutes."

"You got it."

I walked back to his office at top speed. By the time I opened the door, Prithi had a Prada messenger bag over her shoulder. I took it from her. I wouldn't be able to get it out without Carlyle noticing. "We're going to need to make a run for it. I have a car waiting outside. If you hear gunshots, don't look back, don't stop running. Got it?"

She nodded, her growing resolve to stay alive settling on her face.

"Come on. You first. I'll act like you slipped away from me."

I pulled open the door holding her arm. We moved out into the office. She squirmed against me, shaking her arm and pulling. As soon as we were both clear, I let her go. She bolted for the door.

I glanced back at the same time I started chasing. Carlyle had seen, and he was pausing his speech again to aid in the chase. I had been hoping he wouldn't want to be so obvious.

Prithi reached the door ahead of me, and went to open it.

"Stop."

She stopped.

I caught up, pulling my gun from under Campbell's suit jacket. I was hoping to get in and out without these kinds of problems.

"Campbell, what the fuck are you doing?" Carlyle shouted behind me. I opened the door, and we passed through together.

The desk had already been alerted. I shot the guard in the shoulder, and the receptionist in the head. I hated to have to kill her, but she was too dangerous to simply wound. I heard gunshots behind us. Carlyle was packing too.

"Keep going. Get to the Cadillac."

I turned around, facing Carlyle old-west style. I would have loved to drop the mask's illusion just then, to see the look on his face. I had to settle for shooting him in the chest. He was still firing as he dropped. He was a lousy shot.

I regained the chase, following Prithi out the front door. I was breathing heavy, Campbell's old body not suited for running. We crossed the ground towards the parking garage. There was no sign of Amos.

Where the fuck did he go? He'd survived the weres at the Golden Sun. He was too good to have just driven off and left me here.

A police car appeared in the garage. It came to a stop in front of us, the doors opening. I reached out and grabbed Prithi's arm again, jerking her perpendicular to the law enforcement.

"Stop and drop," one of them shouted. "Now!"

"Keep going." I fired two shots at the car. They weren't close to hitting the crooked officers, but they kept them under cover.

"You said you had a car."

"I did."

There was more motion coming from the buildings. It was like a swarm of angry ants, the secondary security, the hidden security beginning to pour out to take on whoever was threatening the Machine. This had gone really bad really fast. I was going to kill that fat-ass if I ever saw him again. He had the easy part of the job.

We were out in the open, quickly getting surrounded. I expected to be shot any second.

He came flying out of the garage, through the front-end of the squad car, slamming it into a spin that collided with the officers. He jumped the curb, headed our way, his window down and one of the rifle ends hanging out of it. He drove and fired at the same time, keeping the oncoming guards back. The Cadillac skidded to a stop next to us.

"Someone call a cab?"

I opened the back door and practically threw Prithi in, sliding behind her, and then reaching over her lap for one of the rifles.

"Where to, Mac?" Amos leaned back to look at us. "Famous Amos' House of Pleasures?"

"Just drive," I replied.

He laughed and hit the gas, kicking up dirt and heading away. We weren't safe yet, we still needed to get through the gate.

"What is that smell?" Amos asked, bringing the rifle back in and concentrating on driving. "Did you piss yourself? It's kind of hot."

Disgusting. "Can you shut the hell up for two minutes?"

"Let me tell you, Baldie... Holy shit that match was unbelievable. I've got the whole thing playing in my mind right now."

I swear Prithi looked like she would rather have been dead. She was tucked between the rear passenger seat, her eyes closed tight.

"Do you mind? Guard at twelve o'clock."

I leaned out the window with the rifle. He was standing in firing position, the way they teach it at the range.

"He'll move."

"You sure?"

He took a shot. Missed.

"Yes. Just don't slow down."

Amos accelerated. The guard didn't even wait for the last second to bail. It didn't matter that the gate was reinforced and there was no way we could have blown it. We skidded to a stop, and I hopped out and ran past the guard and into the booth. I opened the gate, and jumped back in. He stayed head down on the ground the entire time.

Then we were through, and out on the road.

"What now?" Amos asked.

"We need a new ride."

"You know they're going to match me up to the rental?"

"You should have thought about that before you were late picking us up."

"Ah, shit. I saw the cop car come in, I was trying to stay out of sight until the last second."

"You did great at that. Now we need a new ride."

"And someone needs a new pair of panties."

Prithi. I looked over at her. "We made it. You can open your eyes."

She did. A moment later, she climbed onto the back seat.

"Amos, Prithi."

"A pleasure," Amos said. Prithi just looked shell-shocked.

I took the bag and pushed it towards her.

"I know you're traumatized, but we don't have a lot of time. You need to work mobile."

She took the bag with shaking hands, and started unzipping it.

CHAPTER FORTY-EIGHT

The game.

"THERE'S JUST NO WAY," PRITHI said. She had Campbell's laptop on her knees, and was trying typing in different potential passwords. Somehow, that didn't seem very efficient.

"You told me you could hack it?"

"With the right equipment, sure. I didn't know I was going to have to do this while we drove." She pushed herself towards the corner after she said it, afraid I was going to hurt her.

Black had given me the phone for a reason. It was time to see if Adams could come through. I pulled it from a pocket and hit contact list. It immediately started dialing, the info coming up only as 'Outgoing Call'.

"What do you need?" The voice was gruff, and younger than I had expected.

"A new car. Tech to crack a password protected laptop and cell phone. Enough firepower to drop a skin walker. "

"New panties," Amos shouted from the front. "Size extra small. Pants, also extra small."

"I've got your location. I'll send you the address. When you get there, look for Templeton."

The connection dropped.

Nice guy.

It took thirty seconds for the address to pop up, and I let the cell read Amos the directions. It was a warehouse or something just outside of Boston, only twenty minutes or so from where we were. I looked out the back window. Nobody was tailing us yet. Hopefully we could get there without being spotted.

"Just give it up for now," I told Prithi.

She closed the laptop and put it back in the bag. She was still terrified.

"I'm not going to hurt you, even if you can't help. Right now it's enough for me to know I stopped Tarakona from killing you."

"I helped you already." Her voice was weak and low.

"What?"

"I said I helped you already. In the Machine. I didn't know what was going to happen. I swear I didn't. I thought it was all above the table."

"A little less mystery would go a long way."

Her face turned red. "Azeban."

I looked at her. Was she suggesting… "You're Azeban?"

"Yes."

"Dannie said she and Azeban…"

Her face turned more red. "You can be anything you want to be in the Machine. Do anything you want to do. Is Daaé's real name Dannie? She was jacked into the same sub node that you were. Is she still at the Greens?"

The power of the mask chose that moment to fade away. Prithi drew back when Mr. Campbell disappeared. I reached up and pulled the bone artifact from my face, putting it back in my pocket. I couldn't hide my anger when I answered her.

"No. She's dead."

Tears welled up from her eyes again. "How? I… I didn't mean for this to happen. It was just part of the game. That's what they said. Mr. Carlyle came to me, he said there was someone in the Machine with a unique pattern. They wanted to talk to you about it to tweak the Machine, so don't let you exit. I told him it was against policy, but he threatened to fire me. It was easy enough to override that method on your node."

Whatever that meant. "How can you be Azeban? You were in the Machine when we were locked in."

She wiped her eyes with her shirt, and pushed her long black hair aside. There was a small, tattooed stamp on the back of her neck.

"We have our own interfaces to the Machine, a patch that rests on the tattoo and a pair of glasses. It lets us switch back and forth, or even overlay the Machine view with reality. It isn't quite as immersive and takes some getting used to, but it lets us test commits in realtime."

"So you were here and there? That's why you paused when we sat down with you?"

"Yes. I was talking to Mr. Carlyle. I was making the change while I talked to you."

"What about all that shit about Tarakona being the future?"

"It's all a game, right? I mean, I spend twelve, sixteen hours a day in the Machine. I work late so I can stay, and come in on the weekends. I buy information from one source, I sell it to another. I have a whole skyscraper in the Machine from all the credits I've earned. It's all for fun."

She thought the entire thing was a game? "You think the Houses only exist inside the Machine?"

"I thought they did. I thought it was all a big sub-game, you know, like those live-action roleplaying freaks, except a little more realistic? I committed the code and locked your node, which meant Dannie was stuck, too. Then that other guy showed up and said they were coming to kill you... the real you. I got scared, so I switched out, but Mr. Carlyle was watching me, making sure I didn't get up or leave. Then I saw that Dannie was gone from the node, and you were stuck. I waited for her to take you out, but she didn't. So I did."

She looked at me, her lip quivering.

"I didn't know she was dead. I thought she escaped. They let me go home. This morning, they said someone outside of the company found out what I had done. They were going to kill me. Mr. Carlyle told me that. I didn't think it was real."

She started crying again, in loud, wracking sobs.

I couldn't be angry at her. She saved my life. She tried to save Dannie. "Prithi, I need you to try to calm down, okay. What happened to Dannie wasn't your fault. I'm trying to catch up to the asshole that killed her. You can help me with that."

"I want to go home."

"You can't go home. Not today, maybe not ever. It isn't safe for you, and it's really not safe for your family. All of those things you learned about the Houses? It's all real. The espionage, the killing, the ghosts, everything. It's not just inside the Machine."

She cried a little harder, and then calmed herself enough to speak. "You're a ghost?"

"Yeah."

"A wizard?"

"A necromancer."

"They said your pattern was unique. There aren't supposed to be any necromancers."

"We're a dying breed," I said, using the same lame joke a second time. I got a small, nervous laugh from her. "Maybe you can't hack the computer yet, but you can tell me what you know about Tarakona."

"He's real, too?"

"Real enough to kill for."

She sniffled a few times and wiped her eyes again. "There were already whispers when I started working for Parity, when I started using the Azeban avatar. Someone who would challenge the Houses, who would pick them apart one by one. He's been hiring ghosts left and right for different operations, but I heard he has his own operatives that he calls his 'pack'. They're like his family, but they aren't related. Supposedly, they're people he found at homeless shelters and youth camps and stuff like that, brought under his wing, took care of. He's got people planted everywhere, and they're really loyal to him because he saved their lives."

Some of those people might have gotten sick and turned feral. If there was a way to reason with them after... Veronica might not have been lying.

"They say some of them are 'special'. That he handpicks the ones who please him and does something to them to make them... I don't know... better?"

"What does he want?"

"To destroy the Houses, and put the original humans back in their rightful place."

"Has he ever been in the Machine?"

"There's no way for me to know that. Some people claimed he had. Others said he hadn't. The Machine is anonymous. That's why I believed them when they said they wanted to tweak it. I thought they wanted to fix it so people like you wouldn't stand out."

"Do you know anything about what House Red took from him?"

"They always called it his treasure. That's all I know."

I'd gotten two different stories so far, but it seemed as if they both had elements of truth. Whoever Tarakona was, he was powerful, and he did want to make a move against the Houses. With Red it was personal. Probably with Black, too. The others? He would bring them down, because they kept everything stable and smooth. If he wanted to give the world back to the original humans, he would want chaos and fear. He would want an environment where he could start freeing the ferals and give them a chance to fight back.

Where did the stone, the so-called 'treasure', fit in? Where did Jin fit in?

Even better, how the hell was I going to stop it?

CHAPTER FORTY-NINE

Know your enemy.

THE ADDRESS TURNED OUT TO be a large, brick warehouse on the outskirts of Boston. It didn't have a gate around it, or any windows; only a bunch of loading docks and a few heavy metal doors scattered along the dirt and graffiti covered doors.

A semi was waiting when we got there, an eighteen foot shipping container loaded onto its back. The loading bay behind it was open, and an overly-muscled woman with frizzy dark hair was waiting there, smoking a cigarette, legs dangling from the dock.

"I'd ask you if you're the necro, but I think that's pretty clear." She got to her feet and took another puff on her smoke.

"Would you mind putting that out?" I asked.

She laughed. "Afraid you'll get cancer."

"Already have it. I don't want to watch you get it."

She held it between her fingers, looked at it like she had never seen it before, and tossed it to the ground in front of us. "I was almost done with it, anyway. The door over there is unlocked."

We made our way inside the warehouse. I'd expected it to be stocked with equipment suitable for ghosts. Instead, it was filled with diapers.

"You might want to grab a box," Amos said, nudging Prithi. The girl was clearly uncomfortable with everything this far out of her

317

ordinary.

"Amos," I said.

"Just sayin'."

We met the female wrestler further back near the open bay. She had been joined by a tall, skinny guy in a suit while we were making the trip. A fixer. She must have been his bodyguard. He looked at Prithi first, wrinkling his nose.

"You'll find a change of clothes in the office over there. Extra small, as requested."

She seemed nervous to go off on her own, but I reached over and took the laptop bag from her, and she headed to the door the fixer was pointing at.

"You Templeton?" I asked.

"Yes. This is Sasha."

"Baron, and Amos."

He made a small grunt like he didn't care. "It was short notice, so we didn't have time to unload the truck. Your car should be here in the next few minutes."

"What about the Caddy?" Amos asked.

"We'll sink it."

He turned towards the back of the truck. "Sasha?"

She went over and unhitched it, swinging the container doors open.

The inside was filled with all kinds of fancy kit. Guns hung from hooks on the walls, and flat tables with drawers beneath begged to be explored. There was combat armor, helmets, cuffs, knives, even a samurai sword. A laptop rested on a counter at the front, its screen providing the illumination for that part of the container.

"You needed hardware to crack a laptop and a phone. That box has it. You can even do a remote Machine insertion if you want to - we'd just need to stamp your neck." Templeton hopped into the container and surveyed the wall. He lifted a gun from one of the racks. It was small, with the largest cylinder I had ever seen.

"Oh shit," Amos said, moving past me to join the fixer. "I didn't think that thing actually existed." He reached out for it, and Templeton handed it over.

"You said something about skinwalkers. I've never seen one, but if they do exist, the Mark Six can take them out."

"Fuck yeah." Amos hefted it in his grip and looked back at me. "Beats the shit out of those peashooters."

"I only have the one, and no extra rounds. Even for a House, it's a hard item to come by."

"What else you got?"

Templeton led Amos deeper into the truck. I waited outside for Prithi, unconcerned about the weaponry. Amos would get what we needed.

She looked embarrassed when she came out of the office and walked over to us. The shirt and pants had been replaced with a tight, black, long-sleeved lycra turtleneck and tights that squeezed right up against her small frame, leaving little to the imagination. It was something I'd seen plenty of times before on Dannie, so it didn't register as revealing to me. It was clear she felt differently.

"You don't have anything looser?" she asked Sasha.

The ghost glanced over at me and shook her head.

"There's a rig for you at the front. Take the bag and see what you can do with it."

She took it from me and held it in front of her chest, which earned a snort from Sasha. Her face flushed and she started walking stiffly towards the setup inside the container, trying not to move her ass too much when she walked.

"Where did you find her?"

"It's a short story that I'm not going to tell you." I half-smiled and followed behind her.

There was no chair for Prithi to sit in. She leaned down over the laptop and started smacking the keys. A few seconds later she looked back. "I need a lightning cable for the phone, and a CAT5."

The computer had put her in her element, and all of the discomfort that had taken her to it had vanished. There was a pair of glasses laying on the counter, and she picked them up. "Too cool."

I heard some drawers moving, and Sasha handed the cables forward. Prithi pulled everything from the bag and connected them.

"Well?" I asked.

"This isn't like the movies. A good password can take days to crack brute force."

"We don't have days."

"Then its good for you that they have a Machine interface on board."

"Won't they know you've jacked in?"

"Only if I went in with my company avatar, but I'm not going into the full Machine anyway." She pushed her hair aside to clear the stamp, and then tapped a spot an inch above it. "I have an implant connected to the interface. I have some utilities stored in there, some routines for getting intel in the Machine. I can make some alterations to the algorithms. No problem with this setup. An hour, max. I'm not completely useless."

I smiled and put my hand on her shoulder. "I guess not."

She put the glasses on, and found a thin wire with a patch at the end, which she brought up and stuck against her own stamp. She blinked crazy fast for thirty seconds or so, and then her hands started flying across the keys, throwing up windows, taking them down, and causing the screens of the phone and the other computer to flicker.

"Car's here," Sasha said. She started leading me from the container.

"Hey, Baldie, catch." Amos tossed something at me as I passed.

I caught it and held it up. A long coat, feather light, grey and smooth. It looked like carbon fiber.

"Ballistic," Templeton said. "Can stop small arms fire, and some higher calibers."

"What about claws and teeth?"

"A safe assumption."

I carried it out to the car, a black Ford with tinted windows. A third ghost was leaning against the door. "That your Cadillac?"

"It was."

"I'll make it disappear."

"Hang on." I jumped down from the loading dock. "Can you go help my partner pick up the weaponry. I need to pull some stuff from the Caddy."

He shrugged. He knew I just didn't want him to see what I was doing. "Yeah, whatever. Give a holler when you're done." He went over to the bay, and Sasha helped pull him up.

I popped the trunk of both cars, transferring the ice first, and then Danelle and Mr. Timms. All the while I kept glancing back to see if anyone was watching me. Not because I cared if they saw me with a corpse, I was a necromancer after all. What I didn't want was Prithi catching wind that her apparent virtual girlfriend was hanging out in the trunk. She was skittish enough already.

Once I was done, I took off the heavy trench she had given me, and transferred everything to the new one.

"Just for this mission," I said to Dannie, as though she cared which coat I wore. Even if she were alive she wouldn't have given a shit.

I went back to the truck, ducking inside and handing Anonymous the keys to the Cadillac. He vanished without another word. Amos turned and showed me his haul: half a dozen handguns holstered around his surface area, a few knives, a couple of grenades, and the Mark Six.

"Feel like a fucking Army Ranger."

"After way too many hits at the all you can eat buffet."

"Shut up."

I went back to Prithi, whose hands were furious on the keyboard, her eyes darting back and forth, seemingly not even aware of what the appendages were doing.

"I have it," she said. She also knew I was there. Somehow.

"Have what?"

"Campbell's e-mails. There's nothing from anyone named Tarakona, but there are a whole bunch of encrypted missives from Matwau Ravenfeather, talking about 'the takeover'."

That sounded juicy, but who the hell was Matwau Ravenfeather? "Can you read them?"

"It would take too long, I'm indexing on common words. Does 'Sakura' mean anything to you?"

Shit. "Yes. What about it?"

"Comes up a lot, along with mention of the treasure. Whoever this guy is, he must have some connection to Tarakona to have been talking about it. Just looking at the word frequencies, my guess is that Ravenfeather and Tarakona are working together to bring down Sakura and..." She paused.

"What?"

She didn't answer.

"What?"

"Father," she said at last.

"Father what?"

"Matwau Ravenfeather wants to take out his father."

"He told Campbell that?"

"Not directly. I followed his e-mail headers back to the originating server and hacked into his account."

"From here?"

"From the Machine. Bet you didn't know that was possible? There's lots of back-doors in the Machine, if you know where to look. Don't worry, I'm using a new ID. Did you know Ravenfeather's father owns the company right next to where you picked me up?"

"Raven Microsystems? I could have guessed."

Her fingers lifted off the keyboard. She reached up and pulled off the glasses, and snapped the patch from her neck. She turned around and looked up at me.

"Did you know Ravenfeather's father is Mr. Black?"

CHAPTER FIFTY

I liked this better before...

"WHAT?" I FELT LIKE I had been sucker punched.

"Matwau Ravenfeather is Mr. Black's oldest son. There's more, but we need to get going."

I must have looked at her like she was crazy. "What happened to Miss Terrified?"

She gave me a sheepish smile. "I'm still terrified. I hit a... tripwire. I think they know where I am, and since they probably know I'm with you..."

They would be dispatching a team to deal with us.

"Do we know where they are?"

"There's a Feral Control yard outside Poughkeepsie. I hacked the cell tower next to the office and back traced the calls to there."

"Definitely not useless," I said. She smiled and blushed at the compliment.

Templeton's phone rang.

Prithi's eyes met mine. I reached under the coat and drew my gun at the same time I turned on the fixer.

"Don't touch it."

He looked at me. Not afraid. Curious. He started reaching for the cell. Sasha noticed what was happening, and made a move for one of the guns on the wall. Amos reached out and grabbed her arm.

"Hold up she-hulk."

"Don't," I repeated.

"You know who I work for."

"I thought I did."

The phone kept ringing. I moved towards him. "I'm going to pick it up."

"You can't do that. They'll kill me if I don't answer and I'm not dead." His hands slithered towards his pocket.

"I'll kill you if you touch the phone. Black put me on this personally, I think he'll take my side."

I could tell Templeton was trapped, screwed whichever way he turned. I watched his adam's apple bob up and down as he swallowed heavily. His hand kept moving.

"I have to get this," he said.

I kept the gun on him while he pulled the phone from his pant pocket.

He started raising it to his face.

"Shoot him," I heard Prithi say behind me.

I didn't hesitate. One round, right between the eyes. It pinged off the wall behind him and almost hit Amos on the ricochet, burying itself in one of the metal drawers.

The phone fell to the ground and burst into pieces.

Sasha shifted her weight against Amos, turning in his grasp and sending an elbow towards his face. He angled his head, taking the strike off the top and using his own weight as leverage to throw her into the wall. She hit hard and bounced back, pulling a knife from her belt and lashing out. It hit his chest, skidding off the kevlar vest he had hidden beneath his layers, surprising the ghost and giving Amos a massive opening to throw her to the floor.

I turned back to Prithi, who had regained the patch and glasses sometime during the standoff. "We have to go," she said again. "I'm picking up a series of calls from the yard to the tower a few blocks from here. They must have other ghosts in the area."

Shit. I grabbed her arm and tugged her away from the setup, ripping the wire from her neck. Amos was standing on Sasha, holding her down with a huge boot. I put a bullet in her head, too. It felt dirty, but I knew she would have done the same to us.

"Can't trust nobody no more," Amos said. He started for the back of the truck, unclasping one of the submachine guns from his bulk.

The entire container erupted in the deafening echo of bullets pinging off the inside of the enclosure, bullets bouncing around and sinking into whatever they could find. At least one got Amos in the chest, and I felt something smack hard into the coat, pushing it against my leg with solid force. I shoved Prithi to the ground and landed on top of her while Amos tried to turn sideways and press himself behind one of the chests of drawers. Anonymous ducked back behind the inside of the warehouse to reload.

"Son of a-" Amos started saying.

I reached forward and got my hand on Sasha's ankle. I breathed in the power of the fields and exhaled, pushing it into her. "Get up, Sasha."

Her body twitched, and started to move. "What the fuck just happened?" she asked.

"Oh my god," Prithi said, able to see what was happening from her place below me. I hoped she wouldn't wet herself again.

Sasha was on her feet when Anonymous leaned over from the corner and opened up for a second time. I could hear the bullets sinking into her, and the force sent blood and bits of flesh everywhere. My power fed into her, and she was on her feet, but she wasn't going for the asshole like I wanted. She was looking around, trying to figure out that she had been shot, was still being shot. She didn't get that she was dead yet.

I rolled off Prithi and got up behind her. She turned my way.

"What's happening?" she asked, her hands feeling at the new holes in her chest.

"Turn around." I pushed harder, and her body shook. Her confused mind was fighting the commands, and I was overpowering it. I stood behind her, letting her corpse take the hits and firing around it. Anonymous ducked back around the corner, and I emptied the gun to keep him there.

Amos handed me another as I passed.

We moved forward like that, out of the truck and into the warehouse. Anonymous gave up at that point, disappearing back into the building. I could hear his boots echo while he ran.

I dropped Sasha's thread and dashed around her, turning the corner in time to see the ghost pulling open the door to get back outside.

I shot him in the back.

"Let's go," I shouted. I took the short route, jumping down from the loading dock and running to the car. Amos and Prithi appeared a few seconds later, and he took her under the arms and lowered her off the platform.

I heard the rumble of a heavy engine, and a large pickup came tearing around the corner, heading our way. The earth started shaking, breaking up the blacktop in front of us and launching shards of rock forward. I dove behind the car, hearing the stone crack against the metal. The windows must have been bulletproof, because they didn't shatter from the impact.

There was a soft, hollow sound from behind me, and then a loud scream that arched from the warehouse towards the pickup. It was followed by an explosion that sent a wave of heat and pieces of torn steel flying overhead. Amos appeared from back behind the semi once it had all landed. He was holding the Mark Six in his hand.

"Yeeeeeee Haaaaawwwwwwwww," he shouted.

I looked around for Prithi, not seeing her and fearing the worst. She crawled out from behind the wheels of the truck; wheels that had been flattened by the user's assault.

I opened the driver's side door of the car and got in, finding the keys resting in the center console. I pushed the ignition at the same time Prithi and Amos reached the car.

"Are you okay?" I asked her, looking back over my shoulder. Her face was dirty, and she had a tear in the sleeve of her shirt. A small stain of blood surrounded it.

"It hurts, but I'll survive. Can we go?"

I hit the gas, making a tight turn and getting us going in the other direction. I angled around the burned out husk of the pickup and cut out into the street at the same time a second car turned into the warehouse lot. It hit the brakes halfway and started backing up to give chase.

Traffic was light, the usual assortment of soccer moms, blue collars, and the unemployed. I slammed my foot down on the gas and took off, weaving through two lanes of cars. I watched our tail in the rear-view, a Mazda or something with a sharp nose. I could see two women inside. The one sitting shotgun was lowering her window, a rifle in her arms.

I cut left in front of a minivan, sped around a Honda, and slipped back to the right. We were approaching an intersection, a green light leading the way. The Mazda got up in front of the van, and the passenger opened up, cracking bullets off the glass and dinging the metal.

"Christ, can't you go any faster?" Amos asked. He had the Mark Six cradled in his lap, the muzzles of the other weaponry poking out from below his duster.

"I can if you roll yourself out. It's your fat-ass that's slowing us down."

He laughed and looked back at Prithi. "Still dry back there, sweetheart?"

"Go to hell."

Her backbone was growing in a hurry.

The intersection was looming, the light still green. I checked the cross-traffic. "Hang on."

The tires complained while I whipped the car to the left, cutting off the guy in the Mazda's lane and forcing him to slam on the brakes. The ghost in the Mazda was good, and she broke left into oncoming traffic, somehow avoiding getting hit. Prithi smacked her shoulder into the door and cried out in pain.

"Put your belt on," Amos said. He looked out the back. Our tail was still attached. The passenger leaned out, opening fire on the rear of the car. I didn't hear many hits. She was aiming low, trying to wreck the tires.

I cut the car right, passed a Fiat, and came back left. Where the hell were the cops when you needed them? It wasn't typical for a ghost to be so blatant about an attack. We kept to the shadows and underground, to avoid hurting innocents.

"Do you even know where you're going?" Amos asked.

I rounded another car. The light ahead of us turned yellow, and the cars on our side started slowing to stop, leaving us with no clean way through. I moved into the wrong lane and sped up, running nose to nose with an oncoming SUV. The driver cut the wheel and got out of the way just in time, his face pale and eyes wide with terror as we passed within precious inches of one another.

The light was red now, and I hit the accelerator, hoping to get out in front of the vertical traffic and squeeze through the vanishing empty space. I heard horns and screaming tires as I tore past, somehow finding a few feet of space to not get slammed from the side. We reached the far side of the road in one piece, and I made it back over to the right lane.

Glancing up in the mirror, I could see the Mazda had also made it across.

"Amos, you need to take them out. This is the cleanest shot you're going to get."

The red light had paused the traffic behind us, leaving an open space on our side that carried only us and them. Amos put his window down and turned, trying to angle his mass so he could aim the Mark Six.

Thunk!

He pulled the trigger, and something launched from the gun, the rear end of it flaring to life once it was clear. I heard the high-pitched scream again, and the roadway exploded next to our tail.

"Tax payers ain't going to like that," Amos said.

The Mazda returned fire, bullets catching the rear glass and working their way towards the passenger side. Amos brought his meaty arm back in right before the side mirror vanished, ripped away by the assault.

We were almost back on top of the traffic flow, bearing down hard on a Subaru at the rear end.

"One more shot. Don't miss."

Amos grunted and shifted his bulk again, putting his arm out the window.

Thunk!

Another missile launched from the weapon, again going wide, hitting the ground away from the car.

"Fuck!"

"We're out of time." I was almost on top of the Subaru, ready to weave around him.

"Screw this," Amos said. He used his free hand to draw his pistol, and fired into the back of the car. The glass was hardened from one side. Taking hits from both caused it to shatter.

The gunfire from the Mazda began climbing the trunk, bullets bouncing off and threatening to hit us, sinking into the leather seats and padding. Prithi rolled down to the floor, and Amos leaned back with his arm extended, able to sight the weapon with the better angle.

Thunk!

I could feel the heat of the bullet's exhaust when the motor activated and it whined its way out of the car. I followed its contrail in the mirror, guiding it with my eyes into the grill of the Mazda.

The car exploded.

I cut tight around the Subaru and accelerated, at the same time Amos whooped his pleasure next to me.

"You see that shit? Fuckin' ghosts. Nobody shoots at Amos and gets away with it."

Prithi lifted herself up from between the seats, settling back and putting on her belt.

"I liked all this stuff better before it was real."

CHAPTER FIFTY-ONE

No, really. Know your enemy.

WE DITCHED THE FORD. WE didn't have a choice. There was just no way to ignore a shootout like that, or an exploding car. I knew word of it would get back to Black pretty fast, and I wondered what he would think of it.

He wouldn't be happy. We were supposed to stay out of the spotlight, not cause trouble. Trouble was for thugs. So was public violence.

We didn't have a choice in that either.

The car wound up hidden in some brush and trees in a conservation area. We switched over to a brown Econoline van that Amos bought after I dropped him at a used car dealer, reconnecting later once he secured a ride. He'd paid a premium to get it off the lot without spending time filling out paperwork, and he made sure to let me know he expected to get his money back. He also made sure to let me know how comfy the seats were.

Prithi nearly fainted when we transferred Dannie from the trunk of the Ford. I had tried to keep her from seeing it, and in the end had failed. After she recovered from her shock, she sat in the back row of seats and stared at Danelle's lifeless face with tears in her eyes.

"I guess that's why she liked the Machine so much," she said, motioning towards Dannie's legs.

We were on I-84, headed west towards Poughkeepsie. It turned out that the yard Prithi had pointed us towards had been abandoned six months earlier, the 'patients' transferred to other facilities after an undercover expose had revealed some pretty shitty conditions there. Overcrowding, malnutrition, and a crooked director had combined to make a great news story, and to conveniently give Tarakona a base of operations that was close to his targets, but far enough away to go unnoticed.

I wasn't dumb enough to think there was anything convenient about it.

We were a three hour drive away from what I expected would be a showdown between Matwau, Tarakona, Veronica's brother, and any number of skinwalkers and other ferals they had supporting them. It was obvious charging in was going to be a stupid thing to do, and given any kind of choice I wouldn't have gone near the place at all.

Going was most likely suicide.

Not going was definitely suicide.

Mr. Black would see to that.

I still owed them for Dannie, and I let that feeling of revenge and anger help fight against my sense of desperate dread and hopelessness. Even so, it was a tough attitude to master.

I was sitting in the front row of bench seats, laying across them and trying to think. I glanced back at Prithi. "She liked it a lot more after, yeah, but she never let her disability get in the way. She could always take care of herself. And me."

"I got that impression. I wish I could have known her... outside I mean."

It was hard for me to come to grips with the fact that Prithi and Dannie had a relationship of sorts, even if it had been limited to the Machine. It had nothing to do with Prithi's gender, and everything to do with the fact that Dannie never told me about it until she had to. We were best friends, and she thought I would be jealous or something?

"Dannie wasn't into girls."

She smiled. "We could have just been friends. What happens in the Machine stays in the Machine."

Right. I didn't really want to talk about Danelle.

"Tell me more about Black's son."

"I didn't get as much as I could have with more time. From what I did get, it seems like whatever is going down has been in the planning stages for years. Have you ever heard of Moutohora?"

The look I gave her caused her to shrink back against the seat.

"What about it?"

"It came up in the indexing a few times. That must be where Tarakona and Matwau met. The phrase around it was 'back on Moutohora' or something like that. It stood out because I'd never seen the word before. There was also mention of '12 years'."

If Jin was here, I would have asked her if she knew who led the team that had picked up the archaeologist with the stone. Without her here, I was pretty certain I could guess.

"Moutohora is a volcanic island off New Zealand. Black sent a team there to recover an artifact, which I can only assume belongs to Tarakona. Or at least, Tarakona believes it belongs to him. Black takes it, he gets pissed and wants it back. I can understand that. What I don't get is why he would be hanging out there in the first place? What is he, a hermit, or a castaway or something?"

"A wizard," Amos said. He'd been oddly quiet until then. "Maybe he didn't want to deal with the House bullshit, so he exiled himself or something. You know, thanks but no thanks, stay off my lawn. Except Black doesn't give a shit what anybody else wants."

I could buy into that line of thinking. "He knows House Red doesn't have a wizard, and he knows there's this magic rock that has some kind of power that's good enough to keep Red from being gobbled up by the other Houses. He wants to help because he's got the hots for Mrs. Red."

"He also doesn't want to lose an ally," Prithi said. "I've been trading information with the different Houses for years inside the Machine. They have all kinds of secret alliances and treaties, and half of them contradict one another. A good sexual relationship is probably the best way to keep a truce going."

"Mr. Black is powerful-"

She shook her head. "Many of the Houses fear him, yes. He's still only one person. The most powerful one-on-one. Against the combined weight of the rest of the Houses…"

"So Black takes the rock. You think he knew it was Tarakona's and didn't give a shit, or you think he only found out after?"

"It doesn't matter. There was no way once he had it he was ever going to give it back. I think in the beginning he figured Tarakona didn't have the balls to confront him. Except he did. He killed Jin's parents, to show both of them that he could do it right under their noses and they couldn't stop him. He also got to Black's son. Maybe even from day one, before the stone had even left the island."

"Power," Prithi said.

"What?"

"Matwau isn't Mr. Black's heir. His second son, Kotori, is. It could be that he felt slighted."

"Or it could be that he's just a dick," Amos said.

Kotori was the one in Dannie's old photo. I'd never met him, but she always used to talk about what a kind, gentle soul he had. Maybe that was why he'd tried to make an heir with science, because his other kids were failures of a different kind.

Prithi moved from the back seat to the front. I sat up straight so she could take her place next to me. "Either way, the treasure has power. Enough that Mr. Black believes it can save House Red. What if Tarakona offered Matwau even a portion of that power?

What if he enticed him with House Black? There was a mention of something they called the 'bonded'. Do you know what that is?"

"No."

"Come on, Baldie, you don't know what bondage is?"

I shifted my gaze between both of them. "When I was with Black... I knew he could kill me with little more than a thought. Let's say Tarakona offered Matwau enough power to challenge Black. Maybe he already even gave him some of it, enough to convince guys like Carlyle and Campbell to join their cause."

I paused, because it hit me then, harder than my sickness ever had.

"Tarakona didn't kill Jin's parents. Matwau did."

"That's an awful giant leap off an awful short pier," Amos said with a snort.

It was a stretch. A big stretch. It also made sense. "Look, Black has been after this Tarakona for years, right? Mr. Fucking Black. Ten years since he killed Jin's parents, Red's sister, and he can't find him. The most powerful man on the planet, and he can't find him? How the hell does that happen?"

"He joins forces with Black's son, who does the dirty work?" Prithi asked.

"Yes. Black has a statue of himself and his children. He also kept an eye on Dannie even after he kicked her out. He told me how much he cares about his kids, and maybe some of that is bullshit, but I don't think all of it was. It could be he isn't paying attention to what Matwau is doing, or he's looking at the wrong things, and overlooking the fact that he's been planning a coup."

"Wait a second. Dannie is Mr. Black's daughter?" Prithi glanced back to where she was resting.

"She was. It's a long story. "

"Let's say you're right, Skeletor. Let's say Matwau has been taking his pops through the back door. He's got Jin. He's got the stone. He's got these big toothy bastards that shrug off bullets like they're spitballs. He's got whatever shit makes him think he can make his move and survive Black's reprisal." He turned his head so he could look me in the eye. "You get what I'm saying?"

Prithi's face paled. I met his eye and returned the stare until he put his attention back on the road.

He didn't want to say what we all knew was true.

We were going to die.

CHAPTER FIFTY-TWO

Nice evening for a stroll.

SOMEHOW, THE SITUATION MANAGED TO go from impossible, to more impossible. I was counting on the element of surprise, of infiltrating the yard in the darkness, and sneaking my way through. I was planning to make use of Mr. Timms, on sending him out into the night to use his natural curiosity, hunger, and skittishness to find a clean path through the walls and into the area.

My plans fell right to shit. There was no cover around the yard. No trees, no buildings, no tall grass or shadows. There was a straight line of sight from two miles away in every direction. It was perfect for spotting escapees and mowing them down before they could disappear.

It worked the same way for anyone trying to get in.

"What the fuck are we gonna do?" Amos asked. He had pulled the van off the road a couple miles out, into one of the last runs of trees before it became a wide open space.

We couldn't see the yard from here. It was a suggestion on the horizon, the lights of the place casting a small volume of luminescence into a misty night sky. Rain was pattering on the hood, and trees were smacking their branches against the sides with regularity.

It felt like a warning from God.

A warning I was still going to ignore.

I was dead either way, and I had a feeling Matwau and Tarakona would be more forgiving than Black would.

"I don't have a choice. You do."

"Don't do that shit."

"Amos, it's suicide. We both know it. Take Prithi and get her out of here. Help her disappear. You might not have been able to protect them all, but you can save one. Bring Dannie back to Chicago and give her the burial she deserves."

He stared at me for a long time, conflicted. For all his talk, he didn't want to throw his life away. I didn't blame him. I wouldn't have done it either.

"Shit." He reached over to the passenger seat and picked up the Mark Six. "At least take this badass."

I shook my head. "No. It won't help. You wasted all the shots with your shitty aim."

He smiled. "Thought you were an asshole the first time I met you."

"I am."

"I know. You're my kind of asshole though." He held out his massive hand. I took it in mine and shook.

"Prithi, Amos will help get you out of the spotlight of the Houses. You're going to have to stay off the Machine, at least for a while. I know it's supposed to be anonymous, but I think we've proven that isn't always true, especially if the right people are looking for you."

She nodded and leaned over to hug me. "Thank you for saving my life."

It brought back so many memories. How many lives had I saved, before all of this? Enough to balance out the ones I had taken, I hoped. "You're welcome."

"You got a plan, Baldie, or you just gonna knock on the front door."

"I've got a plan."

"You shitting me?"

"Maybe."

I opened the door of the van and stepped out into the rain. I went around back and into the rear, finding my suitcase resting below Dannie. I unzipped it just enough to grab the photo. I took it out, looked at Karen and Molly one last time, and tucked it in my pocket. Then I leaned over and kissed Danelle on the cheek. "I'll see you soon."

I closed the doors and walked back around to the side.

"Amos, thanks for everything. Now get the hell out of here."

He lifted his hand in a wave, which vanished behind the closing door. I moved away from the van, and Amos backed it out into the street, turning it the other way.

Then they were gone.

I stood there for a few minutes, my eyes closed, my senses tuned to the cold moist of the rain slapping my bald head, running down my nose, and from my nose to the ground. I made sure to take the time to savor life.

I put up my hood, and started walking.

CHAPTER FIFTY-THREE

Smells like teen spirit.

VERONICA'S BROTHER MET ME AT the gate.

He looked just like his avatar in the Machine, right down to the wisp of red hair that fell in front of his right eye. He was all smiles when the heavy iron doors parted, the churning of the chains rising above the soft growls of the ferals on the walls. He was backed by a pair of vampires, their bodies stiff, the motions jerky, as though every instinct told them to attack me, but something was holding them back.

"Out for an evening stroll?" he asked.

I put my arms out to the sides. He punched me in the gut. I bent over, but didn't make a sound.

"That feels so much better in real life. I'd turn you to ash where you stand, but he wants to meet you. He's impressed with you, not only for surviving this long, but also for having the balls to show up here. To walk right up to the gate, no less." He laughed at that. "First, the coat, and your weapons. You can keep the hoodie. We wouldn't want you catching pneumonia before you meet the boss."

I shrugged out of the coat and tossed it to him. Then I slowly took the two guns from their shoulder holsters and handed them over.

"Not in the mood to chat?" he asked.

I stared at him without saying anything.

"You aren't going to bother me by not talking. This way."

He led me into the yard. There were a dozen or so ferals spaced throughout, mostly werewolves but also a few vampires and one solitary wendigo. Most were sitting on their haunches, staring at one another, or running their claws through the grass, or being otherwise docile and calm.

He might have been controlling them, or they might have had free will. Either way, they looked... bored.

"You like the pets? It's hard to bring a feral under control. No magic in the world can do it."

I kept looking at them, remaining silent.

"Science. Science is the key to filling the gaps where magic fails. Or perhaps it's the other way around."

We finished crossing the yard, turning left at the base of a thick stone building and walking along the perimeter. We started crossing another part of the yard, towards a tall, square structure on the northern side.

"To think. All of these years of plotting, all of these years of planning. The lies, the deception, the money." He shook his head and laughed. "And a single necromancer who isn't smart enough to die when he's supposed to almost fucked it all up." He looked over at the vampires flanking him, as though he expected them to join him in his mirth. Their reaction combined with mine made him uncomfortable. "Will you say something?"

I turned my head and smirked. That was the best I was going to give him. I could see it was getting under his skin.

He shoved me from behind, making me stumble for a couple of steps. Then he moved in front of me so he could open the door to the building.

It fed into a large, open inner space. It was a gymnasium. I hadn't realized the yard had been a human prison before it had gone to the ferals.

The lights were off, a dim illumination sourced from a circle of candles in the center of the room. Jin was laying strapped to a gurney in the middle of the setup, her profile visible in the candlelight, covered by a light blanket. She probably would have liked to turn her head to see who had just come in. A strap across her forehead prevented that.

The stone rested on a pedestal behind her.

It was glowing.

"There he is."

The voice was a deep baritone, smooth and confident. He was approaching from my left, the three guys from the Greens in step behind him. Seeing his face... there was no doubt he was related to Danelle.

He had the same sharp features, the high cheekbones, the olive skin. He was wearing a red silk robe belted at the waste by a brown rope, which also had a small dagger tucked against it. He was short, shorter than Dannie even. Too short to be such an asshole.

Matwau.

"You look like shit, my friend." He smiled. A warm, inviting smile. "Though, I suppose you've had a rough couple of days, have you not? My apologies." His eyes flicked over to Veronica's brother. "Do you have it?"

He nodded and pulled his hand from the pocket of my trench. Red's necklace hung from it. He tossed it to Matwau, who held it up in front of his eyes. The stone shattered in his grip, revealing the small data chip within.

In that moment, I understood. He hadn't let me live because he wanted to meet me. He wanted the chip. The access key to gain control of House Red's assets. He wanted to make sure it was still in the necklace before he cast me aside. Had all that bullshit about freeing the original humans, the ferals, been no more than that? When it came down to it, were he and Tarakona nothing more than a pair of thieves?

"I've waited a long time for this. House Red and House Black in my hands, the true strength of the ancient world only a few cuts away. My father is a blind, megalomaniacal fool. He tried so hard to keep the House out of my hands. First Danelle, and then Kotori? And if that wasn't enough, he arranged for the House of his mistress, his whore of a mistress to endure by bonding a fucking elf!"

His face clenched in anger, and he took hold of the dagger, lifting it from his belt.

"Ever since Moutohora, I knew what I had to do. Black doesn't know what's best for this world. He only knows what's best for him." He took a few deep breaths to compose himself and closed his fist over the data chip. "Thank you for this."

"You're welcome." I said, my voice muffled.

Then I spit the dice at him.

Everything stopped. It was as if all of time warped around the pair of bone cubes, as they traveled the six feet between him and me. Nobody moved. Nobody spoke. There was no sound, no air, no anything. I wasn't wearing the mask, not yet, but in my mind I could hear the spirit's cold laughter, and the cries of the souls it devoured.

The dice hit him in the chest, and clattered against the planked floor. It was only once they had bounced around and finished settling that the world regained itself.

He looked at me, and then down at them. He didn't know how to react. Nobody did. Not until the darkness rose from them.

Not until the force of the power lashed out.

Snake. Lightning.

His eyes grew wide, and his lip curled. His body convulsing, his tongue sliding in and out of his mouth, his muscles contracting and expanding, contorting him in a twisted dance of death. Next to me, Veronica's brother was suffering the same fate, as were two of the skinwalkers behind him, and the pair of vampire guards. I had offered up six souls, willing to risk that I would have to be one of them to satisfy the spirit. It had made its choice.

It had screwed me.

One of the skinwalkers was still standing, completely unaffected. He stared at Matwau, a look of confusion across his angled face. Then he looked at me.

Veronica's brother had taken my guns and given them to the vamps to hold. I took three quick backwards steps, coming up next to them, punched one hard in a quaking face, and stole the weapon from its hand. The skinwalker changed his shape, from man to something else, something lean and muscular, hairy and clawed. I shot the second vampire in the head, and managed to get my other gun from it while it tumbled to the ground.

The skinwalker leaped towards me, and I opened fire, planting an entire clip of bullets into its shoulders, its chest, its face. I saw an eye explode, and it cried out in pain.

It didn't stop coming.

I ducked down, dropping the empty pistol and getting myself behind the dead vampire. Claws sunk into its flesh, and teeth tore into its throat, ripping away in an effort to reach me. I let go and rolled to the side, coming up and firing three more shots at its head. The wound had made it a little more careful, and it put its hands up to protect itself.

I used the precious seconds to reach up behind my head, to where the mask was resting in the back of the hood. I grabbed it and put it to my face, feeling the bones knitting themselves together around me, hearing the screaming and the echoes, the laughter and the excitement.

Snake. Lightning.

I needed to stay alive for another twenty seconds.

The skinwalker growled and charged again, and I backpedaled away, trying to buy time. I threw myself to the ground to escape a heavy tackle, rolled away and took two more shots that struck it in the neck. It roared in pain, even as I watched the wounds begin to close. I was running out of ammo.

Matwau's knife. It wouldn't do much, but it was a good last resort if I needed to try to stick the other eye. I ran for it, towards the wizard, who was frozen on his hands and knees.

I heard it coming, and I threw myself to the ground, momentum carrying me forward and sliding me across the floor. I stopped only a foot away from Matwau, the knife within easy reach. I started grabbing for it.

He looked up at me.

His eyes were burning in flame, his visage twisted. His lips shook, and his tongue hung from his mouth. The rest of him was still.

He was overcoming the power of the dice.

I took the knife in my hand and turned myself over on my knees, bringing it across and down in one quick stroke. The protruding end of his tongue fell to the floor, and he grunted in pain.

That was when the skinwalker hit me.

I felt the claws dig into my side, puncturing flesh and muscle and bone, and throwing me backwards a good twenty feet. Everything exploded into white hot agony, and I tried to cry out, finding my lungs not quite functional. Tears sprang to my eyes from the pain, and I lifted my head, firing the gun towards the approaching mass through blurry orbs, trying to slow it down.

Then all I heard were clicks. I dropped the gun, and tried to raise the knife. It must have fallen out of my hand when he hit me. My eyes started drooping closed.

The power of a soul, for the power of a soul.

CHAPTER FIFTY-FOUR

What is it with...

"It's about fucking time."

THE power fed into me, changing me into someone, and something, else. I felt the strength, the vitality, the energy, the power. I felt my lungs filling, my ribs healing, my skin closing. The skinwalker was close now, so close.

He came face to face with another of his kind.

I roared with the power of the beast and threw a heavy fist into its face, the force of the blow casting it aside. It growled and skidded on the floor, righting itself and coming back again. I got to my feet and set myself, catching its claws when they came in at me, turning my hips and throwing the monster again. It rolled and got up, charging back a third time. It was a brawler. I was an artist. As a human I didn't stand a chance. As a skinwalker... I caught its arms in my grip and held it, muscle against muscle, desire against desire.

I didn't want to die. I didn't have to die. All I had to do was overpower this thing.

We stayed locked in position, growling at one another, sharp teeth clacking together, spit flying in both directions. I narrowed my eyes and pushed harder, feeling it give an inch at a time, desperate to win the standoff.

It yelped in pain, its arms rocking back. I got it turned around, elbows locked behind its body in a tight submission hold.

It wasn't good enough.

I leaned forward, sinking long, sharp fangs into its neck, tasting the flesh and the blood as it poured from the new wound. It was almost enough to make me puke, almost enough to lose the fight for me. I steeled my will and kept at it, lifting my jaws, shifting them forward, and biting again. It wasn't good enough to just wound the beast. He would heal if I did, just as I had healed. I had to deliver a fatal blow.

I didn't taste the spine when my teeth crushed it. I knew when it happened, because the skinwalker became a lump of fur in my arms. It was only then that I stopped chewing, only then that I stopped fighting. I pulled my face away, refusing to look at the carnage I had wrought. I took heavy breaths, turned, and vomited onto the floor.

I was still bent over when something else hit me. Something bigger and stronger than the skinwalker had been. I didn't see it at first, because the blow slammed me into the rafters against the wall, shaking the entire structure and leaving me face down.

I didn't see it until it picked me up and turned me around, holding me off the ground in an impossibly large hand.

"Ooh are ong oie," Matwau rumbled, his words distorted beyond understanding by the loss of his tongue.

It was true that Tarakona had changed him. It was true that he had given him power. He was massive and scaled, sharp edges running down hundreds of mottled brown segments and plates that covered every inch of him. Small red eyes peered out between heavy, spiked lids, and hot, fetid breath poured from his mouth into my face.

"Excuse me? I didn't quite get that."

He roared at my mockery, rearing back and throwing me to the ground, forcing me off my feet, slamming my back hard enough to break it. He lifted his foot and tried to bring it down on me, but I caught it over my head and pushed, bringing him off balance enough to stumble back a few steps.

In that moment, I wished I had taken the Mark Six.

Instead, I pushed myself backwards, slithering like an upside-down snake. I scrambled along the floor, heading for the dead skinwalker. Matwau was on me again in an instant, kicking me in the side, his scaled foot rending flesh and bone. After the third kick I caught the foot, turning his ankle and bringing him to the ground with me. He hissed in anger and raked his hand across my stomach, opening it up. I shoved backwards one last time, and got my hand on the dead skinwalker's ankle.

"Get up you hairy son of a bitch," I said, sending the power into it. It's eyes shifted and it began to stir, its head rocking in confusion. I pushed harder, sending energy through the thread, forcing it to do my will. The drain on me was enormous, and I could feel my own enhanced constitution quickly slipping away.

It fell on top of Matwau, grabbing his hand with dead strength. He screamed and flailed, ripping into its dead flesh, tearing and cutting it to ribbon.

It didn't notice.

My wounds healed, and I got to my feet. The dead monster was still clinging to the wizard, still trying to fight, biting and scratching with razor hands and teeth. It was enough to annoy, and to buy me some time.

Time to do what?

The knife was on the ground a few feet away. A knife, against whatever he was? It sounded ridiculous.

It was my only chance.

I bent over to pick it up.

The power of the mask wore off.

"Wait. What? Too fucking soon," I said, feeling all of the immense strength sucked away. I lost the connection to my zombie in an instant, nowhere near strong enough to hold him as myself.

I didn't bother to pick up the knife.

I turned to face Matwau, and fell to my knees, sick with weakness.

I coughed.

He threw the corpse aside and stared at me, unmoving. He knew he had won. He knew there was no hurry. I had used every trick I had, and still come up short. He was going to take on Black, and maybe he was going to win. What he would do after that... at least I wouldn't be alive to see it.

He took a step towards me.

"You killed her, you know," I said. "Danelle. Your sister." I wasn't going to let him end me without trying to get in any last remarks. "It wasn't her fault Black didn't want you to have the House, and to be honest... I can see why he would rather give it to your tree-hugging brother. Black might be an megalomaniac, but at least he isn't a glorified thug."

I spit at his feet, the action making me cough again.

"So, come on. Come on and get it over with. Choke me, break me, disembowel me, whatever. I'm done. I'm just fucking done."

I had already made my peace on the walk to the yard. I had already asked the stars to say goodbye to Karen and Molly for me, though I didn't know if they heard my request through the gloom. I had promised Dannie I would see her soon. I didn't think that would be a good thing for either of us. At least we'd be together.

Matwau stared at me without moving. Then he looked over to the center of the gym, where Jin was strapped to the table. She must have been gagged, too, because she hadn't made a sound.

He moved towards me.

I took deep, even breaths. I tried to fight against the terror that was rising up in me, the fear of dying and what waited just beyond. I didn't want this asshole to see me sweat, to see me scared of him. I didn't want to give him the satisfaction.

He came right up to me, my face in line with his hips. I looked up at him, defiant. He looked down at me, pleased. He reached out with his left hand and picked me up by the neck, holding it light enough that I could still breathe. He brought my face to his a second time.

"Aelle as aitch." It didn't sound like much, but I knew what he had said.

He drew his other hand back, and planted it in my gut, the sharp scales ripping me apart once more, causing his hand to sink into my body. He kept his eyes on the dark vacuum of the mask's the entire time, and I was glad he did.

It made it easier for me to stab him in one.

I had tucked the knife into the pocket of the hoodie without him seeing. I had retrieved it when he lifted me. I brought it up and in, sinking it into the deep socket at an ascending angle, hoping that it was long enough to reach his brain.

It must have been, because he dropped me and fell backwards to the ground, dead.

I fell to the ground, too, and I lay on my back, spread eagle and bleeding out. I stared up at the roof of the gymnasium, and tried to remember when I had last played basketball. It must have been before Molly was born. I missed basketball.

I expected I should be frightened. I expected I would have thought only of Grandma Sophie, of the screams of her death, the terror of her final expression. I expected I would have mimicked it while I passed from this world into another. I knew something sinister was waiting for me, and yet I was calm. Unafraid.

The power of a soul, for the power of a soul.

It came as the softest whisper of promise in my mind, shrouded in the echoing stillness of the damned. It was an offer I hadn't been expecting. I'd already used a soul.

Six souls. It is a fair trade.

I heard them. There was one there I didn't expect.

A strong one, yes? Take it.

I did. I took Matwau's power, and I let it come into me. I felt it giving me strength, and putting me back together. I pulled myself to my feet.

I looked down at the olive flesh. I was naked, the robe Matwau had been wearing missing.

There, on my bare chest, was a tattoo of a dragon. It was black to Jin's red, but just as intricate, just as impossibly lifelike. I ran my finger along it, noticing that it had edges and bumps, texture as well as form. Matwau had said something about bonding. The tattoo must have had something to do with it.

I found his robe discarded on the floor and slipped it on. I wondered briefly how the magic would deal with that, since I knew I was still dressed beneath the facade. It was a curiosity for another time. It was great I had killed Matwau, but we were hardly safe. I didn't know if Tarakona was here or not. I didn't know if the ferals outside would decide to come in.

I made my way over to Jin, still motionless on the gurney in the center of the room. As I reached her, I saw that her right breast was exposed, leaving her tattoo visible.

It was glowing, matching the light of the stone positioned behind the table.

She didn't move when she saw me. Her eyes just followed my hands as I reached up and pulled the leather bit from her mouth.

"Tarakona, please don't do this. Please."

Tarakona?

"I only did what my aunt asked me to do. I never wanted this responsibility. The family needed me. What was I supposed to say? Please."

Her eyes were pleading now, sparkling in the light around us.

"Jin. Wait." I reached for the straps that were holding her wrists, and started unbuckling them. "It's me, Conor."

"Conor?"

I got her left hand free, and she reached up and started undoing the clasp on her head.

"Yeah. It's me. Matwau is dead. I just look like him. It's magic from an artifact." I wasn't going to tell her where I had gotten it.

"Who's Matwau?"

I got her other arm free, and she sat herself up, leaning forward and wrapping her arms around me. I could feel her shaking against my shoulder, and I returned her grip, holding her tight and resolving everything I had learned into the best version of the truth I could manage.

Matwau wasn't working with Tarakona. Matwau was Tarakona. He used the discovery and retrieval of the stone from Moutohora as a cover, his chance to create a fictional enemy to move against his father and his father's mistress, and get the ball rolling on the whole thing. Veronica's brother had said science was the bridge between his power and the skinwalkers. He had invented something to create them. Maybe he had given them my treatments? Jin had never said what the others changed into.

Had he wanted to free the ferals, or was that part of the cover, too?

"Matwau who?" Jin repeated, breaking the embrace to look at me, her eyes wet.

"It doesn't matter," I replied. I realized it didn't. Dead was dead. There was no coming back.

Unless I brought them.

I undid the ankle straps and helped Jin down off the gurney. The stone stopped glowing the second her feet hit the floor, the connection between them broken. She shifted the blanket to cover herself and looked over at the mess I had made, not reacting to the artifact at all.

"How much did they give you for this job?"

"Two million."

She laughed. "You need to raise your rates."

I let myself smile.

Something outside exploded.

It was enough to shake the building, sending paint chips down from the ceiling.

"The data chip," I said. "It has to be on the floor somewhere. We need to find it and get out of here."

She started scanning the ground. The chip was tiny, the size of a fingernail. How the hell were we going to find it?

I had forgotten I had Matwau's power. I opened myself up to the fields, listening in on the mixture of the frequencies. I expected a noisy din. What I got instead was melodic, enchanting, beautiful. In that moment, I knew what Veronica and Black had meant when they called death magic a stain. It was a jackhammer to a violin, a spider to a butterfly.

I stood in the center of the room, breathing in the energy and waiting. I was ready to fight.

"I've got it. And your dice," Jin said. I glanced over to where she was kneeling, holding the blanket around herself in one hand, and the chip in the other. "Let's grab the stone and get out of here."

It was a good plan. I stepped towards it and reached out.

The side door to the gym squeaked open.

I turned and put out my hand, ready to rain hell on anything that tried to come in.

"Baldie, you in here?"

Amos' fat head snuck into the doorway. He saw me and froze, unsure. Then he saw the bodies, and Jin standing among them, looking back at him.

"Couldn't wait to get him home?" he asked. He grinned and entered the room. "Robe's a nice look. The Indian Hugh Hefner. I don't know what the fuck you did in here, but did you know there's a whole yard of hippie ferals out there? I'm tempted to scratch behind their ears and try to teach them to fetch."

Prithi came in behind him, an assault rifle cradled in her arms.

She was crouched low, like she was special forces or something.

"I think that shit looks cooler in the Machine," Amos said, putting his hand on her shoulder.

I finished my reach, picking up the stone in my left hand. It was still warm. I clutched it under my arm and carried it to where Amos and Prithi were waiting.

"You're a little late."

"Better late than never."

"He would have killed you."

"Definitely better late."

"Thanks for coming back."

"She made me do it. What is it with chicks threatening to cut my jewels off, anyway?"

CHAPTER FIFTY-FIVE

Don't look back.

"ARE YOU SURE YOU'RE GOING to be safe?"

"I'll be fine. You did your job. It's time for me to go do mine."

We were standing in front of the Japan Airlines baggage check, where Jin had already handed over a suitcase she had bought yesterday, filled with clothes that still had their tags, and used solely to protect her artifact: the strange, plain stone whose magic she refused to reveal to me. She would be gone within the hour, flying first class to Japan. Once she was there, she would take a limo to her aunt's estate near the coast and enter the data key and passcodes that would give her full access and control to all of House Red's assets, and make her title of Miss Red official.

"I don't know. Matwau didn't just get to House Black. He had allies in your House, too. They managed to sit under your aunt's nose for years."

"And now that their leader is gone they'll come back in line. That's how the Houses work. You know that."

She brought out a part of me that no one had been able to since I got sick, and it was a comfort that was dangerously addictive. Dannie had been my best friend, yet we'd never shared that spark of potential. Even in our most intimate moment we'd fallen flat. I was angling for an excuse to go with her, to keep working the job, to stay close.

After Amos arrived, we took our time exploring the yard. We found the tech Matwau had been using to communicate with his followers. It was rigged to self-destruct with one wrong password entry, which Prithi had triggered straight away. She was distraught at the loss. I wasn't concerned. The best we could have gotten was the history of a dead asshole, and a list of his accomplices. Like Jin said, with Matwau gone, they would fall back in line. Especially since they had no way to know that Jin existed, or that she wasn't a wizard. Everyone who did know besides Mr. Black, Amos, and me died that night.

The only other item of interest we found was a log book of names, times, and medications, along with a few vials of liquids with the Parity logo etched in the glass, and a large number of empties. Jin recognized the names from her search for my treatment. They were experimental medicines, intended vaccines against the feral viruses. They kind of worked, turning a small percentage of the ferals into what Black called skinwalkers, and gentling the rest to various degrees. It made some amiable to control. It made others downright docile.

Matwau? He had changed into something entirely different. Had he taken the vaccine? Was that what it had done to him? Studying drug interactions in full-frequency wizards was next to impossible. He must have been desperate to resort to treatments that were more likely to kill him than make him stronger.

Desperate like me.

We burned the place to the ground, of course. It was easy to do with Matwau's magic. Even though the power had worn off after an hour, I could still hear the rhythm of the magical spectrum in my head. I could remember the beauty of the flow, and now I could only wince every time I noticed the pulsing of my own frequency, the scratchy chaos of decay.

"I'm going to miss it," Jin said, shifting her bag from one

shoulder to the other. Her plane was leaving soon, and she still had to go through security.

"My winning personality?"

She smiled and turned to face me, her eyes looking up into mine. "My freedom. Your winning personality goes along with that. I'd offer you a full position with me if I could, Baron. I'd keep you close all the time if I could. I feel safe with you, especially after what happened to Natsumi…" Her voice trailed off.

I watched her eyes. They weren't giving me quite the look Amos had described, but there was definitely feeling there.

"You can't risk it, I know. The Houses don't hire necromancers. Not above the table, anyway. I can't help being who I am, any more than you can help being who you are. It's the life we've fallen into."

A tear formed, and she blinked it to her cheek. "A life I fear, for the choices I have to make, and the choices I can't make. I owe you more than money could ever repay."

I blinked a few times, trying to keep my own emotions at bay. It seemed so easy for her to bring the softest parts out of me. "Does that mean you won't send a team to kill me?"

She laughed at that, and then stepped forward and wrapped her arms around me. She kept looking at me, every part of her inviting. Her head tilted up, my head tilted down, and we met in the middle. A kiss. A long, passion-filled goodbye. It was enough to get the deadest parts of me twitching.

No matter how long it had lasted, it would have been too short. She pulled away and put her hand to my cheek.

"Goodbye, Baron."

"Goodbye, Miss Red."

Then she was gone, turning on her heel and walking towards the checkpoint. I stood and watched while she showed her boarding pass and waited on line. I kept watching while she passed through the metal detector and vanished into the terminal.

She never looked back.
I wasn't going to either.

CHAPTER FIFTY-SIX

The promised land.

I DROVE AMOS' VAN THROUGH the gates of Graceland, taking the road that split the cemetery out towards the back, to where Caroline was buried. It was three in the morning, the best time for a necromancer to be cruising for inventory.

Only I wasn't there to make a withdrawal.

Not today, anyway.

I rolled to a stop and killed the headlights, opening the door and circling around back. I had a flashlight in one of my pockets, and I picked it out and turned it on, waving the beam between the headstones. We didn't have an official plot here, so I was going to put her somewhere that I could always find her. Somewhere that I could come whenever I visited, to sit and remember. Caroline's spot was quiet, out of the way. I figured she wouldn't mind the company.

I opened the back doors of the van and looked down at Danelle, still resting peacefully, though the ice had all melted and she was starting to smell. I reached behind her to the shovel, and made my way over to the spot I had picked.

I started digging.

Amos was going to be pissed, because he wanted to say goodbye. He thought I was going to do this with him, but I had never planned to. From the minute Dannie had died, I knew what I wanted to do, what I needed to do. I knew Amos wouldn't have approved. Hell, I wasn't sure I approved. No, I was sure I didn't.

I finished the hole and went back to where she was resting. I stared at her for a good ten minutes, trying to convince myself to put her in the ground and go. To get on with my life, and let her get on with her death.

It was a pitched battle of conscience that I ultimately lost.

"Dannie." I put my hand on her, feeding her the energy and bringing her back.

Her body shook, and she gasped. Her eyes shifted, looking up at me.

"Why?"

If there was one word that could have cemented my idea that I was making a huge mistake, that was the one. My stomach clenched with guilt. I forged ahead.

"I never got to say goodbye."

She planted her arms and pushed herself into a sitting position. "You say goodbye in a eulogy, Conor. Maybe you write a poem, or leave flowers, or something. You fucking promised."

I felt my eyes beginning to tear. "I know. Shit, I'm sorry, Dannie. I had to. It wasn't supposed to happen like that, you know?"

"Like what? Me trying to save your ass? Of course it was. Sooner or later it was. I wish I was still alive, too. I wish I could still look out for you. You'll have to look out for yourself now. Please let me go, Conor. Put me back to sleep and leave me that way."

"Dannie, I-"

"Don't. Just don't. I know what you want, and I'm asking you not to. I'm begging you not to."

"I have another question. A different question. Why didn't you tell me about Azeban, before the Machine?"

"What? Why the fuck does that matter?"

"I don't know. It was never like you to keep anything from me."

"I was trying to protect you, you ass."

"From what?"

"From yourself."

"I don't understand."

She rolled her eyes. "I don't want to tell you. If you don't get it… it's better that way."

I stared at her, thinking. "Are you saying…"

The dead couldn't cry. If they could, I think she would have been.

"Yes, you idiot. I only agreed with you because I didn't want to lose you."

I took a deep breath and swallowed the massive wave of emotions that threatened to wash me away. Why the hell did I have to ask, anyway?

"Are you happy now? Say goodbye, Conor, and let me go. Say goodbye, before you regret it even more than you already do."

The battle was rejoined. Every part of me knew I should listen, and just cut the thread and put her in the ground. I could bring Amos with me, and we could drop her some flowers and reminisce, and give her a proper goodbye, like everyone else on the planet did.

Everyone who wasn't a necromancer.

I had already tied my heartstrings into a knot with my first question. What other damage would I do with my second?

Shit.

"I can't. I'm sorry Dannie, I can't. I have to know. You're the only one who can tell me."

Her eyes were angry, and sad. She tried to beg me with them. She knew I wouldn't listen.

I was an asshole, after all.

"What's it like, on the other side?"

She didn't say anything. I could feel her resisting, and I pushed more of the power into her, forcing her to do my will. Her face twisted and wrinkled, and her lips started to move.

"Fuck you, Conor."

I pushed harder, thankful for the second hit of meds that had restored me to my regular level of poor health. Her entire body shook from the force.

"It... It's..."

The resistance vanished without warning, the connection snapped. I fell backwards, every nerve in my body telling me it was being stabbed. I hit the ground and clutched at my gut, coughing up a storm and trying to calm the sudden throbbing in my head. What the hell had just happened?

Once the pain subsided, I got to my feet, ready to bring her back again and hear the answer to my question.

Except she hadn't fallen when I did.

She was still sitting upright. Her eyes were still moving.

She was smiling at me.

"Do not dare to compare yourself to those who die when they should, necromancer. You will learn what it means to cheat me. You will come to my door sooner or later. Everyone does. Or... perhaps I will come to you."

The words hung thick in the air, and in my soul, until they were replaced with haunting, terrifying laughter.

Laughter that echoed across the dead of night.

Other Books by M.R. Forbes

http://books.mrforbes.com/?don

Features:

Loads quickly (no click tracking or analytics)

Next book in series displays at top

Provides current information about upcoming releases in the series.

Thank You!

It is readers like you, who take a chance on self-published works that is what makes the very existence of such works possible. Thank you so very much for spending your hard-earned money, time, and energy on this work. It is my sincerest hope that you have enjoyed reading!

Independent authors could not continue to thrive without your support. If you have enjoyed this, or any other independently published work, please consider taking a moment to leave a review at the source of your purchase. Reviews have an immense impact on the overall commercial success of a given work, and your voice can help shape the future of the people whose efforts you have enjoyed.

Thank you again!

About the Author

M.R. Forbes is the creator of a growing catalog of speculative fiction titles, including the epic fantasy Tears of Blood series, the contemporary fantasy Divine series, and the world of Ghosts & Magic. He lives in the pacific northwest with his wife, a cat who thinks she's a dog, and a dog who thinks she's a cat. He eats too many donuts, and he's always happy to hear from readers.

Mailing List: http://bit.ly/XRbZ5n

Website: http://www.mrforbes.com/site/writing

Goodreads: http://www.goodreads.com/author/show/ 6912725.M_R_Forbes

Facebook: http://www.facebook.com/mrforbes.author

Twitter: http://www.twitter.com/mrforbes

Thank you again for reading!

Made in the USA
Lexington, KY
28 October 2018